Berkley titles by Barbara Dunlop

MATCH MADE IN PARADISE
FINDING PARADISE

Finding Paradise

BARBARA DUNLOP

JOVE
New York

A JOVE BOOK
Published by Berkley
An imprint of Penguin Random House LLC
penguinrandomhouse.com

ISBN: 9780593332986

First Edition: November 2021

Printed in the United States of America
1   3   5   7   9   10   8   6   4   2

Book design by George Towne

Finding Paradise

Chapter One

⟶

ENJOYING THE LAST SIP OF A BUBBLY DOM PÉRIGNON from her blown-crystal flute, Marnie Anton paused beneath the vaulted ceilings of LA's Lafayette mansion to ponder irony and the twists of fate.

"I see you need more champagne," Hannah Lafayette observed, her voice light and cheerful as she approached Marnie in the great room. She gave a discreet wave to a nearby waiter who was standing at the ready.

Hannah had grown up in the mansion and was completely comfortable in its grandeur and opulence.

Marnie, on the other hand, had grown up behind an auto shop in Merganser, Kansas.

A crisp-dressed, white-shirted man refilled her glass with the dry, deeply flavored golden champagne that foamed partway up to the rim. In a town full of entertainment power brokers, the late Alastair Lafayette still had an unbeatable wine cellar.

"Thank you." Marnie gave the waiter a truly grateful smile. She might have grown up playing in a wheel alignment pit instead of a wine cellar, but that didn't mean she couldn't appreciate a great vintage.

"I can feel the excitement from here." Hannah gestured to the dozen women chatting and laughing over drinks and hors d'oeuvres in scattered groups around the gracious room.

"You didn't have to do all this." Marnie had been surprised when Hannah and her twin brother, Henry, had so wholeheartedly embraced supporting the Finding Paradise Alaskan matchmaking venture. They were hosting a launch party tonight, giving the selected women a chance to get to know one another before tomorrow's flight to Anchorage, then Fairbanks, then on to the small, rural town of Paradise.

"We're more than happy to help out," Hannah said with what sounded like sincerity. "I know Mia transferred ownership of the house to us, but we still consider it hers too." She paused for a moment, a thread of humor coming into her voice. "And Henry wouldn't have it any other way. He got a haircut, picked up a new suit and shaved at four o'clock this afternoon."

Marnie couldn't help but smile at Henry's eagerness to meet the young, eligible women who were participating in the endeavor.

Her legal client and close friend Mia Westberg was the driving force behind the Alaskan matchmaking project. At twenty-seven, Mia was only two years older than her stepchildren, Hannah and Henry, and over the past few months, they'd battled each other in a drawn-out court case over Mia's husband Alastair's estate. By rights, Marnie and Hannah should still be adversaries.

Marnie had successfully argued for the fashion empire and mansion to go to Mia—as Alastair had directed. But Mia had promptly shared ownership of the company with the twins, handed over the family mansion to them, then ceded control of the company and moved to Paradise, Alaska.

Having met bush pilot Silas Burke and having seen the diamond ring he put on Mia's finger, Marnie didn't blame her friend for falling in love. But Mia had turned a clear court case win into what felt like a partial loss. It was hard for the competitive streak in Marnie to accept the final outcome.

"Scarlett Kensington seems particularly amped up." Hannah continued the conversation like she and Marnie were old friends, nodding to one particular group of women.

Marnie took in Scarlett's flushed cheeks and her brisk hand gestures where she chatted with Olivia Axler and Willow Hale in front of the wide stone fireplace that soared to the ceiling—a portrait of Grandfather Lafayette gazing down from its face. Scarlett was twenty-two and worked as a production assistant in the film industry.

Mia and her cousin Raven, who also lived in Paradise, had carefully selected each applicant, choosing women they thought might fit in best in small-town Alaska. There were plenty of robust, hardworking men in Paradise who were eager to meet new women. And the women here were eager to meet honorable men.

"Scarlett's into surfboarding and parasailing," Marnie said to Hannah, having studied the background of each of the successful applicants. "She also said she likes to hike in the San Gabriel Mountains."

"I guess that's the kind of thing you'd be looking for."

"Willow hang glides, and Olivia's been fly fishing with her grandfather. We built outdoor sports into the algorithm."

"That seems smart," Hannah said, tilting her head to study another of the conversation groups. "From the pictures Mia sent, Paradise is nothing but mountains, trees and rivers. You'd have to be outdoorsy to put up with that."

Marnie had seen those same pictures. "They have a café, a bar, housing—well, cabins and camp trailers mostly. But there's the health center, the school, Galina Expediting's warehouse and West Slope Aviation at the airstrip."

Galina and WSA were the main employers in the town, its reason for existing, in fact.

Hannah pouted her pretty red lips. "Not a single designer boutique, no fine dining, no beachfront, never mind a country club."

Marnie cracked a smile at the justified criticism. "Plus, the bugs and the bears. Definitely not my idea of paradise."

"Whose was it, do you think?" Hannah looked perplexed, giving her champagne flute a small wave of emphasis. "Who got there, looked around and said, 'Ahh, Paradise, that's the right name'?"

Marnie's grin widened. It felt strange to chat amicably with Hannah after the bitterness of the court case.

Marnie had later learned that Hannah's mother, Alastair's ex-wife Theresa, had been the driving force behind the hostility. Still, it was unsettling to have Hannah's attitude turn on a dime like this. Marnie kept expecting Hannah to voice some sharp disagreement or have an angry outburst like she'd done a couple of times in the courtroom.

"Silas is picking them up in Fairbanks?" Hannah asked after a moment of silence.

Marnie nodded. "I'm not sure he's thrilled to be dropped into the middle of the whole undertaking. But he can't say no to Mia."

Hannah took a sip of her own champagne. "Mia made it sound like his boss was the real grouch."

"Most of the guys can't wait to mix and mingle. The entire town is in desperate need of more estrogen. But his boss, Brodie, thinks it'll be disruptive to his airline's operations."

"It probably will."

"True, and he's skeptical that any of the women will settle down in Alaska."

"Even if they do meet their perfect match?" Hannah asked.

"Even then."

"What do you think?"

Marnie had to agree with Brodie—even though they'd chosen women who skewed toward outdoor pursuits. "Would *you* leave LA for Paradise, Alaska, population four hundred?"

"With gravel roads, a single restaurant and an average winter temperature of ten below?" Hannah grimaced.

Marnie lifted her flute in mock toast to their evident agreement. "Exactly."

They both drank, then pondered for a moment.

"I hear the guys are super sexy," Hannah ventured.

"I suppose they'd keep you warm at night," Marnie allowed.

Hannah stretched out her fingers and gazed at her perfect coral manicure. "I'd miss Celeste's esthetic talents . . . and my friends at the club . . . and where would you even wear your Castille or your Faux?"

Marnie couldn't afford either of those fashion designers, but she understood the point. "I have a dozen pairs of perfectly good shoes that would *not* survive gravel roads and muddy pathways."

Hannah's sculpted brows furrowed. "Mia's been wearing those brown leather boots all the time up there, waterproofed, I think."

"Barely a heel." Marnie had seen them in pictures, splattered in mud. They looked tragically practical, reminding her of a time in her life she preferred to forget.

"No calf elongation whatsoever." Hannah glanced down at her own shapely legs beneath the shimmer of her slim, steel-blue cocktail dress. Her stiletto peep toes had obviously been dyed to match the dress, and they looked terrific.

"I'm only five foot two." Marnie needed all the help she could get in the heel department.

Hannah stepped back to take in Marnie's four-inch T-straps. "Those are really nice."

Marnie turned her ankle sideways. "A little platform under the toe helps. Keeps the arches more comfortable when you're standing." She'd learned back in law school that she needed to add to her height if she wanted anyone to take her seriously.

In front of a judge, she always wore slacks to help camouflage the lift of her shoes. She tied her hair back too. The bright copper color seemed to distract male judges, also male opposing attorneys. She'd never figured out why. It was just hair, and plenty of people had hair that color.

"I take it Alaska's not on your bucket list?" Hannah asked.

"My bucket list includes places like London and the Mediterranean."

As for Alaska, Marnie would see the women safely to LAX tomorrow morning and onto the plane. Then she planned to take a little time for herself to recover from the flurry of activity. She hadn't booked any client appointments for tomorrow or for Friday either, planning to extend the weekend, kick back and relax.

Thinking about it, she could use a new manicure herself, maybe a pedicure too. Maybe she'd do an entire spa day.

"I guess we leave the outdoorsy stuff to the hang gliders and the parasailers."

"I've played beach volleyball," Marnie offered with a thread of humor.

She could also navigate by the stars and survive a week in the wilderness with nothing but a pocketknife and a pound of dried beans, but she didn't say so. And she'd sure as hell never do it for fun.

"Tennis for me," Hannah said. "But that's mostly because the Turquoise Racket Club serves such a great brunch."

"I feel like an underachiever," Marnie said.

"You? You're one of the best lawyers in LA!" Hannah paused. "I mean, you beat us without breaking a sweat."

Marnie sent her a sidelong glance, wondering if this was it, if Hannah was about to express her hidden hostility.

"And we had ourselves a top-notch team," Hannah continued offhandedly. "Brettan LaCroix spared no expense."

"There wasn't much they could do with an iron-clad will." Marnie was still tense, still on alert for an argument.

"Mia was a highly flawed defendant. Half the city hated her. The rest thought she was a shameless gold-digger."

"She wasn't." Marnie reflexively defended her friend.

"Turns out not. And you never gave up on her. And you represented her brilliantly. So, I'm saying, you're not an underachiever."

"Oh." Marnie sorted through the conversation in her mind. It didn't seem like Hannah was going to get hostile after all.

"You should come and see us next week," Hannah said.

"For what?" Had Marnie missed something in the exchange?

"To look at giving us some legal advice. You worked with Mia for years, so you know our business."

After a stunned moment, Marnie gathered her wits. "I specialize in family law."

"And it's a family business."

Marnie supposed you could frame it that way.

"So, will you take us on?" Hannah asked.

"Uh, sure, yeah, I'll come by next week." Who would

say no to a new client who owned a mansion and a fashion empire? Not Marnie, that was for sure.

Hannah raised her glass again, and Marnie silently toasted to the most unlikely business relationship in the city.

"I'VE SAID IT ALL ALONG—DISTRACTION, DISRUPTION then fallout." Brodie Seaton, owner of West Slope Aviation, ended his sentence on a firm note of conviction. Then, obviously confident his message had been delivered, he leaned back against the workbench of the airplane hangar in Paradise, Alaska, his arms crossed over his chest.

Aircraft Maintenance Engineer Cobra Stanford didn't disagree with his boss. He'd been skeptical about the Finding Paradise matchmaking scheme from the beginning. But it was above his paygrade and none of his business, so he'd kept his thoughts mostly to himself.

"I'm planning to keep my distance," he said now.

"Wise," Brodie said with a nod. "I wish there were more like you around."

Cobra swung the engine cowl shut on the twin otter bush plane—one of the largest in the fleet—secured it and stepped down off the ladder. The aircraft was fit and ready to make the run to Fairbanks tomorrow to pick up the twelve LA women.

The light dimmed to dark orange through the high hangar windows as the sun set behind the mountains in the late September evening, making the fluorescent ceiling lights appear brighter.

"Are the pilots drawing lots to see who takes the Viking Mine run?" he asked. Whoever took the lengthy flight to Viking was sure to miss the women's big arrival.

"I'm assigning T-Two and Xavier."

Cobra gave an ironic grin. "That's going to go over well."

T-Two, Tobias Erickson, was a laid-back guy, but Xavier O'Keefe was as excited about the LA women's visit as anyone in town.

"They're up in the rotation," Brodie said. "Business is not going to be interrupted by this. Besides, they'll be back before the evening's over."

Cobra moved to the bench and took a clean shop rag from the pile to wipe his hands. "I can take the right seat if that helps."

Cobra had trained as a pilot in the military. Although he didn't keep his hours current enough to serve as pilot in command, he could take the first officer's seat when needed.

"You're just trying to get out of town."

Cobra gave a shrug. "Maybe."

Brodie grinned. "Nice of you to offer, but I'm not making concessions to this madness."

"You let them take over half your staff housing." Cobra turned to rest his hips against the workbench, matching Brodie's posture.

The air compressor finished chugging and hissed to silence and the fluorescent buzz above them filled the space.

"Mia saved my PC-12 from crashing," Brodie said, referring to the time Mia Westberg had cleared airstrip debris in the middle of a flood.

"Plus, Raven wanted this," Cobra added.

Brodie's eyes narrowed as he sent Cobra a sidelong glance. "Keeping the peace between Raven and me is important to the town."

That was true enough. Raven was operations manager at Galina Expediting. Together with Brodie's company, West Slope Aviation, they supplied outlying mining, scientific and wilderness tourism operations all across central Alaska. The two companies made up the majority of Paradise's economy.

"They redecorated half of your housing units—girlified them, according to Peter."

"That wasn't Raven."

Cobra knew Brodie had a soft spot for Raven. He also knew enough to let that particular subject drop. "Mia?"

WSA's chief pilot Silas Burke's new fiancée, Mia, was a former supermodel and had a flair for the artistic. She'd first come to town in June, and she was behind the matchmaking project. She'd also had an impact on the décor over at the Bear and Bar Café, and now she had Silas building her a swanky new house beside the river.

"Who else?" Brodie asked with an arch of his brow. "Dusty rose. My walls are *dusty rose*."

"Is that a real color?" Cobra moved a few steps to the refreshment fridge at the end of the workbench. Since he was off the clock now, he pulled out a couple of beers, holding one up to Brodie as a question.

Brodie nodded, and Cobra tossed him the can.

"You should see the other stuff," Brodie said, sounding like he was in pain. "Watercolor paintings and frilly curtains and something called wainscoting."

"What's wainscoting?" A picture was forming in Cobra's mind. He'd heard sawing and hammering next door to his own WSA staff housing unit for weeks now. He'd never been inclined to check out what Peter and the construction crew were doing.

"It's trim, fancy wooden trim."

"Does it add any structural value?" Cobra popped the top of his beer can.

"A little, maybe, I suppose. But it's white and . . . you know . . . dusty rose."

"So, white and pink?"

Brodie grimaced.

"Like a little girl's bedroom." Cobra covered his smirk with a chug of his beer. It tasted good going down, crisp, cold and refreshing. He realized how long it had been since he'd taken a break. He stretched out his neck and shoulders.

"Sure." Brodie took a drink himself. "Kick a man when he's down."

Cobra's grin broadened. "There is one upside."

Brodie gestured with the can. "I don't want to hear any optimism from you."

"Okay."

It took Brodie less than a minute to crack. "All right. Give it to me."

"Pretty women."

Brodie frowned. "That's not the upside. It's the downside."

"Potato, Potahto."

"No. All downside for me. I'm not interested in any of that, but all of my pilots are."

Cobra guessed Brodie was only interested in Raven—who was pretty herself in a not-so-flashy, down-to-earth way. But he wasn't going to bring her up again.

"Don't tell me you're interested now," Brodie said with mock disgust. "You're the only other guy on Team This-Is-Stupid."

"Not my thing," Cobra said.

Brodie gave him an odd look.

"Short term," Cobra elaborated. "I have zero interest in getting to know a woman who's only sticking around for seventy-two hours. Plus, they're lower-forty-eight, big-city. Could you have found any less likely group of women for this?"

"*I* didn't find them," Brodie pointed out.

"Why not from Anchorage or Wyoming?" Targeting LA had struck Cobra as flawed from the beginning.

"Wyoming?"

"Rural women who don't expect five-star dining and maybe know their way around a shovel or a well pump."

Brodie straightened away from the workbench. "I said that weeks ago. I suggested some perfectly practical screening questions, but I was shouted down. It's pointless to let people think Paradise is all 'sipping brandy in front of an open fire.'"

"It's not an easy life up here."

"It's a great life." Brodie pointed around with his beer can for emphasis. "But it's not cushy by any stretch. And did you see the website they built?"

"I did not." Cobra was surprised that Brodie had.

"All vistas and bonfires, snowmobiles and fun. They showed the Frances' house, like that's typical of where people live around here."

Mrs. France owned the Bear and Bar Café, and the France family had the fanciest house in town.

"They dressed up a section of the Bear and Bar for a photoshoot." Brodie was clearly on a roll, and Cobra settled back to sip his beer and listen. "Tablecloths and silverware and flowers. It's false advertising, I tell you. And Mia— they used Silas and Mia's happily-ever-after story, set him all combed and clean-shaven in his flight suit in the sunshine in front of a freshly washed bush plane, Mia holding his hand all über-citified, like anyone from LA would naturally fit in up here. Do they show the mud? No. Do they show the mosquitoes? No. Mia barely escaped a bear attack. Do they mention that? No."

Cobra was sympathetic but also entertained by how worked up Brodie was getting over the whole crazy idea. He quickly raised his beer to hide his grin.

Brodie caught the expression anyway and scowled. "This isn't a joke."

"I know. But you're headed off the deep end there."

Brodie jabbed his thumb against his chest. "I'm the rare voice of reason."

Cobra polished off the beer then dropped his empty into the recycle bin. "Here's the thing about these women, Brodie. They're small. They're slow. They'll probably wear high heels. I'm liking our chances of a clean escape."

Brodie cracked a smile then too.

Cobra clapped him on the shoulder. "Bob and weave, Brodie. Bob and weave. We'll make it through the weekend."

Chapter Two

MARNIE SQUINTED DOWN THE BRIGHT WHITE CORRI-dor of the terminal at LAX, watching for Olivia Axler to appear. Eleven of the twelve women had already arrived. With less than an hour until preboarding, only Olivia was missing.

"Anyone heard from Olivia?" Marnie asked the others as she sent a text to check on Olivia's whereabouts.

Everyone shook their head, but Marnie's phone pinged.
Checked in and on my way, Olivia had texted.

Marnie blew out a breath of relief.

"All right," she said to get the rest of the group's attention.

They were all freshly shampooed and made up, dressed in low-key but snappy outfits with a range of fashionable shoes and boots. Scarlett wore flats, but Ariel Wallace had worn open toed, spike-heeled shoes—Marnie winced at the pain she'd likely be feeling later.

The rest of the women had gone with a mix of practicality and fashion. On top, they wore a variety of stylish jackets and trendy sweaters. But slacks had been the preferred choice rather than skirts. Ariel had gone with a skirt above her impractical shoes—did she even know where she was going?

Before the group joined the TSA checkpoint line, Marnie began handing out small white envelopes. "This is some spending money. You're welcome to have breakfast and lunch at the Bear and Bar as part of the accommodation package. Dinners are all prearranged and noted in your itinerary. Did everyone test the link?"

There were nods all around.

Olivia rushed up beside her. "Sorry about that. I got stuck in traffic, then I remembered I had a nail file in my carry-on and had to dig through it in the cab to find it. I'm just a hot mess right now."

"The important thing is you're here," Marnie said. She handed Olivia her spending money.

"You'll have two hours between planes in Anchorage. Then Silas, Mia Westberg's fiancé, will meet you at the FBO in Fairbanks. The FBO is outside the public terminal, so you'll have to catch a shuttle. Pick up your luggage at the baggage claim, then follow the signs out the end door to the shuttle pickup. You're looking for—" Marnie consulted her notes.

"Can't you just show us when we get there?" Willow asked.

"Yeah, won't we all be together?" Olivia asked, concerned.

"We're all on the same plane from Anchorage, aren't we?" Scarlett asked.

"I'm not coming to Alaska with you." Marnie looked up to find twelve shocked gazes on her.

"What do you mean you're not coming to Alaska?" Willow asked.

"You're the one who knows everything," Olivia said.

All the women nodded to that.

"Why would you miss all the fun?" Scarlett asked in obvious bewilderment.

"I would've paid way more attention if I knew we'd be on our own." The pitch of Ariel's voice went up. "It's going to be like *Naked and Afraid* out there without you!"

Marnie thought that was a little dramatic.

"You *have* to come," two voices said simultaneously.

Everyone jumped in with words of agreement.

An announcement came over the speaker about luggage security.

"I don't have a ticket," Marnie pointed out.

"Get one," Olivia said, wrapping her hand around Marnie's forearm. "You *have* to come with us."

"That wasn't the plan." Marnie couldn't imagine what she'd said to make them think she'd go all the way to Paradise with them.

"You've worked so hard," Ariel said.

"This isn't fair," Scarlett said. "Who won't let you come? Who can we call? Mia?"

"Mia didn't tell me I couldn't come," Marnie quickly said, not wanting any blame directed at Mia.

"Who did?" Willow asked.

"Nobody. It just never came up."

"So, they didn't say you couldn't," Scarlett said, drawing back, her expression turning contemplative.

"No . . . but I never planned—"

"Quick," Olivia said, urging Marnie toward a customer service desk. "See if you can get on the flight."

"I can't just drop everything and—"

"It's not fair for you to miss out," Ariel said. She dug into her purse. "Use my credit card."

Marnie waved her off. "That's not necessary."

"We'll all chip in," Scarlett said, holding out her envelope of spending money.

Everyone started agreeing and offering their money at once.

Time was ticking, and the TSA line was growing.

"We'll feel terrible if you don't come with us," Willow said, waggling her envelope.

Everyone looked so earnest and so concerned and so worried about her missing the fun that Marnie didn't have the heart to argue anymore.

"Okay, okay, I'll see if I can get a ticket," she finally said, giving up the fight. Part of her was worried they'd miss their flight by standing here arguing. But another part of her thought, "Screw it, why not?" She needed a break after the past frantic weeks anyway.

They all cheered then, their enthusiasm warming her heart.

THERE WAS ROOM FOR HER ON THE FLIGHT, BOTH flights in fact, and Marnie was able to stay with the group all the way to the Fairbanks FBO, where Silas was picking them up in a West Slope Aviation twin otter airplane.

She'd dressed this morning in a white tank top with a royal blue blazer and a chunky silver necklace. Her hair was loose, and her dangling earrings and multiple bracelets weren't exactly Alaskan casual. Neither were her slim black jeggings and her strappy platform wedges.

But here she was, in the middle of Alaska with nothing but a handbag under her arm containing a comb, lipstick, credit card, a few dollars and her phone. She desperately hoped Mia had some extra clothes she could borrow for the weekend, or that she'd at least have time to shop in the little town.

Silas was punctual, showing up in an olive-green flight suit, drawing clearly appreciative attention from the women assembled in the small, utilitarian FBO. Marnie could guess what they were thinking—they were hoping all the men of Paradise looked like Silas. And maybe they did.

To get things started, she did a quick round of introductions. Then Silas led them across the open tarmac into the airplane where they got settled into narrow gray seats. The twin otter airplane was compact, and they took up nearly all the room, with some of their luggage piled on the back-row seats. The plane didn't have a restroom, but Mia had warned them about that, so they were all prepared.

It had been a whirlwind trip. Marnie had spent the lay-over in Anchorage and the few moments she'd had in Fairbanks trying unsuccessfully to call Mia and leaving two voice mail messages. She'd also reached out to her law firm and her clients with active cases, checking for urgent issues and letting them know she'd be out of town over the weekend.

Now, with her phone battery dwindling, the twin engines roaring to life and the huge propellers spinning and vibrating the aircraft, reality hit her head-on. She was in Alaska.

Alaska.

Alarm began to build inside her. She wasn't a spontaneous person, and the little airplane made her feel trapped. Once they were airborne, she'd be swallowed up by the rugged mountains and wild forests that Mia had described in such clear detail. The thought of wolves and moose and grizzly bears made her frightened, then excited, then overwhelmed and jittery with anticipation of the unknown.

They turned onto the runway, increasing their speed as they hurled along. Then they lifted off, and she scanned the enormity of the forest as they banked west and headed toward the vivid autumn mountainside, the white peaks and the endless sky.

She didn't see a single wolf or grizzly bear along the way. At one point, she thought she might have seen a moose standing in a little green pond in the saddle of two mountains. But the plane was too high, and they were going too fast for her to be sure. It could have been a dead tree or a rock, or pretty much anything else. All in all, the lack of animal spotting was a disappointment after Mia's captivating stories.

Back on the ground, she stepped from the airplane down three little stairs to the gravel of the Paradise airstrip. The wind whipped her hair, a cutting, chilly breeze in the thin air. She gathered her blazer closer around her, but it was made for fashion, not warmth, so it didn't help much.

The air was fresh, Marnie would give it that. It held a hint of pine tree and autumn grass and that was all. It was pure and clear as could be. And through it, the mountain peaks were outlined like razors against the canopy of bright azure.

A burly man was hauling suitcases out a small rear cargo door three at a time and stacking them on the rough gravel. Watching his efficient movements, Marnie shifted under the wing to make room for Scarlett, who was coming out behind her.

"Wow," Scarlett said, pausing to take in the vistas. "This is absolutely fabulous."

"Chilly," Marnie responded, rubbing her arms.

The only building in sight was tall and cavernous, dusty blue with a red and white sign advertising West Slope Aviation. She guessed they were the only game at the airport. There were a few other bush planes parked around them. They were smaller than the one they'd just flown in on. Pickup trucks lined one edge of the lot, nosed into the bush that surrounded the place.

"Reminds me of being at altitude," Scarlett said, inhaling deeply. "I'm sure we'll get used to it in a few days."

Marnie figured they'd be used to it just in time to head back to California. A shopping trip was high on her list of urgent activities, and Mia had mentioned a clothing store in town, the Butterfly Boutique. Marnie needed some weather-appropriate clothing. She knew all about hypothermia, and she had no intention of succumbing to it before it was time to go home.

"I count thirteen," a very deep masculine voice said from behind her.

She turned to the sound to see the burly man who'd been moving their luggage talking to a second man, slightly shorter, great looking and with an air of authority.

"How did that happen?" the second man asked, taking in their group with a frown.

"You're asking me?" the larger man responded, drawing Marnie's attention to his square chin, strong brow and his overall scowl.

His neck was sturdy and his shoulders brawny, while his chest was a barrel of strength and power. He looked like he belonged out here in the wilderness, like it was the safest place for him, or at least the safest place for the rest of humanity to keep him.

"This is a problem," the other man said.

Olivia stopped to stand next to Marnie. She craned her neck, gazing around at the vistas. "Is it what you expected?"

"Mostly," Marnie answered, keeping her attention on the two men. Either Mia hadn't listened to her voice mail yet, or she hadn't shared it with these two. Marnie was the thirteenth member of the group, so she was their problem.

"You?" she asked Olivia.

"It's *so* quiet," Olivia answered. "Like, listen."

"Right?" Scarlett responded. "No traffic or music, or any background noise at all. It's as if we've all gone camping in the mountains."

Silas approached the two men, and Marnie wondered if she should join the conversation, maybe offer an explanation about what had happened.

"Thirteen?" the guy with the air of authority asked Silas.

"Was I supposed to leave one of them behind?" Silas countered.

Marnie took a step their way.

"Marnie!" It was Mia's excited voice, and in seconds,

Marnie was swept into a laughing hug. "You came. I can't believe you came."

As Mia drew back from the hug, the other women clustered around them.

"It was a last-minute decision," Marnie said, trying to gauge Mia's expression to see how much inconvenience she was about to cause.

"This is going to be *great*," Mia said. Then she looked around the circle. "It's wonderful to finally see you all together! Let's get you out of this wind."

COBRA WATCHED THE CLUSTER OF WOMEN FILE THEIR way into the little office next to the WSA hangar. They looked exactly how he'd expected, fresh-faced and pretty, dressed in highly impractical clothes, gawking around like they'd never seen a pine tree in their lives.

One of them was dressed like she was headed to a boardroom, her halo of bright copper hair blowing free in the wind. She was a tiny thing, with eyes as green as a glacial lake. He couldn't come up with one single reason why a woman like that would have to come all the way to far-flung Alaska in search of a man.

He had an inexplicable urge to warn her away, to suggest she get right back on that plane and return to civilization. He'd give her five minutes alone in the bush before some predator caught her scent and moved in. As the thought formed, he laughed at himself and shook off the image. Nobody was letting any of these women wander off in the bush on their own.

"So, what now?" Brodie asked Silas, as if the extra woman were Silas's fault.

"Hey, I'm just the pilot." Silas raised his palms.

"You're going to throw your fiancée under the bus?" Brodie demanded.

Cobra couldn't help but smirk. Brodie had cornered Silas with that jab, and they all knew it.

"I'll talk to Mia," Silas said. "Find out how the plans changed."

"They might have to double up," Cobra said, although he didn't know how that would work.

"In single beds?" Brodie asked.

"I can't see one of them sleeping on the floor," Silas pointed out with a frown.

Mrs. France owned the only bed and breakfast in town—three rooms above the Bear and Bar Café. But they were full of the men who'd vacated WSA staff housing to make room for the women in the first place. And it wouldn't be fair to disturb other Paradise families with this silly scheme.

"What we need is another WSA unit," Silas said.

There was a moment of silence, and then both men looked at Cobra. He knew exactly what they were thinking. His WSA housing unit was the next one down from those they'd redecorated. It might have been the natural choice, but it sure wasn't his first choice. Other guys were still living in their housing rooms—guys who'd been in favor of this thing from the start. Let one of them move.

"Seriously?" He looked to Brodie because he knew Brodie would have more sympathy than Silas.

"It makes the most sense," Silas said.

"None of this makes *any* sense," Cobra objected.

"You could bunk above the hangar," Brodie ventured.

Cobra shot them both what he knew to be an intimidating glower. The caretaker suite in a loft of the WSA hangar hadn't been used in years. He didn't mind roughing it when necessary, but that suite was gritty and rundown. He also objected on principle. He'd purposely stayed far away from this thing while everyone else got all amped up. And now he was the guy stuck with fixing the last-minute problem?

"It's just a few nights," Silas said.

"Since when do you care where you sleep, anyway?" Brodie asked.

The three men had spent plenty of time in rugged remote fly-in camps over the years. Cobra could sleep anywhere.

"Fine," Cobra said because he couldn't think up an acceptable reason to refuse. "I'll take one for the team."

"Good man." Brodie clapped him on the shoulder.

"Probably be nicer out here anyway," Cobra said, thinking it wasn't the worst weekend to stay out of town.

"Should we go see what's what?" Silas asked, nodding to the office.

The three men started for the building.

"Raven's coming out in her truck," Silas said as they walked. "Mia brought the SUV." He was clearly doing math inside his head.

"And with your two trucks," Cobra finished the count for him, turning to angle toward the hangar where he was on deadline servicing an airplane, "you can fit all thirteen."

"Me?" Brodie asked. "I've got work to do out here."

"I've already done my part," Cobra called over his shoulder.

"I'm your *boss*," Brodie noted.

"Not for long if this keeps up."

Brodie and Silas both chuckled as Cobra lengthened his strides.

Leaving the others to drive the women into town, Cobra picked up his impact gun and started back to work. But then he caught sight of the pile of luggage he'd left sitting on the gravel next to the plane.

He told himself it wasn't up to him to load it into the pickups.

He covered a bolt and triggered the gun to loosen it.

Brodie and Silas were perfectly capable of moving the pile of suitcases by themselves.

Cobra removed another bolt. Then another and another while the luggage stared accusingly back at him. He hated to see a job left half done.

He removed the final bolt and dropped it into the tray.

Then he set down the impact gun. He didn't know what they were doing in the office all this time, throwing a tea party or something. But he couldn't stand staring at the bags any longer. Plus, he wanted the gaggle of women away from the airstrip and off to town just as soon as possible.

He headed for Silas's truck first. The keys were in the ignition, and he pulled it over to the twin otter, transferring half the bags into it. Then he switched to Brodie's truck and set the remainder of the bags in the pickup box, parking the vehicles in front of the office so they could easily load up the passengers. He told himself he was likely saving Brodie and WSA from a lawsuit by not having the women cross the uneven parking lot again in their ridiculous shoes.

As he exited and slammed the driver's door on Brodie's truck, Raven arrived in hers.

"Hey," she called to him, hopping out. "Everything under control?"

"Absolutely," he said.

"What's wrong?" She drew close, peering at his expression.

Cobra liked Raven. Everyone liked Raven. She was friendly, practical and hardworking, an Alaskan born-and-raised woman who made their lives easier by running Galina Expediting so efficiently.

"Nothing," Cobra answered, neutralizing his expression and taking the edge out of his tone.

She didn't press.

"They all inside?" she asked with an anticipatory smile.

"All present and accounted for," he said. It was on the tip of his tongue to tell her they were more than present and accounted for, but he left that for Brodie and Silas.

"This is going to be fun," she said.

"Fun," Cobra echoed, trying to sound at least slightly enthusiastic.

"You coming in?" She gestured to the office.

"Not right now."

"Busy?"

"Yeah, behind schedule."

"Catch up later then." A bounce in her step, Raven headed for the office door.

Cobra turned for his own domain in the hangar. Although a green-eyed copper-haired woman danced alluringly behind his eyes, he had no plans to catch up on any of it until the weekend was completely over.

Chapter Three

"I DIDN'T MEAN TO CAUSE SUCH A BIG PROBLEM," MAR-
nie said, feeling guilty as Mia led the way into a WSA
housing unit that was currently occupied by one of the
ground crew members. She regretted for about the dozenth
time getting on that plane at LAX—if only the flight had
been full, it would have saved her from making such an
outlandish decision.

She could have been home in her apartment right now,
maybe with a pizza from the Obverse Gourmet, scrolling
through the Bernadette Day Spa menu and planning a luxurious self-care day tomorrow. She was close to needing a
new pedicure, and a deep-tissue massage would have
worked miracles.

"You're not causing a problem," Mia said, still chatting
enthusiastically as she flipped a light switch and illumi-
nated the corners of the room with bright white fluores-
cence.

"I got caught up in the moment," Marnie said, looking
around the austere bedroom in surprise. She wasn't sure

what she'd expected from a single man working in rural Alaska, but it wasn't hospital corners on the bed and a nearly bare dresser top with nothing but a historical crime novel, a flashlight and a shine.

"I'm so glad you did." Mia turned in the middle of the room. "I'm sorry it's so stark."

"Does anyone really live here?" Marnie walked past the bed, the dresser and a compact desk to peep into the bathroom. It was similarly tidy, with a bar of soap on the counter and two towels hanging perfectly straight on the rack.

"Former military."

"Oh, that makes sense." Marnie turned back. At least it explained why you could likely bounce a quarter off the dark gray bed.

"Someone from WSA will come by with fresh sheets and towels later on, but you can leave your . . ." Mia gave her an apologetic grin as her gaze went to Marnie's compact purse. "I guess you don't have any bags to leave, do you?"

"I was hoping to do a little shopping here."

"Butterfly Boutique it is." Mia glanced at her watch. "Or the hardware store. We've got an hour or so until they close."

"The hardware store?" Marnie asked in confusion.

"For boots. They have the good stuff," Mia clarified.

Marnie could tell she meant the kind of shoes that were sturdy, practical and unattractive but would support your ankles, keep your feet bone-dry and repel snakebites.

Marnie knew all about that kind of footwear. She'd rather buy something with a little style and a heel. "The Butterfly Boutique doesn't carry shoes?"

"Some," Mia said, taking in Marnie's wedge sandals. "But you're going to want something for walking. The scavenger hunt is the first activity tomorrow."

"I wasn't planning to do the activities." Marnie wasn't here to participate in the matchmaking weekend. She didn't mind helping with the event. And hanging out with Mia again was going to be a load of fun, but she had no intention of interacting with Alaskan men looking for romance.

She was an introvert at heart, and she loved the city. She was the last person who'd have screened in as a potential match for an Alaskan man, and she wouldn't risk giving anyone the wrong idea about her future. She planned to spend it helping grow Miller and Marsh into a bigger, more successful and highly respected law firm.

Mia's life might have taken a totally unexpected professional and personal curve, but Marnie's future in LA was brighter than she'd ever imagined.

"You don't have to sit them out." Mia reached out to clasp Marnie's shoulder. "Seriously. It's going to be a lot of fun."

Marnie peered into Mia's blue eyes. "Who are you, and what have you done with the ice princess?"

Mia chuckled. "Well, for one thing, she got laid."

Marnie split a grin at the unexpected answer.

"There you are," Mia said approvingly. "Kick back. Relax. You're here now. You might as well have a good time."

"You seem disgustingly happy," Marnie said, taking another look around the room. She sat down on the bed and bounced a little. It wasn't bad; firmer than her own, but she'd manage for a few nights.

"I've been stopping and smelling the roses. It's funny how things that seemed so important—"

"Like a multi-million-dollar corporation and a mansion?" Marnie was still wrapping her head around Mia's decision to walk away from her inheritance.

"Aren't as important as you thought they were," Mia finished, sitting down at the opposite end of the bed and canting her leg to turn sideways.

"I should admire your tranquility," Marnie said.

"But you don't?"

"I do. In some ways."

"But you can't understand it," Mia guessed.

"Not so much. Maybe we're in different places, but it doesn't compute for me. I've only just started building my client base. I can't imagine slowing down my career for—" Marnie gestured around the room.

"I won't be living in staff housing."

"But you are going to live in Paradise."

"With Silas."

"The guy who's so very good in bed."

Mia gave an eyebrow waggle and a secretive grin. "Yeah, him."

Marnie was happy for Mia, puzzled sure, but mostly she was happy. She knew guys like Silas were few and far between. But women like Mia were also few and far between.

Marnie really missed having her in LA.

She tried to shake off her mood by changing the subject. "I have a new client, and you'll never guess who."

"You want me to try?"

"Lafayette Fashion."

Mia looked suitably surprised. "How did that happen?"

"Hannah asked me last night at the cocktail party."

"Didn't think I'd ever see that happen."

"Me neither." Marnie shook her head. "You know it's not the same without you. I miss you."

Mia leaned forward and clasped Marnie's hand. "I miss you too."

Marnie looked down at their hands. "You think you'll ever come back?"

"On vacation, maybe. But Silas won't move there."

"Have you even asked him?"

"He offered."

"He *did*? When?" Marnie couldn't hold back her enthusiasm. "That's so great. It would be perfect."

"I already said no."

Marnie's jaw dropped. "What? You mean, you could have had it all? The company, the house, the great guy— what were you thinking?"

Mia rose to her feet. "That I wanted the great guy to be happy."

Marnie stood too. "What about you? What about you being happy?"

"I love Paradise."

"I know you think you do." Marnie could imagine how easy it might be to convince yourself you wanted what the love of your life wanted.

"No. I really do."

Marnie frowned, skeptical that cultured, sophisticated Mia could—coincidentally—have had that big a change of heart.

"You're going to have to trust me on this," Mia said, clearly reading the doubt in Marnie's expression.

"I remain unconvinced."

Mia clicked her cheek. "Sadly for you, you don't get a vote."

"Sadly for me," Marnie conceded. "Butterfly Boutique?"

"First the hardware store."

"I admire this new you, but I really miss the old Mia right now."

"Would the ice princess have taken no for an answer?"

Marnie conceded that point. "The hardware store it is."

AS HE PASSED BY BILL'S HARDWARE STORE A FEW hours later, Cobra heard music coming from the Bear and Bar Café. The aroma of grilled burgers and homemade gravy wafted over the sidewalk, reminding him that he'd worked through dinner. The scents might have been enticing on his empty stomach, but he was committed to his plan to avoid the partygoers.

The WSA cafeteria grill would be shut down this late, but he could always pick up some cold snacks there to take back to the hangar. He'd grab himself something for breakfast too.

He'd blown most of the dust out of the hangar's caretaker suite, but none of the appliances were in working order. They'd disassembled the fridge a couple of years back—raiding it for parts—and the stove had at least one blown fuse. Not that he planned to take up cooking over the weekend.

He'd parked his pickup near the corner of Main Street, intending to grab a pillow and blanket from WSA storage. He'd also pick up a few things from his room. He assumed the woman using it would be at the mixer by now, so he wouldn't disturb her. She was likely flirting with Xavier or Jackson, or maybe with AJ from Galina Expediting. Who knew what her tastes were in men?

Pilots T and T-Two, fraternal twin brothers, were coming the other way on the wooden sidewalk. They stopped to open the door to the Bear and Bar.

"The party's rolling," T-Two said, holding back the door and waving Cobra in.

"I'm not . . ." Before Cobra could refuse, the aroma of Mrs. France's signature gravy hit him full-on. The appeal of fruit and a cold ham sandwich instantly shrank to nothing, and his stomach perked up at the thought of a Super Bear Burger and some fries slathered in gravy. "Sure," he said instead and walked inside.

There were only thirteen of them, he reasoned. The Bear and Bar was large enough to give him space. On the restaurant side there were a dozen square tables, lined along the front windows and scattered through the dining room. The lounge side featured both high tables and dining tables, barstools and a couple of pool tables. A guy could always lay low over there, or he could head out to the back deck if he wanted to hide completely.

He scanned the crowd, seeing that it was thicker than usual. No surprise in that. A few people were sitting, but most were standing, mingling, sipping drinks and having conversations. He had a vague impression of well-dressed women with pretty, flashing smiles. But he didn't let his gaze linger on anyone in particular.

Then he caught sight of her copper hair. She was facing away from him, and he let himself pause for a look. She seemed shorter than she had at the airstrip. Maybe it was because she was standing next to Silas and Mia. Silas was six-two, while Mia was a former model and taller than average.

Cobra pushed his attention past her to the bar. There was a quiet spot at the far end, with a few empty stools near the wall. He ambled over and sat up, catching the bartender's eye.

"Hey, Cobra." Bartender Badger rewiped the surface in front of him.

"How're you doing?"

"We're hoppin'. What can I get you?"

"Amber Ice," Cobra ordered. "And a burger and fries?"

"Super Bear and gravy?" Badger confirmed, although it was little more than a formality, since Cobra ordered it all the time.

"Yes, please."

Badger moved farther down the bar and filled a mug from the tap. "Didn't expect to see you in here tonight."

Cobra's cynicism about the event wasn't a secret from Badger. "I was hungry."

"They all seem happy," Badger said, setting the foamy mug down in front of Cobra.

"The women or the guys?"

"Both teams." Badger canted his head sideways and Cobra followed the direction of his gaze. "AJ's been chatting up that brunette in the green sweater. But when T and T-Two walked in, she got distracted."

T and T-Two, Tristen and Tobias Erickson, were nicknamed because T had arrived first in town, and then T-Two had followed shortly after. Their Norwegian heritage

Cobra perked up at the sound. It was husky-soft, slightly melodic, threaded with unmistakable concern. And it was her. He was certain of that.

"Good," she said, her voice flowing like honey around him. "Don't."

He slowly swiveled on the barstool and met her green eyes.

She took what looked like a startled step back.

He would have left the barstool to give her some privacy but standing would have made him tower over her in the narrow space, and he didn't want to be intimidating.

"Just let it lie," she said into the phone, her gaze not leaving his. "Okay. Bye."

"I didn't mean to startle you," he said as an apology.

"No, no, you didn't." She was obviously lying, but he let it go, assuming she was trying to ease his guilt.

Their gazes held for a moment longer, his curious, hers wary. He knew he had that effect on people, especially women. There was something about his rugged looks and his size that made them nervous. It usually helped if he broke the silence.

He moderated his tone, keeping it as friendly as he could manage. "You're here with the visitors." It wasn't a question, since he'd seen her arrive on the twin otter.

"No," she said, tucking her phone back into a little clutch purse. "I mean, not really. I'm not one of them."

"You were on the plane," he pointed out.

"Yes, but I'm . . ." She gave a nervous little laugh. It was too tight in her throat to prove she'd relaxed at all. "I'm sounding embarrassed."

"Not really." He was the one lying now.

There was a hint of a blush on her pale cheeks, which looked cute with her copper hair. Getting off the plane, she'd been dressed for business. She was more casual now in a pair of black jeans and a cropped pale yellow pullover with a pair of leather ankle boots on her feet. It was the change of shoes that made her shorter, he realized. It hadn't been his imagination.

She hesitantly held out her hand, small, soft-looking, thin delicate skin with a perfect pearlescent manicure.

He was afraid to touch it.

"I'm Marnie Anton, lawyer, one of the organizers of the event."

It would be rude not to shake, so he gently and carefully took her hand, his swallowing it up. He'd meant the contact to be brief, to let go right away, but energy leapt from her skin to his, streaming up his arm to his shoulder. "Conrad Stanford, but everyone calls me Cobra. The nickname is from the military."

"Military?" She sounded hopeful and maybe a little less intimidated now.

"Air force."

She tilted her head and gave him the first hint of a smile. "You don't look like a Conrad."

He quirked a small smile of his own. "Probably why they gave me a nickname." He knew he had to let go of her hand. As he did, he let the pad of his thumb surreptitiously stroke the back of it.

"It suits you," she said, and her smile squeezed his solar plexus—in a good way, in a fascinating way.

A beat went past in silence again.

"So . . . you're not here looking for a husband?"

She shook her head.

"Well, I'm not looking for a wife."

"It's good we got that out of the way."

The crowd shifted, and a couple of people moved in too close for comfort behind her. She took a half step his way.

He fought the urge to reach out, to put a protective arm around her waist. It was an irrational impulse. She wasn't in any danger from random partygoers.

"I'm not sticking around," he said, even though he was

curious about her. "I'm just here to pick up a few things for the weekend."

She looked puzzled.

"Not in the café," he elaborated. "In my room."

"Your room?"

"The WSA staff housing barracks."

Her eyes squinted then she grimaced. "Uh-oh."

He glanced around to see what had her worried. Nothing looked wrong. "What?"

"You just said you were in the military."

"Sure. Yeah." He didn't know why she'd gone back to that, unless maybe it made her feel safer around him.

"I think . . . maybe . . ." She bit her bottom lip. "I just saw your hospital corners."

He glanced down at himself, baffled by such an odd euphemism. "My what?"

"The ones on your bed."

It took a second for her words to sink in—this was the woman staying in his room.

"I'm sorry," she quickly said into the beat of silence. "It was a last-minute thing. We were already at the airport. I wasn't supposed to come along, but then everybody wanted me . . . for continuity, really. But they also thought I'd be missing out on the fun." She drew back, cringing as if she was expecting an angry outburst from him. "So . . . here I am."

He wasn't about to get angry with her. Okay, sure, it was an annoyance that he had to move out to the airstrip. And he wished they'd been more organized, and he supposed he wished she wasn't an impulsive person.

"Don't worry about it," he said. Then he rose from the barstool. "I do have to pick up a few things if you don't mind."

"No, no. Whatever you need." She glanced around the lively room. "Okay if I walk back with you?"

"Sure," he said, surprised by the question.

He realized he'd prefer it if she did. He couldn't say why, especially since she wasn't interested in meeting men, but he didn't want to leave her here looking eligible among his friends and colleagues.

MARNIE WAS RELIEVED TO MAKE AN EARLY EXIT FROM the Bear and Bar, even if it was with a mountain of a man whose rugged face and bulky biceps and sturdy shoulders said he'd probably lived for years on the wild side. A faded blue T-shirt was stretched across his broad chest, and a pair of black cargo pants hung over scuffed work boots that thumped hollowly as he walked along the wooden sidewalk.

She was far more introvert than extrovert, and a big party wasn't her idea of fun at the best of times. And now she needed to sort through the jolt of her assistant Bexley Wright's phone call.

She told herself to ignore it, to set it aside, not to let something so far away worry her. But she hadn't heard from her father in five years, not since they'd marched him out of the Wichita courtroom in handcuffs. It was too easy to get rattled by him suddenly reaching out.

"You're friends with Mia in LA?" Cobra asked conversationally as they rounded the corner from Main Street onto Red Avenue.

A single streetlight stood at the intersection of the two streets, though it was too early in the evening to need the illumination. Along Red Avenue, pickup trucks and a few battered-looking SUVs were parked against the raised wooden sidewalk. Most of them were muddy along the bottom. All of them were dusty on the top.

"Yes, she's . . . a friend," Marnie answered. She found herself stretching her spine and raising her shoulders, unsettled by the difference in their heights. She wished she were wearing a pair of her regular shoes to give her a boost.

"Is there a *but* in there?" Cobra asked. His voice was rumbling, gentle, but with a distinct thread of steel underlying the low tone.

"No *but*," she said airily. There was nothing at all uncertain about her friendship with Mia.

"You don't sound completely sure about that."

"Maybe there was an *and*," she admitted.

"*And*?"

She couldn't help but smile at his persistence. "And she's also a client. I'm her lawyer."

"Ah," he said.

That got her curious. "What *ah*?"

"So, her big court case, that was you."

Marnie was surprised he knew about it, then realized Mia's circumstance must have caused quite a stir while she was hiding out in a town this size. "That was me."

"Were you disappointed with the outcome?"

"No, why?"

"I heard she lost her house and control of her business."

Marnie didn't like that characterization. "She didn't *lose* anything. We *won*. She was being magnanimous and generous to the twins. Mia's like that."

"Oh."

They fell silent for a few paces, then arrived at his room. He gestured for her to go first up the three steps to the door.

Marnie stopped on the square porch at the top and inserted the key Mia had given her.

"You locked the door?" Cobra asked from behind.

She turned to look at him, confused by the question.

"I never bother," he said.

"That's you." She gestured at him up and down. "I mean, who in their right mind is going to give you a hard time?"

He gave an indulgent-looking smile and a shake of his head. "Nobody locks their doors in Paradise. You'd be perfectly safe."

She wiggled and jiggled the key, finally getting the sticky doorknob to turn. "It would freak me out to know it was unlocked." She'd never be able to sleep like that. And every time she came back here, she'd worry someone was hiding inside.

"You'd get used to it," he said.

She doubted that. As they walked inside, her phone rang again.

Cobra flipped the light switch while she moved to the middle of the compact room and extracted the phone from her purse. The number was unknown, causing anxiety to lurch in her stomach. The odds were remote that it had anything to do with her father or her family, but she wasn't taking the chance.

Her finger hovered over the buttons as she debated what to do. She closed her eyes and muttered an expletive, annoyed that her father had the power to get inside her head like this. She gave a little shake and declined the call.

"Everything okay?" Cobra asked, and she realized he'd seen her hesitation.

"Unknown number," she said, which was the truth.

He considered her for a moment. "That's it?"

"That's it," she said breezily, dropping her phone back into her bag and setting the bag on the stripped-down bed, next to a pile of folded sheets and blankets.

"You really shouldn't play poker," he said.

"Who says I play poker?" She understood what he meant, but the call was none of his business.

He seemed amused by her misdirection and moved past her to the little closet where he extracted a blue and gray duffel bag. "I take that back. You should definitely play poker with me."

She knew she should let it go. "Are you saying you can guess what I'm thinking?"

"I'm saying you're bad at bluffing." He spread the bag open on his bed.

"It really was an unknown number." She hadn't blown off a friend or colleague or anything like that.

He passed by her again, moving to the dresser. "I could almost hear the debate inside your head."

She knew he was exaggerating. "Now who's bluffing?"

He lifted a neatly folded stack of three T-shirts from the top drawer.

She couldn't help sneaking a peek inside the dresser. It looked every bit as tidy as the room. It seemed he wore boxers, black boxers. She quickly averted her eyes, realizing she'd seen too much already.

"Right there," he said, pausing to point at her eyes, stopping just short of touching her face. "It's a tell. You had an emotional reaction to the number."

It took her a second to speak. "I didn't know the number."

"Hmmm." He went silent.

She shook her head at the trick. "Oh, no, no. You don't get to say *hmmm* and then wait. You're fishing, like a carnival tarot card reader, looking for me to give something away so you can sound smart."

He quirked an amused grin. "I'm not trying to predict your future. I'm just saying, you've got no more than a pair of sixes."

"Three of a kind," she said, stifling her own grin. "Queens."

"Then I guess you take the pot." His gaze was warm now, full of good humor as he set the T-shirts into the bottom of the duffel.

He moved a stack of boxers and socks, seeming completely unconcerned that she was standing watching him pack his underwear. Then he switched drawers and pulled out some black work pants.

"I'm a lawyer," she said.

"So you said." He moved to the little bathroom.

She trailed behind him and leaned on the door jamb while he opened the cabinet, not sure why she was still bothered but genuinely wondering if she'd overestimated her own litigating talents. "I know how to keep my emotions to myself."

He collected a razor and a can of shaving cream. "Not so much." He caught her gaze in the mirror.

"I argue in court. I'm good at keeping a straight face."

"Was it particularly unsettling, then?" He crouched down and located a black leather shaving kit. "Whatever you saw on the phone."

"No."

He dropped the razor and shaving cream into the kit and arched a brow. "Both things can't be true. Either it was nothing and you have a terrible poker face. Or it was something unsettling that broke through your usual reserve."

"Why are you doing this?" she asked as he straightened back up.

He gave a shrug. "I honestly don't know. We can drop it. You need the soap?" He pointed to the white bar in a little plastic dish at the edge of the sink.

"I've got cleanser."

"Great." He closed the lid on the dish and tossed it into the shaving kit. He added his toothbrush and toothpaste then pulled back the shower curtain and paused there. "This is awkward."

"*Fine*," she blurted out. "Someone in my family is trying to get hold of me, and I thought the unknown number might be them. I haven't heard from them in years, and I don't particularly want to hear from them now. That's it. That's all."

"Oh."

She waited. "*Oh?* That's all I get after you pushed and pushed?"

He turned back to her. "How about this? Maybe it'll help. I know all about difficult families. I avoid mine too."

Oddly, it did help. "Would you take their call?"

"Depends." He rocked his head a little as if he was considering the question. "I'd probably do what you did, be suspicious and decline the call. Then I'd mentally run through scenarios about what it was they could possibly want."

"Exactly!" she said, relieved that he seemed to be a kindred spirit.

He took another moment, just standing there taking up most of the space in the room. "But that wasn't the awkward thing."

She blinked, confused.

He cocked his head toward the shower. "I was hoping to sneak in a shower before I headed back out to the hangar. Would you mind?"

Marnie felt her face heat. "Oh."

"Don't do that," he said with a sympathetic smile, easing slightly forward, shrinking the room even more. "I'm glad you explained about the call."

She closed her eyes for a brief second. When she opened them, he seemed closer still. His steel-gray eyes held a trace of humor, but it was overlaid with compassion.

He didn't look so rugged and untamed anymore. He looked . . . gorgeous. He also looked very strong and very sexy.

Her heart fluttered and her chest warmed. *Wow.*

"Would you mind?" he repeated.

She didn't mind anything, anything at all.

"I won't use all the hot water," he promised.

She brought her head back from the clouds and roused herself to answer. "Yes. Sure. Of course. Please."

He flicked the white plastic curtain shut again. "I'll take all of those yeses."

It took her a moment to take a step away from him, and as she turned to shut the door, her mind filled with a vision of him naked and covered in soapsuds.

"Wow," she whispered out loud this time, leaning back against the bathroom door to catch her breath.

Chapter Four

"COMING OUT," COBRA CALLED TO GIVE MARNIE FAIR warning as he opened the bathroom door. A few seconds later, he walked out and met her shocked expression.

She stared over her tablet at his bare chest and the navy-blue towel wrapped around his hips. Clearly, she hadn't understood his announcement was made so she could avert her eyes.

Her gaze zeroed in on the jagged scar that crossed his lower-right ribcage. It was ugly but fully healed and his only true battle scar.

He'd mostly worked on base when he was overseas with the air force, but he'd once been part of a relocation convoy that came under fire on a dusty road near the Syrian border. Luckily, his wound hadn't been life threatening, and the Rangers with them had quickly cleared the area.

His other scars had far less interesting stories. There was one beside his left eyebrow from a bar fight in Adana, Turkey. He'd been in the right that night. The other guy was being a colossal asshole. So much so that the owner hadn't even called the authorities, just thanked Cobra for helping out. But most of them were simply from living a life around men and machinery.

"I didn't mean to startle you," he told her apologetically.

"No." She waved away his concern. "My fault. I was caught up in reading."

He saw that she'd made up the bed, removed her shoes, pulled her hair into a high ponytail and was curled up against the wall, leaning on a pillow.

He'd never brought a woman to his room. But if he ever did, he hoped she looked exactly like Marnie, all fresh, sweet and gracious.

The outside door suddenly opened and T-Two stepped inside. "Hey, Cobra, what's—" He stopped short, took in Marnie, took in Cobra's state of undress and quickly took a step back. "Sorry, man."

Marnie's eyes went round with embarrassment.

"It's not . . . that," Cobra said, turning to his dresser to get himself some clothes.

"I'm staying here," Marnie quickly told T-Two, pointing to the bed, then switching direction to point to the room.

"None of my business," he responded, still looking apologetic.

"I mean I'm *staying* here. And he's not . . . staying here." She gestured to Cobra. "He's just showering."

It was obvious to everyone she was only making things worse.

"What's up?" Cobra asked T-Two.

"I can come back—"

"Get a grip," Cobra told them both with frustration. To T-Two he said, "I'm not sleeping with her." To Marnie he said, "T-Two won't gossip."

"There's nothing to gossip *about*," Marnie said, her voice going slightly high-pitched.

"Then we're all good," T-Two said to her. He looked her

over with obvious interest, and Cobra's core tightened with reflexive jealousy.

"You are fully dressed," T-Two casually observed.

"I am," Marnie agreed, with a ring in her voice that said it proved her point.

"You here for a reason?" Cobra asked him. "Or just to shoot the breeze?"

T-Two gave him an odd look.

Too late, Cobra realized his impatient tone made him sound like he was interested in Marnie. "I'll get dressed." He grabbed a T-shirt, a pair of boxers and some jeans, and headed into the bathroom.

As he put on his clothes, he heard the soft mutter of T-Two's and Marnie's voices. He couldn't make out the words, but she did laugh at one point. Great. He was so glad to be helping T-Two chat her up. He raked back his short, damp hair and walked barefoot to the bedroom.

T-Two was in the desk chair, while Marnie was cross-legged on the bed, her tablet set aside.

"—even though I was born seven minutes before him, and I'm slightly taller," T-Two was saying, obviously relaying the story of how he and his brother both ended up in Paradise two years ago.

"Tobias," Marnie said, as if trying his real name on for size. "That suits you. I think I'll use it." She looked up. "Not like Conrad here."

Part of Cobra was happy she remembered his real name, another part wondered why she didn't like it.

T-Two seemed to consider her pronouncement. "He needs a three-piece suit and a pair of Oxfords to pull off a name like that."

"Even if you shorten it," Marnie said. "Con? Rad? Nah."

"But you like Tobias?" Cobra couldn't help but ask. He considered joining Marnie on the bed but settled instead for bracing himself against the dresser top.

"Tobias is cute."

Cobra scoffed out a laugh.

"I'll take cute," T-Two said with a waggle of his eyebrows in Marnie's direction.

"She's not here to meet anyone," Cobra told him.

T-Two looked at Cobra in puzzlement.

"She's a lawyer."

"I'm a lawyer," Marnie concurred with a nod.

"She's one of the organizers," Cobra said. "Of the event. She's Mia's friend."

"O . . . kay," T-Two said slowly and searchingly.

"I'm not looking for a husband," Marnie added. "And I'm definitely not staying in Alaska."

"What have you got against Alaska?" T-Two asked, clearly rising to the defense of his adopted state.

"It's . . . uh . . . cold and remote and empty?"

Cobra couldn't argue with that.

"It might not be for everyone." It was clear T-Two was going to take a shot at selling Alaska to the LA lawyer.

Cobra settled back to watch. He didn't know much about Marnie, but what he did know told him T-Two was going to lose the debate.

"Twenty hours of daylight in midsummer," T-Two said.

"Only four hours in January," she countered.

Cobra was surprised she knew that.

She caught his doubtful expression. "I've done a lot of research on Alaska in the past couple of months." She turned back to T-Two. "Go ahead. Bring it on."

"Freshest air in the entire country," he said.

"Hawaii," she said.

Cobra smirked.

"Wide-open spaces," T-Two tried.

"With nothing in them."

"Wildlife."

"Grizzly bears, wolves, moose that can kick as high as your head."

"The foxes are cute."

Marnie grinned. "I'll give you that one. But Pomeranians are cuter, and they're domesticated."

"You have a dog?" Cobra asked. For some reason, he hadn't pictured her as a dog person.

"No dog. No pets. I'm out of my apartment too much. It would be cruel."

"See that," T-Two told her with aplomb. "Foxes take care of themselves. They wander by, look cute then go off and hunt up their own dinner. Now that's a low maintenance pet."

Marnie shook her head. "No. Not buying foxes as pets."

"What about the beautiful vistas?"

"I can see the ocean from my balcony."

"Man." T-Two shook his head. "You're a tough sell. But I'm not giving up."

"You wanted something?" Cobra asked him, not particularly excited about listening to T-Two chat up Marnie any longer.

"Oh, yeah. The rear brakes are squealing on the blue F-150. Brodie asked if you could take a look before Dean takes it down the road tomorrow."

"Sure." Cobra straightened away from the dresser, trying to give T-Two the signal to leave. "I'm headed back out to the hangar in a bit."

T-Two got it, rising and glancing from Cobra to Marnie and back again, a speculative gleam coming into his eyes.

Cobra gazed levelly back. If speculating on Cobra's interest in Marnie kept T-Two away from her, great. She'd made it clear she didn't want to be bothered with any of the Paradise guys. And Cobra liked Marnie. He figured this was doing her a favor.

T-Two said goodbye and left, closing the door behind him.

"He seems nice," Marnie said. "And he sure loves Alaska."

"The Erickson brothers are talented bush pilots. Alaska's a good place for them."

"What about you?" She moved forward to the edge of the bed.

"What about me?"

"Is Alaska a good place for you?"

"Yes." Of that, he was certain. There was room to breathe here. Hard work was respected. And it was far, far away from Seattle.

"Hmmm."

"You're *hmmm*-ing me now?"

"Yes. I'm waiting for you to give something secret away."

"Not going to happen."

She interlaced her fingers together and touched them to the bottom of her chin. "Where did you grow up?"

"Seattle."

"You didn't even make it that hard."

"It's not a secret."

"What do you consider a secret?"

He grinned and sat himself down on the chair T-Two had vacated. "Nice try."

She seemed to contemplate a moment longer. "I'll give up one, if you give up one."

Her green eyes were shining in the light, her skin glowing smooth silk. Her full red lips flashed a smile that showed off perfectly straight white teeth, and it struck him that she was spectacularly gorgeous. He didn't know how he'd missed the full force of it before now.

He propped his elbows on his knees and leaned forward, speaking softly. "You first."

MARNIE TRIED TO COME UP WITH THE RIGHT SECRET, something innocuous enough to share with a stranger but juicy enough to get Cobra to dish when it was his turn. She wanted to know what lurked beneath that tough, scarred exterior.

"I'm a thief," she said.

His eyes widened. "You steal things?"

"Stole. Once. It was before I passed the bar."

He made a show of glancing around the room. "Are my things safe around you?"

"I'm over it."

"What did you steal?"

"Cake, a cupcake. A beautiful, wonderful cupcake. It was confetti vanilla, piled high with fluffy pink buttercream icing with silver sprinkles and a little star on top." Even now she fondly remembered the sweet, creamy taste.

He looked distinctly entertained by the confession. "Why did you do that?"

"My family wasn't very well off, so we never spent money on frivolous things. I was thirteen. My mother had died that year, and it was my birthday, but nobody remembered."

"Your family forgot your birthday?" Cobra's brow furrowed, his expression going from entertained to troubled.

"It was only my dad and my brother then, plus my uncle. They were . . ." She chose her words carefully. "Well . . . focused on work and . . . on other things. But it was grocery day. So, my dad took us all to the Town Market. I spotted this elaborate cupcake just sitting there on the bakery table in a little plastic container that would fit so neatly into my shoulder bag." It was crystal clear in her memory to this day. "I couldn't resist. I snagged it, took it home, and when everyone else had gone to bed, I lit a candle. I didn't have a real birthday candle, just the regular kind. So, I lit it and held the cupcake in front, so the flame danced over the icing and kind of looked like a birthday candle." She smiled, remembering the satisfying effect. "I sang Happy Birthday to myself, really quiet so nobody would hear, then I blew out the candle." She paused for a breath. "Best cupcake I ever ate."

Cobra sat still, his dark eyes clouding. "That's a really sad story."

"You think?" She looked back on it with a bit of amusement now, a little bit of guilt too since a willingness to steal had to say something about the core of her moral fiber. The memory sometimes gave her a shiver of fear, because she would have been in deep trouble if she'd been caught. "I cut the container into teeny, tiny little pieces before I hid it way down in the trash bin. And nobody in the world knows except you."

"I can't believe your family forgot your birthday."

"We weren't a celebrating kind of family, not for anything. Your turn now." She waited, but he didn't speak. She inched a little closer. "You can't wimp out on me, Cobra."

He cleared his throat. "Mine's nowhere near as endearing as yours."

"Thievery's not endearing. Come on. Give."

"All right. I betrayed my brother."

"You have a brother?"

"*That's* your question?"

"Yeah. You have a brother?"

"Two. Barrick and Miles."

"Are you oldest?"

"In the middle."

"Which one did you betray?"

He cocked his head. "Are you going to let me tell the story?"

She made a zipping motion over her lips.

"It was Barrick. He had this girlfriend in college. He went to UW, so he still lived at home. Anyway, the two of them had a big fight one night. I was out in the garage working on a car, and she stormed from the house and saw me there. For some reason, she decided I needed to know what an ass of a brother I had. I didn't disagree, and well, one thing led to another and we—"

"You *slept* with your brother's girlfriend?" Marnie was thinking that definitely beat a pilfered cupcake.

"*No.*" Cobra looked appalled. "I kissed her."

Marnie sat back. "You *kissed* her? That's your big secret? Some little kiss back in college?"

"It was a big kiss, a long kiss, a kiss that almost turned into something else. But I stopped just in time."

"But that's it?"

"I felt guilty about it for years. I might not have been crazy about my brother, but it was a jerk move."

"Did you steal her from him? Did you start dating her yourself?"

"No." Cobra compressed his lips over what looked like a smirk. "They made up. They're married now."

Marnie fought her own reflexive grin. "That must make for one awkward Thanksgiving dinner."

"She pretends it never happened, and I sure never gave her away. Plus, I moved to Alaska, so we don't see each other much." He paused. "Nobody knows that secret either. Well, Josephine, but she's not telling."

Marnie couldn't help but think about the burden that had to cause for Josephine. "That must be hard. To be married to someone and have to hold that in your soul forever."

"It would bother you?"

"I'm barely over the cupcake, and I don't live with the baker."

Cobra chuckled. "You don't know Josephine—cold as ice and twice as determined. I'm sure she blocked it from her mind years ago."

"How would you even do that?" Marnie wished she could erase bad memories. If she could, her family's criminal trial would be a blank slate. She'd like that.

"She makes the world work the way she wants it to work." Cobra stood from the chair then and went back to the bathroom, returning with his shaving kit to drop it into the duffel bag.

He pulled on a pair of socks, shrugged a blue flannel button-front shirt over his T-shirt, and stepped into his scuffed leather boots, obviously preparing to leave.

Marnie wished he'd stick around a little longer. He was unexpectedly entertaining. But she knew he still had work to do tonight.

Watching him, she couldn't help speculating about his kiss. How had it felt to be Josephine, to have Cobra's strong arms wrapped around you, the woodsy scent of his skin, the taste of his full lips? A ripple of desire coursed through her, imagining the thrill.

She wondered if Cobra regretted kissing Josephine.

He lifted the duffel bag and took a final glance around the room. "Well, this has been . . . interesting."

"Was it at least a good kiss?" She blurted the question out before she could stop herself.

His eyes crinkled with a smile. "I was barely seventeen. There were no bad kisses."

It wasn't exactly an answer, but she assumed that meant he'd liked it. She waited a moment, but he didn't elaborate.

"I guess, I'll see you . . . around town?" she asked.

"Unlikely," he said, glancing down at his duffel bag. "I'll be living and working at the airstrip while you're all here."

The answer was disappointing. She would have liked to see him again.

"Come back if you need anything else." Her voice sounded husky, like there was an invitation embedded in there. She hadn't meant it that way. Or maybe she had. It was hard to be sure with him standing so close.

He searched her eyes. His voice was low too. "I will."

Something crackled between them, attraction, energy, maybe their shared secrets. Or maybe it was just that they'd each expected something different from the other.

"I've got some work to do," he said, into the silence.

"Right, the brake shoes on the half-ton."

He drew back in obvious confusion.

She thought maybe she'd remembered wrong. "Isn't that what Tobias said?"

"It is," Cobra answered, but he still looked at her like she'd said something outlandish.

She waited, but again he didn't elaborate.

After a minute, he drew a breath and his eyes softened to ash. "Goodnight, Marnie."

"Night."

He took a step back, then another, then he twisted the doorknob and was gone.

Marnie sat back down on the bed . . . his bed. She flopped backward and let her mind fully explore the possibilities of kissing Cobra.

Chapter Five

COBRA WORKED LATE ON THE TRUCK BRAKES THEN crawled out of bed in the early morning and realized how poor the hangar heating system was at keeping the caretaker suite warm. It was cold enough that the window had frosted overnight. With another long day of work ahead of him, he decided to head into town for a hot breakfast at the WSA cafeteria.

By the time he got back, the sun had melted the frost, but he'd already made up his mind to light up the wood boiler stationed outside the hangar. It was a seasonal system—generating way too much heat for the summer or early fall. He usually waited until mid-October to fire it up, but wood fuel was free for the hauling, and he could open the bay door to keep things in balance. It would definitely keep him warm overnight.

He got the boiler humming, pumping heat into the hangar, then turned his attention to the beaver that was in for an oil leak. He took off the engine cowls, then headed into the parts room to find an O-ring for the tach drive.

He heard several trucks drive past the hangar and into the parking lot. It would be the pilots and possibly some of the Galina Expediting staff with delivery trucks. The frost had melted from the control surfaces, and it was time to get the planes in the air.

All summer long, orders were sorted into manifests in the Galina warehouse, then loaded on a variety of bush planes for delivery to central Alaskan mines and tourism operations, scientific and exploration camps. Now that the season was winding down, more cargo came out of operations than went in, but there was still a steady stream of flying. By late October, flying work would be down to nearly nothing.

He heard a woman's voice outside. At first, he thought it was Hailey, WSA's only female pilot, but the voice didn't sound right. It wasn't Raven. He wondered if it could be Mia here with Silas. But another woman answered, then another spoke, and another. He closed his eyes, realizing they'd brought the LA women back out to the airstrip for some unfathomable reason.

Although frustration was his first emotion, his thoughts quickly switched to Marnie, and he felt curious instead. He'd fallen asleep last night with an image of her in his mind. She'd looked enchanting curled up on his bed, a beckoning smile on her face. When he woke this morning, he still pictured her clearly.

He'd looked around for her at the WSA cafeteria this morning but quickly realized they'd give the women breakfast at the Bear and Bar. It was nicer there, proper tables and real chairs instead of picnic tables and benches, table service instead of the cafeteria lineup. The food at WSA was satisfying, but it was designed to keep hardworking men fueled up all day long, not to appeal to the palates of women who were likely used to pesto avocado camembert fusion on their sprouted wheat toast—or something like that.

On sober reflection, it was just as well she hadn't been there. He recognized the signs, and the last thing he needed was to become infatuated with a woman who'd barely be here long enough to unpack her suitcase.

He found the O-ring and headed back into the main hangar, stopping short when he saw someone peering into the beaver bush plane's engine. From this angle, all he saw were legs, jean-covered legs that were definitely female.

Oh, no, no, no. He picked up his pace. The last thing he needed was some curious lookie-loo injuring herself by poking around an engine. Cobra's hangar was *not* part of the tour.

"Hey," he called out as he ducked under the wing.

The bright copper hair registered as she turned to face him.

Marnie.

He stopped short, dialing back his frustration and swallowing the terse rebuke and warning on the tip of his tongue. "Be careful," he said instead.

"Morning," she said with a pretty smile that targeted the center of his chest. "I've never seen a radial engine up close."

The statement momentarily stopped his train of thought. "Why did you call it a radial engine?"

She gestured to the cylinders, running her finger around the configuration. "Because it's . . . radial."

"I thought you were a lawyer." He set the O-ring down on the top of his toolbox.

"I am a lawyer."

"With a hobby in mechanics?" He was trying to work this out.

Last night she'd somehow known that rear brakes on the half-ton were shoes and not pads, and she was just about the last person he'd expect to have an interest in mechanics. She was adorable and delicate. He'd be willing to bet her small, soft hands had never once touched a wrench or a screwdriver.

"I grew up behind an automotive shop. I was a curious kid."

That explained part of it. "As a little girl you were curious about mechanics?"

"My father considered a working knowledge of internal combustion engines to be a basic life skill."

Cobra couldn't exactly argue with that, even if there was something off in her tone when she said it. If he had to guess, he'd say she hadn't been a willing pupil. But it was very progressive of her father to teach her.

"I can check the fluid levels and belts," she said. "Not to mention change a tire if I ever get a flat."

"They don't have auto shops in LA?"

She stepped back from the open cowling. "They do. And I call them if I'm dressed for work."

"You shouldn't change a tire on the side of a busy road." He didn't like the picture that painted in his mind, the cars whizzing past. And he particularly didn't like to think about the kind of men who might be tempted to stop and pretend to help her when she was in such a vulnerable position.

"I'd call the shop," she said. "If for no other reason than to protect my manicure."

"There are plenty of other reasons to call a bonded professional. Safety, for example."

"They're doing flightseeing tours out there," she said, changing the topic and looking through the open door to the parking lot and the airstrip beyond.

"Probably up to the Pedestal Glacier and along the Paradise Valley to Briar Falls. You'll also get a great view of the creek falls off the airstrip as you're taking off." Cobra wouldn't mind taking her flying himself. He wondered how Brodie would react if he offered.

"Not really my thing," she said.

"Are you sure? People pay big money for that tour."

"I saw enough mountain vistas on the way in," she said. Then she grimaced. "I sometimes get a little airsick."

"Ouch." He could understand her reluctance. Some passengers had very bad experiences in small planes. Everything, the bumps, the jolts, the turns and altitude changes, were sharper and more sudden than in an airliner.

Her hand went reflexively to her stomach. "I think I'll play this one safe."

Cobra felt guilty wasting work time standing here talking to her, so he stepped up to the engine and reached inside to unfasten the tach drive.

"I didn't notice that last night," she said.

Puzzled, he turned his head.

She was pointing to the back of his neck. "Can I?"

He could guess what it was she'd seen. "Sure." He stilled for her.

She reached up to the collar of his coveralls and gently pulled it down, her fingertips grazing the back of his neck and sending a wave of desire plummeting through him.

He gasped and hoped she hadn't heard.

"It's a snake," she said as she revealed the tattoo. "Bend a little."

He did, and her breath puffed lightly against his skin. He gripped hard on the ratchet handle wrench.

It took her a minute to speak. It felt like a long, long minute. "It's not too ugly."

He chuckled, breaking the spell. "You don't like tattoos?"

"I don't like snakes. But it's stylized enough to be . . . inoffensive."

He straightened and joked. "Inoffensive. That's truly what I was striving for when I got it."

She went quiet then.

He turned, worried he'd been rude. "I didn't mean—"

But she didn't look offended. She looked . . . desirable. Her lips were soft, pink, slightly parted. Her eyes were wide, sparkling like emeralds in the sunbeams. The skin of her cheeks looked so touchable and soft. His hands were far too rough and dirty to touch her but, man, he was tempted.

She took a half step closer, making it even harder for him to resist. But he steeled himself, tightening his grip on the wrench and curling his left hand into a fist by his side.

She tipped her chin and tilted her head to exactly the right angle for a kiss. "Didn't mean what?" she asked softly.

The wrench clanged to the ground, bouncing off the oil-stained concrete.

He cupped her cheek with one hand and wrapped his arm around the base of her spine, lowering his lips to meet hers.

The kiss all but exploded between them. Her mouth was mobile, soft and sweet. He tried to be gentle, but instinct took over, and he kissed her harder, deeper, pressing her against his—

He abruptly let go, dragging himself back, horrified that he'd ruined her clothes with the grease on his coveralls. She was wearing a pink blouse for God's sake, pale pink, all soft and silky, clinging to her slim shoulders.

"What?" she asked, breathless, looking confused.

"I'm sorry."

"Why?"

"Look at you." There was an oil smear on the front of her shirt, and he could have kicked himself for his stupidity.

She looked down for a minute. "Oh."

There was a streak of dirt on her cheek where he'd touched her.

He pointed. "There."

She rubbed the spot away. "Better?"

"Yes. I'm sorry, Marnie. I don't know what I was thinking."

"Probably the same thing I was thinking."

He waited, hoping she'd tell him exactly what that was. But she didn't.

"Your shirt is ruined," he guiltily pointed out. "I'll buy you a new one."

"That's not necessary. Really. I'm the one who wandered into a repair shop dressed like this."

"I'm the guy who pulled you into his arms."

Her green-eyed gaze met his again—like soft moss after a cool shower. "Mistake on both our parts."

He didn't agree that any of it was her fault. All she'd done was stand there looking desirable. He was the one who'd lost control.

"But no real harm," she said, squaring her shoulders and glancing to the beaver engine. "You have work to do. I should leave you to it."

Yes, he did have work to do, but he didn't want her to leave.

Still, he didn't stop her, and she walked away, out through the bay door, back to the airstrip and the group of women where she belonged.

MARNIE, MIA AND RAVEN DECIDED TO SIT OUT THE AFternoon's scavenger hunt, opting to have a visit instead. Breena had the event well in hand. She'd received permission to use Finding Paradise as a technical project in one of her courses, so she'd developed a custom app for the scavenger hunt and downloaded it onto the participants' phones.

Split into groups, they were given a starting point in town and, using clues, had to upload photos of assigned items—things like moose hair tufting on leather mittens at Greenway Gifts, the grizzly bear carving behind Caldwell Corner Gas, and the eagles' nest at the end of the block by the school.

The app was impressive. Breena had showed it to Marnie earlier. When completed, a detailed map of the town appeared on screen, while colorful confetti and balloons burst out to celebrate the achievement.

Marnie, Mia and Raven had convened at Raven's cabin where Mia was living while she and Silas built a house nearby. Having visited Mia at the Lafayette mansion, Marnie was shocked to find her living in such battered, shabby surroundings. It reminded Marnie uncomfortably of the old house where she'd grown up in Merganser, Kansas.

The floor was faded linoleum, pitched and hollowed. The countertops were made of raw wood, painted white with open shelves above them that held mismatched dishes and a collection of dry goods.

Marnie was sitting gingerly on a saggy, faded red brocade sofa in a tiny living room around the corner from the kitchen. Mia and Raven were curled up across from her, each looking perfectly at home in stained beige armchairs. Between them was a battered coffee table, against the wall was a black wood stove with glowing coals that radiated heat.

"Too early for wine?" Raven asked.

"It's almost three." Mia unwound her legs, stepped into her shoes and moved into the kitchen, taking a bottle of wine from a shelf below the counter. "Old World red?"

"Works for me," Raven said.

"Sure," Marnie added her agreement. "Love some." She glanced further around the rooms, wondering whether to gently phrase a question about Mia's thoughts on living in this cabin or diplomatically keep her mouth shut.

Raven took in Marnie's expression and chuckled. "You look just like Mia did the first day she came here."

Marnie tried to school her features, not wanting to insult either of them.

"Horror was my reaction," Mia called from the kitchen. "Well, horror and terror."

"Terror?" Marnie asked with a reflexive glance into the

corners, wondering if there was some creepy-crawly thing she had to worry about and if she should lift her feet to avoid it.

"Silas scared the crap out of me," Mia said. "His grim attitude, angry eyes and all that rugged, muscled, broad-shouldered height."

Marnie had met Silas, once in LA and again yesterday. He seemed thoughtful and easy-going, and completely devoted to Mia. Although he was tall and fit, he was more handsome than anything. He wasn't particularly rugged, at least compared to Cobra.

Marnie pressed her lips together, feeling the echo of Cobra's kiss. She remembered his arm so firmly around her, pressing her close, overwhelming her senses with want and passion. The memory was so vivid that her skin warmed even now, and desire threatened to swamp her all over again.

"You should tell her," Raven said to Mia, eager anticipation in her expression.

"Tell me what?" Marnie asked, liking the idea of distraction.

Mia opened her hands. "I guess I have to tell her now."

Raven grinned. "It's funny. Plus, she's your lawyer. It's not like she can divulge your secret to anyone."

"Secret?" Marnie repeated, genuinely interested now.

Mia gathered three acrylic tumblers of red wine in her hands and returned to the living room.

Marnie carefully took the first one from the cluster. The plastic was lined with cracks, and the glass was covered in pink and green beach umbrellas.

"We don't much stand on ceremony," Mia said.

Remembering the fine crystal stemware at the Lafayette mansion, Marnie knew that was an understatement.

"It's a very nice Bordeaux." Mia handed a glass to Raven and took her seat again, kicking off her shoes to curl her jean-clad legs under her once more.

"She makes me ship it in special," Raven said.

"There's a savings when you buy it by the case," Mia said.

"You're worried about money?" Marnie found that impossible to believe.

"Not worried. I just noticed is all."

"Are you going to tell me or what?" Marnie asked, taking a sip and discovering it was a very nice wine, despite its humble presentation.

"She thought Silas was a serial killer," Raven said, a thread of glee in her voice.

Mia shot her a glare. "Sure, just blurt it right out there."

"It's not like you weren't going to tell her." Raven took a sip.

"Why would you think that?" Marnie asked with a laugh. "What did he do? Was it threatening?" She couldn't picture Silas doing anything threatening. She hadn't so much as seen him frown at Mia.

"Brought her straight from the airstrip to here," Raven said.

"Whose story is this?" Mia asked her.

"Sorry. Carry on."

Mia turned back to Marnie. "We left the airport, just me and him, him all grumpy and annoyed at having to deal with a big-city princess. Then, no explanation, no nothing, we wheel in here. You must admit, from the outside, this place looks like a killer's lair."

"Hey," Raven said with mock offense.

Mia ignored her. "He left me alone in the car and hauled my bags off inside. I figured he was up to something, and I didn't have any mace, so I thought I better get the hell out while I could. I tried to drive away."

"She hit a tree," Raven said.

"I hit a tree," Mia admitted. "Silas caught me, took over the wheel and yelled at me for being nuts."

"It wasn't nuts," Marnie said. It might be funny in retrospect, but a woman should act on her instinct when it came to threatening men.

"Thank you," Mia said with obvious satisfaction.

"It might not be the prettiest house in the world," Raven said.

"It's . . ." Marnie had been about to say *practical*, but it wasn't even particularly practical since it had aging furniture, a rustic closet of a kitchen, no phone service and substandard plumbing.

"Functional," Mia said. "And you do get used to the eccentricities."

"We just installed a cell signal booster," Raven said. "And after the plumbers finish Mia's house, they're going to fix up my bathroom," Raven said.

"Don't go into the bathroom," Mia warned Marnie. "At least not without instructions."

"Instructions?" Marnie hoped she wouldn't need to use the bathroom.

"We'll worry about that later," Raven said. Her phone dinged, and she checked it out. "Breena says the scavenger hunt is going great guns." Her eyes went a little wide. "Scarlett climbed a tree to get a shot of the eagles' nest."

Mia's brows shot up. "Is she okay?"

"Did she fall?" Marnie asked.

"The eagles are very protective. They're fast, really big, sharp talons, sharp beaks."

Marnie cringed at the thought of being swooped at by an eagle.

"Scarlett's fine, and the picture's great, but it sounds like it got exciting for a few minutes. Breena's sending out some new safety instructions."

"Maybe she should send a chaperone with each of the groups," Mia said.

"Xavier would chaperone Scarlett," Raven said with a calculating grin.

"You saw that too?" Mia asked.

"What?" Marnie answered, feeling out of the loop yet again.

"Didn't you see them dancing last night?" Mia asked. "Out on the deck."

"It was cold," Raven said. "But that didn't seem to slow them down."

"I left early," Marnie confessed, her thoughts going back to Cobra.

"Tired?" Raven asked.

Marnie wasn't about to make something up. "Cobra needed some things from his room, so . . . you know . . . we went to get them."

Both women gaped at her in silence.

"What?" Marnie asked.

"Together?" Raven asked.

"Yes. Why?"

"If you ask me, Cobra's the scary one," Mia said.

"All those scars," Raven said. "He's so quiet. You can never tell what he's thinking. And he stares with those intense wolverine eyes."

"You think he's quiet?" Marnie agreed on the intense eyes part. She found them sexy. But he hadn't seemed quiet. He'd been positively chatty last night.

"You didn't notice?" Mia asked.

"Did you do a lot of the talking?" Raven asked.

"I . . . don't . . ." Marnie thought back.

He was an easy man to talk to. He was easy to listen to, too. And he was very easy to kiss—extraordinarily easy to kiss. She couldn't stop a fond smile of remembrance.

"What?" Mia prompted, looking curious.

"Sometimes quiet," Marnie said, schooling her features. The man was quiet when it counted.

Chapter Six

COBRA HADN'T PLANNED TO JOIN IN ON THE TOWN cookout and campfire taking place in the field off the end of Red Avenue on Saturday. But while he'd grabbed a late lunch in the WSA cafeteria, staff had started mobilizing for the event. He wasn't going to sit on his hands while others carried picnic tables, chairs and grills over to the site, or while they hauled, bucked and split enough firewood for the night's bonfires.

So as the event got under way—WSA and Galina staff arriving at the end of their work days, families coming down to join in the fun, a group of kids kicking a soccer ball around by the goal at the far end of the field, and the LA women making their way over from the nearby WSA housing—Cobra was still splitting the deadfall trees they'd salvaged from the nearby bush.

They'd decided on three fires to keep them small and accommodate more people. The kids couldn't exactly roast marshmallows around a giant ten-foot blaze. To make sure there was fuel enough for the night, Cobra and Brodie had stacked close to a cord between the three pits.

"At least none of them are wearing skirts today," Brodie observed, pausing to watch the women who were loitering about a hundred feet away.

Cobra didn't look up. He wanted to know if Marnie was there, but he didn't want to see her. If he did, he knew he'd stare blatantly at her beauty. In all likelihood, she'd catch him. And he'd embarrass them both with the naked hunger in his eyes.

Their kiss had been humming in the back of his mind all day long. It had been one hell of a kiss, rocking him to his core, making him question every kiss that came before it. Logic told him a single kiss couldn't be that much different than all the others. It had been weeks, maybe a couple of months since he'd kissed a woman, so maybe that was the problem. He should make a trip into Anchorage soon and get himself a social life.

"The bugs will be disappointed by that," he responded to Brodie, swinging his ax and burying it in a round of pine, splitting the dry wood into two halves.

"My guess is they learned a thing or two yesterday afternoon."

Cobra lifted one of the split halves and steadied it on his chopping block before stepping back to swing. "What was yesterday afternoon?"

"Scavenger hunt. Breena sent them out to the eagles' nest to take a picture. I expect by now they're fully familiar with our abundant insect life."

Cobra gave a dry chuckle as he split the half and tossed two pieces onto the woodpile. "Experience is a great teacher. I saw you donated flightseeing tours."

Brodie tossed his own split pieces onto the growing pile. "Sure. Why not?" He set up another round for himself and began speaking philosophically. "Maybe some of them go back to LA, maybe they share their photos, maybe they mention West Slope Aviation or Paradise, Alaska, and we get some tourism business out of it."

"Hadn't thought of it that way."

"Did you meet Scarlett?"

"Nope." The only woman Cobra had met was Marnie, and she wasn't even one of them.

"She's a production assistant for a Hollywood film company."

"You liked her?"

Brodie drew back in what looked like horror. "*No.*"

Cobra wasn't following. "Then what?"

"Hollywood film companies need locations." He swept his arm around the vista of the valley. "Can you think of a better wilderness location than Paradise?"

"You think she'll bring a Hollywood film here?" The odds had to be low on that.

"I know it's a long shot," Brodie said. "But if you consider all potential economic outcomes, the odds go up. For example, Ariel Wallace distributes organic products. Maybe she comes up with an idea for natural glacier water. I can see Paradise Valley glacier water being a big seller, can't you?"

Cobra tossed his final stick of wood and buried his ax deep in the chopping block. "You're trying to turn this into an economic development endeavor?"

"Why not?"

"They're like mail-order brides," Cobra said.

Brodie frowned. "Not exactly."

"Okay. Fair enough. Not mail-order brides." Cobra knew the statement was insulting.

They were most likely perfectly wonderful women. From the little he'd heard, they were each smart and successful in their own right. Plus, he trusted Raven. She wouldn't introduce anyone flaky to the town.

"Raven was very selective," Brodie said, sounding defensive.

"My bad. It sounds like they're all very accomplished."

"Very."

"I know Raven has the best interests of the town at heart."

"She does." Brodie buried his own ax into his chopping block, tossing his last two sticks onto the woodpile. "She doesn't always nail it the first time. But she does try."

"Nothing against Raven," Cobra said, reminding himself to tiptoe around Brodie when it came to Raven.

Brodie's gaze moved to the cluster of people around the picnic tables and the grills. "I know." He was clearly gazing at Raven.

She was deep in an animated conversation with John Reed, the head cook. From her gestures, he'd guess she had an opinion on the placement of the grills.

Brodie looked amused. He also looked delighted, his expression softening as he watched the exchange.

There wasn't a chance Brodie would be interested in Scarlett or anyone else from LA.

Cobra didn't know what the deal was—if Raven wasn't interested, or if Brodie hadn't asked her. Curious, he probed for more information. "She's smart, hardworking and really pretty."

Brodie looked up, doing a double take. "What?"

"Raven. If a guy was looking for someone who'd fit in Paradise, you couldn't beat Raven."

Brodie's lips thinned. "We all need to stay away from Raven."

"We do? I mean, I know we always have."

Brodie gave a sharp nod. "And we need to keep it that way."

"Because?"

"The obvious."

"Which is?"

"She makes the whole town run. Somebody does her wrong or breaks her heart, and she's outta here. Then where will we be?"

"Have you ever talked to her about it?" Who knew, Raven might appreciate a date or two, maybe even a date with Brodie. She sure didn't seem like the type to randomly hook up if she went to Fairbanks or Anchorage.

"Yes," Brodie said.

"Really?" The answer surprised Cobra. "You and her?"

"Sort of. We skirted the issue once or twice. She agrees with the logic."

"Are you sure about that?" As they talked, Cobra caught sight of Xavier messing with one of the propane-powered mosquito traps.

"Positive."

"Okay." Cobra didn't know why he was still pushing.

Brodie was old enough to decide who was his friend and who was his romantic interest, and Cobra didn't have a stake in Raven's social life one way or the other.

"I'll go give Xavier a hand," Cobra said. "He looks frustrated."

Brodie nodded, and Cobra headed across the field to where Xavier was crouched in front of a trap.

"Problem?" Cobra asked him as he approached.

"Can't get the burner to stay lit."

"Bottle full?"

Xavier stood and lifted the propane bottle to test its weight. "I'd say three-quarters."

"Does it have a kit?" Cobra looked under the burner as he asked the question, locating the small maintenance kit clipped onto the stand. He unbuckled it. "We should reset the valve pin."

He was glad to find the kit fully stocked, including a reset tool. He twisted it into the valve, then he reset the regulator and cleared the lines for good measure before he stood back. "Give it another try. If that doesn't do it, we might have to take it to the shop."

Xavier relit the burner, and they both heard the propane hissing and the small burst as it lit up.

"Done," Xavier said, sounding satisfied.

Cobra replaced the kit and buckled it in.

"You changed your mind," Xavier said.

"About?" Cobra asked as he rose.

"This. Them. The women. Did you decide you liked one of them?"

"I didn't change my mind." Cobra liked Marnie, but Marnie wasn't one of the women, so she didn't count.

"You're here."

"Only to help out."

"So, none of them caught your eye?"

"None of them. You?"

Xavier responded with a covert grin and shifted his focus to the women gathered around the picnic tables.

"Who?" Cobra asked, following his line of sight.

"Light brown hair, up in a ponytail, with the green jacket and jeans. Name's Scarlett."

"Hollywood production assistant," Cobra said, putting the name with her face.

A worried look crossed Xavier's face. "You've met her?"

"No. Brodie has."

"Brodie?" Xavier looked even more worried.

"He wants her to bring a movie to Paradise. To use us as a location."

Xavier looked relieved. "Oh. Okay. That's a good idea."

"It's a long shot of an idea."

"But he's not attracted to her or anything."

"No. Definitely not."

Xavier smiled. "Sounds like the field is open."

"Sounds like." Cobra's gaze slipped from the five and a half foot tall, slim woman to the smiling copper-haired Marnie who stood close by. He let himself stare for a full minute before he forced his attention back to the mosquito trap. "I think we're good here."

"Great. Thanks, man." Xavier gave him a little salute as he headed for the picnic tables and the cluster of people settling in for the cookout.

MARNIE FELT ODDLY AT HOME AT THE COMMUNITY gathering. Some of her few good memories from growing up in Merganser were the summer potluck picnics where she could play with her school friends on a Saturday and somebody always brought dessert.

Now, she pushed up the sleeves of her olive-green cable-knit sweater and offered her services to the cook who looked to be in charge at the line of grills. Two men were juggling six grills between them.

"Oh, no, no, no," the man demurred. "You're our guest."

"It's a community picnic," she said, while at the same time picking up the flipper. She knew how these things worked. Offers of assistance were turned down. Actual work was gratefully accepted. Plus, she knew her way around a grill. Right now, a row of burgers at the far end needed flipping, so she did.

"You don't have to do that," he said.

She grinned right back at the man in the white apron. "I'm part of the community; at least I am for the weekend. I can help out." Then she nodded. "Your brats are going to burn."

That got his attention.

"I'm Marnie, by the way," she called out while he rescued the sizzling brats.

"John." He looked to be in his midforties, slightly rounded in the middle with a friendly face and warm blue eyes.

"Nice to meet you, John."

"Raven's not going to like this," he said with a shake of his head.

"Leave Raven to me. Got another apron?"

He obviously wasn't about to give her one himself, since that would make him complicit, but his flick of a glance told her where they were stacked, so she snagged one and put it on.

She lost his attention after that when the burgers on one of the other grills needed him.

People filed past the line of grills with their buns at the ready. She fell into a rhythm with John and another cook named Fredo.

Mia appeared in front of her. "Hey! What are you doing back there?"

"Cooking some of the best burgers you'll ever eat." Marnie slid one on top of the tomato slice on Mia's bun.

"You shouldn't be working."

"I'm an organizer, not a guest." Marnie was having fun, feeling useful and saying hi to people in the brief, casual way she preferred. Plus, she liked John and Fredo.

"You're a volunteer, not an employee," Mia said, looking around as if she was trying to figure out how this had happened.

"Don't look at me," John called over. "I tried to stop her."

"He did," Marnie affirmed. Then she shrugged. "Too bad I'm more persuasive than he is."

"Come out here and eat," Mia said, awkwardly waving her forward with a plastic cup of what looked like red wine.

"In a few minutes," Marnie said.

"We're slowing down," John said, moving in beside her and firmly removing the flipper from her hand.

"Those are ready," she told him, and pointed.

"You're telling me how to do my job now?"

"No, no." She didn't want to insult him, but he only grinned at her.

"Over here," Mia said, motioning to a picnic table where Raven had already sat down.

"I'll be right there." Marnie untied her apron and dropped it on the back of a chair.

"Thanks for the help," John said.

"Call me back if you need me."

"It's under control."

Marnie made up her own bun, got a burger from Fredo and joined Mia and Raven at the picnic table with Scarlett and Xavier.

"You need wine," Mia said to her, and immediately hopped up.

"I can get my own—" Marnie started, but Mia was already on her way, so she gave up, settled in and took a bite of her juicy burger. It was delicious—a soft, dense bun, crisp tomato, perfectly grilled meat patty and slightly melted tangy cheddar cheese. She swallowed. "Yum."

"Aren't these buns to die for?" Scarlett asked her as she took another bite.

"Home-baked daily at the Bear and Bar," Xavier said to Scarlett. "The best in the whole country."

Raven nodded approvingly at him. "Way to wave the town flag there, Xavier."

Xavier smiled slyly. "I got the memo."

"T-Two's got a good patter going too," Marnie said.

Raven looked surprised. "You've been hanging out with T-Two?"

"He was with Cobra."

"Cobra again?" Raven asked, looking curious.

Marnie kept her focus on the table, fighting the urge to scan the crowd for him. She'd spotted him early on, off in the distance chopping firewood. Even from far away, he looked distractingly sexy.

Luckily, tending the grill had kept her occupied.

Mia had arrived with Marnie's wine. "What's this about Cobra?" she asked as she settled back down on the bench.

"We were talking about T-Two," Marnie answered. "When I first got here, he came to Cobra's room."

"Because?" Mia prompted.

"Because he needed Cobra to do the brake shoes on a half-ton at the airstrip. What I was *saying* is T-Two spouted a list of the five best things about living in Alaska." Marnie took a breath followed by a drink of her wine, discovering it was very good too. "Nice," she said holding up her glass to check out the rich color in the waning light.

"We should have thought to put the five best things on a wallet card," Raven said to Mia, sounding like she was serious.

"What were they?" Mia asked Marnie.

Marnie searched her memory. "Fresh air, long daylight, great vistas, wildlife, cute foxes."

"Cute foxes?" Mia asked.

"I countered with fierce grizzly bears."

"Countered?" Scarlett asked, looking puzzled.

"Grizzly bears aren't so bad," Mia said with a self-satisfied grin. "You just have to show them who's boss."

Everyone chuckled, since they all knew the story of how Mia had fended off a grizzly and two cubs with a can of bear spray.

She tapped the red canister strapped to her belt. "Never leave home without it."

"Should we all have one of those?" Marnie asked, wondering for the first time about animal safety.

"We're all in town or in large groups, so I think it's okay," Raven said.

"But it's not a bad idea," Mia said.

"I can set it up," Xavier offered.

Scarlett sent a surreptitious but admiring smile his way.

Marnie realized the Finding Paradise project at least had a toehold on success with those two. It was a surprise—a happy surprise.

Marnie's phone buzzed in her pocket. She set down her

burger to check and saw it was Bexley from her office. She worried a client might have a problem and quickly accepted the call.

"My assistant," she said to the others at the table as she rose to step away. "Hi, Bexley."

"Hi, yourself." Bexley sounded cheerful, and Marnie's worry level dropped. "A super-rush package came for you."

"You're in the office?" It was unusual but not unheard of for Bexley to work on a Saturday.

"Just for a couple of hours. I thought it might be important."

Marnie wasn't expecting anything specific, but disclosure files might have arrived on any number of cases. She moved a few feet away to keep from disturbing everyone else. "Who's it from?"

"Bingalo Rodeo Drive."

That didn't make any sense. "Are you sure?"

"I'm reading the label right now."

"I didn't order anything from them." Bingalo was a highly exclusive shop.

"It's got your name on it. Want me to open it and see?"

"I guess. You'll probably have to send it back."

"Maybe they got the name wrong." Bexley's voice changed as she switched to hands-free.

"Maybe." But that didn't make much sense. It wasn't as though Marnie's name and address were in their customer database.

While Bexley opened the package, Marnie went to snag the last bite of her burger, popping it into her mouth before she picked up her wine.

"Wow," Bexley said.

Marnie stepped back from the table again, quickly swallowing. "Wow, what?"

"It's *gorgeous*."

"What is it?"

"A blouse. Do you ever have good taste."

"I didn't pick it. I didn't buy it."

"It's silk, a band collar, little peek-a-boo vee with flat lace at the front, cap sleeves, and so, so soft. Pale pink, a blush or maybe a crepe. I'll shoot you a picture."

The word *pink* broke through Marnie's confusion. "Oh no."

"What?" Bexley asked. "Is it bad? What's wrong?"

Marnie scanned the crowd for Cobra now. "He didn't."

"Who? Didn't what?"

"There was an accident," Marnie told her. "My pink blouse got stained yesterday morning. But it was only yesterday . . ." She didn't see how it was possible for Cobra to pull it off so fast, or even shop for anything beyond steel-toed boots and dungarees.

She looked at Mia, wondering if she might have helped him. But if Mia knew what was going on, she'd be watching Marnie right now, waiting for her reaction. Plus, Cobra had been embarrassed by the kiss. He didn't seem like the kind of guy who'd share what had happened with Mia or anyone else.

"Was it somebody's fault?"

"No, but he thought it was." The picture pinged in her phone, and Marnie took a quick look. The blouse was exquisite.

"Who's *he*?" Bexley asked.

"Not important." Marnie's stomach clenched at the thought of the cost. "Thanks. Really, thanks, Bexley. I hope you're headed home now."

"In about five minutes. Enjoy the rest of your weekend."

"You too. I'll see you Tuesday."

"Bye." Bexley ended the call, and Marnie pocketed her phone.

Overwhelmed by the magnitude of the gesture, she scanned the crowd for Cobra again while she removed her used paper plate from the table.

"Everything okay?" Mia asked, looking quizzically at Marnie's expression.

"Good." Marnie gave an unconcerned smile. "Just routine stuff. I'm going to toss this."

"No more cooking for you," Mia admonished with a wag of her finger.

"Promise. I'm going to take a wander around, maybe meet a few people."

"Really?" Mia looked surprised.

Marnie spotted Cobra in the distance then. "I'll catch up later."

COBRA HAD PLANNED TO BE LONG GONE BY NOW. BUT he'd stayed for a couple of burgers, and then work had started on laying the wood for the bonfires.

"Cobra?" The sound of Marnie's voice broke through his concentration, obliterating hours of his effort to focus on other things. "Cobra?" she repeated, drawing closer behind him.

He took a beat before turning, preparing himself for the sight of her close-up and hoping it didn't flatline his brain the way he worried it might.

It did. But only for a second, and then he found his voice. "Hi."

Her skin seemed to glow in the twilight. Loose strands of her hair shimmered pale copper around her face, lifting ever so slightly in the light breeze. Her eyes were emerald-bright, fringed with dark lashes. Her lips were full. And her supple form was outlined against a soft, clingy sweater and jeans that molded along the curves of her thighs and calves.

"I can't believe you did it," she said.

He glanced reflexively back at the bonfire setup, seeing nothing out of place. "Did what?"

"The blouse," she said on a note of exasperation.

"Oh, that."

"Yes, that."

"I didn't think it would ship so soon."

"That's your excuse?"

"I thought you'd get it when you were back in LA."

"I bought the first one at the Butterfly Boutique. You went to *Bingalo*?"

Apprehension hit him. Had he screwed this up? "Is there something wrong with Bingalo?"

Their website had looked great, classy, top-rated by whoever it was that rated those things—lots of gold stars and glowing words. And the woman he'd spoken with on the phone seemed to know exactly what she was doing.

He'd admit, he hadn't spent a whole lot of time shopping. He hadn't had a whole lot of time to blow on it.

"Hey, Cobra," Brodie called loudly from across the field. He made a circular motion with his arm. "Light it up."

Cobra made his way to the fire.

"It's expensive," Marnie said, following. "Like, *really* expensive."

He struck a match to the kindling and watched as the flames curled into the wood. "I owed you."

"You didn't—"

"I ruined your blouse, my fault." He turned from the fire to look at her. The yellow light flickered against the side of her face.

Every second, every nuance, every feeling of their kiss bloomed viscerally through his mind, his body, his very bones.

As he stared, her gaze softened to moss and her lips parted.

Before he could stop himself, his hand moved her way.

The fire gave a loud pop, and he reflexively wrapped an arm around her waist, twisting to shelter her and pushing her away from the shower of sparks. He stopped a few feet farther from the fire, keeping his hold on her in case she was off-balance, also because he couldn't bear to let her go.

"This keeps up," he tried for a joke, "it's going to cost me a fortune."

"Huh?" She tipped her chin upward, looking straight up at him, looking gorgeous from this angle, sinfully sexy.

"The sparks can burn holes in your clothes. You shouldn't sit around a bonfire in anything you care about."

A voice called out, "Nice," as those nearby gravitated to the fire.

Cobra reluctantly let her go and eased back.

People began moving lawn chairs into the circle of warmth. The cooking staff arrived, erecting tables and setting up a working area to serve cookies, marshmallows and hot chocolate.

"I can get you a chair," Cobra offered, at war with himself over whether to let her go or keep her as close as he possibly could.

"Hey, Marnie." John approached them with a hearty greeting. "Does your offer still hold?"

"Of course," she was quick to answer.

"Just for half an hour or so."

"Happy to help out." She sounded genuinely happy.

Cobra looked back and forth between the two, gauging their expressions, wondering if there was anything between them. John was sure to be attracted to Marnie, any man would. But he was on the old side for her. Plus, Marnie had made it clear she wasn't looking for a relationship.

Still, Cobra couldn't quite squelch his jealousy at their easy conversation.

"We've been split into three teams," John said. "And I was hoping to give Fredo a bit of time with his kids."

"No problem. Where do you need me?"

"Hot chocolate station?"

"I can do that." She gave Cobra a parting glance. "Thanks for saving me from the sparks."

"Sure."

"And thanks for the blouse, even though—"

"Stop," he said. "It's done."

She frowned. "I hope you at least asked the price before you ordered it."

"No need." He paused. "I just told the woman to send you the best one she had."

Marnie rolled her eyes then. "Now I'm afraid to wear it."

"Wear it." His tone was insistent, and he held her gaze for good measure. "Wear it."

She gave him a shy smile but then turned away without answering one way or the other.

"Are you planning to sit here?" Carrying an armload of lawn chairs with his wife and three young kids, Badger was clearly looking for a spot in the rapidly filling area around the fire.

"All yours," Cobra said, stepping out of the way.

He worked his way to the back of the crowd, leaving the choice spots to the families but finding a spot where he had a clear view of Marnie. She'd wrapped herself in a big white apron and was smiling and chatting as she ladled hot chocolate into mugs for the children and adults lining up for dessert.

The kids who'd been chasing soccer balls and racing around the forest edge all afternoon would roast a marshmallow or two, eat a cookie, drink the creamy hot chocolate and eventually be bundled off to bed. The adults would then sweeten their mugs of hot chocolate with liquor, and the event would move to a different phase.

What made it different tonight was the presence of all those LA women. Cobra might have been set against them coming, but right now they were certainly energizing the evening. Maybe Raven and Mia weren't so misguided after all.

Brodie appeared beside him with a beer in his hand. His voice was dire and laden with unease. "Xavier, Dean, AJ, Jackson."

Cobra raised his brow in a question.

"All of them. They're going to be moping around for the whole of next week. Why are we the only ones who can see how this game ends?"

Cobra scanned the crowd and saw each of the men Brodie mentioned in lively or intense conversations with one of the LA women. "They're big boys. They'll shake it off."

Brodie eyed him with skepticism. "Aren't you the optimist today."

Cobra let his gaze rest on Marnie again. "No reason it can't be fleeting."

He was talking to himself more than to Brodie. She might have been an unexpected breath of fresh air in his world, but he could keep his head on straight. He had no intention of moping around next week after she was gone.

"It won't be fleeting," Brodie said.

"Voice of experience?" Cobra was certain now of Brodie's attraction to Raven, and he kept his tone casual. "You know you can talk about it."

"I am talking about it."

"I mean about Raven."

Brodie's tone darkened. "There's *nothing* going on between me and Raven."

"I *know.*"

"So, why bring it up?"

"Because I know what it's like to want someone you can't have." The experience was in Cobra's past, and just a little bit in his present too.

Brodie opened his mouth, looking like he was warming up to a serious rant.

"Look." Cobra checked around them to make sure nobody was close enough to overhear. Then he leaned in for good measure. "Tell me, don't tell me. I just want you to know you can."

Brodie snapped his jaw shut.

"Holding that all inside? You're gonna blow, man. Watching these other guys go after who they want is obviously killing you."

"I'm not dead," Brodie ground out.

Cobra gave a dark chuckle. "Might be easier if you were."

"She's . . ." Brodie clenched his jaw tight, obviously fighting the urge to speak up.

Cobra waited a moment then looked at Marnie again. "I know."

Chapter Seven

MARNIE'S WSA ROOM WAS RIGHT NEXT DOOR TO RA-
ven's. So, as the picnic ended, the two women walked
across the field toward the lights on Red Avenue. The dark
sky above was chock-full of stars, layers of them, bright
and twinkling in a three-dimensional vista that Marnie
remembered from the open plains of Kansas. The wind
was crisp now, and the mountains had disappeared into
blackness.

"You want to come inside?" Raven asked as they
mounted the short staircase that led to their shared porch.

"Sure." Marnie wasn't tired. She was still jazzed from
all the activity.

She hadn't talked to Cobra again, only seen him from
afar. But even watching him was energizing. She'd played
their conversation over and over inside her head, deciding
he'd showed a lot of class by replacing her blouse. She
wasn't annoyed about it anymore. In fact, she was looking
forward to wearing it.

Raven's room was a mirror image of Marnie's. It was

more cluttered and lived-in than über-squared-away Cobra's, but that seemed only natural.

"I smuggled something back for us," Raven said, reaching under her jacket and producing a stainless-steel thermos.

Guessing it was hot chocolate, Marnie unzipped her newly purchased black jacket and shrugged it off in the close, warm air of the bedroom.

"Grab a seat." Raven gestured to the only chair in the room as she set the thermos on the dresser and opened the small corner closet.

Marnie hung her jacket over the back of the chair and turned it from the little desk to face the bed.

"Brandy?" Raven asked, holding up a half-full bottle.

"You bet. Can I help?"

"Absolutely not." Raven set down the bottle and ducked into the bathroom, calling over her shoulder, "You've done nothing but cook and serve all evening long."

Marnie smiled. "I grew up in a small town."

Raven reappeared with a white ceramic mug in each hand. "You did?"

"Merganser, Kansas."

"I thought you grew up in LA." She gestured up and down at Marnie with one of the mugs. "You're so . . . citified."

"It's a learned look, believe me. I've been to dozens if not hundreds of community picnics. I know the drill."

"You did seem at home."

"It gave me something to do. I'm not wild about standing around cocktail-party style and chatting with strangers."

"Well, the cooks sure love you to death." Raven poured a measure of brandy into each of the cups.

"You should always make friends with the cooks," Marnie said.

"Words of wisdom." Raven opened the thermos with a little hiss of pressure and added the hot chocolate.

"That smells wonderful," Marnie said. She'd ended up

serving it for much of the evening but hadn't gotten around to drinking any.

Raven handed Marnie one of the mugs, then peeled off her boots and settled herself on the bed, leaning back against the wall. "I saw you were talking to Cobra at the fire."

"I was." Marnie took a sip. The hot chocolate tasted every bit as good as it smelled—creamy, rich and sweet.

Raven crossed her legs and cradled her mug between both hands. "He actually carried a conversation with you."

"He did."

"That's unusual."

"Wouldn't it be more unusual if he didn't?"

Raven grinned. "Your conversation seemed intense." She lifted her brows and left a pregnant pause.

"He bought me a blouse."

The answer clearly confused Raven, as Marnie had expected it would, particularly without context.

"At the flightseeing tours," Marnie continued. "I went into the shop for a look at one of the planes. I accidentally got some grease on my blouse and Cobra felt like it was his fault. So, he ordered a new one, and it was delivered to my assistant at the office."

"He knows where you work?"

"You can find my office address online, or Breena knows. Or any of the others know. You wouldn't have to be a super-spy to find out."

"Was it his fault? The grease, I mean."

"No. Hence the tense conversation. His gesture was way off the charts."

Raven paused for a drink. "Why did he think it was his fault?"

Marnie couldn't decide what to say to that. It wasn't as if anything real had happened. It was a silly slip-up, a moment in time, a simple kiss between a man and a woman.

Raven shifted forward, obviously curious. "There's

something. I can see it in your eyes. It's a good story. Did you trip, break something, touch something you shouldn't?"

Marnie grinned and shook her head. "No. I know my way around a repair shop."

"You do?"

"Merganser, Kansas." Marnie smoothly changed the subject. "Mia said you grew up in Alaska on a gold mine."

"I did. Me, three brothers and my dad. Mom died when I was seven."

"I'm so sorry. I lost my mom when I was twelve. You never truly get over it."

Raven nodded to that. "It was tough at times, being the only girl in such an isolated location."

Marnie raised her hand school-room style and waggled her fingers. She could relate. "Only girl here too. One brother, plus my dad and my uncle. We were on a couple of acres just outside town. Tumbleweed Fuel and Service." Some of her isolation had been geographic, but a big part of it had come from her family's suspicious worldview.

"Hence, knowing your way around a repair shop."

"Right," Marnie agreed.

"And the grease stain?" Raven tilted her head and leaned slightly forward again.

Marnie had hoped they'd dropped that. On the other hand, she saw no real reason to lie. "He kissed me."

Raven's jaw went slack.

"Don't get the wrong idea. It was nothing. On a whim. But"—Marnie gestured to the front of her sweater with her free hand—"coveralls, grease, pale pink blouse. Disaster."

"You kissed Cobra?"

"Technically, he kissed me. But sure, I kissed him back. He's a good kisser." Marnie kept her tone light, but her chest tightened and her skin warmed with the memory.

"So, today's conversation, was it about the kiss?"

Marnie shook her head. "Didn't mention it."

"Oh. Probably nothing then." Raven nodded sagely.

Marnie was surprised but gratified by Raven's easy dismissal.

"I kissed Brodie," Raven said in the next breath.

"I didn't know you and Brodie were a—"

"We're not."

"Were you before?"

"No. Never. It was just a one-time thing. We were out of town, and we'd had a big win on . . . well, road repairs. It sounds boring, but it was important. We were celebrating. It was a congratulations gesture, nothing more than that. So, I know exactly what you're talking about."

"Right," Marnie said, realizing that Raven did understand. "Impulsive actions and romantic interest are two very different things."

"Exactly."

IF A GUY WAS GOING TO BE IMPULSIVE, HE SHOULD DO it on a Sunday.

Cobra was normally methodical. He understood systematic, meticulous work kept planes in the air and saved lives, and he respected that. But it *was* a Sunday, and Riley Stern was a good friend. So, he abandoned his plans for the hundred-hour maintenance on the islander airplane.

"Sure," he answered Riley on the phone, swinging his legs from the bed in the caretaker's suite, appreciating the warm floor beneath his feet. It had been well worth firing up the wood boiler.

"Yeah?" Riley sounded relieved. "We didn't expect this much interest in white water rafting. I thought two rafts would be plenty."

Riley owned Rapid Release, the local white water rafting company and one of the few tourist attractions in Paradise. He was often away for a week or more at a time, taking tourists on wilderness adventures. It was rare for him to do single day trips from town, rarer still for him to need all three of his rafts at the same time.

"Can you bring the outboard to the hangar?" Cobra asked.

"I'm on my way now."

Cobra stepped into a pair of pants. "What if I'd said no?"

Riley gave a chopped laugh, showing he thought the suggestion was absurd. "I'm five minutes out."

"I hope you brought coffee."

"And cinnamon buns."

"At least you know how to bribe a guy."

Bear and Bar cinnamon buns were legendarily large, tasty and filling.

Cobra ended the call. He got dressed and ready, and was heading down the corrugated metal staircase when he heard Riley's truck pull in.

He turned on the overhead lights and opened a bay door.

Riley circled his truck to back it inside. The forty-horsepower motor was lying in the open box.

Cobra pulled down the tailgate for a look.

"Water pump impeller failed a couple of weeks back," Riley said. "I just got the new one in last week."

Cobra slid the outboard toward him, checking the bolt size on the leg then moving to his toolbox for a socket. "We should be able to change it out in a couple of hours."

Riley pulled the coffee and warm cinnamon buns from the passenger side of the pickup.

Smelling the combined aromas, Cobra decided to start with breakfast. He set down the socket.

Riley put the food on the workbench, and Cobra joined him, helping himself to a cup of black coffee and tearing a chunk off one of the cinnamon buns.

"What time are you launching?" Cobra asked.

"Eleven is the plan."

"Doable." It was a little after seven now.

"We're putting in above the gorge. An hour and a half to the sandbar, stop for lunch, then through the rapids, over the mini-falls and into town. You busy today?"

Cobra paused midbite, his suspicions flickering. "Why?"

"I need an extra raft pilot."

"So, you want me to fix the outboard *and* run the raft down the river?"

"I know you're a full-service kind of guy."

"I've been trying to stay away from the circus."

"Breena is meeting us at the sandbar with lunch. You won't be a babysitter, just a boat pilot. You know that river better than most, and I'd really hate to lose a raft full of tourists."

"They're not tourists."

"They're not locals."

"True." Cobra wasn't about to argue the point any further.

"So . . . ?" Riley pressed.

"All of them are taking the trip?" Cobra asked.

He wasn't going to pretend Marnie didn't enter into the equation for him. He'd like to see her again, and today was the last day of the matchmaking event. A fancy wind-up dinner and dance was planned for tonight, then they were all taking the twin otter back to Fairbanks early tomorrow morning.

"All of them, even Raven and Mia."

"Raven's doing something recreational?"

Riley tipped a flattened hand back and forth. "Part work, part recreation, since she organized it."

"Still," Cobra said. "It's not like her to have fun."

Riley grinned.

"No disrespect," Cobra quickly put in. He hadn't meant it that way. Her work ethic was noble.

"I know," Riley agreed. "If anything, we need more like her. So, you in?"

"Sure," Cobra said, since it sounded as though Marnie

was likely to be there. If this was going to be his last chance, it might be nice to say goodbye.

They finished eating, replaced the impeller and had the rafts towed up to the put-in by ten thirty.

Cobra and Riley each drove a company pickup, while Riley's employee Nicholas Constantine drove the van filled with life jackets, helmets and equipment. Between them, the three men set up the rafts on the rocky shore, readying them for the trip. A cool breeze swept down from the glacier, rustling the dry fireweed stalks and the remnants of golden leaves still clinging to the poplar trees on the hillsides.

"What do you think of all this?" Nicholas asked Cobra as they connected the fuel lines.

"The river trip?"

"The women."

"Oh. I'm against it."

"Against women?" Nicholas's grin showed he was joking.

"Not in general," Cobra returned easily.

Nicholas turned toward the road where an engine sounded in the distance. "I think it was a really good idea."

"How so?" Cobra scanned his way around the raft, checking for the first-aid kit, extra life jackets and the emergency paddles.

"They all seem nice, and so pretty."

"You think any of them would actually move here?"

"I think they're at least open to considering it. I mean, why else would they come?"

Cobra had to admit, he hadn't thought of it that way.

The town school bus pulled up with Kenneth at the wheel.

As the women filed out, Cobra was glad to see they were dressed warmly, all of them looking like they'd layered up beneath their Rapid Response nylon splash suits.

He watched until he saw Marnie leave the bus. The splash suit practically swamped her slight frame. She wore plain canvas trainers on her feet. The shoes were scuffed and worn, so he guessed she must have borrowed them. Her hair was braided close to her head, and her eyes were covered in sunglasses.

She looked gorgeous.

Riley gathered them all together for a safety briefing while Nicholas handed out life jackets and helmets.

Cobra perched on a boulder to change from his boots into his lightweight trainers then left the boots and his wallet and keys in the van. Kenneth had brought AJ, Xavier and Breena along to ferry the other vehicles back to town so they could meet the rafts at the boat launch after the ride.

Cobra zipped himself into a life jacket and tightened the chinstrap on his helmet.

Riley would lead in the first raft, followed by Nicholas, while Cobra would bring up the rear. If there were mechanical problems along the way, it would be easier for Cobra to pull in behind the troubled raft than to turn back and fight the current to get to them.

He was disappointed to see Marnie in raft number two with Nicholas—not that they would have been chatting along the way. Cobra would be busy driving, and she'd be busy hanging on and possibly screaming for dear life as they bounced up and down in the rapids. She was up front in the raft, so she'd get a very exciting ride.

Xavier settled Scarlett at the back of Cobra's raft and was busy saying goodbye to her. He was reminding Scarlett and everyone else to properly hang on to the woven straps that wrapped around the big blue tube.

"Any questions?" Cobra asked after Xavier stopped talking.

"We're not going over a waterfall or anything, are we?" a woman at the front asked. Cobra remembered her name was Olivia.

"There's a small falls near the end," he said.

A couple of the women gasped, and eyes widened all around.

"Nothing to worry about," he assured them. "The raft will easily handle it. I'm Cobra, for any of you I haven't met yet. Olivia, Willow, Ariel, Scarlett and . . ." There was one woman he didn't remember, short dark hair under her pale blue helmet, a little nervous looking.

"Kathleen," she said.

"It's going to be fun, Kathleen."

"It's going to be *awesome*," the woman named Willow said with a whoop. She'd strapped a camera to her helmet and was clearly ready for fun.

"She hang glides," Scarlett told him.

"It starts out gently," Cobra said to them all as he positioned the raft, getting ready to push off and hop in himself. "You'll all be comfortable and used to the motion before we hit any really rough water, so don't worry."

He checked out the other rafts. Riley was pushing off, Raven in the raft with him along with four other women. Nicholas was watching the progress as Riley successfully fired up the outboard and headed into the middle of the river.

Marnie and Mia were in Nicholas's raft. Mia in the middle and Marnie up front, looking eager, the bright orange life jacket further engulfing her, her hands properly positioned on the straps. She was going to have a bouncy ride at the bow, and he hoped the motion didn't bother her stomach. He wondered if she'd taken a motion sickness pill beforehand.

Cobra kept an eye on her as Nicholas pushed off, settled into his seat and started the motor, turning the raft downstream. As they headed for the bend, Cobra pushed off himself, leaving Xavier standing onshore waving to Scarlett. Sitting down, he locked the outboard leg in the water and fired it up.

"Ready?" he called to the women, receiving nods and smiles from them all. He added a little power and sent them heading in the right direction.

They started out with gentle rollers. A larger one broke over the raft, and everyone shrieked then laughed as the cold water hit them. The boulders at the shore, the fall colors and the birds flying over them slipped along as they rolled their way around a bend in the river.

The river narrowed after the bend. Cliffs rose up on either side, and they picked up speed, bouncing more sharply over the rolls and hollows.

"Do you *see* that?" Willow called out, pointing ahead to a stretch of bubbling white rapids.

"Don't let go," Cobra warned her.

She quickly put her hand back in place.

"Get ready," he told them all, goosing the throttle for a second to make sure they were positioned correctly to catch the fun of the rapids without scraping up against the boulder field on the west shore.

They hit the rapids to shrieks and laughter that turned to oohs and aahs as they came out the other end and the raft settled.

"Can we do that again?" Kathleen asked.

"You ever paddle that stretch?" Willow asked.

"We could sure use that in a film," Scarlett said.

Cobra couldn't help remembering Brodie's idea of using Paradise as a film location. "There are more rapids ahead," he told Kathleen.

The women all cheered.

"I've paddled it with Riley and some others," Cobra answered Willow's question. "But the motor gives a little more control."

"For us wimpy paddlers?" Olivia asked.

"For less experienced paddlers," Cobra said.

"I don't want to paddle," Ariel said.

"I'm perfectly happy with a motor," Kathleen agreed.

"I'd love to paddle it," Willow said, a look of anticipation on her face. "I love so much about this place. I haven't met the right guy here yet, but maybe I should look harder. This stuff is so much fun!"

"Here we go again," Cobra warned them. An even rougher stretch of white water was coming up.

The raft bounced over the rougher rapids, water splashing across the bow, wetting everyone's faces. They shrieked louder still as they rocked their way through a bubbling, narrow channel and shot out the other side.

By the time Cobra pulled the raft onto the sandbar where Breena and Badger had driven in on ATVs to set up a folding table and a grill, the women were chatting fast, their excitement level high as they greeted their friends from the other rafts and exchanged stories.

MARNIE STOOD IN THE SUNSHINE ON THE SANDBAR with Mia, finishing their chicken wraps and sweet, creamy coffee. The wraps had a Tex-Mex flair, and the hot spices hit the spot after the cool ride down the river.

"Have you done this before?" she asked Mia.

"First time for me. Silas has a boat and says we can take river trips next summer. But we've been too busy building the house to have any fun."

The statement amused Marnie. "Really? No fun at all? Spending your nights cuddled up with Silas?"

"Okay, I'm having *some* fun."

"That's a relief. I'd hate to think you'd given it all up for nothing."

"It wasn't for nothing. And I didn't give it *all* up."

"You gave up a lot."

"And I got a lot." Then Mia looked like inspiration had struck. "You should come see the house before you go. They've finished the flooring and installed the kitchen cabinets. We're about ready to move in."

"I'd love to see it. Will we have time before dinner?" Since they were flying out tomorrow morning, there weren't many options.

"We should have." Mia drained her cup.

"You must be looking forward to moving." Marnie pictured Raven's rustic little cabin.

"Raven's place isn't so bad."

Marnie pasted Mia with a look of disbelief. "Seriously? Not so bad?"

"I got used to it over the summer."

"Talk like that, and the princess sorority's going to kick your butt to the curb."

"It's amazing what you can get used to if you try."

Marnie knew she could get used to almost anything. She'd spent years living with few creature comforts and even fewer indulgences. But she didn't want that life now, not when she had a choice.

"I've gotten used to year-round sunshine and day spas," she said.

"Not to mention evening cocktails on the Brandy Bistro deck."

"See, you do miss it."

"In my weak moments." Mia focused on a spot beyond Marnie's left ear. "Will you take a look at that."

"What?" Marnie turned to see where Mia was looking, and her breath caught in her throat.

"It's a moose and a calf," Mia said. "No, wait, two calves." The animals were only fifty feet away, standing partway in the water.

"Should we be scared?" Marnie took a step back so she was level with Mia instead of being closest to the wild animals.

"Hey, Riley," Mia called softly over her shoulder.

Riley looked up from where he was talking with Scarlett and Willow.

Mia pointed.

"Cobra," Riley called in the same soft tone. "Moose."

Marnie's attention went to Cobra crouched beside one of the rafts. He rose, and she inhaled, taking a good long look at his form and his face. She'd expected him to come talk to her during the lunch stop, but he hadn't. She didn't know what to make of that.

"Keep still and quiet," Riley told them all. "They're far enough away, but we don't want to startle them."

Willow put on her helmet and switched on the camera, a huge grin coming over her face. "This is fantastic," she whispered.

"Shhh," Riley said.

"Can they hear us?" she asked him.

"See the size of their ears?" As he spoke, the mama moose's ears twitched, moving in all directions.

Marnie caught Cobra's eyes and held them.

A small gasp came up from a bunch of the women, but he didn't break their gaze, and neither did she. She tried to read his expression. She tried a little smile to see if she'd get a reaction.

"It's coming." Scarlett sounded startled.

"This way," Kathleen added.

"Everyone walk slowly over to the rafts," Riley instructed. "You don't have to get in. Just be ready."

Everyone moved toward the river, all except Cobra, who came Marnie's way instead. She met him partway, and he urged them toward the raft.

"Do we get in now?" Scarlett asked.

"Will you look at them," Willow said in a tone of awe.

Riley and Nicholas moved to stand next to Cobra, blocking the moose from the women. All three of the men raised their arms, moving them slowly in the air like they were herding cattle.

The moose stopped, and the calves stopped with her.

She turned her head, as if she were focusing on them with one eye. Then with a snort of disgust, she turned to the trees and took off at an ungainly gallop.

Willow was the first to speak. "I got it all." She was standing next to Riley where she had a clear view of the moose.

"You want to be careful around those," Riley told her.

"You were standing right here," she said.

"You think I can protect you from a moose?"

Willow looked confused. "No. I meant I was in no more danger than you were."

Riley rolled his eyes. "You don't think I know moose behavior better than you?"

"That's why I took your lead."

Breena had made her way back to the grill. "We're shutting these down. Last call for wraps."

"I'll take one if they're left," Nicholas said.

"We've got three," Breena said. "And monster cookies for dessert." She held up a box.

"Cookies, yes," Mia said, surprising Marnie as she headed for dessert.

"Cookie?" Cobra appeared beside Marnie.

"Not for me." Marnie had already overindulged calorie-wise this weekend, and the name monster cookie implied a size and sweetness that would take her a long time to work off.

"You sure?"

"My hips are sure."

He grinned. "Nothing wrong with your hips."

"I know, and I'm keeping it that way. But go ahead." The cookies were looking very popular.

"I'm good," he said, gazing at the cluster of people around Breena. "Your stomach okay?"

"Why? The wraps tasted great."

"I meant from motion sickness."

"Oh. No. I feel fine."

"Good." He paused for a minute and she thought about Raven saying he was usually quiet. "So, you're liking the trip?"

"It's exciting. Very wet." She gestured around the beach. "If it weren't sunny, this could be quite miserable."

He looked to the sky. "We could build a campfire if we needed it. It is getting late in the season for rafting. Riley's out of the field now."

"The field?"

"Most of his river trips are longer, weekends or weeks long."

"So, camping?"

"Camping."

"With tiny, little tents and dried food, like that?"

"Like that. You can take more gear on a raft than if you're backpacking or canoeing, but it's rustic."

"I'm not a fan of rustic."

He chuckled. "Never would have guessed."

She gave him a frown. "Are you mocking me?"

He returned her gaze with good humor. "No. I admire someone who knows what they want."

Marnie had known what she wanted—more precisely known what she *didn't* want—since she was a young girl. "I'm not sure why anyone would choose hard, cold and grimy when you could have soft, warm and clean."

"Hard to imagine," he said.

She tried to guess what he was thinking. "Are you happy here?"

He pointed to the sandbar. "Here?"

"In Paradise."

"Yes. I'm not so much for warm and cushy."

She could see that. And she could admire that. "I guess you know what you want too."

He sobered and something shifted in his gaze—boring into her, sucking the air from her lungs.

The sun seemed hotter, and the river roared louder, and the dried leaves scuttled sharply over the bare rock behind.

"In fact, I do know what I want," he said.

"All right," Riley called out from the lead raft. "Let's get back on the water."

Chapter Eight

WHAT COBRA WANTED WAS MARNIE. HE HADN'T SAID the words out loud, but they were a full-on shout inside his head.

The second leg of the river was shorter than the first, but it held some of the most exciting features. They started off with a stretch they called the Washing Machine, where water bubbled white and frothy among the rocks. It was tricky to navigate, with a very specific path through.

It culminated in a whirlpool, and Cobra cut back the power on the outboard and let the raft spin around a few times before he corrected their course and headed into a flat stretch. Predictably, his passengers loved it.

There were a couple more rapid sections before they rounded a tight corner into a steep gorge where the temperature dropped about five degrees. At the outlet of the gorge was the highlight of the trip, a shallow, tiered waterfall where the bow of the raft got airborne for a few seconds over the final drop.

"This is the exciting part," Cobra called to his passengers. He dialed back the power again, wanting to make sure Riley was safely through the feature and Nicholas was far enough ahead before he made his start.

The sound of the falls came up around them, and the women's eyes got wide.

"The waterfall?" Willow asked, excitement in her tone and a wide grin splitting her face.

"Everybody ready?" he asked.

There was a chorus of yeses and nods all round.

He could see Riley out the other end, and Nicholas was crossing the calm stretch before the final drop. He hit the power and sent them over the first lip, aiming for the channel just east of Billy Goat Rock. After that he'd traverse the river to the far eastern shore, taking a narrow channel between two jutting boulders. It looked dangerous, but it was the safest way through, fast but deep.

They rocketed out the far end, wallowing through a field of rolling rapids to three giant waves and the down-rush into the calm stretch. He caught a glimpse of Nicholas heading into the last waterfall. Something looked off with his approach. Cobra squinted and saw Nicholas frantically twist his head to check the outboard.

Cobra swore under his breath, knowing something had gone wrong. But his attention had to stay on his own raft. He churned through a field of rapids and over a drop, as the women whooped with excitement and water sprayed up to soak them all.

He looked up as soon as he could, seeing Nicholas's raft sideways, off the route, heading for a dangerous drop-off.

"Hang on tight," Cobra shouted to his passengers while he poured on the power.

"What's—" Scarlett started to ask, but then she looked at Cobra's expression and clamped her jaw shut.

To Cobra's horror, Nicholas's raft took the falls in the wrong spot. It tilted to one side, sending Marnie flying out and splashing into the water.

Cobra's stomach dropped to his toes, and a surge of adrenaline charged his system. He strained to see her in the dark green water as he took his own raft through the center of the channel, bypassing the features they usually ran for fun, taking the safest and fastest way forward.

Nicholas's raft righted itself, with everyone else still clinging on. He looked frantically back, but without power there was nothing he could do to help.

Cobra spotted a flash of orange in the river and swore out loud this time.

Marnie was caught in a whirlpool, getting dragged under the water.

He pointed the raft her way and gunned the motor.

"Marnie!" Scarlett screamed.

"Get her!" Olivia shouted.

"Go, Cobra, go!" Willow leaned forward as if she thought her aerodynamics would help them move faster.

Cobra watched the orange life jacket. He saw Marnie come up for a breath, but then she was gone again, and he lost his visual.

He was almost there . . . just another minute.

He spotted her and cranked the steering. Then he cut the power to stop the prop from cutting her. He leaned way over the side of the raft and plunged his arm into the water.

She wasn't there.

He couldn't feel her.

Sheer, blind panic took over.

He reached again, felt frantically around. His hand brushed her life jacket and grabbed onto a corner with a death grip, hauling her bodily out of the water, dragging her into the raft, onto his lap, wrapping his arm tight around her.

She coughed up some water.

The raft was spinning in the whirlpool, and he restarted the motor, righted the raft and headed for the calm water.

"You okay?" he asked Marnie, holding her tighter

against him. His heart was still beating out of control and his lungs labored to oxygenate his bunched muscles.

She was freezing cold in his arms, and he was flashing back to the second when he'd thought he'd lost her.

She managed a nod.

"You hurt? Hit your head?"

When she shook her head no, his heart rate finally began to steady.

The other women gaped at her in alarm.

"I'm okay," she rasped to them. "I'm okay."

Willow had the presence of mind to wave at the raft where Nicholas was standing and give him a thumbs-up.

Nicholas slumped in his seat and buried his face in his hands.

The rest of the trip was through relatively calm water, and Nicholas would be able to steer with the paddle. He was out of danger now.

Cobra tucked Marnie's freezing hands into his palm, assuring himself she was safe, she was fine, he hadn't lost her. "We'll get you warm soon. We're only twenty minutes out."

Her teeth were chattering, her lips were blue, and she was shaking against him. She was showing the early signs of hypothermia, but that was better than the late signs of hypothermia.

"Feeling cold is a good sign," he told her.

"Then I'm doing great, all things considered," she said, voice shaky.

"It's when your body stops trying to warm itself up that you're in real trouble."

"I know."

He adjusted his hold, pressing his chest against her back and splitting his thighs to hold her in between them for warmth, not sure he'd ever be able to let her go.

They caught up to Nicholas, and Cobra could see Riley was backtracking. He must have guessed something was wrong.

"You okay?" Nicholas called out to Marnie, his face pale and drawn.

"She's good," Cobra answered for her. "Freezing cold. We're going in fast."

"Good. Man, I'm sorry," Nicholas said.

Marnie shook her head at him. She'd obviously known the outboard quit on him.

"Nothing you could do," Cobra assured him. "At least you didn't flip all the way over."

But Nicholas just shook his head in regret, obviously replaying the incident over and over, wondering what he might have done differently.

Cobra understood. It might not have been Nicholas's fault, but it would likely take the guy a while to get over the accident.

"What happened?" Riley shouted out as he arrived on the scene.

"Marnie went in," Cobra called back.

"Cobra fished her out," Willow added. "You should have seen him."

"She needs to warm up," Cobra said. "We'll see you back there."

Riley gave him a wave, and Cobra twisted the throttle, pointing the raft for town.

MARNIE WAS TOASTY WARM NOW, A WOOL BLANKET wrapped around her as she sipped a cup of tea next to the wood stove in the Rapid Response reception lounge. The dozen seats were filled, and many people were left standing as they chatted about the thrills of the river trip.

Everyone had finally stopped fussing over her. She was grateful for that. Her spill had been frightening and freezing, but it was over now, and she was perfectly fine.

"I got the whole thing on video," Willow said, taking the chair next to Marnie. "You mind if I post it?"

"I don't think it would be the best advertisement for Paradise," she said. It would be hard for Mia and Raven to get the next batch of women up here if they thought their lives might be in danger.

Willow blew out a breath. "Good point. But do you want a copy?"

Marnie was about to say no. She didn't particularly want to relive those few minutes.

"Cobra was amazing," Willow said as she scrolled through her phone.

"Sure," Marnie said instead. "I'll take a copy." She was probably nuts to do it, but she knew she'd watch the footage of Cobra after she got back to LA.

"You should have seen the expressions on his face," Willow continued. "I swear, if he hadn't grabbed you on the second try, he'd have dove right in after you."

Marnie doubted that. Nobody would willingly go into that icy swirling water. Plus, he would have been sucked under along with her, and what would have been the point of that? She shuddered now, remembering the strength of the current.

Willow touched her arm. "You sure you're okay?"

"Perfect. You should go get ready for tonight." It was coming up on five o'clock, and cocktails at the dinner dance finale started at six.

Willow looked up and gave a sigh.

Marnie saw she was checking out Scarlett and Xavier, who were talking in a corner, heads bent together.

"Not much point," Willow said wistfully.

"Are you telling me you've met every guy in town?"

"I have now. Riley and Nicholas were the only ones missing."

"Missing?"

"They were on a river trip until last night, so nobody'd met them."

Marnie hadn't known that. Then again, she hadn't exactly taken inventory.

"Ah, well," she said. "It was worth a try."

"And it was a blast," Willow said, gazing around. "I really do love it here."

"Enough to stay?" Marnie couldn't conceive of that. She was looking forward to the mild ocean air and temperate waves washing over sun-warmed sand. Everything about Alaska was *cold*.

Willow shrugged her shoulders. "Maybe. I'd think about it. I wouldn't have applied for this if I wasn't willing to consider the possibility."

"Too bad, then. Looks like Scarlett and Xavier might be our best possibility." Marnie's gaze strayed to Cobra, who was talking intently with Riley and Nicholas. She guessed debriefing on the trip and the accident.

"Scarlett wants to bring a film here," Willow said.

"A white water adventure?" Marnie guessed.

"It's a great excuse for her to come back."

"I guess it's a long way to come if it were only for a vacation."

Cobra was in profile to Marnie, his shoulders straight, his chin jutting as he emphatically made a point about something. She recalled the second his hand had gripped her life jacket, her intense feeling of relief, his strength as he'd hauled her up like she weighed nothing at all, then the warmth of his body wrapped around hers when she'd felt like she'd shake right out of her skin.

There were times in her life when strong men had been intimidating.

This wasn't one of them.

"And ridiculously expensive," Willow said. "Even if I would like to jump off Mulligan or Dwarf Peak."

"You learned the local peaks?" Marnie was surprised by the detail.

"Hell yeah. This would be a hang gliding paradise. I mean, you'd need a chopper to get up to the top. But if I had unlimited funds, I'd do it in a heartbeat. I might be the first person ever to try."

An idea popped into Marnie's head and she voiced it. "Get Scarlett to write it into her script. You can be the stunt double."

Willow drew back, a contemplative expression coming over her face. "That's not a bad idea." She paused. "I mean, seriously, that's a great idea. I'm going to talk to Scarlett."

"Talk to her at the dance. Now, go get ready."

"I will. You coming?"

"In a minute." Marnie wanted to hang back and properly thank Cobra.

She waited a couple of minutes for the three men to finish talking. When they didn't, she folded the blanket, intending to interrupt them.

But Brodie appeared in the doorway just then. He glanced around and made a beeline for Cobra, interrupting the conversation and making a long statement.

Cobra's brows went up. He asked a question then nodded.

His gaze slid to Marnie, and he gave her a smile.

She smiled back, feeling warmer still.

He let Brodie finish talking, then he nodded his assent to whatever was happening and came swiftly to Marnie's side.

She opened her mouth, but he was faster.

"You're going to the thing tonight, right?"

She nodded.

"I gotta go. But I'll see you there?"

"Uh, sure, but—"

"Great. Sorry, I have to run."

"That's fine—"

He was already leaving, picking up Brodie on the way to the door, their heads bent together, continuing the discussion.

Raven came her way. "I've got my truck outside. You want a ride?"

It was only a few blocks to the WSA housing, but Marnie was naked under the dry Rapid Response jumpsuit, her wet clothes in a bag on the floor. She'd be happy for the ride.

"Yes, please," she said. "Do you know what's up with Brodie?"

Raven looked around. "Brodie's here?"

"He just left with Cobra."

"Oh. Is something up?"

"I don't know. Never mind. Let's go get dressed. Mia found something cute for me at the Butterfly Boutique. Although I'd rather bundle up for warmth than anything else."

"It'll be warm at the Bear and Bar, really warm with all those bodies dancing."

"That will be nice."

"So, you might as well look beautiful."

Marnie realized she wanted to look beautiful. She was looking forward to seeing Cobra tonight, and she wanted to look beautiful for her last night in Paradise—and with him.

MARNIE HATED THAT SHE WAS WATCHING FOR COBRA, glancing to see who'd come in whenever the Bear and Bar door opened. But it was nearly eight o'clock, the dinner was over, and he still hadn't arrived.

The place had been transformed for the occasion, looking more like a wedding than a northern café, with bunting streaming from the ceilings, crisp white tablecloths on tables that were now being shunted to the side to make a dance floor. Breena was moving tiny hurricane lamps from the tabletops to the ends of the bar, creating quite a beautiful display in the dim light.

Marnie felt like she ought to help out.

Willow touched her arm, getting her attention.

Their table was at the edge of the room, so they'd stayed

put, chatting and sipping on the wine that had been served with dinner—one of Mia's purchases, judging by the excellent flavor.

"Scarlett says she has a friend with a script," Willow told Marnie.

"An outdoor adventure," Xavier added from the next table over.

"A *potential* script," Scarlett emphasized.

"We have the mountains, the river, the forests and a long, long magic hour," Xavier continued with enthusiasm. His interest in keeping Scarlett in town was obvious to everyone.

"Magic hour?" Marnie asked.

"Lingering daylight at sunrise and sunset. The camera loves it."

"Oh." That was news to Marnie.

Raven arrived and pulled up a chair. "What are we talking about?"

"Scarlett's film," Willow said.

"Here in Paradise," Xavier said.

"That's a thing?" Raven asked, glancing at Marnie.

"Sounds like maybe," Marnie said.

"It's an *idea*," Scarlett put in. "We're hashing it out."

"I'm going to do stunts," Willow said.

"Scarlett's friend has a script," Xavier said.

"Wilderness adventure," Marnie added.

"Wait . . ." Raven looked around the two tables. "Like, for real?"

"We're getting ahead of ourselves," Scarlett spoke up emphatically. "A film takes money, a whole lot of money. You need investors, and my friend hasn't had a full-length feature produced before, so attracting money to—"

"How much money?" Raven asked as she located a clean glass and a half-full bottle of wine on the table.

"Hundreds of thousands, at a minimum," Scarlett said

as Raven poured herself a drink. "Even more to do it in a remote location like this."

Raven stopped pouring and turned around in her chair. "Hey, Mia!"

Mia's head popped up from where she was talking with Silas and T-Two. She looked around for the source of her name. "Huh?"

"Over here." Raven waved at her.

Mia gave a word and a smile to Silas and then came over to join them. "What's up?"

"Scarlett needs an investor."

Mia looked to Scarlett. "An investor in what?"

"We're doing a film," Willow said. "Here in Paradise."

"Her friend has a script already written," Raven said. "A wilderness adventure."

"With superheroes," Willow added.

Marnie's curiosity perked up. "Superheroes?"

"It's going to be expensive," Raven said. "So, we naturally thought of you."

Mia grinned and nudged Raven on the shoulder. "Northern superheroes?"

"Wilderness superheroes," Xavier said. "The Wild Men or something."

"Women," Willow said. "Women too."

"Sounds exciting," Mia said.

"So, are you in?" Raven asked.

"Whoa, whoa, wait," Scarlett said. "I'm a production assistant. I've never been a full-on producer."

"Could you hire experienced people?" Mia asked, looking like she was giving the idea serious thought.

"Sure," Scarlett said. "But—"

"Tell me how it works." Mia looked around for a chair, and Xavier immediately hopped up, offering his.

Scarlett looked really nervous now, glancing self-consciously around the group. "I . . . uh . . ." She swallowed. "I'd need a director, a photography unit, lighting, editing, actors, of course."

"Stunt doubles," Willow put in.

"Grips, electric," Scarlett continued. "Transportation and logistics."

"I can do transportation and logistics," Raven said.

"Editorial, hair and makeup."

"Yolanda and Bette at the salon," Xavier said.

Marnie found herself caught up in the enthusiasm. "I can do legal."

"Marnie can do legal," Raven said with a grin.

"You can see it adds up fast," Scarlett said.

Mia was listening intently to Scarlett. "Say you make it. What happens then? Would you stream it? Broadcast it?"

"It'd be tough to find a broadcaster, and you'd have to sell it to a streaming service. I have a few connections in LA, but I've never tried to sell a film myself."

Mia's brows went up. "Connections? You mean like rich LA people who go to parties?"

"In mansions," Marnie couldn't help but add, seeing the direction Mia was going.

"Yes," Scarlett said with a nod. "Those kinds of connections."

"You think the twins would help?" Marnie asked Mia.

"They'd better," Raven said.

"I'm sure they would," Mia said.

Scarlett was glancing from person to person, looking shell-shocked.

"Can your friend send us the script?" Mia asked Scarlett.

Scarlett swallowed again, more slowly and deliberately this time while Xavier put a comforting hand on her shoulder. "You know it would cost . . ."

"Mid six figures," Raven said, "maybe more."

"But we'd make at least some of it back, right?" Willow asked, glancing around for confirmation.

"We'd try to get distribution agreements up front," Scarlett answered her. "But it's risky."

"Is it fun?" Mia asked.

Marnie tried to hide her grin. The new Mia was highly in favor of getting fun out of life, and she wasn't afraid to spend money.

Scarlett didn't seem to know what had hit her. She nodded to Mia, looking like she'd pretty much lost the power of speech.

"Seems worth it," Mia said.

"We're *doing* this?" Willow asked, looking a little shell-shocked herself.

"The script would need work," Xavier said. "To customize it for Paradise."

"Customize away," Mia said, coming to her feet. "Can you put together a budget?" she asked Scarlett.

Scarlett nodded wordlessly once again.

"Then do it."

Marnie rose with Mia, following her away from the table as excited chatter broke out behind them.

"You've made her life," Marnie said as they walked.

"It's a good idea. Plus, it'll keep Brodie on our side. Silas said he wanted to turn this into an economic development venture."

"You know it's high risk, right?" Marnie felt honor bound to point that out.

Mia shrugged. "Life is high risk."

"Do you know what happened to Cobra?" Marnie blurted out her real question as they approached Silas's table.

"He's at the hangar, why?"

Marnie's chest hollowed out with dejection. "I . . . uh . . . owe him a thank-you. For rescuing me."

"You know he didn't do it for the gratitude."

"I know." It was a bitter disappointment, nonetheless. "He decided not to come?"

"He's fixing the twin otter." Mia glanced around the room and lowered her voice. "We don't want to panic anyone, but tomorrow's flight to Fairbanks is at risk."

"Seriously?" Marnie felt a glimmer of hope. Then she realized what it meant. Their flight out of Fairbanks was in the morning, and right after that they had a tight connection in Anchorage.

Mia nodded, looking worried. "It's not going well. Brodie says Cobra might be pulling an all-nighter."

UNDER THE BELLY OF THE TWIN OTTER, COBRA STARED up at the time-consuming series of bolts required to get access to the fuel system.

He heard the side door of the hangar bang shut, and he wondered who'd taken pity on him and left the party to stop by. He hoped they'd brought him a steak or some of the fresh-grilled halibut. The leftover snack food in the caretaker's suite wasn't really doing it for him.

Footsteps approached on the concrete.

Cobra turned his head and was surprised to see bare legs, a woman's legs with wedge sandals over shimmering purple toenails.

Marnie tipped her head down to look at him. "Hi."

"Hey," he said, his mood lifting as he quickly wiped his hands to shift out from under the aircraft. "What are you doing here?"

"Looking for you." She straightened as he stood.

"Yeah . . . well . . ." He gestured to the twin otter. "I'm sorry I didn't show up at the party."

"I'm sorry you have to work."

"Nature of the job," he said, wishing it weren't, wishing he could simply drop everything and take Marnie back to the dance floor at the Bear and Bar.

"Mia said you're saving our butts."

"I'm trying."

She paused for a minute, her gaze softening. "I came to say thank you for saving my life."

"No need. It was part of my job."

"No need?" She took a step closer. "I was going down for the third time. I could barely keep my head above the water, and I was losing my breath."

His heart banged hard against his chest wall. It was either from the memory of almost losing her or from the power of having her close—hard to tell which. "I'm just glad I got there in time."

She cracked a smile. "You and me both."

They fell silent again.

"You should go," he said, even if it was the last thing he wanted. "Have some fun on your last night."

Her pretty lips turned slightly pouty, sexily pouty, irresistibly pouty. "You don't want me to hang around?"

Yes! He wanted to shout. But he swallowed the word, trying to keep it light instead. "You hanging around here in pretty clothes gets expensive for me."

She looked down at her outfit, a sparkling silver tank top and a short black skirt. Her hair was swept up, accenting her gorgeous eyes. Her neckline was scooped low and her creamy shoulders were bare, smooth and irresistible.

"Got another set of coveralls?"

"Not a chance."

"You don't think I could help?"

"I think covering up that outfit would be a crime."

She smiled then, her eyes glowing, her lips looking more kissable by the second. "I'm not leaving," she said saucily.

"You don't think I could kick you out?"

"You won't."

"What makes you so sure?"

"You'd have to touch me to—" She abruptly halted, going quiet while the air charged with particles of energy. "I meant you'd get me dirty."

"I know what you meant." He also knew what he wanted.

"You going to make me hunt down the coveralls by myself?"

"It's your last night in town," he said.

"I know."

"The party must be rockin' by now."

She shrugged. "If you don't get the otter fixed by morning, it won't be our last night in town."

"That's not your problem."

She glanced around, zeroing in on the back wall. She pointed. "Storage closet?"

She was right.

"You're impossible."

"You're amazing. I'm alive and standing here because of you. The least I can do is pitch in. What are we doing anyway?" She canted sideways to look under the plane.

He asked himself why he was arguing. He wasn't about to let her do any heavy work, but his evening would be a million times better with Marnie there to entertain him while he worked.

"They got a fuel indicator light for the number one engine on takeoff. That's when you need your power the most, so it's a very dangerous situation. I've checked the electrical system, nothing there, and now I have to trace through the fuel lines."

"That shouldn't take long," she said.

"Maybe not on your average automobile, but the fuel system on a twin-engine aircraft is slightly more complex. And it's hard to access. I was about to remove the panels."

"I can twist a wrench," she said.

"*You* can carry on a conversation while I work."

She cocked her head sideways. "Are you calling me decorative?"

She was extraordinarily decorative, but that wasn't what he meant. "I'm calling you entertaining."

"That's just as bad."

"You want the coveralls or not?"

Her outfit was making him nervous, and not just because he wanted to drag her into his arms like he'd done the last time. There were endless other sources of stains in the hangar. A thousand things she could brush up against.

"Yes," she said.

He nodded to where she'd pointed. "Storage closet."

She grinned and all but hop-stepped that way.

He couldn't help but chuckle. "Observation only," he warned.

"Don't be silly," she called back over her shoulder. "I'm an able-bodied assistant, and you're on a hard deadline."

Marnie suited up faster than he'd expected. She'd had to roll up both the legs and the sleeves of the dark green coveralls, and they were still miles too big. She ducked under the belly of the plane with a ratchet handle, checked out the panel he was loosening up, sized up the bolts and selected a socket.

"You really did grow up in a shop," he said as she started on a bolt.

"You think I'd make that up? I mean, 'I'm secretly an Icelandic princess' is something you might make up. But 'I secretly know the difference between a slotted and a Phillips-head screwdriver'? Who's that going to impress?"

"Me."

She nudged him with her elbow. "You're weird."

"And you're not?"

"I suppose," she said, moving to the next bolt. "Is this what your dad did?"

It was hard for Cobra not to laugh at the question. "You mean, was he an AME?"

"Yes. Did he inspire you to go into the trade?"

"Not in the least. My dad's an accountant, and my mom's an engineer. If they could have picked, I'd be a lawyer."

Marnie surprised him with a smile. "Well, my dad would have loved another tradesman in the family."

"He must be proud of you."

"Not so much. But he'd sure have been proud of you." She took in the entirety of Cobra from his head to his toes, ending on his hands.

"That's ridiculous." Who wouldn't be bursting with pride over Marnie?

"What about your brothers?" She paused. "You said Barrick was the oldest?"

"Barrick works in the state senator's office. Miles is a doctor, a dermatologist."

She seemed to consider the answer, continuing to twist off the bolts and plunk them into the tray. "So, you're the only one who's—"

"Disappointing?" He'd heard it a thousand times, but it still wasn't fun to hear it from her.

"I was going to say useful." She paused in her work, looking quite sincere.

"Miles is a doctor."

"A dermatologist. He's not exactly out there saving babies."

"Like I am," Cobra scoffed.

"You never know. If a plane falls out of the sky, it could have a baby on it."

"Are you mocking me?" He paused now too.

She twisted her body toward him. "Not in the least. You do important work. Do they make you feel like you don't?"

"Yes." He didn't see any point in lying. His family's disappointment in him was acute and mentioned often.

She reached out and touched his arm, wrapping her hand over his biceps. "Their loss."

"I don't see how." He glanced down at her hand, feeling its warmth, feeling the blood pulse under his skin.

"You moved to Alaska. That's how." Her eyes were dark in the shadow of the plane, like evening in an evergreen forest.

He covered her hand with his, linking their fingers together. "You're . . ." He didn't know what to say.

"An equal disappointment to my own family."

"They have zero right to be disappointed." Cobra wished her father were here right now so he could tell him so. "And that's an entirely different scenario. They're jealous of your success."

She extracted her hand from his and went back to work. "I doubt very much they'd see it that way."

He wanted to grab her hand back, to hold it tight against his chest, pull her into his arms, forget about the repair, forget about anything and everything except Marnie.

"Last one on this side," she said, and he quickly braced his hands against the large panel of sheet metal to stabilize it.

Chapter Nine

"EVERYONE WILL BE PERFECTLY SAFE, RIGHT?" MARNIE asked as she scrubbed her hands at the big sink next to the hangar's workbench. She was exhausted but satisfied with what they'd accomplished over the past long hours.

"Perfectly safe," Cobra answered as he wiped down his tools and placed them back in his rolling toolbox.

"So, you know for sure the blockage was the problem."

"I know it for sure," he said. "Plus, we'll test the engine."

"That seems prudent."

He smiled as he came her way. "I'm nothing if not prudent."

She shifted to make room for him at the sink, propping herself back against the workbench while he washed his hands. She looked around but didn't see any chairs near the workbench.

"You want a beer?" he asked, opening a battered fridge beside the sink.

"Depends," she said, amused that they had a shortage of chairs but a handy beer supply.

He looked up from the open door. "On?"

"Is it late, late night, or early, early morning?"

He grinned at her joke. "For the purpose of my being thirsty, it's late, late night."

"Then yes."

He pulled two cans from the fridge and pushed the door shut behind himself, crossing to where she was leaning. He pulled the tab on one of the cans and handed it to her.

"Why no chairs in here?" she asked.

"You want to sit down?"

"You don't?"

He set his beer down on the workbench then bracketed her hips with his hands.

She reacted to his touch with an instant rush of heat and desire.

He lifted her straight up and sat her on the workbench. "There." He retrieved his can of beer and popped it open with a hiss.

They were closer to eye level now, and the hum of attraction eddied through her body. She lifted her can in a toast. "I believe you saved the day."

"Clearing a fuel line isn't exactly leaping tall buildings."

"Thirteen women can catch their flights home because of you."

His deep gray eyes crinkled in the corners as he lightly touched his can to hers. "I guess I am pretty amazing."

"Pretty amazing," she said, surprised at how deeply she meant it.

They each took a drink.

"I guess this is it," she said.

"It really shouldn't have ended this way."

Her chest tightened and her heart thudded hard at the potential implication of his words. Was he saying something more should have happened between them, something passionate, something sexual?

"You should have enjoyed the party and gotten a decent night's sleep tonight. Not gotten stuck with this." He gestured around them.

She swallowed her disappointment. "It's too late for sleep." She'd have time to drive back to her room and pack up her few things, and that was about it. "Maybe I'll upgrade to first class, get one of those pods and sleep on the way home."

"Let me do it. I'll upgrade your ticket."

"Oh no you won't. That blouse you bought me cost more than an upgrade."

He tilted his head. "I don't see the connection."

"The connection is you paying for things. You shouldn't have bought me the blouse."

He gave an almost imperceptible shake of his head and his gaze softened and dropped to her chest. "At least your clothes are safe this time, fully protected from grease and grime."

"I feel fully protected." She did, from grease and from grime and from anything else with Cobra standing so close.

He eased in, bracing his hands against the lip of the bench, one on each side of her. "I want you to feel safe."

"I do." She took in his face, trying to imprint it in her brain so she could save it for later, his dark eyes and straight nose, his full lips, his square chin now covered in a whisker shadow.

She caught a glimpse of his tattoo, captivating and sexy, like a secret glimpse inside him. Before she could check the impulse, she was reaching out, stroking her fingertip over the black ink.

He sucked in a quick breath and dropped his shoulder to give her better access.

His skin was hot and smooth. His energy pulsed through her fingers and along her arm, enveloping her shoulder, her neck, her breasts.

He eased forward, and she let her knees drop apart so he could get closer still.

His hand cupped her cheek, thumb smoothing slowly back, his fingers cradling her neck, giving the slightest pressure to pull her forward.

She went along, leaning in as his mouth slanted over hers in a hot, sizzling, freewheeling kiss. His arm went around her waist, pulling her close, wedging his body against hers.

She dragged down the zipper of his coveralls, and he shrugged them away. She explored his shoulder through the thin T-shirt, his powerful arms, the definition of his chest.

He stripped off his shirt and kissed her harder, devouring her mouth, sending shock waves of pleasure and need down her spine. She traced the ridge of his scar as he unzipped her coveralls.

Her arms tangled in her sleeves, and he chuckled low, getting her loose.

They stilled then, staring at each other in awe and amazement. His hands slipped under her tank top, caressing her stomach, deliberately circling higher and higher. Eyes darkening, he peeled the top off over her head, and they met skin to skin.

Their kisses started slowly, growing longer and deeper, passion building while they struggled out of their clothes. They wrapped their bodies together, meshing tightly, waves of pleasure ebbing and flowing with every kiss and every caress.

Their passion rose higher, and higher again, until her every nerve zinged to life, pleasure pulsating faster and faster through her chest, her limbs, her mind. She teetered on forever before bursting with release and slowly going limp in his arms.

Cobra rubbed his palms along her bare back, stroking her hair, kissing her temple, her lips, her neck. Then he tucked her head into the crook of his shoulder and gathered her against his slick body.

"I don't know what to—" He froze as a pair of lights flashed across the high ceiling of the hangar.

"What's that?" Marnie asked, a burst of panic seizing her chest.

"Silas," Cobra said. He was already moving, tugging down her skirt, handing over her tank top and panties, organizing his own clothes back around him.

She struggled into her tank top, yanked it down over her waist then stuffed her arms into the sleeves of the coveralls and zipped them up to her chin.

He stepped back, inhaling deeply, taking in every inch of her where she still sat on the workbench.

He leaned forward and smoothed her hair and stroked the pad of his thumb over her tingling lips before drawing back. "I look okay?" he asked.

She checked him out and nodded.

"You look perfect."

The side door opened, and Cobra took a step sideways, turning on the water at the sink and pretending to be busy.

Silas stopped short when he spotted Marnie.

"Hi," she said.

His gaze narrowed as he walked forward, clearly curious about what she was doing in the hangar at five thirty in the morning.

She pretended his surprise was at the coveralls and gestured to her outfit. "I know. I helped Cobra fix the plane."

"She did," Cobra said, his voice surprisingly calm and chill. "Bet you wouldn't have guessed that." He shook his wet hands and turned to Silas, his expression as impressively unflustered as his voice.

A tense knot loosened inside Marnie's stomach.

Silas looked back and forth between them one more time. "You got it fixed?" he asked Cobra.

"I was about to text you," Cobra answered. "Blockage in

a fuel line to the number one engine. It's cleared. We're ready to do an engine run-up."

COBRA PASSED THE LUGGAGE A BAG AT A TIME TO BRO-die, who was inside the tail of the twin otter packing it in while T and T-Two climbed into the cockpit. Clusters of women stood on the gravel lot, seeming remarkably upset at leaving their new Paradise friends.

Xavier was holding Scarlett in his arms, rocking her like he didn't want to let her go.

"They seem to have hit it off," Cobra said to Brodie.

"She's coming back," Brodie said with an amused grin.

"Seriously?" Cobra would have bet money against any long-term relationships coming out of this.

"Didn't you hear the news?"

"News?" Surely there hadn't been an engagement in such a short time. Cobra hoped not for Xavier's sake. People didn't fall for each other in a heartbeat. Not so fast. Not like that.

His gaze shifted to where Marnie was talking to Raven, taking a lingering look.

"They're making a movie," Brodie said.

Cobra felt Marnie's sunny smile all the way to his toes. "Who's making a movie?"

"Scarlett knows a script writer, and Willow's doing stunts, there's river rafting and hang gliding and superheroes, and Mia's investing money in it."

"You mean *here*?" Cobra couldn't believe the film idea had turned real.

"They cooked it up yesterday, finalized something at the party last night. You missed one hell of a party."

"You think?"

Through the cargo door, Brodie looked half guilty, half amused. "Sorry you had to miss the fun."

Cobra's gaze strayed to Marnie again. He couldn't say

he was one bit sorry he'd missed the party. He'd give up a dinner dance for a night with Marnie under an airplane any day of the week. And that was before their lovemaking. He'd give up just about anything to make love with Marnie.

She caught him staring at her and gave him a hesitant smile.

He tried to guess what she was thinking. Was it satisfaction? Was it regret?

"Is that the lot of them?" Brodie prompted, coming out through the small door.

Cobra quickly lifted one of the remaining three bags and slid it inside. "Last three."

They finished packing them in, and Brodie secured the compartment door.

As he walked away, Cobra looked for Marnie again. They hadn't had a chance for a proper goodbye, not that they could have a private one here, not that he knew what he'd say to her if he could get her in private. One thing was for sure, he'd hug her every bit as hard as Xavier was hugging Scarlett.

He spotted Willow then. She seemed to be debating with Riley about something.

It hit Cobra then that Riley was here; so was Nicholas, so was practically every living, breathing male in Paradise— the single ones, anyway. Silas was here too, but he was with Mia, who was still making the rounds of goodbyes.

Cobra saw Marnie then. She was talking to Willow, laughing, looking happy and excited about going home. With gold leaves scattered over the airstrip and snow dusting the tops of the mountains, he couldn't really blame her for that.

She looked incredibly fresh and astonishingly beautiful for someone who'd stayed up all night. He wondered if she'd had a chance to upgrade her ticket. He wondered if there was any way for him to do it from here. He didn't have her ticket or flight number, or even her airline for that matter. But there were only so many airlines flying Anchorage to LA. He'd bet he could take care of it with her name alone.

She saw him looking, said something to Willow, then came his way.

"Hi," she said, her pretty hair lifting in the breeze.

"Hi," he said back, his hands itching to reach for her.

"I guess this is it," she said.

"Looks like it is."

"Well." She glanced around, seeming like she was at a loss for words.

"It was great meeting you, Marnie."

She looked back at him, seeming relieved at his casual farewell. "It was great meeting you too."

Women began boarding the plane, climbing the narrow steps and waving as they ducked through the door.

Cobra didn't want to make Marnie uncomfortable, but he didn't want to stand here and pretend they were merely acquaintances. "I hope you're . . . okay with what happened this morning."

She glanced to her toes for a second, but she also smiled, and a cute pink flush came into her cheeks. She stepped a little closer. "I'm absolutely okay with what happened this morning."

He breathed a sigh of relief, tension he hadn't known he'd been holding rushing out of his body. "It's probably obvious, but so am I."

Her smile turned to a smirk. "It was a little bit obvious."

He shook his head at her teasing.

They both went silent.

He cleared his throat, desperately wishing he could ask her to stay. But that was miles away from ever being in the cards.

"I hope you enjoy the blouse," he said to fill the silence.

"I'm sure I will. It's really beautiful."

"Will you send me a picture?"

Her expression faltered, and he could have kicked himself for asking.

"Sure," she said quietly.

He wanted to apologize, but he couldn't come up with the right words.

They fell silent again.

She bit down on her bottom lip. "Would it be weird if I hugged you?"

It took all he had to hold still. "Do you care if people ask questions?"

She tilted her head. "Do you care if we lie?"

"Not a bit."

"Great." She all but threw herself into his arms.

He wrapped her close and squeezed her tight for just as long as he dared. But then he released his hold and stepped back before anyone could become truly suspicious.

"I'm going to miss you, Cobra," she said then turned away before he could respond.

She all but trotted across the gravel and quickly took the stairs, ducking and disappearing into the plane.

He clenched his jaw, telling himself to buck up. It was far from the end of the world. She was an unexpectedly charming woman who'd livened up a weekend he'd dreaded. And now it was over, and life would go back to normal.

The last of the women filed into the plane.

Mia and Raven stood side-by-side, waving at the faces in the twin otter windows. Cobra looked for Marnie but realized she must have taken a seat on the other side of the plane.

Brodie started to fold the ladder and secure the door, but Mia rushed forward and stopped him. Then she boarded the plane herself.

Cobra guessed it was for one final goodbye. Women really seemed to draw these things out.

He waited too, although he wasn't sure why. The fuel system was working fine, and the test flight had been perfect. There was nothing for him to do to help with the take-off. If Mia wanted to individually hug every passenger on-board while the twin otter burned aviation fuel, that wasn't his problem.

Cobra turned away, heading for the hangar, forcing his mind away from Marnie and onto the next hundred-hour maintenance on the schedule.

He heard the engine speed change, and the gravel crunch as the plane moved ahead, taxiing up the access road for the strip.

As the sound diminished, he heard Raven and Mia talking. But then a third voice chimed in—Marnie's.

Cobra whipped around, shocked to see her with them. The twin otter was still taxiing, so that didn't make sense.

His first thought was that something was wrong, and he instantly strode her way. But all three women were smiling, laughing even, sending a wave of relief through him. He started to smile too, but quickly controlled his expression—looking delighted at the turn of events would inevitably raise questions.

"I thought you were leaving," he said in a deliberately neutral tone. They all looked his way. By their expressions, he knew his words had been more abrupt than he'd intended.

"We talked her into staying," Mia said defensively, linking her arm with Marnie's.

"Don't worry, you'll get your room back," Raven added, like he cared about that.

"She's got some lawyering to do for us," Mia said, while Cobra looked to Marnie.

Unease came into her eyes, and she slid her gaze from his. He could have kicked himself, realizing how his surprise might have come across as disappointment. He wanted to backtrack, to tell her he was happy she'd stayed, *thrilled* that she'd stayed. But he couldn't say that in front of Mia and Raven.

"She's staying at our new place," Mia said. "We're moving the furniture in today."

"I get my cabin back," Raven said.

"So, everything's back to normal," Mia said. "And I have a brand-new house with a *very* comfortable guest room."

Cobra tried to catch Marnie's eyes and convey an unspoken apology, but the three women turned away, and he was left kicking himself for his stupidity.

MARNIE TRIED TO STUFF THE MEMORY OF COBRA'S EXpression to the back of her mind as she gazed around the living room of Mia's new house. He'd been more than gracious before she got on the plane, hugging her goodbye, telling her he'd enjoyed their time together, acting sad to see her go and asking for a picture of the blouse. It would have been the perfect ending to a perfect fling—if only she'd held up her end of the bargain and flown out of his life.

"What do you think?" Mia asked her gesturing around the expansive living and dining room.

Marnie refocused her attention, taking in the huge stone fireplace, the bank of windows overlooking the river and the soaring ceilings. "I *love* it."

She did. It wasn't as magnificent as the mansion in LA, but it was spacious and beautiful, with warm wood on the ceilings, red-toned beams highlighting the walls, and the fireplace as a feature at one end. Their voices echoed in the empty room. The air was cool since the double front doors were standing open. Plastic sheeting covered the floors, crackling under Kenneth's and AJ's feet as they carried a mattress through the door.

"North-side bedroom." Mia pointed for them.

Raven came in next, dressed for work, tablet in her hand. "I've got three trucks coming from the warehouse," she said to Mia. "Bedrooms and loft first, appliances second, then living room last."

"Perfect," Mia said.

"Your kitchen won't be up and running until tomorrow."

"It'll take us another day to unpack the dishes anyway."

Silas appeared from a hallway past the dining area. "I'll do a Bear and Bar run later on."

"Get them to make lots of burgers," Mia told him as he put an arm around her and gave her an affectionate kiss at her hairline. "You'll have plenty of hungry people."

Marnie shook the thoughts of Cobra from her mind. That interlude was over and done. The best thing she could do now was respect his space and stay out of his way—which shouldn't be too hard, given all the work there was to do helping Mia move in. And that was before she even started researching entertainment and film law or helping Mia set up the new production company.

She was excited about the film project. She wouldn't have considered expanding into entertainment law, but she could see it now as a good fit, especially since Hannah and Henry wanted her help with the fashion business.

She was confident the new adventures would take over her brain and consume her emotional energy—better that than thinking about Cobra and speculating on his sudden coldness when he found out she was staying longer than planned.

Other groups of men entered with more loads of furniture, a box spring, a dresser, a stack of drawers.

"We need you to show us where to put everything," Silas said to Mia.

"Happy to direct traffic." She looked excited.

"I'm heading back to the warehouse." Raven stepped out of the way for Kenneth and AJ, who were lugging in another king-size mattress.

"Other bedroom?" Kenneth asked Mia.

"South side." She pointed past the fireplace to a hallway that led off the other end of the living room. "Go ahead and take a look around," she said to Marnie before following Silas to the master bedroom.

Activity all around her, Marnie wandered into the kitchen. It was spacious, with cherrywood cabinets and burgundy countertops. The appliances hadn't arrived yet, but the stovetop and a double oven were built right in.

She peeped through cupboards and closets and wandered into the glassed-in octagonal breakfast nook that practically hung over the river. She imagined drinking coffee there with the morning sun reflecting on the mountains. Next to it was a glass door leading to a sundeck with an even wider panoramic view.

Between the living room and the kitchen was a feature staircase that led to an open loft. Marnie climbed the stairs, running her fingertips along the smooth natural-wood railing. The upstairs space was bigger than she'd expected, with a bathroom and walk-in closet that meant it could be used as a bedroom. It would also make a fantastic office or family room. Astonishingly, the view was even better from up here. She could see miles down the river and into a mountain pass still filled with gold and red autumn trees.

A few things had been moved upstairs already—two cream-colored armchairs, a low table and a big rectangular box filled with something that likely needed assembly.

Curious, she dropped to her knees on the plastic-sheeted carpet and folded open the top of the box. It was filled with polished maple wood panels, posts and hardware. She guessed it was a shelving unit, and a set of instructions in seven different languages confirmed her assumption.

She looked around the room and tried to decide where it might go. It was twenty-four inches high and had three sections, making it twelve feet long, perfect to fit under the windows. She removed the top pieces and set them below the windowsill against the cream-colored wall to test the fit. It was going to look great.

A small toolkit came with the set, so she fastened the bottom shelf to the posts and the braces. It went easily and smoothly together—the sign of an expensive piece of furniture. After she stepped back for another look, she gave into the impulse to carry on, curious to see how the finished product would turn out.

As she settled the last panel on the pegs, footsteps sounded on the stairs.

"*There* you are," Mia said from behind her. "What are you doing?"

Marnie came to her feet, surveying her work. "It looks great, doesn't it?"

Mia came alongside her. "We have people to do that."

"I know. I'm a person, and I just did it."

Mia nudged her arm. "I meant the guys. You're too valuable to waste on furniture assembly."

"It was fun. Do you like it?"

"I do. It looks great."

"Will this be your office?"

"Den more than an office. I don't know what kind of work I'll end up doing. We'll put a sofa in here, a pullout in case we need more than one guest room. It'll get the afternoon sun, so on cold winter days, it should be very cozy."

"This whole place is terrific. That kitchen is huge."

Mia laughed. "We used the plans from the Wildflower Lake Lodge villas. But Silas kept adding to them, a few feet here, a few feet there, a garage, a bonus room above the garage, an arctic entry, an extra closet."

"He wants you to be comfortable."

"I'm way more than comfortable. Did you check out the guest room?"

"Not yet."

"No rush. It's full of guys debating how to assemble the bed frame."

"I can help," Marnie offered.

Mia ignored the offer. "Scarlett had her friend send me the original script. The email was full of caveats about changes they're planning to make for filming in Paradise. I think they're nervous that I won't be able to see how it'll work here."

"Have you read any of it?"

"Just a page or two. I'm not going to be the best judge of the writing."

"I'll reach out to the office today and find an entertainment law contact. We want to get this right."

"We do."

"You're completely sure you want to do this?" Marnie asked again. "Sure you want to spend all that money?"

Mia shrugged. "I've got money. And I have to do *something* with it. I'm tired of watching it pile up in my bank account."

"You could invest it." Marnie had made that suggestion in the past.

"I am investing it. We're making a movie."

"That's more of a gamble than an investment."

"Westberg Productions International—what do you think?"

"International?"

"I'm thinking we might have to go on location, maybe somewhere warm come January."

Marnie grinned. "Now you're being realistic."

Men's voices sounded over the rail in the living room.

Marnie's stomach clenched as she recognized one as Cobra's. The very last thing she wanted to do was face him again and see that guarded expression in his eyes.

"T brought it from the strip," Cobra was saying.

"She's around here with Mia somewhere," Silas responded.

Marnie took a surreptitious step toward the back wall in case Cobra glanced up and could see her.

"I'll set up an LLC," she said to Mia, keeping her voice very low.

Mia lowered her own voice to match. "Is that a secret?"

"I'll let her know," Silas said.

Marnie couldn't make out Cobra's answer.

"No," she said to Mia, as close to normal volume as she dared. "I'll make sure you can operate internationally. I'm guessing Scarlett will need some advice too."

It was going to take a lot of research to make sure Marnie got this right.

"Whatever she needs," Mia said with a dismissive wave of her hand.

"—whoever's idea it was," Cobra was saying.

"Don't just give me a blank check," Marnie responded to Mia, wondering what Cobra had meant by his words. What idea? Did he hate the idea? Was he talking about the fact that she'd stayed behind?

"It's going to be an exciting winter," Silas said on a laugh.

"Why not?" Mia asked.

"Huh?" Marnie blinked, having lost the thread of their conversation.

"Are you saying I can't trust you?" Mia asked.

"Of course, you can trust me. I'm your lawyer."

"—a few more hours tonight," Cobra was saying.

"Then do whatever you need to do," Mia continued. "Xavier's got a thing for Scarlett, and she likes him back, and Willow just plain wants to hang out in Paradise."

"That's the season," Silas said.

"Plus, Brodie's finally on board with our plans," Mia continued, paying no attention to Cobra and Silas's conversation. "When you get back to LA, we'll start on the next group."

"Catch you later then," Cobra said, and Marnie breathed a sigh of relief.

"What do you think?" Mia asked.

"About which part?" Marnie asked, having lost all meaning of Mia's words.

"Getting ready for the next matchmaking group. We'll have to wait until spring for the trip, but we can start taking applications right away."

"Already?" The first women weren't even back home in LA yet.

"No sense in waiting," Mia said. "We should take the town's enthusiasm and roll with it."

Chapter Ten

COBRA PRIDED HIMSELF ON ROLLING WITH THE punches, and he'd do it this time too. He was nothing but glad Marnie was still in town, confident he'd eventually get a chance to see her, even if she had seemed elusive the past couple of days.

He knew from Silas that she was setting up a company for Scarlett's film. He also knew she and Mia were unpacking dishes, positioning lamps and hanging pictures in the new chalet. The two women were obviously close friends. It only made sense they'd be spending time together.

As for him, he was gearing up as planned for the annual Klondike Challenge, exactly like he did every year. On the workbench at WSA, he pushed a cleaning patch through the barrel of his .30-06 target rifle.

"There's a new event this year," Brodie said, looking up from the Klondike Challenge mailout. The three-day competition was Central Alaska's quirky northern games weekend, held to close out the fall season.

"What's that?" Cobra discarded the tarnished patch and looped a fresh one on the end of the rod.

"The Green Energy Challenge. It's a team event on a stationary bike array. The winners generate the most kilowatts in thirty minutes. It's sponsored by Glacial Solar, that renewable energy start-up in Fairbanks."

"That seems appropriately progressive."

"I thought so. They've also changed the name of the Wife Packing Contest to the Partner Packing Contest."

"I'd say that one was long overdue."

"I guess Silas and Mia can enter for us this year."

Cobra couldn't help thinking about Marnie and how light she'd be to pack. "Silas might want to get in some road training." The race was about half a mile long.

"Did you talk to Raven about a rifle?" Brodie asked.

"Last year she used the .270."

"She came fifth."

"I'm not sure it was the rifle's fault." The .270 was lighter with less of a kick than the .30-06—a nice gun for someone Raven's size.

Cobra had promised to work with her over the summer on target practice. But the summer season had been so challenging, they hadn't found the time.

"We need two men and two women for the Green Energy Challenge contest," Brodie said.

"T and T-Two are constantly mountain biking."

"Silas says Mia's a runner. She might have strong legs."

"She's pretty skinny."

"True."

"Breena would be good," Cobra said. "Too bad she's back in Anchorage."

"We can't put Raven in everything," Brodie said. "The two of us should do Firewood Stacking again this year."

"Hell yeah," Cobra said. Brodie and Raven had taken first place in Firewood Stacking the last two years running.

"We run out of women really fast around here," Brodie said.

"Maybe we should get Willow to come back," Cobra joked. "She was sporty."

"I bet she bikes." Brodie seemed to be seriously contemplating the idea. Then inspiration seemed to cross his face. "What about Marnie?"

"Biking?" Cobra couldn't see that. "She barely weighs a hundred pounds." Then he realized he had an opening here to learn about Marnie's plans. "You think she'll still be around by then?"

"Good point," Brodie said, not providing the slightest scrap of useful information.

Cobra tried not to be exasperated by his burning desire for information about her. Still, he couldn't stop himself from trying another angle. "I could ask her," he said casually.

"You going over there?"

Cobra shrugged as he replaced the rifle bolt and closed the action. "Sure. I can stop by. I'll ask Silas and Mia about doing the Partner Packing."

"Are you going out to the range now?"

Cobra shook his head, having only just changed his mind. "Tomorrow."

Brodie gave a considered nod, paused then looked and sounded far too casual. "I'll talk to Raven about a gun."

"Sure. That would be good." Cobra didn't let on that he thought Brodie was making an excuse to see Raven the same way Cobra was taking the excuse to see Marnie. Instead, he put the rifle into its case and locked it in the cabinet.

It was only a few minutes to Silas and Mia's new house. The driveway was long and rutted, curving slightly through the woods before it opened up into their meadow. Silas had plans to improve it with gravel. Hauling three-quarter-inch crush up the supply road would be expensive, but it would definitely help—especially during the spring thaw.

WSA's big 615 loader was running close to the house, and Cobra could see Silas in the cab. When Silas spotted Cobra's truck, he shut down the machine and climbed out while Cobra parked out of the way and walked over.

"Looking good," Cobra said, scanning the work Silas had done in leveling an area in front of the three-car garage.

"The finishing touches take forever," Silas said. "One bite at a time."

"Let me know if you need help."

Silas nodded. "Thanks. I will."

Cobra glanced at the 615 and couldn't help but joke. "So, Mia's machine-operating days are over?"

During a flood emergency earlier in the summer, Mia had used the 615 to clear debris from the airstrip, likely saving Silas's life when he'd been forced to land his plane there.

"She retired with honors," Silas said, smacking his glove-covered hand on the top of the machine's yellow bucket.

Cobra glanced around, hoping to catch a glimpse of Marnie or Mia. Mia's SUV was parked in the open garage. That was encouraging.

"Brodie and I were talking about the Klondike Challenge," he said to Silas.

"You looking for donations?"

"Between WSA and Galina, I think the finances are under control. Brodie said Mia's a runner. Does she also bike?"

"Was a runner," Silas said. "Since the grizzly bear incident, she's stayed away from roadwork. We've ordered a treadmill." He nodded to the room above the garage. "That way her running's not wildlife or weather dependent."

"There's a new event this year, the Green Energy Challenge. A team of two men and two women on stationary bikes."

"Doing what?"

"Generating energy. Highest kilowatt count wins. We're

thinking it'll likely be T and T-Two for the guys, but we need to fill the women's spots too."

"I can ask her," Silas said.

"She home now?" Cobra asked, glancing at the house.

"I think they're upstairs. Come on." Silas peeled off his work gloves and headed for the front door.

The entryway flooring was still partially covered in plastic, but the furnishings were in place now, and paintings had been hung on the walls, with other art objects and books set out around the living room.

"Wow," Cobra said in appreciation of the progress.

"I know," Silas said in agreement. "It's sure not WSA housing."

"I might be a little jealous." Not that Cobra needed anything near this nice. But he'd appreciate having his own kitchen and living room.

When he'd first moved to Paradise, he hadn't known how long the job would last. But it had been a few years, and for the first time, he wondered about building something for himself. He liked Silas's location too—slightly outside town, quiet and where he could hear the faint rush of the river.

"Mia?" Silas called up the stairs.

He got only silence in response.

"Mia?" he called again, louder, moving toward the bottom of the stairs.

They both waited.

"I thought they were up there," Silas said. "They must have gone over to Raven's."

"Mia's SUV is in the garage."

"They usually walk or take an ATV. Brodie and I widened the path. I can ask her later."

Cobra forced down his disappointment. "Do you happen to know when Marnie is leaving?"

"Not sure. She hasn't said."

"We wondered if she might ride a bike."

Silas coughed out a laugh.

Cobra frowned.

"Don't get me wrong," Silas said. "She's awesome, but I don't see a lot of strength in those hundred pounds."

Cobra knew Silas was right. He hadn't truly considered Marnie a candidate for biking, but it had given him an excuse to ask about her.

"WHY ARE WE IN THE BATHROOM?" MIA STAGE-whispered to Marnie.

Marnie had rushed them in here from the open loft and closed the door as soon as she'd heard Cobra's voice. Now she was perched on the raised-tile platform at the end of the oversize tub. Mia had taken the vanity chair.

"I don't want to tell you," Marnie admitted.

"Tell me what?"

Marnie frowned at the illogical statement. She'd just said she didn't want to tell Mia the reason.

"Is it bad? Are you sick?" Mia asked.

"No. I'm fine. Nothing bad. It's . . . kind of a secret."

Mia pulled a face. "Since when don't you tell me secrets?"

"It's not *you* I don't want to tell."

Mia lifted her hands and glanced around. "Well, I'm the only one here."

"I don't want to tell you something you can't tell Silas." Marnie wouldn't ask Mia to keep a secret from her fiancé.

"Is it *about* Silas?" Mia looked worried.

Marnie knew she was making things worse. "No."

"Will it hurt Silas?"

"It has absolutely nothing to do with Silas."

Mia looked relieved. She went silent for a beat. "You know, I don't have to tell Silas everything. I mean if it were something that was none of his business . . ."

"It is. None of his business."

"Great." Mia smiled. "Let's hear it."

Marnie gave in. "It's Cobra," she admitted.

Mia glanced to the closed door, obviously knowing he was out there. "What about Cobra?"

"I don't want to see him."

Mia frowned in concern then. "Why? What did he do?" She started to rise. "Should I—"

"No!" Marnie interjected, then quickly covered her mouth against the outburst.

"No, what?"

"No, don't do anything. He didn't do anything. He was fine. He was great."

"Then, why . . . ?"

Marnie squeezed her eyes shut for a second and balled up her hands. "We had a thing."

"A thing?"

"A sex thing."

Mia opened her mouth, but Marnie held up her hand to stop the ridiculous back and forth. "We had sex. Me . . . and Cobra . . . we had sex."

Now Mia looked baffled. "When? Where? Wait." She stood, quickly crossing to the door and cracked it open.

Panic flashed through Marnie's stomach. "Don't do *that*."

"I'll be super quiet." Mia put her finger to her lips and eased the door silently open. She looked back at Marnie with a triumphant grin.

Marnie frantically shook her head, but Mia put her finger up in a one-minute gesture and slipped out of the bathroom.

Unease rolling through her, Marnie held her breath until Mia came back with their two half-full glasses of chardonnay.

She set one down on the counter and quickly shut the door again.

"You broke cover for *wine*?" Marnie could hardly believe it.

Mia handed over Marnie's glass. "Don't tell me this isn't a wine-worthy conversation."

Marnie had to admit it was. But it had still been a foolish chance to take. Then again, Mia had gotten away with it, and now they had wine.

"What are they talking about down there?" Marnie asked.

"All I heard was wife packing and chainsaw chucking."

"That makes no sense."

Mia shrugged as she took her chair again. "It's what they said."

"Nothing about me?"

"Nothing about you. Did you want it to be about you?"

"No." Marnie didn't. Not really. A big part of her wanted to know what Cobra was thinking about her. But an even bigger part of her absolutely did not.

"So." Mia shimmied forward, leaned in and lifted her glass. "You and Cobra and sex. Dish."

"We had sex." As she said the words, Marnie had to shake off the visceral memory.

"Yeah, I'm going to need more than that."

"The night we fixed the twin otter. It was a long night, a tricky repair, and we were happy that we got it done in time, celebrating, really."

"In the hangar?"

Marnie nodded. "On the workbench. Well, sort of on the workbench, but sort of—" She stopped herself again, the vivid memories crowding inside her head.

Mia snickered, then she sobered. "Who am I to talk? Silas and I once *celebrated* in the cab of the 615 loader."

"That big thing outside?" Marnie pointed in the general direction of the driveway where Silas had been running the loud, rumbling machine all afternoon.

"That's the one."

Marnie laughed. "Well, at least it's roomy."

"Not as roomy as you'd think. But, back to Cobra."

Marnie sighed. "It was almost morning, and Silas showed up."

"Silas *caught* you? Then why is it—"

"No. No. We heard him coming in time. But then we had to test the otter's engine, and everyone started showing up for the flight."

"So, you didn't talk about it at all?"

"A little, just to say goodbye while I was boarding. He was great, really sweet, really . . ." Marnie's memories took over once again, and she felt a hitch in her chest. She took a drink of her wine to wash it away.

Mia looked confused. "So . . . what's the problem?"

"You saw his expression after I stayed."

"What expression?"

Marnie waved her glass. "He looked . . . surprised, disappointed, alarmed."

"He was afraid he wouldn't get his room back," Mia said.

Marnie gave Mia a dubious frown. "Yeah, that wasn't it. It would have been perfect for him, a wonderful weekend fling that he never had to think about again—if only I'd flown away like I was supposed to."

"You don't know that."

"I think I do. And honestly"—Marnie paused—"I'd rather not find out for sure." She squared her shoulders, her tone perking up as she voiced her plan. "So, I lay low, we finish the legal work, I leave and all is well—weekend-fling memory perfectly preserved."

Mia pondered for a moment, tapping her fingernails against her mostly empty wineglass. "I suppose," she ventured slowly.

Marnie would admit it wasn't a perfect plan. "It's the best plan I've come up with. And, believe me, I've thought about it . . . a lot."

Mia seemed to accept the logic. "But it was a good fling?"

Marnie took another drink of her wine. "It was a great fling."

They sat in silence for a few moments.

"So," Mia ventured. "He's not as scary as we thought?"

Marnie shook her head. "He's chatty too. You and Raven keep saying he's so quiet. He's not quiet."

"Really," Mia intoned musingly. "Obviously, he likes you."

Or he'd *liked* her—certainly in the moment he had. Or he'd seemed to.

Thinking back, he'd come across as skillful and smooth, like maybe he'd done it all before. And maybe he had. Maybe he was that good at having a fling because he'd practiced—a weekend in Anchorage here and there, nothing long-term, nothing serious. Marnie could see there'd be no end of willing women.

"We need more wine," Mia said, rising from her chair.

What Marnie really needed was to put this behind her and move on.

COBRA DROVE OUT TO THE MAKESHIFT TARGET RANGE a couple of miles from Raven's cabin. He pulled his truck behind hers, parking off to the side in the burnished red fireweed stalks at the end of the narrow dirt road. He'd brought his .30-06 for him and both the .270 and the .308 for her to try. He could hear through the trees that she was shooting already, the crack of her rifle sharp as it echoed back from the hillside.

He slung a bag with his pistol cases and ammunition over his shoulder and pulled the three rifle cases from the small back seat of his extended cab. The shots fell silent, the forest going still and quiet around him, the birds obviously frightened away by the rifle shots.

After a moment, a squirrel scolded him from a nearby

tree. Another answered it, and a branch rustled above him. The wind was calm, the air crisp in the shade of the towering fir trees. Snow was creeping down the mountainside, telling him they had only a few weeks before it fell and stuck in Paradise.

He headed down the footpath to the range, hearing Raven take another couple shots. Then he heard her voice and wondered if Brodie had come out with her. She laughed, and he tried to imagine what was funny about target shooting.

"Once or twice," another voice said, and Cobra stopped still.

It was Marnie.

"You never told me that." Mia added her voice to the conversation.

"It doesn't come up very often in LA," Marnie answered.

Cobra rounded the final corner of the path, the canyon and the firing platforms coming into view. Then he paused at the sight of Marnie.

She was exactly as he'd remembered, better than he'd remembered, her copper hair pulled back but bright in the sunshine, the profile of her smile dazzling white, her lips soft, her laugh musical, the curves of her lithe body perfect in every single way.

Raven stood up from the little bench in her firing lane and handed Marnie the rifle.

Cobra lurched forward, thinking to stop her, afraid someone would get hurt, wondering what on earth Raven could be thinking. He was about to call out when he saw that Marnie knew what she was doing. She handled the rifle like a pro, checking the safety, opening the action and keeping the barrel at a safe angle as she settled herself on the bench.

She put hearing protection over her ears and slipped on her protective eyewear. Then she leaned forward, planting her elbows on the table, her trigger finger safely to the side, looking through the scope.

"What do you want me to hit?" she asked Raven.

"Use target five. It's fifty yards."

"You got it."

Fascinated, Cobra stood back to watch.

Marnie stilled, paused then pulled the trigger. The sound ricocheted. Her shoulder barely moved as the rifle kicked back. It was a .30-30, not a huge rifle, but it had a firm enough recoil to leave a mark, especially when you considered her size and strength.

She took a second shot, then a third.

Raven checked the target through a set of binoculars. Her voice went high with apparent excitement. "No *way*. How did you do that?"

Marnie shrugged and set the rifle on the platform and stripped off the hearing protection.

Mia took the binoculars from Raven and looked through them for a moment. "You hit the bull's-eye," she said to Marnie on a note of astonishment.

"Try a hundred yards," Raven said with obvious enthusiasm. "Target nine."

"Okay." Marnie replaced the spent ammunition. This time, she fired off three shots in succession.

Raven was quick with the binoculars.

"Did she hit it?" Mia asked, talking loudly over their hearing protection.

"Dead center," Raven answered, stripping hers off and staring at Marnie in astonishment.

Cobra started forward, amazed himself. What else had Marnie been hiding?

Chatting among themselves, the women didn't hear him until he was almost there.

"*There* you are," Raven said as he approached.

Marnie turned, saw him, and her smile instantly disappeared.

"She's a deadeye," Raven said.

"That's a terrible nickname," Mia said.

"Have you been holding out on us?" Cobra joked, trying to lighten the atmosphere between the two of them.

"Nobody asked me about shooting," Marnie said, her tone flat.

Raven gave her an odd look.

Mia glanced speculatively from Marnie to Cobra and back again. It didn't take a rocket scientist to guess Marnie had told her something.

Cobra set his rifles and ammunition on the stand in the next lane to free up his hands. He took the binoculars from Raven and raised them, focusing on the two targets. His eyes widened a little. To say Marnie had made a tight grouping was an understatement.

"Do you have a military background?" he asked her, trying to imagine how an LA lawyer had learned to shoot like a sniper.

"No," she said, turning away from him and reloading the gun.

He wasn't about to give up. "Where'd you learn to shoot like that?"

Leaving the safety on, she raised the gun and put her eye to the scope. "I was raised by survivalists."

Mia reacted first. "No way."

Raven laughed.

"In Merganser, Kansas?" Cobra asked.

Marnie didn't answer.

"You never told me that," he said. And they'd talked about her childhood.

Both Raven and Mia looked him over in confusion.

"Why would she tell you?" Raven asked.

"It's not something I talk about," Marnie said. "Everybody ready?" She gave them a minute to put on their safety gear before taking a couple of shots at the two-hundred-yard target.

Cobra looked through the binoculars to the overlapping

holes she'd put in the center of the bull's-eye. "Okay, now you're just showing off."

He caught a glimpse of her self-satisfied smile. He liked it so much better than her scowl.

"You have to try Cobra's guns," Raven said. "They're higher quality than mine."

"You prefer a .270 or a .308?" Cobra asked Marnie, arranging the three rifle cases on the stand next to where she was shooting.

Instead of answering, she rose from her seat, backing up as she spoke to Raven. "I don't want to get in the way of your practice."

Raven grasped her by the arm to stop her progress. "How long can you stay in Paradise?"

Marnie blinked. "A couple more days, why?"

"Any chance you can stretch it?"

Cobra understood where Raven was going with this, but it took Marnie a moment.

"Oh, no," she said with a definitive shake of her head. "That's not going to work."

"We *need* you," Raven said. "Paradise needs you."

"For the Klondike Challenge?" Mia asked, catching on a second behind everyone else.

"Yes," Raven said emphatically. She gestured to the targets down the range. "You'd win it easily. I came fifth last year in the women's competition, and you're way better than me."

"Not a chance," Marnie said.

Cobra wanted to urge her to stay. But given her attitude toward him right now, he was worried he'd drive her away.

"You don't like my guest room?" Mia asked in an obvious ploy to corner Marnie.

"Oh no you don't," Marnie retorted, seeing right through Mia.

"I'm insulted," Mia said on a huff, crossing her arms and raising her nose in the air.

"Not going to work," Marnie told her.

"Turn it into a vacation," Raven suggested.

Cobra bit back his own thoughts.

"I have clients," Marnie said.

"I'm your favorite client," Mia said. "And I need you here."

Cobra gave Mia a smile and a nod. That was an inspired counter argument.

"You're not my only client."

"Hannah and Henry are important clients of your firm now, and I'd bet they'd be fine with you staying here for a while."

"You can't call Hannah and Henry," Marnie said in a warning tone.

"I call them all the time," Mia said airily.

Cobra wanted to cheer her on.

Marnie looked disconcerted by that. "I can't ask Gretchen Miller to cover for me for two more weeks."

"Why not?" Mia asked. "You're bringing increased Lafayette business to the firm, and you're expanding into entertainment law. Trust me, *that's* going to be lucrative."

Cobra fought a grin at Mia's convincing delivery.

"Everyone needs to take a vacation sometime," Raven added. "Come on, Marnie. Paradise came second last year, a close second. You could take us straight to the top."

"Serious bragging rights," Cobra offered helpfully, earning him an annoyed look from Marnie. "You'd be the town hero."

"I don't want to be the town hero," she told him.

"Why not?" Mia asked.

"Brodie would be thrilled," Raven said. "And if you make Brodie happy, let's just say he'll get very cooperative on our future matchmaking rounds."

"It's true," Mia said. "After I saved his plane from crashing in the flood, Brodie was putty in my hands."

"Really?" Cobra had a hard time believing Brodie would completely roll over for anyone, even for someone who'd saved his plane and his pilot.

"Really," Mia said with conviction.

Raven took Marnie's hands. "Say yes. It's only a couple of weeks."

Marnie shook her head.

"I think that's a yes," Mia said.

It looked like a hard no to Cobra, and he was sorely disappointed. He wanted two more weeks with Marnie. He'd take anything he could get, but two weeks sounded exceptional—if only he could get her to talk to him again.

"I'll ask," Marnie said with exaggerated resignation.

Raven whooped with joy.

"I'll *ask*," Marnie repeated for emphasis.

"They'll say yes," Mia said. "I can guarantee they'll say yes."

Marnie's eyes narrowed at Mia. "You're going to lobby them, aren't you?"

Mia produced her phone and wiggled it in the air, causing Cobra to fight off yet another smile. "I am."

"Can I stop you?"

"You don't want to stop me. We'll have fun. And you deserve a break."

Marnie rolled her eyes at that. "My life at the law firm isn't all that tough."

Mia pressed on the screen with her thumb.

"How are you with pistols?" Cobra asked Marnie, since it looked like Mia had all but won the argument.

Marnie gave him a menacing look—hard to do given the differences in their sizes, but she pulled it off.

He ignored it. "I've brought a .270 and a .308. You might like the .270. The action is smooth, and it has a nice trigger."

Raven moved to pack her rifle in its case.

"Gretchen?" Mia said into her phone, taking a couple of steps away from the rest. "It's Mia Westberg. I was wondering—"

"I'm ignoring you," Marnie said to Cobra.

"I got that."

She made a shooing motion with her hands. "So back off."

"You know I can't do that."

She put her hands on her hips and tipped her chin even higher. "Why not?"

He wanted to say she'd invaded his dreams and his waking hours and thoughts of her had taken over his life. "Because you took three shots and only made one hole, and—"

"My mistake."

"—and I have higher-performing firearms."

Mia waved her phone as she called out to Marnie. "You're good to stay."

"Inevitable," Marnie whispered in an undertone as her chin dropped.

Cobra's chest warmed at the thought of her staying in town. His fingers flexed, and it was all he could do not to reach out to her.

Chapter Eleven

A DOZEN THOUGHTS RUSHED THROUGH MARNIE'S mind as she squeezed off a final shot from the 9mm pistol. Among them, that Cobra wasn't exaggerating about his high-performing firearms.

Also, that Mia was a good friend *and* an important client, and Marnie really was doing legal work for her here in Paradise. Although Marnie felt guilty about staying, she was happy to hang out with Mia awhile longer. She also admitted that Cobra—who was shooting his own .357 revolver a few lanes down—had gotten under her skin like no man ever before.

She dropped the empty magazine from the 9mm. Her arm was getting tired, and she knew it was time for a break.

The people of Paradise had set up a rustic but very functional shooting range in a small box canyon that provided natural safety barriers. Meadow grasses and flower stalks shifted in the light wind in front of rows of stands. The targets were set up at intervals all the way up to four-hundred yards. They had to manually replace the paper targets, but Cobra had done that after he arrived.

She went to the binoculars now to check her accuracy at fifty yards. She was glad Cobra was at the far end of the stalls. If he were sitting next to her, she'd have been jumpy, messing up her aim.

"How does it look?" he asked, coming her way.

Raven had left to take her own gear back to her truck, and Mia had . . .

Marnie looked around, wondering where Mia had disappeared to. "Not bad," she answered Cobra.

He sat down at the next bench and put his hand out for the binoculars.

"What about you?" she asked instead of handing them over.

He gestured out on the range. "Target six."

She put the binoculars to her eyes and focused.

He was good. He was *really* good.

"My turn," he said, and gently drew the binoculars from her hand. His fingers brushed hers, sending a current of awareness skittering along her skin.

She sucked in a breath. "Good shooting," she managed to politely tell him.

He raised the binoculars to look at her target, then he whistled under his breath. "Survivalists, you say? They taught you well."

"You're better," she responded, rubbing her hand where he'd touched her, trying to erase the ridiculous sensation.

"I had professional training."

"I was a child prodigy."

He smiled at that, and she felt it to her core. She wished he'd move away again. Then she wished he would move even closer. Then she wished she'd get her own emotions under control already.

"I can also replace the seals in a water pump," she rattled off to fill the silence. "Operate a ham radio and identify every edible plant in the greater Midwest."

He was gazing at her now, his dark eyes both probing and puzzled at the same time. "Impressive."

"Thank you." She wasn't sure what else to say.

"Seriously. The world needs more women like you."

She scoffed at that. Her survivalist skills were the least practical thing about her these days.

"But there aren't other women like you." His voice turned gravelly and humor lit his eyes. "Listen, I know you said you're not looking for a husband, and I'm really not looking for a wife, but—"

"Ha, ha," she mocked, guessing where he was going.

"Would you consider marrying me?"

She wasn't ready to joke around with him. "Not a chance."

"No?"

"No."

"Well, that's disappointing," he said easily, still looking amused by his own joke.

"You'll get over it."

"Tough to find a woman who can replace the seals in a water pump."

"I don't do things like that anymore." She found herself lightening up.

His brow quirked upward. "No real call for it in LA?"

"One of the reasons I moved there."

Their gazes met and held, the scent of gunpowder overlaying the drying grasses and leaves.

"Are you going to tell me?" he asked, his voice low and intimate.

"Tell you what?"

"Why you're avoiding me."

"I'm not."

He went silent, letting the faraway squirrel chatter fill the air around them.

Marnie wished Mia or Raven would get back here.

"Why are you lying to me?" he asked.

"I'm not lying," she said, feeling guiltier for lying about lying than the original lie. Interesting, that.

"Marnie."

Her frustration was clear in her tone. "What?"

"What's going on?"

"Do we *have* to do this?"

"Yes, we do."

"Fine." She tested a couple of explanatory sentences inside her head. Neither of them worked.

"You're not doing it," he noted.

"I'm thinking about it."

"Okay." He waited.

She took the plunge. "I didn't want to be . . . you know . . ."

He cocked his head. "If I knew, I wouldn't be asking."

She squared her shoulders then and glanced around to make sure they were still alone. She pivoted her body on the bench to face him full-on. "You didn't sign up for this, and I didn't want to be that woman."

His brow furrowed. "What woman?"

"The one-night stand who never went away."

He drew back. "One-night stand?"

She pasted him with a warning look. "Keep it down."

He lowered his voice, leaning closer. "A one-night stand? Is that what you think happened between us?"

There was no other way to describe it. "It was one night, and . . . well, you were standing." She didn't know why she'd added that irreverent ending. It just popped into her head.

His gaze darkened further. "That wasn't what I wanted."

"To be standing?" she asked flippantly, trying to keep ahead of her emotions.

"A one-night stand." He kept his voice low, but the strain in it was obvious.

"I was leaving the next day."

"There was nothing we could do about that." He paused.

"I mean, nothing that we knew of at the time, anyway." He reached out to touch her hand.

She pulled away, and he gave a frustrated sigh.

"What did you want, Cobra?"

"I don't know. Ten nights, thirty nights." His deep voice vibrated through her, drawing her in like a magnet. He leaned closer still. "What did you want? What *do* you want?"

Raven's voice reached them, followed by Mia's.

"Tell me," he said with urgency, glancing toward the trail and the voices, clearly expecting the two women to appear at any second.

"I don't know," Marnie answered. "I haven't thought it through." She'd thought about him plenty, but she hadn't let herself consider the possibility of anything more happening between them.

Mia and Raven appeared in her peripheral vision, and she straightened, realizing how close she and Cobra had gotten to each other.

Cobra straightened away as well, his gaze still holding hers. "Think it through. Give it a chance."

"Cobra." She didn't know what she was asking.

"We're both adults," he elaborated. "We can be discreet if that's what you want. Just don't—"

"How'd the 9mm work for you?" Raven called out to Marnie, crossing the last few yards between them. "Did you like it?"

"It's a perfect match," Cobra answered for her, taking a beat before he moved his gaze from Marnie to Raven. "She's incredible."

Marnie was slower to shift her attention.

Just don't . . . his cut-off words echoed in her mind. Just don't, *what*?

COBRA'S STATEMENT STILL ECHOED INSIDE MARNIE'S head as the Klondike Challenge team gathered at the Bear and Bar the next night. Brodie surprised her with his involvement. Given his attitude on their matchmaking scheme, she hadn't seen him as a community leader. But there he was in front of the bar explaining the timing and logistics of the Klondike Challenge that was taking place in just over a week in the Alaskan town of Balsam Ridge, two hundred miles away.

According to Brodie, WSA would fly the participants to Balsam Ridge where they'd be provided with luxury tent accommodations. Marnie was also surprised to learn that it was such a big event. Communities from all over Alaska would be there, winding up everyone's season as winter set in.

At a table next to the window with Mia and Raven, Marnie eased back in her chair to bring Cobra into view. He was closer to the bar than they were, facing front, and she could see his profile.

Watching him now, she vividly remembered the taste of his lips, the touch of his hands and the silky feel of his hot, smooth skin. She wanted it again. She wanted all of it all over again.

Brodie was talking about meals now—a central cafeteria and a barbecue pit. He listed the names of the current Paradise team members, noting some spots hadn't yet been filled and they needed two women for the new Green Energy Challenge. Then he opened the floor to questions.

Marnie only half listened, restless, frustrated at being this near to Cobra, wanting to talk to him, to pick up where they'd left off yesterday and ask him the question that was burning in her mind.

He smiled at something Brodie said, and some people laughed. She realized it must have been a joke.

She quickly grinned, pretending she'd been listening. Then she joined in the applause with the rest of the crowded room.

Brodie took a mock bow, and conversation came up around the room.

"Do you cycle?" Raven asked her.

Marnie shook her head. "Walking the city streets is my best exercise."

Mia looked around at the crowd of mostly men. "I wonder who might . . ."

Silas appeared behind her and rested his hands on her shoulders.

She immediately smiled and looked up at him.

He gave her a quick peck. "I told Brodie you'd try out for the cycling."

"Me?" Mia asked in obvious surprise.

"You run."

She reached down to touch her slender thighs. "I don't have a lot of power in these."

"We don't have a lot of choices."

"Hey!" Mia said in mock offense.

Marnie took the moment to casually rise from the table. She started to explain that she was going to the ladies' room but then realized nobody was paying any attention. She moved away, scanning the room until she spotted Cobra.

He was around the corner, standing between the pool tables and the dividing wall, talking with T-Two.

She started his way, greeting a few people she recognized along the way—AJ, Kenneth and Xavier, who looked a little down and was probably missing Scarlett. The music had been turned up after Brodie's talk, and people were three-deep at the bar ordering drinks. She was thirsty too, but she was much more interested in talking to Cobra.

He saw her coming, met her gaze and stilled.

She took a couple steps closer before pausing, not wanting to interrupt.

He said something more to T-Two, and T-Two clapped him on the shoulder before walking away.

A little smile came up on Cobra's face. He leaned his shoulder against the wall and cocked his head, obviously waiting to see what she'd do. It wasn't quite a contest, but she knew it was her move.

She took a step, then another and another until she was standing in front of him.

"Just don't . . . *what*?" she opened.

His smile grew a little, and his dark gaze softened.

"Is what you said to me yesterday," she elaborated.

"I know what I said to you."

She moved closer still, lowering her tone. "And?"

"Freeze me out." The deep timbre of his voice reached all the way to her bones. "Just don't freeze me out."

"I don't want to freeze you out." Fighting to keep from swaying into his arms, she took the final plunge. "I want to let you in."

He sobered and slipped an arm around her waist, turning her, guiding her toward the back door to the patio.

She went willingly, and the voices and music faded behind them as they stepped outside.

Marnie's jacket was light. The change in temperature gave her a shiver, and Cobra pulled her closer. The moon hung bright above the snowy mountain peaks, its brilliance casting shadows from the picnic tables and the patio railing. Their footfalls echoed as they crossed the wooden deck.

A black shape moved beyond the rail, smooth, undulating. It was the biggest dog—

Cobra stopped short, and his grip tightened around her.

"Is that a . . . ?" Her voice trailed away as the shape stopped short too.

Cobra pivoted, blocking her with his body, walking her swiftly back to the restaurant door.

"Wha—" she started as he grasped the handle.

"Bear," he said, shoving her unceremoniously inside and shutting the door behind them. He moved fast, pulling her along by the hand as he headed into the main restaurant area. "Bear right outside," he shouted over the music.

Conversation paused.

He left her at the end of the bar, going behind it and shutting off the music.

His voice was forceful, and everyone paid attention. "Mia's grizzly's outside on Red Avenue."

"With the cubs?" Brodie asked.

"Yes," Cobra answered.

Marnie hadn't seen the cubs. She was just as glad she hadn't known there were three bears. Not that there'd been time to be afraid. Cobra had moved too fast for her to think. But now fear rose up in her chest, speeding up her heart, making her struggle to catch her breath.

They'd almost walked into some *bears*.

Another man stood from a barstool, turning to the crowd with an air of authority. "Anyone else seen them lately?"

There were headshakes all around.

"Probably just passing through again," Silas put in.

"I hope so," the other man said.

Cobra came to stand beside Marnie again. He took her hand, holding it surreptitiously between their thighs. "You okay?"

She nodded.

Mia joked to Silas, "I hope they don't remember me." Her voice was clear enough that other people heard, and a ripple of laughter went through the crowd.

"Nobody leaves alone," the man said.

"Who's that?" Marnie asked Cobra.

"Troy Corbett, chief of police. Also, the only police."

"Volunteers for escorts?" Troy looked around the room.

Cobra and a bunch of other men raised their hands.

"Take your guns."

"Are you armed?" Marnie asked Cobra, looking him over with surprise.

"There's a rifle in my truck. Plus, bear spray. But we won't have to shoot anything. Mia's bear was hanging around for weeks in the summer, and there were no other incidents. She only ended up in trouble because she ran right into it."

"Are you saying it wasn't the bear's fault?"

"It had cubs, and Mia startled it. If it was an aggressive bear, we'd have known by now."

"You're very understanding."

Mia appeared beside them.

"You have your very own bear—bears?" Marnie couldn't help but joke to her.

"I didn't know they were mine."

"T-Two tried to sell me on foxes as pets, but this beats that." Marnie hoped Cobra would appreciate her joke.

"I hope I'm never that close to them again," Mia said. "Silas is bringing the truck to the front door."

Marnie glanced to Cobra. It was easy to read his expression, and she was thinking the same thing—if she left with Mia, she wasn't going back to Cobra's room.

If she left with Cobra, she'd have to out their relationship to Mia and Silas.

Cobra quirked his brow, clearly leaving the choice to her.

She didn't know what to do.

"I can pick you up for target practice tomorrow," he said, obviously giving her a third option.

She was grateful—disappointed to be saying goodnight this soon, but grateful for his solution.

IN SILAS AND MIA'S DRIVEWAY, COBRA HEARD THE whine of a chainsaw. He caught movement beyond the house and saw Silas step back from a pile of logs, his bright orange saw dangling from his left hand.

Silas gave him a wave, and Cobra walked that way.

"You look busy," Cobra said as he approached.

Silas shut off the saw. "Figured I better stack up a few cords before the snow flies."

"Did you put in a wood boiler?" Cobra looked around. He didn't remember seeing one while the house had been under construction.

"This is for the fireplace," Silas said.

"Need a hand?" Cobra asked, seeing the gas-powered wood splitter set up nearby and spotting an extra pair of work gloves on the open tailgate of Silas's truck.

"Sure," Silas said. "You here to help me work?"

Cobra cocked his head toward the house. "Marnie and I are going shooting, but I've got time."

It was an unwritten code in Paradise that you didn't walk away from neighborly work without an ironclad excuse. It was a good code, and the target practice could wait a while longer.

"They're inside—reading a script or starting a film company or something."

Cobra rolled up the sleeves of his heavy cotton work shirt, not surprised to hear Marnie was working hard.

"When I left, they were debating company names," Silas said. "Also, if it should be a single purpose LLC or an umbrella corporation to take on multiple films."

"They sound serious."

"They're a force of nature, those two. It's impressive."

Cobra pulled on the gloves, nodding to the substantial woodpile. "Unlike you, you slacker."

Silas grinned and pulled on the chainsaw starter, revving it up. "At least we get to have some fun."

Cobra didn't disagree with that. It was good to be outside, breathing the fresh air, working their muscles, the blood coursing through their veins. And there was something therapeutic about watching a woodpile grow high, knowing it would keep you warm in the winter. He'd much rather do that than stare at some legal document.

He started up the splitter, set the first round of firewood in the cradle and pulled the lever to move the wedge through the center. As Silas bucked the logs into lengths,

Cobra split and stacked them under the makeshift shed. Between the two of them, they got through the whole pile in less than an hour.

"Beer?" Silas asked, wiping the sweat from his brow and stepping back to admire the tightly stacked woodpile.

"Absolutely," Cobra answered, shutting down the splitter and wheeling it under a corner of the woodshed to keep it out of the weather.

Silas put his saw in the case and moved his truck into the garage.

Cobra brushed the sawdust from his clothes as he walked to the house. He headed in through the side door to the arctic entry to wash up at the deep laundry sink.

Cleaned up, they entered the kitchen where Silas grabbed a couple of beers from the fridge.

Cobra could hear Mia and Marnie talking up in the loft, their voices indistinct. He might not have been able to make out the words, but he still liked the cadence of Marnie's voice.

Silas set the beer bottles down on the table. "Hey, Mia?" he called up the stairs.

"Yes?" she answered.

"Cobra's here for Marnie."

The two women said a few more words as Cobra took one of the wooden chairs at the big, oval table and twisted the cap off his beer.

"We're on our way," Mia called down.

Cobra found his gaze fixed on the staircase and realized he was holding his breath waiting for Marnie to appear. He shook himself out of it and took a drink. He was thirsty and the cold liquid felt good going down.

"Nothing on the docket at WSA for tomorrow," Silas noted.

They both knew work was slowing and would drop off a cliff by the end of October. "You two staying for the winter?" Cobra asked.

Silas generally stayed over the winter with Brodie, while most of the pilots took significant vacations down south. Having Mia around might have changed things.

"Haven't decided yet," Silas said. He took another drink. "Maybe we're making a movie this winter. Who knows?"

Cobra chuckled as Mia came into view. Marnie followed, and Cobra was hit with an intense wave of pleasure at the sight of her.

"Hi, Cobra," Mia said. "You two are off to the range?"

"We are," Cobra answered, dragging his attention from Marnie.

Silas tapped his beer on the table. "I applaud your dedication."

"Anything for the team," Cobra said, taking a deep swallow of his beer, anxious to get going.

He caught the warmth of Marnie's gaze on him. He loved it, but he didn't necessarily want Silas or Mia to see it.

"You ready?" he asked her.

She canted her head toward the guest room. "I'll grab my jacket."

"You want to toss a few sticks of firewood in the truck?" Silas asked. "For the warm-up shack?"

"We'll be fine," Cobra said.

It was chilly outside, but it was sunny enough. Marnie might have looked all delicate LA lawyer, but he knew she was tougher than she let on.

Mia sent Silas a pointed look.

"I'll throw some wood in the box for you," Silas said.

"Don't worry about me," Marnie said to Mia. "Really."

"I'm not going to let you freeze to death." Mia gave Cobra a reproving look. "We want her to like it here."

"Fine," he said, rising to help Silas. "We'll fire up the wood stove in the shack."

"You don't—" Marnie started.

But Mia touched her shoulder. "Let them go be manly."

"This is silly."

"But not a big deal," Cobra told her. "I'll meet you out front."

Cobra backed his truck up to the woodpile and they stacked a dozen pieces of firewood into the box.

"You got matches?" Silas asked.

"You my babysitter now?" Cobra asked, somewhat offended.

"No. But I answer to Mia, and she might ask."

"I can survive a good week with the gear stashed in my truck."

"Okay, then." Silas patted the box of the truck. "You kids have fun."

"Tell Mia I'll bring Marnie back alive."

"You better."

Cobra climbed into the driver's seat and firmly shut the door.

Marnie was waiting on the front porch and hopped in before he could even think about getting out to open her door.

Relieved they were finally alone, his frustration disappeared. He gave her a warm smile, drinking in her beautiful eyes and dazzling hair, struggling not to fixate on her lips and make himself half crazy.

She smiled back, flashing white teeth as he pulled away.

"I feel like this took us a while," she said, shifting her body sideways and raising her knee up on the bench seat to face him. She wore a tidy little pair of jeans, a mottled purple sweater, a short, black windbreaker and a pair of sensible leather boots.

He was willing to bet she'd bought the boots in Paradise. They didn't seem like the kind of thing she'd wear in LA.

"Where to?" he asked.

"I thought we were going shooting."

"We can shoot if you want. You feel like you need the practice?"

"I'm a bit rusty," she said.

He tried not to be disappointed. He'd happily hang out with her anywhere, but if they were focused on target practice, they wouldn't be focused on each other.

"Why?" she asked.

"Why what?"

She gave him a look that said he wasn't fooling her. "Are you trying to entice me back to your lair?"

"My *lair*?"

"You have designs on my body?"

He had plenty of designs on her body, but he hadn't expected to pick her up and rush off to the nearest bed for passionate sex. Well, sure, he wanted to do that. But he hadn't expected it.

"No," he said. "I mean, I wasn't thinking about your body." Not completely, anyway. "I was thinking we could take a drive or a walk or something. We could go see the waterfall above the airstrip. There's a nice trail from the hangar. It's a little steep."

"I don't mind steep."

"Yeah?" He'd rather walk beside her than shoot beside her. That way he could look at her, talk to her, maybe hold her hand all afternoon.

He slowed for the end of the driveway and took a left for the airstrip.

Chapter Twelve

THE WATERFALL TRAIL WAS NARROW. IT WAS STEEP enough in a few places that Marnie had to use her hands to scramble up the rocky patches. So she was slightly winded but mostly exhilarated when they came to a near-vertical rock face about fifteen feet high.

"You feel comfortable climbing this?" Cobra asked. "We're almost there."

She sized it up, looking at the slope of the rock and the potential foot and handholds. It was dry granite, no moss or weeds that might make her feet slip. And her boots had good treads. She was glad of that today.

"The bottom part looks okay," she said, moving sideways for a new angle. "The last five feet or so look challenging."

"I'll go first," he said. "Then I can guide you from the top."

"Sure." She wiped her hands on her jeans, making sure they were thoroughly dry.

"Or we can turn around here," he offered.

She shook her head. "I'll give it a shot."

In answer, he wrapped an arm around her shoulders and gave her a brief encouraging squeeze. "If it's too tricky, I'll come back down."

"You've done this before, right?"

The way he'd talked earlier, she thought he'd climbed the trail numerous times.

"It's been a while," he said. "I don't remember it looking this steep."

"Probably because you were with your outdoor buddies, not some city girl."

"Probably," he agreed. "I've only had to consider my own skillset before."

She wasn't insulted. She knew he hadn't meant to criticize her ability. She was a city girl now, and she was the one hesitating, not him.

"Carry on," she said, stepping back to watch him climb.

The first part seemed easy enough, and he took the route she would have picked. The closer he got to the top, the more difficult it was to see where he was stepping. But he quickly cleared the top and turned around.

He crouched down and pointed. "You can't see it from there, but there's a wide ledge tucked inside a crevice. Anchor your left foot there. Hold on to this shelf." He pointed again. "And I'll be able to grab your hand."

"If you say so," she called back up.

"Are you nervous?"

She shook her head. "No." If it was as easy as he made it sound, she'd be fine.

She followed the route Cobra had taken until she could see the ledge.

"Good," he said.

She pulled herself up another step, then wedged her foot into the crevice.

"Grab here," he said, and pointed.

She reached and pulled herself up, feeling unsteady for just a moment, but then he grasped her other hand.

His grip was strong and sure, and she was completely confident he would hold her. Even if everything else went wrong, he'd pull her over the top.

"Put your toe on the little ledge to your right. Next to your knee."

She did. That foothold definitely felt precarious. But Cobra took most of her weight and seconds later she was over the top, first on her knees and then standing.

"Perfect," he said with a beaming smile.

She peeped over the edge and felt vertigo for a second.

"Don't look down," he warned.

She looked around instead.

They'd come up on a high, flat meadow, the river's gorge off in the distance. The wildflowers had long since died, and the leaves and grasses had turned gold and red. The meadow was knee-high on her, looking waist-high in some places where it stretched out around them.

"Listen," he said, holding still.

She did, and she could hear the faint rush of water.

"Is that the falls?"

"That's them."

They started toward the sound, their hands still linked, his warm and dry, square and callused, with long, strong fingers. She liked the sensation that went up her arm, like his energy was flowing into her, lighting her up, bringing her to life.

"You must have hiked with your family a lot," he said.

"What makes you think that?"

"You said you knew edible plants."

"We did go on weekend wilderness treks. They weren't much fun, though."

"No?"

"It's hard to enjoy yourself when you're training for nuclear fallout, germ warfare or the collapse of the world economic system."

"So, no happy campfire songs?"

"No gooey marshmallows or hot dog roasts. Just reconstituted freeze-dried meat. Sort of a sludge, really." She shuddered at the memory.

"Sounds worse than the military."

"Did they make you eat freeze-dried food?"

"Meals, Ready to Eat in the field sometimes. A lot of stews and pasta. Not the greatest, but okay if you're hungry. Mostly I was on base maintaining and repairing planes."

"And learning to shoot, obviously."

"Everybody learns to shoot."

Marnie spotted a patch of green plants with waxy leaves and dark red berries clustered in their centers. "Lingonberries?" She'd seen them in books but not in the wild.

He looked to where she pointed. "We call them lowbush cranberries. Tart but quite tasty."

"So." She lifted her brows. "A snack?"

He gestured to the patch. "By all means."

She crouched to her knees and picked a couple of the ripest-looking ones, popping them into her mouth. They made her mouth pucker, and Cobra laughed at her.

"Tart is right," she said, swallowing.

"Mrs. France turns them into jam and pies. I suspect she uses plenty of sugar. They're good in muffins too."

"Ooh. These would be great in muffins." Marnie nibbled a few more.

"You bake?" Cobra asked as he picked himself a handful.

Marnie shook her head. "Not in years. My kitchen's small, and there's a great bakery just down the block."

"I bet they don't have wild cranberry muffins straight from the source." He tossed the handful into his mouth.

She sat all the way down and picked another berry, the

dry grass cracking, a few insects buzzing around her. "Baking was work to me as a kid. We baked all the staples, whole-grain bread and buns, biscuits, pancakes."

"Nothing exciting like a birthday cake or some brownies?" She shook her head.

He settled himself on the ground. "My mom baked birthday cakes. I imagine she still does. She didn't make bread or anything, just the fun stuff like Christmas cookies— shortbread and sugar cookies shaped like Christmas trees and bells."

"With icing and sprinkles on top?"

"With icing and sprinkles."

Marnie gave a sigh. "I think I'd like your mom." She nibbled another berry.

An odd expression crossed his face. "We can take some berries back with us if you want them."

She realized she didn't. She wanted the taste of lowbush cranberries to be special to this place, this day, this moment in time with Cobra.

"Your lips are turning red," he said.

She reflexively turned them inward to lick off the stain.

His gaze intensified as he watched the motion, and her lips tingled with desire that made its way to her chest.

"Want to bring those lips over here?" he asked softly.

She did—no question about it. She uncurled her legs and moved his way.

He reached for her, circling her waist and easing her into his lap, settling her there, cradled across his thighs.

He smoothed back her hair and cupped her cheek. His sweet breath fanned her face. "It feels like I've waited forever for this."

"You've kissed me before," she pointed out.

"Not really. Not like this. Not deliberate and slow with all the time in the world."

He kissed her gently, fleetingly, like butterfly wings passing over her lips.

She'd been waiting forever too. "More," she whispered, stretching up.

He smiled and met her halfway, his lips coming firmly against hers, soft, tender, mobile. It was a great kiss, a perfect kiss, the best kiss of her life.

She angled toward him and wrapped her arms around his neck, pressing herself flat against his chest. Their kiss went on and on. She never wanted it to end.

He laid back on the dry meadow grasses, bringing her down on top, and she stretched out, loving the feel of their bodies pressed so intimately together. His forearm splayed across her back, and he stroked her hair, inhaling deeply, kissing her neck and her collarbone, then nudging her sweater and jacket aside to kiss her shoulder.

She sat up, straddling him, and unzipped her jacket.

He grasped both sides before she could peel it off. "Not here."

"Why not?"

"It's too cold, for one thing."

"I'm hot." She fought a losing battle against the strength of his grip.

"Our last time was on a workbench."

She shrugged. "We're adventurous."

"You deserve a bed, someplace warm."

"It's not like we're never going to do it again."

He sat up then, his arms bracketing her. "Yeah?"

"I'm here for two weeks. You think we're going to stop after today?"

"Not unless you want to." He zipped up her jacket.

"Hey!"

"Hey, what?"

"I thought I was winning that argument."

"Look," he said, nodding to something behind her.

"Is that a distraction?"

"No. Look."

She twisted her neck and let out a little gasp, seeing the

most graceful, leggy, wild-looking creature padding along the far edge of the meadow.

"Lynx," he whispered in her ear.

It was much bigger than a domestic cat, with a fluffy mottled taupe coat, too-long lanky legs, sharp ears and a wild face with yellow eyes.

"Is it dangerous?" she whispered to Cobra as the creature grew closer.

"It'll bolt if it sees us."

The lynx turned to them then. It reared a little, looking shocked to find them sitting there. And Cobra was right. It instantly turned away and bounded over the meadow, disappearing over the edge of the riverbank.

"That's rare to see," Cobra told her.

"It was beautiful."

He rose to his feet, drawing her up with him. "Want to go see the falls?"

"Not really."

He chuckled, swiping his fingertip across her nose. "You're impatient."

"I am."

"I've still got a room above the hangar."

"I thought you moved back to your room."

"The hangar's closer. It's warm and private. By the time we look at the falls and walk out of here, everybody will be gone for the day." He made it sound tempting.

She slipped her hand into his. "Show me the falls."

THE FALLS HAD BEEN SPECTACULAR, BUT THEY DIDN'T hold a candle to making love with Cobra.

Now, lying in his arms, the room dark except for an outdoor light shining through the window, she felt utterly peaceful and utterly cocooned in bliss.

Her phone rang.

"No." She half groaned the word into Cobra's bare chest.

His arm tightened around her. "Ignore it."

"It might be Mia."

"What? You want to chat?"

"She'll worry."

He gave a long-suffering sigh and loosened his hold.

Marnie rolled away, reaching down to the floor and feeling around for her jeans. She located the right pocket and slipped the phone out, hoisting herself up and flipping onto her back.

Unknown number.

Her heart sank, and her jaw set in frustration at the intrusion.

"What?" Cobra asked, shifting closer as the ringing continued.

She declined the call and dropped the phone back down on the pile of her pants.

"I saw," he admitted.

"Damn it," she ground out, snuggling back up against him, trying to recapture her bliss.

"You still think it's your family?" Cobra asked, feathering his fingertips along her arm.

"My dad." Her gut told her it was him. "But I don't know for sure."

"I could answer for you," he offered. "If he calls again. Find out what he wants."

"You mean scare him off."

"If that's what you want me to do."

"He won't want anything good, and I don't want to have to think about him." She tucked the covers more tightly around her, stopping a draft.

"You're thinking about him now," Cobra pointed out.

"I'll stop."

They were silent for a minute.

"Have you stopped?" he asked.

Instead of answering, she made an inarticulate sound of frustration deep in her throat.

"Maybe it's not him."

"Maybe it's not."

Cobra shifted. "Me . . . I might be tempted to find out for sure."

"And if it *is* him?" That was her worry.

"Knowing for sure what he wants might be better than wondering about it."

"Oh no it won't." Marnie was certain of that.

They were silent for another moment.

Marnie tried to relax again, focusing on the warmth of Cobra's skin. She rested her palm on his chest, feeling his heartbeat, working hard to get her father off her mind. But the image of her family on that last day, her father, brother and uncle being led from the courtroom in handcuffs, was stuck on a loop in her brain.

"He's tried twice now," Cobra said, speaking softly against her hair.

"Three times," she responded.

He pulled back to look at her. "Yeah?"

She nodded.

"Then he's not likely to stop."

She nodded to that too.

"If it was me," Cobra started again.

"It's not you."

"I'd be too curious not to pick up. I'd assume something was wrong or something was right—someone in the family was sick or pregnant or engaged or something."

"You said your brother was married."

"Barrick's married. Miles is single."

"Do they call you with happy news?" She tipped her head back to look at him. Her family hadn't had happy news in a long time—then again, she doubted there was much happy news coming out of the state prison.

"They do. Or they text me. You wonder why your father hasn't texted?"

"They don't have the technology." If anything, her father was calling from a prison pay phone.

"Who doesn't have a cell phone?" Cobra sounded perplexed, and she realized her error. "Are they worried about the government spying?"

"Something like that." She took the offered explanation.

Cobra stage-whispered his response—an obvious thread of a joke in his tone. "They might not be so far wrong, you know. The government's eyes and ears are everywhere."

She played along, her tension starting to ease. "Do you have insider information on that, *Sergeant* Stanford?"

"No insider information. And, technically, it's Master Sergeant Stanford."

"Yeah . . ." she drawled in a doubtful voice. "I won't be calling you that."

"No?" He gathered her closer in his arms. "I think I'd like it if you did."

She extracted her hand and mockingly held it out for him to shake. "In that case, Marnie Anton, Esquire. Nice to meet you, Master Sergeant Stanford."

"Esquire?"

She nodded.

He shook her hand. "Probably a little too formal while we're naked."

"True." She pretended to contemplate. "I think I'll call you . . ."

"Cobra's already a nickname."

"That's fair."

"What's your nickname?"

"I don't have a nickname."

"Never?"

She shook her head.

"Not even when you were a kid or in college or something?" he asked.

"Nope."

"I don't believe you. Is it bad? Is it embarrassing?"

"My parents called me Marnie. They were not the frivolous sort."

"And in college?"

"I was a serious student. I wasn't into clubs and sororities."

"I call that good judgment."

"Why thank you, Master Sergeant."

He settled her more comfortably in his arms again and nuzzled the top of her head. "I think I'll call you—"

"You don't get to pick my nickname."

"Sure, I do."

"Oh no you don't."

"Cupcake."

"What?" She tried to sit up, but he held on tight. "*No.*"

"You're sweet and delicious, and we both know you have a weakness for them."

She pulled her hand back to bop him on the chest, but he trapped her wrist to stop her.

"You can't call me Cupcake," she said.

He was chuckling at her protests. "You can't exactly stop me."

She twisted her body, straddling his and staring down into his eyes. "Maybe not."

"Definitely not."

"But I can bribe you." She flexed her hips and placed her palms flat on his chest. Then she curved her lips in a sultry smile.

"Bribe me how?" His voice was strangled.

She leaned down and placed her warm lips in the center of his chest. Then she slowly kissed her way upward.

He groaned, and his hands flexed around her thighs.

She made it to his neck, then his stubbled chin, then the corner of his mouth. "What was it you were going to call me?"

"Beautiful," he breathed.

"Better," she whispered.

"Wonderful," he said.

"Getting closer all the time." She softly kissed his lips.

"Fabulous," he said, and flipped her over, easing down on top.

"Fabulous isn't a nickname."

Humor flashed in his eyes. "Then I guess we're back to Cupcake."

She opened her mouth to object, but he kissed her deeply and in seconds she forgot what they were arguing about.

COBRA WAS IN A GREAT MOOD TODAY. HE FELT ENER-gized and alert, upbeat and optimistic as he gauged the weight of the ax in his hand. It had been a while since he'd done much throwing, but he didn't care if he made it into this particular event or not. Silas threw well; so did Brodie. And last year T, T-Two and Jackson had all made a good showing.

Whoever won the preliminaries today would do well for Paradise in the Klondike Challenge.

The Galina staff had set up a row of freshly repainted targets, big rounds of rough cedar they'd cut years ago, taken from a tree trunk Raven had hauled up from the coast.

"You look confident," Silas said as the two men stood side-by-side.

"Not worried about it one way or the other," Cobra said.

"It's not like you won't make the Paradise team. Nobody can touch you on sharpshooting."

"Seems unlikely." There was no sense in pretending it wasn't true. Cobra would be on the team for rifles and pis-tols if nothing else.

"You know," Silas said in a studiously casual tone that caught Cobra's attention. "I expected to hear your rifle shots from my yard yesterday."

"Yeah?" Cobra looked up and down the line of ax throw-ers as six men took their places behind the line, fifteen feet in front of the targets.

"Didn't hear a thing." Silas held his ax over his head, practicing the lineup.

"We walked to the falls instead."

Silas lowered his ax and turned. "Marnie said you stopped by the hangar."

"We did both." Cobra faced Silas, annoyed with the inquisition. "What's this about?"

"Just asking. You two seem . . ." Silas's expression finished the accusation.

"Are you worried about her getting hurt?" Cobra was being completely upfront with Marnie, and he resented Silas thinking anything else.

Silas coughed out a laugh.

"What's funny?"

"Dude, I'm not worried about *her*."

Cobra did a double take as the argument took a strange turn.

Silas shook his head. "You have no idea the world of hurt you're walking into."

"I'm not walking into anything." Cobra was getting to know a very interesting and beautiful woman, that was all.

A three-whistle blast split the air, telling the throwers to get ready.

Silas turned to face the target. "You like her."

There was no point in denying it anymore. "So what?"

"So, she's LA tried and true. She's going to leave you."

Cobra had a fleeting vision of his high school sweetheart, Shelby—although the two situations were completely different. "I know that," he said impatiently to Silas.

"There were twelve other women to pick from," Silas said.

Cobra hadn't *picked* Marnie. She wasn't here to be chosen.

The whistle sounded a single long blast, and Silas threw his ax, hitting just outside the bull's-eye.

Cobra turned to the target and put his mind on the contest, hoisting the ax over his head, lining up, eyeballing the base and the bull's-eye before swinging and letting it go. He buried it in the first ring.

Silas's throw was better. "Off your game?"

"Are you trying to be annoying?"

Troy Corbett, who was acting as the official, gave two short whistle blasts, signaling that the competitors could walk onto the throwing range and retrieve their axes.

"I'm trying to get your attention," Silas said as they walked forward. "Do whatever you want."

"I wasn't waiting for your permission."

Silas grinned knowingly again, annoying Cobra. "Just don't come crying to me."

"Crying? Seriously?" Cobra jerked the ax out of the target. He hadn't run crying to anyone since he was six years old and split open his knee going over Barrick's homemade bike jump on the concrete driveway at their house.

Cobra turned to find Marnie, Mia and Raven heading their way across the meadow. He zeroed in on Marnie's smile, his mood lifting, his chest tightening and his hormones buzzing with the memory of yesterday's lovemaking. Her eyes sparkled as she looked back at him, her bright hair glistening in the sun.

"I guess I'm too late," Silas said flatly.

"I don't know what you're talking about."

"Sorry, man." Silas clapped him on the shoulder. "Really sorry. Let me know if you need to talk."

Cobra shrugged the hand away. "Back off."

"Backing off."

Cobra switched his attention to Marnie again. He knew full well she was leaving Paradise. He wouldn't fall for her like he had for Shelby. He was walking into this thing with his eyes wide open, and he had no intention of slowing down.

"Morning," he said to all three women, but mostly to her.

"Who's winning?" Raven asked.

"I didn't see." Cobra looked up and down the row, realizing he'd have normally checked out Jackson's, Brodie's, T's and T-Two's throws.

"Cobra blew it," Silas said. "He seemed distracted."

Cobra shot him a hard look, but Silas just grinned, stepping up to Mia and giving her a quick kiss at her hairline.

"You're trying out for the women's team?" Silas asked Raven.

Raven gave a firm nod and rubbed her hands together in anticipation. "I'm all ready for this."

Troy gave three more whistle blasts, and Cobra took a last look at Marnie before turning to the line.

"Going to impress her?" Silas asked.

"Get out of my head," Cobra muttered. He took a stance and focused. Truth was, he did want to impress Marnie. He wasn't sure that skilled ax throwing would do it, but he'd give it his all.

The whistle sounded and everyone threw.

Cobra landed a solid bull's-eye, and he heard cheering behind him.

He checked up and down the targets for the other throws. Silas had bettered his first throw, Brodie's was on the first ring, while the others were close to the bull's-eye but not touching it.

Walking back with his ax, he met Marnie at the line.

"Did you win?" she asked, looking impressed.

It was a silly, small thing to feel proud of, but he did. "Best two out of three. My first throw was weak, and all these guys are good. How are you doing?"

"Good."

"Yeah?" He searched her expression, looking for any signs of regret.

"Yeah."

He liked the emerald glow in her eyes. "Glad to hear that."

The whistle blasted to line them up one more time.

"Good luck," she told him.

Cobra turned back, rotating his shoulders, determined to have another good throw.

Silas stepped up beside him, and Cobra gave him a sidelong warning look.

"Not saying a word," Silas said, readying for the throw.

Cobra hit the bull's-eye straight on again, making him and Silas the team designates. Jackson came third to be the alternate.

Troy called for the women's tryouts.

"That's me," Raven said, as Brodie walked over.

"Congrats," he said to Cobra and Silas. "You had me beat today."

"Thanks," Cobra answered. "You know you're guaranteed in Firewood Stacking."

Brodie nodded. "Nobody else was even interested."

"It's not like anyone could put up a challenge." And unless one of the other communities had found a ringer for the event, the Brodie/Raven team guaranteed points for Paradise.

Brodie's attention moved to the competition, and Cobra looked around for Marnie.

He spotted her several yards away watching Raven and the other women line up to throw.

"Congratulations," Marnie said as he joined her.

He shrugged. "It's all in fun."

"I take it you can enter multiple events?"

"As many as you want. Raven's doing Firewood Stacking. She's sure to be in Ax Throwing too. She always ends up in multiple events."

"I thought there'd be more interest in this one," Marnie said, looking at the three women lined up.

Cobra wasn't surprised at all. The women in Paradise skewed both older and younger, Mrs. France and Dixie, the

Galina bookkeeper, at one end, and Breena, who was out at university, at the other. There weren't many town residents like pilot Hailey Barrosse, young adult women who were physically suited to the Klondike Challenge events.

"Can anyone try this?" Marnie asked.

"You know how to throw an ax?"

She gave him a look.

"I don't know why I asked that. Yes. Go for it."

She grinned and headed for the target next to Raven.

Raven looked her up and down, and Cobra had to admit, Marnie looked a little out of place in skinny jeans, heeled boots and a short, green, rhinestone-decorated jacket that she must have borrowed from Mia. Her hair was up in a messy bun, and her earrings dangled sparkly and low. Man, she was sexy.

Silas appeared at Cobra's side, taking in the sight of Marnie. "Is that safe?"

"She's fine."

Silas took a step back, obviously concerned the ax might fly prematurely out of Marnie's hands and sail the twenty yards to where they stood.

Cobra wasn't worried. The whistle blew, and he watched her form. Good backswing, nice grasp, good lineup. She let the ax go and it spun forward, catching the corner of the bull's-eye.

He gave a whoop and clapped his hands.

Silas checked Cobra from under his arched brow.

"What?" Cobra asked. "It was a good throw."

"Where'd she learn *that*?" Silas asked.

"Kansas."

"I thought she was from LA."

"Not originally."

"You kiss her yet?"

"None of your business."

"So, that's a yes."

Silas didn't know the half of it, and Cobra wasn't about to tell him, at least not without Marnie's okay.

MARNIE MADE THE AX THROWING TEAM, BUT SHE FELT guilty when she saw disappointment on the face of Bear and Bar waitress Bonnie Kline. Had she thought of it, she would have blown her second and third throws on purpose and let Bonnie take second to Raven.

She didn't mind bumping Raven from the sharpshooting competitions, since it was Raven who'd encouraged her to enter. But she hadn't intended to displace anyone else who wanted to participate in the Klondike Challenge.

After a day of tryouts, including Chainsaw Chucking and Snowshoe Racing, they were in Cobra's pickup heading back to Mia and Silas's house. Marnie could have ridden with Mia and Silas, but it had seemed natural to walk back to the parking lot with Cobra, and here she was.

"I should have let Bonnie come second," she said.

"There was no need to do that."

"I'm not here to get in the way of anyone's fun."

"Good to know." There was an odd inflection in Cobra's tone as he took the turn into Mia and Silas's driveway.

"What?" she asked.

"What?" he said back, glancing her way.

She watched him for a minute then decided it must have been her imagination.

He stopped the truck in front of the garage, and she was already halfway out when he came around. He propped one hand on the doorframe, seeming to wait to see if she needed any help. It was on the tip of her tongue to make a sarcastic remark about her ability to exit a vehicle, but he was so obviously being a gentleman that she kept it to herself.

They went through the arctic entry and into the kitchen.

"Silas is firing up the grill," Mia called from where she was running water in the sink.

Cobra gave Marnie's hand a parting squeeze and headed for the sundeck door.

"It's so weird to see you cooking," Marnie said as she passed the breakfast nook and joined Mia in the kitchen.

"It's not exactly cooking. The burgers are premade, and the buns are from the Bear and Bar. I'm just washing vegetables."

"How many years did you have a chef?"

"Chefs," Mia answered with a laugh as she shut off the tap, shaking excess water from the colander. "There were three of them all told."

"For the two of you?"

"Mornings, evenings, weekends and parties. It's more work than you think."

"And here you are, doing it for yourself. What can I do to help?" Marnie glanced around at the tomatoes, lettuce, pickles and onions set out on the counter.

"Cut up anything you like. Sharp knives are in the butcher block, and there's another cutting board in the bottom drawer next to the fridge."

"I love your kitchen," Marnie said as she gathered up the implements. She decided to slice the onions first, in case they planned to sauté them.

"It's bigger than the plans we borrowed from Wildflower Lake Lodge. Silas expanded almost everything."

"Your guest room is huge."

"The bedrooms at the lodge are plenty roomy too. That's what tourists want more than a big kitchen. You know, we should get Silas to fly us up there someday. You'd love it."

"Sure." It was hard for Marnie to wrap her head around Mia having a live-in pilot, but she was learning to go with the flow. She sliced through the crackling onion skin and peeled it back. In her peripheral vision, she could see Cobra and Silas on the sundeck talking over the barbecue.

"So . . ." Mia said as she dried the lettuce leaves with a paper towel.

"So . . ." Marnie repeated, wondering what she meant.

"So, Cobra?!"

Marnie supposed the inquisition was inevitable. "What about Cobra?"

Mia's voice went singsong. "He doesn't seem so annoyed that you extended your stay in Paradise."

Marnie glanced Cobra's way and her gaze settled on him.

"And you're looking pretty sappy over there," Mia continued.

"He's not annoyed," Marnie agreed.

"And how do you feel about him?"

Marnie reminded herself to carry on with the onions. "Well, he's sexy," she said, stating the obvious.

Mia dried off her hands and moved closer. "I can see the rugged appeal. What else?"

Marnie sliced through the peeled onion and her eyes began to sting. "He's funny too. And smart and compassionate. I wouldn't have a fling based on sex appeal alone."

"What really happened yesterday?"

"I told you, we stopped by the hangar." Marnie let her smug expression fill in the lovemaking details.

Mia's eyes twinkled in mirth. "Is the workbench your go-to spot now?"

Marnie rolled her eyes at that, then she blinked because they were starting to water. "There's a suite upstairs, remember?"

"You upgraded."

"We did."

"Cobra should be the one to take you to Wildflower Lake Lodge. Now *that's* an upgrade."

Twin tears trickled down Marnie's face, and she was only halfway through slicing the onion. She looked up as the sundeck door opened.

"—and he broke the pulley, lost his grip on the snowmobile and started a small avalanche that buried the truck," Silas said while Cobra chuckled.

Then Cobra caught sight of her. His expression instantly fell, and he strode forward. "What's wrong? Are you all right?" He took her wrists to check out her hands. "Did you cut yourself?"

"The onions," she managed with a sniffle and a watery smile. "I'm fine."

"She's cutting onions," Mia said, her eyebrows raised in interest at his reaction.

It seemed to take Cobra a moment to let his guard down. "Oh." He slowly released her wrists.

"Grill's hot," Silas said in an upbeat voice. "Since Marnie's not dying or anything."

"Nope, not dying, just hungry," Marnie said, appreciating Silas moving the conversation along.

"Burger patties are in the fridge," Mia said.

Silas started for them. "Can you grab the barbecue tools from the entry room?" he asked Cobra. "They're in the top cupboard across from the dryer."

"On it," Cobra said. He stroked the pad of his thumb across Marnie's cheek to erase a tear and gave her a sheepish smile.

"He's got it very, very bad," Mia whispered in her ear as he walked away.

Chapter Thirteen

SINCE THERE WAS NO POINT IN PRETENDING ANYMORE, Marnie had invited Cobra to spend the night. The huge soft bed, the thick carpet, fine furniture and beautifully appointed bathroom seemed amusingly luxurious after the workbench and the tiny suite.

She awoke early in his arms, warm and comfortable, her head nestled into the crook of his shoulder.

"I like this," he whispered against her messy hair.

She smiled to herself and sighed, snuggling up closer. "I like it too." Waking in Cobra's arms felt like a luxury.

"I wish I didn't have to go to work," he said, his fingertips trailing along her shoulder.

"You sure you have to leave so early?" She pressed her damp lips teasingly against his chest. Kissing once, then once again.

He groaned. "You're a cruel woman."

"I'm really quite friendly."

He chuckled. "In a torturous kind of way."

"Why do you have to go right now?" She kissed him again, hoping to change his mind.

He tipped her head back, thwarting her attempt at another kiss. Then he smoothed her hair. "So planes don't fall out of the air."

"Oh. So, nothing important."

"I wish it wasn't." He drew her into a hug. "I'll see you later?"

"I hope so." She'd be counting the minutes.

He slowly loosened his arms then slipped from the bed. He paused and gazed down at her with warm, dark eyes. "Don't move."

"Ever?"

His lips curved into a smile. "I'd love that."

She smiled back.

"For now," he said.

She snuggled in, dozing as he showered and waking fully when he brought her a sweet coffee with whipped cream.

He kissed her goodbye one more time, promising to finish work as early as he could.

As the bedroom door closed behind him, she sat up, leaning back against the headboard. But she was barely two sips into the coffee when her phone rang, vibrating against the bedside table.

It was the unknown number again, and she groaned in frustration. This was getting ridiculous. She glared at the screen for a moment. Then she picked it up and stared at it, trying to divine who might be calling.

Her thumb hovered over the decline button while Cobra's words came back to her. *Curious*, he'd said. Better to know than not to know. She knew if she took the call she could at least stop wondering.

She shifted her thumb to accept. Then she closed her eyes and pressed, raising the phone to her ear. "Hello?"

"Marnie?" It was a raspy male voice that instantly stiffened her spine.

"Yes?"

"It's your father."

"I know who you are."

"I've been trying to call for days now."

Marnie ignored the barely veiled annoyance in his tone. "Is there something you want?"

"Didn't that woman give you the message?" The annoyance wasn't veiled now.

Marnie shook her head in disbelief. Even after all this time, he was demanding. "I've been out of town."

"Where?"

"What do you want, Dad?" If he didn't get to the point soon, she was ending the call.

"Your family needs you."

Dread filled her, and she closed her eyes. "Why?"

"We have a parole board hearing."

"You're getting parole?" She didn't know why she was surprised. They'd been in jail for years on a nonviolent crime. It was inevitable that parole would come up eventually.

"We need you to speak at the hearing."

"Me? You think *I* can speak for you?" After their deception and their lies? They'd played her for a fool. She didn't have anything good to say about them.

"You're a hotshot lawyer now. You can tell *us* what to say."

"The truth?" she suggested mockingly, which was exactly what she'd do in front of a parole board—not that she'd ever be in front of one on his behalf.

"You know what I mean." He sounded exasperated now. "The tricks. The right words. The things these people look for."

"I'm not a criminal lawyer." Even as she said the words, she hated that she felt the need to give an excuse. She should simply say no. He hadn't done a single thing to earn either her legal advice or her support as a daughter.

"You know you came out of this all right. While the rest of us were sweating our asses off, taking risks, you—"

"Don't you dare turn this on me. I was a child."

He snorted. "Old enough to turn your back on your family."

"Because you deserved it. You made your decisions. You made your choices. You're on your own now. Goodbye."

"Wait!"

She hesitated, hating herself for the lurch of guilt that hit her. None of this, not a single bit of it was her fault. She'd learned the hard way that her family was poison. It was dangerous for her to get too close. Still, she put the phone back to her ear. "What?"

"The least you can do is help." It was his cajoling voice. He'd used it on her mother when all else failed.

Marnie wouldn't fall for it. And she wouldn't let him worm his way back into her life. "Tell the parole board the truth, and good luck."

She ended the call and tossed the phone to the middle of the bed, glaring at it. After a few seconds, she picked it up and set it to silent.

Then she swallowed the coffee, angry with her father for ruining that little pleasure. As her heart rate slowed to normal, she made her way to the shower, determined to forget about him, to fill her day with things that kept her mind busy and off her family.

She dressed in jeans, layering up with a T-shirt and soft sweater, deciding to find something around the house that needed doing. It was about time she paid back Mia's hospitality anyway.

An hour later, Mia found her in the loft sorting her way through a box of books and organizing them on the shelves below the windows.

"What are you doing up here?" Mia asked, a cup of coffee in each hand.

"Being useful. You have a lot of mystery novels."

"I brought some of my favorites. I was picturing cold winter nights curled up in front of a warm fire." She set the two coffees on the low table and sat down on the floor next to Marnie. "Looking for something to read?"

"Looking to keep busy and repay your hospitality."

"What's to repay? I strong-armed you into staying, and you're doing legal work for me."

"You're paying me for the legal work."

"So?" Mia stretched her arm back to the table and handed Marnie one of the coffees. Then she took the other for herself. "The production company can pay its own way."

"The production company doesn't exist yet."

"But it will, thanks to you. Things take a little longer when you're trying to do them so remotely."

Marnie had discovered that. She took a sip, pondering their distance from . . . well, everything. "When you first left LA, I remember you saying you felt safe up here."

"I did feel safe."

"I can see why. I didn't understand it at the time, but there's this feeling"—Marnie gazed out the window—"this feeling that nothing can touch you, nobody can find you. It's reassuring."

Mia shifted a little closer, a small frown on her face as she picked up on Marnie's slight change in tone. "Has something gone wrong?"

Marnie sighed. "I just had a call from my father."

"From Kansas?" Mia knew that Marnie was estranged from her family, but that was all.

Marnie had never told anyone her family was in prison. At first, she'd been afraid of the stigma of having felons for relatives. Now she was more afraid of the pity. "Yes, from Kansas."

Mia looked relieved. "The way you were talking, I thought he might have followed you to LA."

"No, no. He's reaching out, wanting to reconnect." Marnie gave a little shudder. The sound of his voice still grated on her—never mind the demands he'd tried to make.

"What did you tell him?"

"To back off and leave me alone."

"Did he listen?"

"I don't know. My phone's on silent now."

"Good. Keep it that way." It was Mia's turn to look around. "So, you need to take your mind off him."

"Yes."

"I have just the thing."

"More books?"

"Film stuff. There's a new version of the script, and Hannah called. They've agreed to host a party for Scarlett."

"That's great! And that's really nice of them."

"Hannah loves any excuse for a party, and Henry wants to invite pretty actresses."

"Are they inviting actresses?"

"Maybe a few to appease Henry. They're making a list of notables from the broadcasting community, hoping they'll come. Scarlett says we need a director. Turns out a good director brings a good team with them."

"Open up the wine cellar and everybody will come."

"That's a great idea," Mia said with enthusiasm.

"You weren't planning to serve wine?" That didn't make sense to Marnie.

"The tour part," Mia said, typing something into her phone. "Alastair did that occasionally, tours of the wine cellar with tastings and amusing anecdotes."

"Hannah and Henry don't strike me as the amusing wine anecdote types."

"True," Mia said, screwing up her face. "We might have to invite a vintner or two for the storytelling part."

"Oh, sure," Marnie said flippantly. "As one does."

"It's not as crazy as you'd think. With A-list guests who are potential customers, winery reps will happily attend. They'll even bring along some wine. If you set it up right, everything builds on everything else. It's the same as Scarlett's idea of getting the right director to bring in the right team."

Marnie understood the concept. Success attracted success. "Can Hannah orchestrate something like that?"

Mia gave a shrewd, enthusiastic grin. "Hannah was born to orchestrate things like that."

MARNIE WAS HAPPY TO LEAVE THE ENTERTAINING TO Hannah and the script reading to Mia. She'd started work on boilerplate contracts for a director, the talent and the crew. If Hannah and Scarlett's schmoozing efforts worked, she wanted to be ready to sign people up for the project.

She was at the dining room table with a laptop, while Mia sat curled up on the sofa reading through the script.

The sound system was playing soft classical music in the background. Marnie didn't recognize many of the arrangements, but their tone seemed to suit the mood.

"There are winter scenes in this," Mia said.

"Is that good or bad?"

"Good, assuming we can get things under way this fall. It'll give us something to do after the snow falls."

"Us?" Marnie asked. "This half of us will be enjoying the sunshine of LA."

"I meant the generic us. Scarlett and Willow, Raven and Yolanda. And you only if we need you."

"If you need me, you can call me in LA." Marnie cut a creativity clause in the director's contract and pasted it into another section.

The side door opened abruptly, and Silas headed through the entry room, his expression tight.

"Something wrong?" Mia came immediately to her feet. Marnie sat up straighter.

"The bears were in the schoolyard."

Marnie's stomach tightened in concern.

"Oh no," Mia said, her eyes round in horror. "Is everyone safe?"

Silas went to a closet and pulled out his compact flight bag. "One of the cubs charged a group of kids. Luckily, Ms. MacFarlane was there and got them all inside. The bears took off, but we need to chase them out of town."

"What do you need?" Mia asked, moving toward Silas.

Marnie rose from her chair, not sure what she could do to help but more than willing to step in.

"Can you take the radio base at the airstrip?" Silas asked Mia.

"Sure. Absolutely."

"Shannon's gone to the school to be with her grandkids. We're going to put a few planes in the air."

"To find the bears?" Marnie guessed.

Silas nodded while Mia gathered her jacket and boots from the entry room.

"If we find them," Silas continued, "you can direct the ATVs."

"What will they do on the ATVs?" Marnie understood the danger, but she hated to think they were going to kill the bears.

"The bears need to associate Paradise with unpleasant experiences." He seemed to take note of her expression. "Beanbags and rubber bullets on the rump. They'll sting but won't injure them. Kind of like a person being hit by a paintball."

"I've never been hit by a paintball."

"Neither have I," Mia said as she laced up her boots.

"Well, it hurts enough to get your attention," Silas said. "It should be enough to keep them away."

"Can I help?" Marnie asked.

"Stay inside while we're gone," Mia said. "Just as a precaution. We'll call when we know something."

"You sure that's all?" Marnie asked, not knowing what she could do toward the effort but wanting to help.

Silas shook his head in answer while he stood by the door waiting for Mia. "It's under control. Text alerts have gone out, so people know to sit tight where they are. You're not the only one waiting it out."

Marnie felt a little better knowing that.

"I'll call you when I can," Mia said as she passed by Silas and the two of them headed out the door.

After it shut tight behind them, the background music seemed louder. It didn't seem to suit the mood anymore, so Marnie turned it off and the house went silent.

She couldn't decide if she should worry about everyone's safety—then thought probably not. Given the efficiency of the town's response, something like this must have happened before. If they'd gone to the trouble of having a preplanned text alert system and an air search plan for rogue bears, it must have been for a reason.

She found herself smiling. This sure wasn't LA anymore.

Slightly restless, she wandered the house for a few minutes, then she opened herself a soft drink to sip and went back to the laptop, turning her mind to the contracts, doing some searches to learn more of the creative control nuances between the writer, the director and the executive producer.

As time slipped past, she heard a plane in the distance and wondered if they'd spotted the bears yet. She wondered then about who would take off on ATVs to shoot rubber bullets. Maybe Cobra since he was such a good shot.

A shudder ran along her spine at the thought of Cobra chasing after three grizzly bears. Surely, he'd be good at something like that. Still . . . they were grizzly bears.

A truck door banged loudly out front, startling her. She hadn't expected Mia and Silas back this soon. She hoped it meant they'd located the bears and successfully chased them off.

She listened for the side door to open, but they didn't come right in.

There was a crash at the back of the house, louder this time.

Marnie moved quickly, wondering why they would come up to the sundeck and hoping nobody had fallen on the stairs.

One look through the glass told Marnie they hadn't.

It wasn't Mia and Silas out there. It was a bear, a huge, brown bear, fur bristling on its neck and hump as it nosed the barbecue.

She snapped her hand from the door handle and paced backward, a chill coming over her as she wondered if bears knew how to break glass.

She crept silently from the kitchen, slipping around the corner and taking the loft staircase to the top. She didn't know why her instinct took her there. The bear had already climbed the sundeck stairs—if it broke into the house, the loft stairs weren't going to slow it down.

Would it be able to follow her scent and find her? Would it be interested in chasing her? She peeped out the window and saw the two cubs milling around at the bottom of the sundeck stairs.

She fumbled for her phone then, pressing Mia's contact, breathing heavily as the call rang through then went to voice mail. Her heart thudded through Mia's breezy message.

"They're here," Marnie said in a raspy voice. Then she cleared her throat. "The bears are at your house. Right now." She hung up and dialed again but still got voice mail.

She tried Cobra but didn't get through on his line either. While she scrolled through her contacts for Raven's number, the phone rang in her hand. Relieved, she took the call, not caring if it was Mia or Cobra or anyone else, just grateful someone would know to send help.

"They're here," she said, voice shaky. "On the sundeck. At the grill."

"Marnie?" a man's voice said. "Is that you?"

It took her a moment to zero in on the voice, then another moment to switch gears.

"It's Ethan," her brother said.

Her father had obviously sent reinforcements. "This isn't a good time."

"I know, I know."

"I mean, this *really* isn't—"

"Dad said you wouldn't talk to him."

Marnie clenched her teeth. "That's not true."

"We get that you're still angry," Ethan continued.

"Angry?" Talk about an understatement.

"But it's more complicated than—"

"Can I call you back?" The last thing she wanted to do—*now* of all times—was talk to anyone in her family.

"You can't call me back," he said.

There was a clunk, then a bang, then a jangle below her. "Well, I can't talk now."

"I don't have much time."

"I can't—"

"Listen, Marnie," he rolled right over her. "Just *listen*. Hear me out. Maybe I don't deserve your help. I damn sure know Dad doesn't deserve it. But I'm asking anyway. We've been in here a long time."

"That's how a jail sentence works." She sounded bitter, and she was. They'd lied to her, lied to her right up to the very second the documented facts overwhelmed them. On top of everything else, she'd felt like a fool.

"It's on Tuesday," he said. "I know we can't force you, but the hearing's on Tuesday. That's it. That's my piece. I've said it."

There was a shout in the background, and a sudden visual of her brother in prison came into her mind.

The line went dead just as something thudded dully against the side of the house, vibrating the floor beneath her feet. Marnie was jolted back to the present. Her heart sped up further as the barbecue banged and clattered around the sundeck. The barbecue wasn't edible, and the bear was going to figure that out pretty soon.

Then a plane sounded overhead, and Marnie's phone rang again. This time it was Mia.

"Hi," Marnie's voice was shaky.

"They're on their way to you now," Mia called into the phone. "Silas can see the bears from the air. Cobra and Riley are only a few miles out. You okay?"

Marnie drew a breath. "I'm fine, but the bear is destroying your barbecue."

"We'll buy a new one. Where are you?"

"Upstairs. In the loft."

"Good. Don't go near the kitchen windows."

There was no chance Marnie would do that. "I won't."

"They'll get to you soon, so just sit tight, okay? Don't worry, you'll be okay."

"Okay, thanks." Marnie tried to keep the fear out of her voice.

"The cavalry's coming."

"I know." Marnie trusted Cobra over anybody to deal with the bears.

"Just stay on the line with me."

"I'm fine. You go back to work." Marnie knew Mia was the radio link between the planes and the ATVs.

"I can—"

"Not necessary. I'm okay. Really, I am. Direct traffic—that's more important."

"Sure?"

"Yes."

"Okay." Mia ended the call.

Marnie listened hard then as she crept back to the window to peep down at all three bears pawing through the barbecue debris. After a few minutes, she heard the sound of ATVs in the distance. From her vantage point, she could tell the bears heard it too.

The mother stood on her hind legs, her head swiveling in the direction of the sound. She seemed to ponder it for a minute, sniffed the air, then decided the ATVs weren't worth fighting, or the barbecue wasn't worth the effort—hard to tell which. She dropped to all fours and galloped down the stairs. Her cubs followed, and they all took off up the river with Cobra and Riley hot on their heels.

Marnie slid down the wall to sit on the floor, her breathing shallow and her heart lodged in her throat.

It was over, she told herself. The bears were gone, and she was safe.

She gripped her phone tightly as the sound of the ATVs disappeared.

Her hold left a red line along her palm. As she stared at the mark, the memory of Ethan's call came back: what he'd asked, what she'd said and what he'd wanted.

Six years ago, feeling so incredibly betrayed, she'd decided she owed them nothing, none of them. But now she thought about Ethan, how he'd been only sixteen when their mother had died. Their father might have lied to Marnie, but Ethan had been dragged into the thick of the nightmare. And he'd paid. He'd paid with his freedom, while she'd been given a chance at a normal life, far away from them.

COBRA PULLED MARNIE CLOSE, BUT IT FELT LIKE SHE was far away.

The excitement had died down, and they were finally alone in her room, the house quiet around them.

"What are you thinking?" he asked, gently setting her back from him to gaze at her expression.

He wouldn't blame her for being rattled by the bears. She'd joked around afterward, and she'd been safe inside, but it must have been frightening all the same.

"Nothing," she said with a headshake.

"You can't think nothing. Brains don't work that way."

"Nothing important."

"You know the bears are long gone." He wondered if she was still rattled and didn't want to admit it.

"It's not the bears."

"You sure?"

She made an effort at a smile. "I'm sure."

"The film?" He knew they'd been working on it, and possibly something had gone wrong.

"No." It was clear she wasn't in the mood for a heart-to-heart talk.

He tried to lighten the mood. "Cupcakes?"

She finally smiled. "No."

"Me?" he joked.

She stretched her neck to look up at him. "Yes."

"That's a lie, Cupcake. But thanks for trying."

"How can I not be thinking about you? You're right here." She flattened her hand against his chest.

He decided to let it drop. "Okay. Let's go with me." He gave her a tender kiss. "Is it something I can do anything about?" he whispered.

She shook her head.

"I'm here, you know. If you need anything."

"Yeah?" She stepped forward, tipping her head up in an obvious invitation. "Anything?"

"Especially that."

Her smile widened and she pulled up on the hem of his T-shirt. "Good."

He shrugged out of it and peeled her sweater over her

head, pulling her into his arms, reveling in the feel of her skin against his.

"You've got bear spray?" he asked even as her kisses pushed everything else from his mind.

"Who cares about bear spray?" Her hands went to the button on his pants.

"I want you to be safe."

"I'm safe right now."

He chuckled. "That you are."

He kissed her more deeply then, slowly removing their clothes and tumbling into the bed, making long, sweet love.

Afterward, he gathered her up, laying her on top of himself, loving the feel of her slight weight and the warmth of her skin. She laid her head down on his shoulder and went quiet. Her fingers toyed with the edge of the sheet.

"What's wrong?" he whispered. He knew it was something. There'd been an energy to her lovemaking, a slightly frantic edge he hadn't felt before.

She drew a deep breath. "I've been thinking."

"No kidding."

"I think . . . maybe . . . it's time for me to head home."

Cobra stilled.

"I know that's not exactly what I'd planned."

He felt as though his blood had dropped ten degrees.

"But there are some things . . ." she trailed off.

Cobra struggled to find his voice. "Did something happen I don't know about?"

"No."

He didn't believe her. "What happened?"

"Nothing specific."

He struggled to figure out what it could have been. "*Are* you still freaked out about the bears? Between me and some bear spray, you have all the protection you need."

"It's not about the bears."

"Then what is it about?"

"Nothing."

"Did I—"

"It's not you." She shifted so she could see his face. "I promise, it's not you."

"Then why?" If he couldn't zero in on the problem, he couldn't solve it.

"A week and a half ago, I left home thinking I'd only be at the airport for an hour, just to send off the girls."

"So what?" That couldn't suddenly be news.

"There's milk in my fridge, fruit on my counter, my plants need water."

"This is about your plants?" He couldn't believe she'd leave him for her plants. He'd buy her a hundred new plants if he needed to.

"It's about my life. My life's not here." She pointed at the window. "It's out there. I might not be in it right now, but it keeps rolling on without me."

He reached for another argument. "What about the Klondike Challenge?"

She paused over the question, biting down on her bottom lip. "I don't want to let everyone down."

"Then don't. Stay at least that long."

"I can't."

"Can't or won't?" He knew he sounded annoyed. He also knew he had no right to be annoyed.

"I'm sorry," she said softly, her cheek going back down on his chest.

He had no right to be angry, no right to keep her here, but his hold tightened on her anyway.

"Damn," he whispered, feeling a hard blast of despair. "Silas told me it would be like this."

She stilled, and he knew he'd said the wrong thing.

"We're not Silas and Mia," she said, her tone flat.

"I know."

"This was always going to end."

"I know that too." He had.

She drew away from him and sat up, holding the quilt

against her chest. "You knew I wasn't one of them. I never gave you the wrong idea."

He sat up beside her. "That's not what I meant." He didn't want her to misunderstand. "I never expected you to stay. Silas said it would hurt to lose you, and it does."

She nodded, looking miserable herself.

Her expression gave him hope, and he ran his fingertips up her arm to her shoulder, kissing her gently there. "A few more days?"

"I can't." She turned to look at him, her green eyes soft as new moss.

He tried to steel himself against the pain, but it didn't work. "When?"

"Tomorrow."

Chapter Fourteen

WICHITA, KANSAS, HADN'T CHANGED MUCH SINCE THE trial. After an overnight stop at her apartment in LA to water her plants and pack a few things, Marnie had checked into the Red Brick Inn on the edge of town. The view wasn't much to speak of—a parking lot and the back side of a heritage building. But the hotel featured spacious rooms, free wireless, complimentary breakfast and was just a ten-minute taxi ride to the prison.

Nobody knew she was here, not her father, not Ethan. She was still debating whether to speak for them, and what her obligation might be to her brother. She had another day before the hearing, and she wondered if meeting with them might give her an answer.

She'd unpacked some dress slacks, blouses and a couple of blazers, plus a pair of high but comfortable ankle boots in case was a lot of walking over the grounds and into the prison complex—assuming she decided to go.

Feeling travel-worn and edgy, with nothing to fill her afternoon, she ran herself a bath in the oversize tub. She hoped an aromatic soak would clear her mind, soothe her nerves, maybe give her some clarity so she'd know what to do.

A long time later, having wavered a dozen times on her decision, she decided she had to get out of these four walls. She called housekeeping for fresh towels, refreshed her makeup in the steamy bathroom and twisted her hair into a quick updo. Her stomach was jumpy, but she knew she had to eat, and she'd seen several restaurants along the block on her way from the airport.

Looking good enough to go out in public, she dropped a pair of walking shoes on the floor in front of a chair. She sat down then, feeling the strain of her choice, knowing every minute brought her closer to having to make it.

She flashed back to Paradise, and to Mia's disappointment when she'd said she was leaving early. She'd let a whole lot of people down, and had probably angered some of them—like Brodie—by screwing up the Klondike Challenge team.

Her thoughts inevitably moved to Cobra. She could still feel his arms around her, hear his voice, smell his clean woodsy scent. The man had no right to be so sexy. He also had no right to seem so compassionate. She'd been on the very verge of confessing or telling him she'd heard from her father again.

But Cobra would have asked questions. He would have pushed and prodded like he always did, and she'd have told him. She knew she'd have cracked and told him her secret when all she wanted to do was bottle it up, stuff it down and keep it firmly and completely in her past.

Which was why she was here, why she was even considering helping them—hoping to end it once and for all.

Trouble was, she didn't know if this would end it or make it worse.

She could sure use a drink.

Her room had a little fridge outside the bathroom, but it

was empty. This wasn't a stocked-minibar kind of hotel. If it had been, she might have poured herself something strong.

A knock sounded at the door, and she stepped over her shoes, crossing the tightly woven carpet to the door.

Expecting housekeeping, she pulled it open. She instantly froze in shock.

Cobra was standing in the hallway, his head cocked to one side, his gaze disapproving.

She gave herself a quick shake and blinked to clear her eyes, convinced she must be hallucinating, wondering if she'd fallen asleep in the bathtub and the rest of this was a dream.

"Cupcake." He gave a lazy shake of his head. "You've been holding out on me."

"How . . ." Baffled by his arrival, she looked up and down the empty hallway.

"Mia told me you'd talked to your dad. Why didn't you *say* something?"

Marnie struggled to speak through her shock. "How did you find me?"

"There aren't many Antons in Merganser, Kansas."

"This is Wichita."

"There aren't any prisons in Merganser."

She fell silent, embarrassment heating her face. "So, you figured it out."

"I have access to the internet."

"You stalked me?"

"No. Mia mentioned your dad had called, and I was worried."

Marnie clenched her jaw. This was the last conversation she wanted to be having.

"Why wouldn't you *tell* me?" he asked.

"I don't tell anyone my family is in prison."

He waited, frowning.

She cracked first. "It doesn't instill confidence in my clients, okay?"

"Every family has their black sheep."

She scoffed out a laugh. "You? With your engineer dad, your doctor brother and the senator's aide?"

He gave a cold laugh. "You do get it, right?"

She didn't get anything right now.

"*I'm* the black sheep."

"No, you're not—"

"You mind if I come in?"

She was brought back again to his unexpected appearance. "How did you even get my room number?"

"I asked at the desk."

"They're not supposed to tell you."

"I asked very nicely."

Marnie thought of the fresh-faced young man who'd checked her in. "You mean you intimidated that poor desk clerk."

"I really wanted to find you."

She arched her brow.

"I don't think he wanted me to have to ask a third time." Cobra looked meaningfully over her shoulder.

She realized they were off on a tangent. It wasn't like she planned to lodge a complaint with the manager. "Fine. Sure. Okay. Come on in."

He smiled as he walked past her into the room. "You know, you always say yes four or five times?"

"I must mean it then."

He looked around as she shut the door, stopping at the edge of the bed to turn around. "So, he called. You came. But why?"

She didn't have a simple answer, so she didn't try. "You want a drink? I really need a drink."

"Sure." He glanced around the room. "I'll take whatever you've got."

She returned to her shoes and sat down to put them on. "I've got nothing. We'll have to go out."

"Anywhere in particular?"

She came to her feet. "Someplace with a full bar."

"Good thing I showed up when I did, then."

"It won't be a bender," she said.

"Bend away. I'll make sure you get home safe."

"Ever the gentleman," she drawled.

"I do try." He opened the door and held it for her to walk out.

She was finding she didn't hate that he was here. She wasn't sure she was glad he was here and that he knew about her family, but at least he was a distraction. And now that he knew the truth, she could talk to him. That was something good.

They stopped at the elevator and he pressed the button.

"You know you could have just called," she said, thinking about the distance he'd flown. At least one of the legs must have been overnight. He had to be exhausted.

"I didn't want to call. I wanted to see you. I wanted to know *why*."

The doors slid open, and they walked inside.

"How did he persuade you?" Cobra asked as the elevator started down. "You were adamant you didn't even want to talk to him."

"My brother called too."

"And?"

"He reminded me that I've been free all these years while they've been locked up."

There was an edge to Cobra's voice. "That's because you didn't commit a crime."

"I know." But she wondered if that was more due to principles or circumstances. She couldn't help thinking Ethan's choices might have been stark.

"You don't sound all that sure," Cobra said.

"I *know* I didn't commit a crime," she emphasized.

He gave an exaggerated sigh as the doors slid open on the lobby level. Then patience and humor rolled into his expression. "A certain vanilla buttercream cupcake notwithstanding."

A family walked up to the elevator, mom, dad and two kids all weighed down with luggage.

Marnie allowed herself a little smile as she shifted out of their way. She started across the lobby but spotted a small lounge tucked beyond the check-in desk. "Look. Liquor." She changed direction.

"That didn't take long," Cobra said as he followed.

She passed under an archway into a peaceful, burgundy-carpeted room with a horseshoe-shaped bar and satin-smooth wood tables scattered around the edges. There was a vacant one in a corner beside the window, so she took it, sliding into a cream-colored padded vinyl seat.

Cobra sat down across from her, and the waitress immediately set two cardboard coasters on the table. "Good evening," she said. "Welcome to the Iron Horse. Can I start you off with a drink?"

"Vodka martini," Marnie said. "Double with three olives."

"Works for me," Cobra said.

"Would you like to look at some dinner menus?"

"I think we better," he answered holding out his hand while the woman grinned.

WATCHING MARNIE SIP HER MARTINI, COBRA COULD barely believe he'd caught up to her so easily. Last night, when Mia had mentioned that Marnie had talked to her father, Cobra had erupted with shock and frustration—his reaction so sharp that Silas had all but put him into a wall.

Silas had been right. Cobra should never have snapped at Mia. And he wasn't angry with Marnie either, even though she'd lied to him about why she was leaving Paradise. He was angry with Victor Anton and Marnie's brother, Ethan, for guilting her into coming down here.

"And the bears?" Marnie asked, continuing the thread of their superficial conversation then tugging an olive off the skewer with her teeth. Neither of them seemed to want to circle back just yet to her reason for being in Wichita.

"Xavier spotted the bears twenty miles north and still moving away," Cobra said.

"That's good. I was afraid at first that you might have to kill them."

"We're a long way from that." Cobra twisted his glass by the stem. "Sometimes wildlife officers will trap and relocate a problem bear. Though that's a lot harder with three of them. And you end up plunking them into the middle of another grizzly's range, which causes conflict. This way the bears get to move wherever they want. It's safer all around."

She concentrated on dabbing the remaining olives in the wide-brimmed glass. "There's a parole hearing." She looked up then. "Tuesday. They have a parole hearing on Tuesday."

"Ahh." Cobra nodded, appreciating the significant piece of information. "That's why the pressure was on."

"Yes. They want me to make a statement on their behalf."

He reached out to cover her hand. "Do you want to do that?"

"No, I really don't."

"You don't have to. You can just walk away."

"Maybe." But she shook her head as if she were torn.

Cobra knew about complicated families—maybe not as complicated as hers. But he did understand the push and pull of emotions. "Why not walk?"

She heaved a sigh. "Ethan. He was older, but we were kids together. I went one way. He went another. It occurs to me now that he didn't have a choice."

"Are you sure about that?" Cobra wasn't buying Ethan's innocence. From what Cobra had read online, Ethan was a grown man when he was arrested.

"I'm not sure about anything. That's why I want to talk to them." She polished off the martini. "Tomorrow."

"Eat something," he said, pushing the shared southwestern appetizer platter her way.

She absently picked up a mini empanada. "You don't think a hangover will look good on me?"

"I don't think it'll feel good on you. If you've come all the way here, you've obviously decided to see them."

She drew a sigh and dipped the morsel into a bowl of fresh guacamole. "I did come all this way."

"You don't have to do anything you don't want to," he said gently.

She chewed while thinking. "How about this: if I look them in the eyes, I can walk away and never feel guilty."

That line of reasoning made sense to Cobra. He helped himself to a jalapeño popper. "Okay. I'll stick around." He ate it whole.

"You can't," Marnie said with a shake of her head. "You have planes to fix."

"The planes can wait. You're not walking into a state prison by yourself."

She frowned. "It's perfectly safe. And what are you saying? That I'm some sort of delicate little damsel in distress?"

"I'm saying that you're beautiful, and that prison is full of criminals and, yes, you're a delicate little damsel compared to them and to me."

"So, you're going to protect me, big bad snake-man?"

"*Snake-man?*" The name struck him as funny.

"Don't you laugh at me."

"I'm not." He struggled to control his expression. "I wasn't planning to flash my tattoo for intimidation."

"What were you planning to do?"

"I don't know. Just be there with you, I guess."

"People visit prison all the time. There are guards in there, you know. I believe they're armed."

"There might be guards but shit still happens." Plus, he didn't trust her family for one second.

She opened her mouth, clearly ready to argue some more.

"Do you like me, Marnie? I mean, I know it's complicated and everything, but you like me, don't you?"

"What kind of a question is that?"

"I think you meant to say: yes, of course, I do, absolutely."

This time, she was the one struggling not to smile.

"Good," he said, satisfied he'd made his point. "Then think about me for a second."

"How is this about you?"

"Do you have any idea how hard it would be for me to sit out here, with you in there—waiting and wondering what was going on?" He'd go nuts wondering what was happening.

She rocked back in her chair, looking incredulous now. "I'm twenty-seven years old. I'll be twenty-eight soon. I've survived all that time without your protection. I think I'll be fine for this too."

He went for another jalapeño popper, nodding his acceptance of her argument as he chewed and swallowed. Inside his head, he was regrouping. "Ever been inside a state prison?"

"Have you?"

"Yes."

"You're lying."

"Okay, it was a military prison."

She sat up straight, her eyes going round. "You were arrested?"

"No. One of our pilots was arrested. He was mouthing off to a superior. Didn't end well."

"That's it?"

"He got five days."

"That's the sum-total of your prison expertise?"

"Would you rather I was convicted?"

"*No.* No, of course not."

"Glad to hear it." He chose a spicy egg roll this time. "So, what's the harm? Of me coming along?"

She bought herself some time by dipping a chip in the guacamole. It was clear she was the one regrouping this time.

"Is it just your ego?" He tried to work his way through her likely objection. "You don't want to look weak?"

"It's them," she said softly, sounding vulnerably honest. She redipped the chip before biting down on it. Some crumbs dropped to the table, and she brushed them on her little plate.

He wasn't sure what she meant, so he waited.

She swallowed and set down the rest of the chip. "They embarrass me."

He gave a chopped laugh of surprise. "Well, that's a switch."

She looked confused. "A switch from what?"

"I'm the one who embarrasses my family."

She looked horrified. "You are not."

"They expected me to get a graduate degree. And they hate that I work with my hands."

"There's something wrong with your family."

"They're uptight. And so are their friends." He couldn't stop himself from picturing Marnie at the annual club picnic. For some reason, he had a very specific image of her in a mint-green dress with flat lace, breezy sleeves and buttons down the front. "They'd like you a lot." He had no idea where it had come from.

"I'm not sure how to take that," she said.

"It's a compliment. I know I can handle your family, Marnie, from one black sheep to the others."

"There's no comparison."

He gave a shrug. "Doesn't matter."

"Fine," she said in an exasperated tone that told him it was a big concession. "Sure, okay, yes, you can come."

"I love it when you give me four yeses."

* * *

IT WAS HARD TO SAY WHICH STRUCK MARNIE MORE, that her father looked smaller than she remembered or that Ethan looked bigger. She came to her feet as the three men walked into the prison visiting room. Cobra stood beside her at the shiny metal table with six attached seats.

"Well, well, well," her father opened, glancing from Marnie to Cobra then back again.

"Hello, Dad."

"You decided to grace us with your presence."

She felt Cobra stiffen beside her.

Victor's hair was gray and thinning, and his skin looked loose on his frame, but his eyes were the same penetrating hazel, brown with what looked like a green underlay. He was fifty-eight now, but he looked much older.

She supposed being stuck inside most of the day didn't help.

"Hi, Marnie," Ethan said. He looked like he'd grown an inch or two since she'd last seen him. His shoulders were broader, and his arms had filled out. He'd obviously been using whatever fitness facilities they had in the prison.

She gave her brother a nod and briefly met her uncle Stuart's pale gaze. He looked a lot like her father, aging and unhappy. She'd never had much to do with him growing up. He gave off a vibe that said he didn't much like kids.

Cobra touched the back of her chair, nodding for her to sit down.

She did.

"And who's this?" her father asked, looking pointedly at Cobra as everyone took their seats.

"A friend. Conrad, this is Victor Anton."

"Marnie's father," Victor said. Neither man offered to shake hands.

"They told me the hearing was at eleven," she opened, wanting to take control of the conversation.

Her dad leaned slightly forward. "You think you can fit us in?"

"Dad," Ethan said quietly.

"Oh, no, no, no." Victor waved a wrinkled hand. "We all know how busy our Marnie is. Took me nearly a week to get her on the phone. And even then she wouldn't commit one way or the other."

Cobra shifted in his seat.

"But here she is," her father continued. "Here to save the day. Looking for our gratitude, are you?"

Marnie didn't expect gratitude. She knew her father hated for her to be in a position of power. She didn't want power. She just wanted to get this over and done with.

"I started writing a statement. They said I'd have ten minutes." So far, she didn't have enough to fill even five minutes.

"What does it say?" her father asked.

"Not much, so far."

Her father made a frustrated sound in the back of his throat.

Ethan stepped in. "Dad, she's trying to help."

"She's enjoying this."

"I'm not," Marnie cut in, struggling to keep her voice even.

"Will you vouch for all of us?" her uncle Stuart asked.

She inhaled deeply. "I plan to be honest."

"*There* it is," Victor said, waving his hand with a flourish. "She's not here to help us at all."

"I am," Marnie said, gripping her hands in her lap.

"Why?" Victor demanded.

"Because you asked," she snapped.

He locked gazes with her, searching her expression. "What's your angle?"

She was tired of being hit with his criticism. She wanted nothing more than to get this over and done with, so she went with blunt honesty. "Getting you out of my life for good."

His jaw went hard. "You've always been an ungrateful little—"

"That's *it*." Cobra brought the flat of his hand down on the table, and the sound echoed. "You"—he pointed to Stuart—"will take whatever you get. And you"—he turned to Ethan—"I can't peg you yet, but you should thank your lucky stars Marnie is who she is. And, *you*"—it was Victor's turn—"better change your attitude before tomorrow, or you're going to be stuck inside these walls until every second of your sentence is served. None of you deserve Marnie's help, but for some reason she's still willing to give it. She'll speak tomorrow, say whatever it is she wants to say, and that's the end of it. She's done. With all of you."

Her father opened his mouth, face red and blotchy.

Marnie reflexively cringed in anticipation of the outburst.

"Are you *kidding* me?" Cobra demanded in a dark tone before Victor could say anything.

"You have *no business*—"

"Dad," Ethan interrupted.

"Stop!" Marnie shouted to them all. Her skin crawled with anxiety like it had so many times in the past.

A stunned silence followed her demand.

"I'm here to . . ." She paused and closed her eyes for a second, awash with regret at leaving Alaska for this. The peace of mind wasn't going to be worth it. She stood, and Cobra quickly followed suit. "Tomorrow." With the final word, she turned and started for the door.

Cobra came up beside her in the hallway. "Sorry."

"For what?" She was filled with anger at her father, not at Cobra.

"I promised myself I'd keep quiet."

She coughed out a slightly hysterical laugh. "None of that was your fault."

They stopped at a barred gate while a guard checked their visitor badges.

"Are they always like that?" Cobra asked.

"It's been years. But, yeah, it's all coming back to me now."

"He treated you like that when you were a little girl?" Cobra looked like he was about to march back into the visiting room and confront her father.

"I didn't challenge him when I was a little girl. And it was easier when my mom was alive." Her mother had always been careful to keep things smooth and calm when her father was around. Marnie realized how much work that must have been for her.

The guard let them through the gate, and they checked out at the front desk.

"Your father's never . . ." Cobra's voice was tight as they walked down the sidewalk to his rental car.

She looked up.

Cobra lifted his brow. "He's never completely lost his temper, right?"

"You mean, hit me?"

Cobra nodded stiffly.

"No."

Cobra blew out a breath.

"You waited until we were outside to ask that, didn't you?" She guessed he hadn't trusted himself in case her answer was yes.

"I did."

"My father demanded. He ordered. He yelled. I saw him cuff Ethan once when Ethan accidentally shot off a rifle. But I think that was more shock than uncontrolled anger."

"I can't believe you came back to help them."

"I'm glad I did."

Cobra glanced over his shoulder. "Seriously? After that performance?"

"This is the end of it. And I'm glad to know they'll be out of my life. I know it didn't look like much, but that's the first time I've ever stood up to him."

Cobra wrapped an arm around her shoulder. "You were terrific."

"You were intimidating."

He hit the fob to unlock the car doors. "I couldn't believe their attitudes. I couldn't believe they'd be so stupid. You were there to help them."

"My dad thought I was there to rub their noses in it."

"So what? Even if you were. They need you way more than you need them."

The way he said it reinforced her new feeling of confidence.

She scooted ahead of him and opened her car door.

"Hey," he called out.

She turned back to him, looking over the open door with a grin. "I am a strong and capable woman."

"Too capable to let me be a gentleman?"

"Yes."

He came up close. "That was only one yes. That means you're not sure."

"I'm not following your logic." The door was already open, so it was a moot point.

He brushed a fingertip across her nose. "Logic says I'm going to keep being a gentleman."

She pouted her lips and purposely softened her gaze. "Not all the time, I hope."

A glow came into his eyes. "No." He leaned in and brushed his lips against hers. "Not all the time."

COBRA WAS WATCHING THE SUN COME UP THROUGH the hotel room window when Marnie shifted in his arms.

"I don't want this day to start," she said, her voice sounding like she'd been awake for a while.

He gathered her closer, glancing at the bedside clock and seeing it was barely past seven. "We've still got time."

"I keep rehearsing it in my mind."

"You don't need to rehearse the truth."

"Clearly, you've never made an opening argument in court."

"That is true." He rarely thought about his own conversations before they happened.

"They'll want to know about character."

Cobra hoped they did. And he hoped her statement kept Victor in prison. The man didn't deserve parole. "You can't change who they are."

She sat up, forcing a gust of cool air under the covers. "I didn't come here to deliberately hurt them."

He sat up beside her, debating whether to put on a pot of coffee or reach for the phone and call room service. The little coffee maker in the corner would be faster.

He rose from the bed and pulled on his boxers, looking back over his shoulder as he headed for the coffee maker. "Do you have any good memories of growing up?"

She reached for a robe and put her arms in the sleeves, pulling her hair from the collar and tucking it behind her ears. "The day I got a full scholarship to KU. But my dad tried to talk me out of going."

"Your father tried to talk you *out* of going to college?" Cobra couldn't wrap his mind around a parent doing that. His parents had offered every enticement under the sun to enroll.

"He didn't trust academia. Said it was full of socialists and I wouldn't learn anything useful for the real world."

"He didn't think law school was useful?" Cobra dropped a pod into the coffee maker and began filling the carafe in the little sink.

"It wasn't law school then. I was accepted into the liberal arts program."

"Then I can see his point."

A pillow hit him in the back of the head, making him spill the cold water across his arm.

"I retract my statement," he said through a laugh, reaching for a paper napkin to dry himself.

"Too late. You revealed your bias."

"Are you sure you want to stay mad? I'm brewing . . ." He checked the package. "Colombian Premium Roast."

"Any of that hazelnut creamer left?"

He gave a little shudder. "You are definitely not a purist."

"Yeah?" She started across the floor, tightening the robe around her waist. "Any more insults you want to toss my way, Snake-Man?" She softened her words by stretching up and kissing his tattoo.

"My parents would have burned sage bundles or danced naked under the full moon to get me into college." He felt her laughter where she pressed against his back as he poured the water into the coffee machine.

"I didn't know you were raised by Pagans," she said.

"Not Pagans, just desperate. They were convinced I was destroying my future."

"By joining the military?"

The coffee maker gurgled and hissed, filling the air with a welcome aroma.

"By pursuing mechanics instead of finance or medicine or law."

"What did Barrick study?"

"He has an MBA, just like—" Cobra stopped himself, not sure why his mind was going in that direction.

"Just like who?" Marnie asked, taking two clean white coffee cups from a shelf and placing them on the counter. They were tiny little things that wouldn't hold enough caffeine to start half his brain.

"Nothing."

"What do you mean, nothing?"

"It was nobody important."

She peeled the seal from a little cup of hazelnut creamer and poured it into one of the cups. "Ahh, a girl."

"Not a girl." He didn't know why he was hesitating, since it didn't matter anymore. It was water under a very long-ago bridge. "It was some guy. My nemesis back then, or so I thought. He was a guy who stole a girl . . . from me."

Marnie looked intrigued now. "Do tell."

"His name was Charles, Charles Hudson-Hyde. Our parents run in the same circle, and he was everything my parents would have wanted in a son, and more."

"Such a regal name. Was he British royalty?"

"Seattle royalty. He and his pals were the A-listers at Bern Academy."

"Wait. You went to a school called Bern Academy?"

"You can understand why I was such a disappointment to my parents." He filled her cup first.

"Did you wear blazers and sweaters with little crests on the pockets?" She mixed in her creamer with a little stir stick.

"Not willingly. But you sure would have looked cute in that little kilt and the knee socks."

"Down, boy."

He was warming up to the image. "White blouse and a silky bow tie?"

She obviously wasn't buying into it. "Tell me about the girl."

Cobra took a swallow of coffee. "Shelby King. My parents never forgave me for letting her go."

"Where did she go?"

"She and Charles went off to Yale. They were planning to live in New York City and make a killing in investment banking."

"That had to hurt."

"She told me it was nothing personal."

Marnie gave a chuckle of disbelief.

Cobra didn't care one way or the other anymore. It no longer mattered. "Shelby was determined to marry an

MBA or some such equivalent. Anyone with a cushy office job and a six-figure salary."

"And you were a mechanic."

"Not then, I wasn't. But it was pretty clear which direction I was going—a blue-collar job and ending the day with grease under my fingernails."

"Sounds like a woman fixated on the superficial. Are they still together?"

"I have no idea. All I know is she made her choice, and I made mine."

"The United States Air Force."

"Don't regret it for a second." He polished off the coffee and poured himself another cup. "What about you? Did you date in college?"

"No, I had to keep my grades up. It was an academic scholarship, and I didn't want to lose it."

He sure couldn't blame her for that. "You didn't want to have to go back home."

"I went back in the summers, but never for good. Then one day the FBI swooped in."

"You were *there*?" Cobra hadn't considered that Marnie might have been arrested along with her family.

"No. I was in law school by then, full of new knowledge, full of righteous anger at the authorities. We might not have been a normal family, but I thought the charges were bogus."

"Uh-oh."

"So, I came home to help—absolutely certain I would prove their innocence."

"But they weren't innocent," he said, trying to guess how betrayed she must have felt by that.

She moved to the sofa, and he followed, taking the opposite end.

"They'd been lying to me for years. Partly my own fault, really."

"It wasn't your fault." He was positive of that.

"It never occurred to me that out-of-state luxury cars had no reason to be dropped off at Tumbleweed Fuel and Service in Merganser, Kansas. Not that I wandered around in the back lot. I mostly saw what they brought into the shop."

Cobra clamped his jaw. "They raised a young girl in the middle of all that?"

"My upbringing left plenty to be desired."

He didn't know whether to admire her for coming back to help these flawed people or offer again to get her out of Kansas before the hearing started. "Are you sure you still want to do this?"

"I don't want to do this. But I do want it to end."

"The hearing might not end it." Cobra was worried that Victor and maybe the others would be denied parole. If that happened, they'd come after Marnie again for the next parole hearing.

"It'll end it for me."

"No matter what?" he asked.

"No matter what."

Chapter Fifteen

MARNIE ENTERED A DRAB ROOM WITH NO WINDOWS and pale green walls. Her escort showed her to a chair behind a scarred, rickety table with uneven legs. Her father was already seated in front of the panel, his back to her. He didn't turn around to look.

Seeing him there alone, she wondered if she was going to have to speak three separate times.

Three people, two men and one woman, sat at a long table at the front of the room with notebooks at the ready, pens in their hands. The woman had short gray hair and wore glasses and a ruddy orange blazer. Her mouth was pinched, as though she didn't smile much.

Marnie supposed she didn't have a particularly fun job.

"You're Ms. Marnie Anton?" the woman asked.

The two men turned their attention to her as well. One looked to be in his thirties, nicely dressed, reasonably attractive, wearing a red tie that clashed with the orange blazer. The other man was older, balding, with bushy eyebrows that protruded from his forehead.

"Yes," Marnie said then cleared her throat. "Yes, I am."

She saw her father's shoulders stiffen, but he still didn't turn.

"You have a statement to make on behalf of Victor Anton?"

"I only wrote one statement," she said. "For all three. Is that okay?"

"You can say whatever you'd like," the younger man said.

"Do I have to say it three times?"

The panel members looked at each other.

They leaned their heads close together, and the woman whispered. The younger man whispered back. The older man looked at Marnie, then returned his attention to their conversation.

Marnie struggled to school her features. They looked so intent, so concerned about getting protocol right.

Then they all sat back.

"You can say it once," the woman told her. "We'll note it for the other hearings."

Marnie was relieved. "Thank you."

"Please," the older man said with a hand gesture.

Marnie began talking, filling the time with facts about their family activities, baking and hiking, school and gardening. She left out the target practice. She noted her parents were frugal with money, that they lived a simple, independent lifestyle. As much as possible, she made it sound like they were an ordinary family. After Cobra's question from yesterday, she confirmed that her father was curt but not violent.

She'd dredged up some memories of Ethan helping her with homework and standing up for her once at school. It was as close as she could come to vouching for their character. She did state that she knew of no additional crimes any of her family members had committed.

When she stopped talking, she realized she'd used up most of the ten minutes. She was proud of herself for that.

"When is the last time you saw Victor Anton?" the older man asked her.

"Yesterday." She didn't add that it was the first time she'd seen her father in six years.

"Stuart Anton?"

"Yesterday."

"And Ethan Anton."

"Same."

"So, yesterday?"

"Yes."

"Would any of them be living with you, should they be granted parole?" the younger man asked.

The orange-blazer woman looked over her glasses. "They can't leave the state without special permission."

Marnie was startled by the question. "No. They won't be living with me."

"Have you ever been arrested or charged with a crime?" the woman asked.

"No." Marnie started to feel uncomfortable.

"Felony, misdemeanor?"

"No."

"There were no charges brought against you when the rest of your family was arrested?"

"None. Why are you asking me this?"

"We'll ask the questions, if you don't mind," bushy brows said.

Marnie sat back in her chair, feeling chastised. She wondered if she should mention she was a lawyer, an officer of the court, so ought to have some credibility.

"So, if paroled, none of your family members would be residing with you?"

"That's what I said."

The three of them stared reprovingly at her.

"No," she answered, starting to get the feeling they were more worried about her influence on her family than her family's influence on her. It was almost laughable.

"Thank you for speaking with us today, Ms. Anton," the younger man said.

Relieved, she gathered her purse, rising from the chair.

Her escort was waiting outside the door and walked her from the interview room to the front desk of the prison where she signed back out again.

A sense of freedom and relief washed over her as she walked along a chain-link fence and spotted Cobra waiting in the parking lot. He was beside the rental car and came her way as soon as he saw her.

"How did it go?" he asked, turning to walk with her.

"Strange."

"In a bad way?"

"They wanted to know if any of my family members were coming to live with me."

Cobra coughed out a sharp laugh. "Hard no on that. So, we're done?"

"Looks like we're done."

"Airport?"

The question jolted Marnie. She hadn't expected him to be so eager to go his own way. She'd thought they might spend another night together, especially after the rough day she'd had.

"Sure," she said, swallowing her disappointment. "We'll have to go pack and check out of the hotel."

He opened the door for her. "Already done."

She paused, even more startled to hear that. "You checked us out of the hotel?"

"I did it while you were in the hearing. Suitcases are in the trunk. I called ahead to the airline too."

She felt almost dizzy with hurt and disillusionment. "Oh. Uh, great."

She hadn't arranged for a ticket home yet, but she supposed she could buy one at the airport. She might have to cool her heels on the concourse for a while, but there should be plenty of flights into LA today, since it was a hub city.

She was hungry now that the hearing was over, so she could use up some time having lunch and maybe a consolatory drink after Cobra boarded his flight. She wondered if their goodbye would be stilted in a public airport. Then again, he didn't seem interested in a heartfelt lingering farewell.

They left the parking lot and made their way to the highway.

"You're quiet," Cobra said as they sped along in sync with the light traffic. He seemed relaxed, his tone animated, as if he was anticipating something good.

"Nothing much to say, really," Marnie responded. She wasn't feeling anywhere near as upbeat as him.

"At least it's over," he said, exiting onto the parkway.

"I guess it is."

He glanced over. "I thought you'd be happy."

She hoped he was only talking about the hearing, but he could also be talking about their relationship. "Relieved, I suppose."

"Relieved is good." He pulled into the rental return line.

He handed the attendant the keys and popped open the trunk.

Marnie went for her suitcase, but Cobra was faster, stacking his duffel across her roller bag and towing them as a unit while they walked to the terminal.

He moved swiftly and with purpose, while she hustled to keep up.

She spotted the customer service counter and started to veer off, but Cobra kept going toward the escalators. Was he not even going to wait for her to get her ticket?

"Hey," she called out, and he immediately stopped and turned.

"Something wrong?" He walked back against the stream of pedestrians.

"I need my suitcase." She guessed he'd forgotten he still had it.

He looked down. "Why?"

She pointed to the lines at the customer service counter. "I need to buy a ticket."

He looked confused. "I bought your ticket online when I bought mine."

"You did?"

"Of course. You think I wouldn't buy you a ticket?"

To be fair, that would be in keeping with her experience of him. She remembered his offer to upgrade her to first class the day she'd planned to leave Alaska. "Oh. Thanks."

He gave her a grin. "Come on. We don't have a whole lot of time to waste."

Her opinion of him softening a little, she started walking again. "How long until my flight?" She was still thinking about their goodbye.

"A little under an hour. But security shouldn't take long this time of day."

They rose on the escalator, coming to the departures level. The lines were long at the check-in desks, but there were kiosks available.

"Do you want to check your bag?" Cobra asked. "I got first-class tickets, so there'll be plenty of room for carry-on if you prefer."

"You bought me a first-class ticket?"

"It's a long flight. The layover is in Seattle."

It was a circuitous route to take to LA. Then again, he'd booked last-minute, so there might not have been a lot of choices.

"I can carry the bag on," she said. "Thanks for doing that." Her feelings for him warmed further and her regret at leaving him became more acute.

They were approaching the security line, and it looked nice and short.

"You should probably check your phone to make sure

the boarding pass came through." He was scrolling through his own phone. "I sent it by text."

She pulled her phone from her purse and saw the airline message. "It's here." She touched the link—seat 2A to Seattle. He'd even gotten her a window seat.

They made their way through the beeps and bustle of security and out the other side to stop in front of the departing flights board. Marnie found her gate then looked around for the direction signs.

"Are you this way too?" she asked Cobra, pointing to the left as other passengers walked around them.

"Are you looking for the restroom?" he asked, pulling the suitcase in close beside them.

"No. I'm gate six. You?"

He looked puzzled again. "Gate six."

"Oh, you're going through Seattle too?" That made perfect sense. Seattle was the obvious stopover for flights to Anchorage.

It occurred to her then that he might have done it on purpose—booked her through Seattle so they wouldn't have to say goodbye right here and now. They'd be together during the first leg of their trips, giving them a little more time.

He touched her arm, gently urging her off to the side where they were out of traffic. "Marnie, what do you think is going on here?"

She didn't exactly understand the question. "We're getting on an airplane?" And they were doing it together. She was much happier about the extra few hours with him than was remotely good for her psyche. But there it was.

He glanced off into the distance for a moment, looking uncomfortable, then looked at her. "I bought you a ticket to Alaska."

Her jaw went slack and her shoulders dropped, while the sounds around her turned to a buzz in her ears.

"You have nearly a week left on your vacation, so I

thought you'd want to relax in Alaska for the rest of your time off—you know, hang with Mia . . . with me," he said.

"But—"

"You don't want to go back to Alaska?"

"It's not that." Joy blossomed within her.

He took in her growing smile. "You thought I was rushing you off to LAX as fast as possible? You really thought I was saying goodbye like this?"

She nodded, face warming slightly.

He chuckled. "That was definitely not my plan."

"Alaska?" she said, trying to wrap her mind around it.

He drew her into a hug. "Unless you'd rather go to LA."

She shook her head against his chest. She wanted to go where Cobra was going.

THEIR FLIGHT FROM SEATTLE WAS ONLY A COUPLE hours late arriving in Anchorage, but it was enough for them to miss their connection to Fairbanks. Cobra's first instinct was to call Brodie to see if someone could pick them up here tonight. But he quickly dismissed the idea.

He had Marnie all to himself for the evening. Why would he want to give that up?

Instead, he scrolled through his phone, finding the number for Mast Mountain Resort.

"What now?" Marnie asked, gazing around at the kiosks and the swirl of passengers standing around waiting and walking through the concourse.

"We'll have to spend the night," Cobra said.

She blew out what sounded like a disappointed breath. "Airport hotel."

"We can do better than that," he said, finding the right listing.

"Yeah?" She perked up.

"How do you feel about whales?"

Marnie looked perplexed. "Who doesn't like whales?"

"I was hoping you'd say that." He tapped the phone number to connect.

"What do you mean?" she asked as the line rang through. "What are you doing?"

"Want to go see some?" he asked, feeling smug about his idea.

"Where?"

"Good evening." A woman answered his call. "Icy Bay Charters. This is Nora speaking. How can I help you?"

"Hello, Nora. This is Conrad Stanford. I'm interested in chartering a boat overnight. Do you have any availability?"

Marnie's brows jumped up, her eyes widening.

"How many passengers?"

"Just two, but we'd like something nice."

"Romantic nice?" she asked, and he could hear the smile in her voice.

"Yes."

"We have the Skipper Five or the Master Belgrade. The Skipper is eighty-five feet, luxury all the way but in the higher price range. The Belgrade is smaller and available at a lower rate. Both will give you an amazing harbor experience."

"The Skipper," Cobra said. "Is pickup available from the airport?"

"Are you serious?" Marnie stage-whispered.

He grinned at her.

"Yes, of course," Nora said. "Do you know the airport?"

"I do."

"Perfect. I'll have the driver meet you at the ground transportation island in thirty minutes. It'll be an SUV. The Icy Bay Charters logo is on the windshield."

"We'll be there," he said.

"Would you like an estimate over the phone?"

"Not necessary."

"Then once you're here, I'll outline the meal options and we can go over the contract."

"Thanks, Nora. Goodbye."

"What did you just do?" Marnie demanded as he ended the call.

She looked more concerned than excited, and he started to second-guess himself. Had he bulldozed through that too fast? He'd planned on it being a romantic adventure.

"We're going to see some whales," he said, stilling and watching her expression.

"On a boat?"

Then it hit him. "Will you get seasick?"

"Is it a small boat?"

"Eighty-five feet."

"That's not a small boat."

"It's not."

"It's the sharp jolts that get me, not the rolling motion."

He blew out a breath of relief, glad he wouldn't have to scramble to change plans. "Oh, good."

"So, we're sleeping on a boat?"

"I thought it would be romantic."

Her expression relaxed and she smiled. "Impulsive. But yes, romantic."

He gave her shoulders a squeeze. "Do you need anything before we get picked up?"

She shook her head as they started to walk. "Do you really think we'll see whales?"

"If we're lucky. They're out there, just swimming around."

"I'd like to see whales," she said, looking eager now.

They made their way to the ground transportation island, and Cobra was surprised to find the Icy Bay Charters SUV was already waiting for them.

The driver was in a neat uniform and very professional. He whisked them smoothly to the marina where they chose a five-course dinner including fresh halibut and crab cocktail, and soon they were on the upper deck of the Skipper Five, leaning on the aft rail to watch the city disappear as they headed out into Cook Inlet.

"How are you feeling?" he asked her. It had obviously been a long and emotional day.

"Light," she said, fighting the wind for control of a wayward strand of her hair. "Relieved, like I'm leaving my troubles behind me back on shore."

"Maybe we should just keep going." He trapped her hair with his hand and held it.

"You think? How long would it take us to get to LA?"

"LA? I meant the other way. We could find a nice little fishing resort in the Aleutians and tell our friends that we're never coming home."

"Forage for salmon and king crab?" She seemed to find the idea amusing.

"It's been done."

"I doubt they'd need a lot of legal work at a fishing resort." Clearly, she wasn't imagining the same getaway as him.

"In your get-away-from-it-all fantasy, you open a law office?"

"I have to work somewhere."

He was the one who chuckled now. "You really do love your job."

She nodded to that. "And you love yours."

"True," he agreed. He loved his job, and his colleagues at WSA, even Paradise, although it was nice to get away from it once in a while.

The idea of chucking it all for Marnie was fleeting. Enticing, but fleeting.

"Still." She inhaled deeply. "Just for a little while. It's nice to forget about everything."

He pulled her closer, touching his chin to the top of her head. "It really is."

"Look!" She pointed. "Is that—"

"A humpback." He saw it too, breaking the surface on the starboard side.

"Wow, that is big," she said as the whale's barnacle-crusted back arched out of the water, its tail breaking the surface then smacking back down.

It was only thirty feet out from the boat, and a small wave rolled their way.

"There's another," Marnie said, excitement in her voice.

"This is closer than I've ever been," he said, taking in the breathtaking size of the animals.

"Oh!" she cried out as one of the whales breached the surface, its white underbelly flashing in the long rays of the sun.

It splashed down, and Cobra reflexively wrapped himself around Marnie to protect her from the salt spray. But they both still got wet.

She laughed, shaking out her wet hands. "Good thing we brought a change of clothes."

The pod of a dozen whales paralleled the boat for about half an hour, breaking the surface as they swam, spraying from their blowholes, and occasionally breaching as they moved farther away before disappearing into the depths.

"Mr. Stanford, ma'am." A crew member who'd earlier introduced himself as Paul approached them from behind.

"That was thrilling," Marnie told him as they turned.

Paul gave her a bright smile. "It's nice when the whales cooperate. When you're ready, the chef has set up dinner on the view lounge on the main deck. You'll be just in time for the sunset."

"Thank you, Paul."

"I think this is a perfect date," Marnie said as they made their way down to the roomy master cabin.

They changed into dry clothes then climbed back up to the main deck, finding an elegantly set table surrounded by glass on three sides. The view was spectacular, the sun streaking the sky pink above the gentle waves, the rocky shoreline and the mountain peaks.

They sat down to a bottle of wine and a smoked salmon avocado appetizer.

Marnie gave a contented sigh as she took a sip of the chardonnay. Her cheeks were rosy, her green eyes bright and her gorgeous hair was combed out and fluffed up, framing her beautiful face.

"Happy?" he couldn't help but ask.

"This day is ending so much better than it started out." She paused. "Thank you, Cobra. For being here."

"Don't thank me. I'm enjoying this as much as you are."

"And for coming after me." She turned her blown-crystal glass by its stem. "I didn't realize how much I needed a friend."

He reached out and took her hand. "Anytime, Marnie. Anytime you need anything." He meant it more than he could say.

She grinned and selected a crostini from the tray between them. "Right now, I need something to eat."

"Agreed," he said, following her lead. It had been a long time since their meal on the plane. He was determined to savor their dinner and every minute of their impromptu cruise. He only hoped it didn't end too soon.

Chapter Sixteen

TOO SOON THEY WERE LANDING BACK IN PARADISE.

"Thanks for picking us up," Cobra said to Brodie as they tied the Cessna down at the Paradise airstrip after the trip in from Fairbanks.

Mia and Raven had come out to meet Marnie, and the three women were hugging and laughing in the parking lot.

She might have been only fifty feet away, but Cobra missed her already.

"Was this your plan all along?" Brodie asked, nodding toward Marnie as he put tension on a strap. "Bringing her back here?"

Cobra pushed a wheel chock into place. "I didn't have a plan," he admitted. "I still don't have one. I'm making this up as I go along."

Just then he caught a glimpse of Silas coming out of the office, jolting him further back to reality. Silas was too far away for Cobra to see his expression, but he could guess what it was.

"So, what's next?" Brodie asked.

"Next I owe Mia a big apology for snapping at her before I left."

"You think Silas will let you near her?" It was clear Brodie had heard the story of Cobra's outburst.

"I'll start with him."

"Good idea."

"It was a knee-jerk reaction," Cobra said, although Brodie wasn't the one who deserved an explanation.

"I know how that goes."

"Marnie's family is a piece of work." Cobra didn't plan to mention the criminal angle, even if it was public information for anyone who cared to look.

"I get it. You were scared—"

"I wasn't scared." Cobra wasn't driven by fear.

"I meant, for her."

"Oh."

"Yeah."

"Maybe." When Cobra found out she was taking on her father—and worse, that her father was a criminal—he'd dropped everything and hopped on a red-eye. His only thought had been to get between Marnie and the man harassing her.

"State prison?" Brodie asked him.

"I guess everyone knows that by now." Cobra regretted that part.

"Just a few of us."

"It isn't general town gossip?"

Brodie shook his head.

"Good. Thanks." Cobra started for Silas.

"Good luck," Brodie called from behind him.

Silas saw Cobra coming his way and stopped short. His eyes narrowed and he stood his ground, arms crossed, feet planted apart.

"I was way out of line," Cobra said as he came to a halt.

"You were," Silas said, his jaw tense, chin jutting.

"It was from shock."

"Doesn't excuse it."

"I know." Cobra deeply regretted his outburst.

"Get it under control, man."

"I will. I am." Cobra slid his gaze to Marnie, last night's emotions returning in force. "She said her family was trouble, but I didn't know the half of it."

The edge went out of Silas's voice. "And you needed to fix it."

"I had to try."

"And you brought her back."

Cobra could guess where this was going. "She wanted to come back."

Silas gave a slight shake of his head. "You're only putting it off, you know."

"You don't have to keep warning me about that." Cobra knew he was treading on dangerous ground where his feelings for Marnie were concerned, but he had it under control. They were both adults and were fully aware of their circumstances. Neither of them would be taken by surprise.

"Someone better warn you. Because it'll be even worse when she leaves next week."

"I'll take the week." Hell, Cobra would take an hour or a day, whatever he could get with Marnie. If he was on a pathway to heartache, so be it. There was nothing he could do to stop it even if he wanted to. He cocked his head toward where the three women were talking. "I was going to apologize to Mia again. You okay with that?"

"It's not up to me."

"I'll take that as a yes." Cobra paused. "I really am sorry."

"So, tell her."

With a nod, Cobra made his way to the women, zeroing in on Mia, wanting to get this done.

She met his gaze as he approached.

"Got a minute?" he asked her.

"Sure." It was hard to gauge her mood, but she followed him a few feet away.

"I want to apologize," he said.

"Did you know her dad was in jail?"

Cobra shook his head. "Not right then." He didn't have that as an excuse for his reaction. "I knew they were estranged, that she didn't want to see him or talk to him. I knew he was trying to get hold of her and it had her rattled."

"I'm glad you went," Mia said with the briefest of glances over her shoulder at Marnie.

"I never should have shouted at you." Standing here in front of her, he was more regretful than ever.

Mia gave a ghost of a smile. "Tell me you wanted to protect her."

"I wanted to protect her."

"Good."

He wanted to be sure he was reading Mia right. "So, you and me, we're okay?"

"We're okay." She held up a warning finger. "But don't you dare hurt her."

"I'm not planning on it."

The last thing he would do was hurt Marnie.

"Just so we're clear," Mia said.

"Yes, ma'am."

"So, you're coming over tonight?"

The invitation warmed him and filled him with relief. "If it's okay with you."

She moved in a little closer. "I know how it feels to be under a ticking clock."

THE TOWN OF BALSAM RIDGE WAS BIGGER THAN PARADISE. It was nestled on the edge of Denali State Park, on the shores of a wide, meandering river. Marnie was more than impressed with the setup for the Klondike Challenge—

what seemed like miles of temporary facilities stretching up the valley from the town.

Most of the events would take place in a central field to the north of the town. It was surrounded on three sides by rolling meadows that were dotted with tent encampments. Raven said the field was once a hay farming operation, but the short growing season made it unprofitable, so it had been abandoned years ago.

Each of the teams set up their own camp on the periphery. The camps themselves had turned into a friendly competition over the years. Since expediting and transportation was a Paradise specialty, the Team Paradise camp was one of the best. For the past three days, Galina had been loading freight and WSA had been flying the cargo into Balsam Ridge, while Peter Gambina and his recruits, including Cobra, had built wooden floors and frames for the Paradise wall tents.

"This one is ours," Raven said to Marnie, opening the door to one of the roomy tents.

Although there was a huge cafeteria tent for all the teams, John Reed and Fredo had also set up a portable kitchen and barbecue area in the middle of the town's semi-circle of tents.

"Are we worried about bears?" Marnie asked as she walked in through the doorway. The tent was a few hundred yards from where the forest started up the mountainside.

"Way too many people around this weekend," Raven said.

Marnie took in the pale canvas walls that were lit up with sunshine. Roll-up windows on three sides let in sunlight and fresh air. The floor was smooth and spotlessly clean, with two comfy-looking little beds set up at the far end. A small table was between the beds with a battery lamp on top. And they had a cute little wood stove near the wall by the door, with two bright blue, foldable director-style chairs in front.

"This is amazing," she said.

"Not what you pictured when we said *tents*, I bet." Raven set her bag at the foot of one of the beds.

Marnie rolled her suitcase over to the other. "I'm in awe." She tested the bed and found the foam mattress nicely firm. "I used to think my family did this well."

"Camping?" Raven unzipped her bag.

"Growing up, my parents taught me how to cope with the end of the world, building lean-tos and rotating canned goods in the backyard bunker. You Alaskans built a town in three days. If the worst happens, I'm liking your chances of survival."

"You had a backyard bunker?"

"It wasn't very big. I wouldn't have wanted to spend a weekend in it, never mind months waiting for the nuclear fallout to disappear or for the zombies to move on."

Raven sat down on the bed and spread her arms. "You're saying this is better."

"So much better."

"We've got a good location, only a short walk to the wash tent." Raven pointed behind herself with her thumb. "But we should go together or take bear spray."

"So, there are bears."

"Not likely, but better to be safe."

"If I learned anything growing up, it's to be prepared."

"We can pick up canisters from Fredo."

Silas and Xavier, their pilots for the flight over, had been crystal clear that no bear spray was permitted inside the airplane. Canisters could accidentally deploy, and pepper spray in a pilot's eyes would blind them and cause a catastrophe.

Marnie noticed a fold-out luggage rack at the side of her bed. "They thought of everything." She moved aside her suitcase and set it up at the foot, plunking the suitcase on top.

"We can't exactly unpack," Raven said, doing the same.

"I feel like I've been living on the road for weeks now."

Not that it had been all bad. She liked hanging out with Mia and Raven too. And the yacht interlude with Cobra had been a dream. She still smiled to herself remembering their night on the water. But she'd had only one night at home in the past few weeks, and all she'd done there was sleep, shower, water her plants and pack a new bag for Kansas.

"Have you heard how the parole hearing went?" Raven asked. Then she looked flustered. "I'm sorry. I shouldn't have asked that."

"It's okay." While Marnie wasn't broadcasting the fact that her father and brother were convicted felons, she was through hiding it. "I got a text message from my brother yesterday. They all got parole."

"Will you stay in contact with him?"

"Nope. I didn't answer, and he probably didn't expect me to. I was clear . . . I guess it's more accurate to say Cobra was clear that I was done with them."

"Quite the thing," Raven said musingly.

"Never seeing my family again?" It didn't feel like much of a big thing to Marnie. It had been years since she'd seen them, and she couldn't imagine them being any kind of a positive force in her life.

"Cobra following you to Kansas."

"Oh, that."

Raven sat back down on the edge of her bed. "So, that kiss you mentioned . . ."

Marnie sat down opposite. "We kissed again." She rocked her head. "And . . . we did more."

Raven grinned at the revelation. "More impulsive actions?"

"Some extremely impulsive actions."

"Anything beyond impulsive?"

"You mean romance?" Dinner on the yacht had sure felt like romance. And if Cobra lived in LA, she'd be more than interested. But he didn't live in LA, so she couldn't let herself go there. It wouldn't work between them. They both knew that.

"Are you falling for Cobra?" Raven asked.

"As in rethinking my entire life because he's a nice guy and good in bed?"

Raven chuckled. "You have to admit, those are two important prerequisites."

"If anyone could keep me warm in Alaska . . ." Marnie ventured. "But, no, my life plan is intact." She had a career to think about, and that career now included entertainment law, which she found fascinating. LA was her city. Paradise was a lark.

"So, just a fling?" Raven asked.

"Just a fling."

Raven's expression turned speculative.

"Are you thinking about Brodie?"

Raven was silent for a long moment. "There are days"—she pursed her lips—"when I wonder if I could, you know, maybe just once . . ." She squeezed her eyes shut. "And then sanity returns."

"Don't you hate it when that happens?" Marnie admired Raven's strength of character. The woman had perfectly valid reasons for staying out of Brodie's arms, and she was sticking to her principles.

"Do I *ever*." Raven braced her hands on either side of herself on the bed. "To be honest, I was hoping you'd talk me into it."

"Do you *want* me to talk you into it?" That struck Marnie as backward.

"I don't know." Raven scrunched up her face. "Maybe I want you to try."

Marnie tried to follow the line of reasoning. "Because if I can talk you into it, then it was inevitable."

"And if you can't, then I'm stronger than I think."

"You want to pro and con this?"

Raven sat up straight and flexed her shoulders.

Marnie thought back to making love with Cobra. "I have to say, it would be a *whole* lot of fun."

Raven reached out and snapped her fingers. "Hey, we're pro and conning me, not you."

"Sorry." Marnie grinned and refocused. "What've you got?"

"It *would* be a whole lot of fun."

"Pro."

"But it would be temporary."

"Probably." Marnie knew the lightning that had struck with Mia and Silas was rare.

Raven's expression faltered. "And then there's the afterward."

"That's the trouble." Marnie had pushed off thinking about that reckoning for her and Cobra.

Raven drummed her fingertips on her knee. "There has to be more than that."

"You'd get to know Brodie better," Marnie offered.

"I know him pretty well."

"Not intimately. And you never know where it might lead."

"A white dress and flowers?" Raven looked extremely doubtful about that.

"Probably not," Marnie had to admit.

The door opened, and Mia breezed in. "There you guys are." She looked back and forth between them, taking in the focus on their expressions. "What are we talking about?"

"Sex," Marnie said.

"Cobra," Raven said overtop.

Mia turned a folding chair to face them and plunked down. "Why would you start that without me?"

"Sorry," Marnie said on a laugh.

Mia leaned forward. "So, catch me up."

Before they could start talking, the door opened again,

and Silas stepped in. He walked over and turned the other chair to place it beside Mia.

"We're talking about sex," Mia warned him as he sat down.

Silas drew back, his eyes widening as he took in the circle. "Sounds like I'm just in time."

Mia socked him in the shoulder. "We're not talking about sex in front of you."

Laughter danced in the depths of his eyes, and he leaned her way, lowering his voice. "We talk about sex all the time."

"Not Marnie and Cobra sex."

Marnie held her palms up defensively. "Okay, new topic." As her words came out, Cobra arrived, catching the final words of the conversation.

"What's the old topic?" he asked.

Silas smirked.

Marnie gave up trying to hide it. "Our sex life."

Cobra glanced at the amused expressions around the room before taking it in stride. "I hope you made me sound good."

"He was *great*," Marnie quickly told everyone with an exaggerated nod.

Cobra strutted victorious across the tent to sit next to Marnie on the single bed. He took her hand in both of his.

"I've never seen him act like that," Mia said to Silas.

Raven looked confused as well. "What have you done to our Cobra?" she asked Marnie.

Cobra gave Marnie a puzzled look. "What exactly did you tell them?"

"Nothing," she said, deciding it was time to end the joke. If deflecting from Raven and Brodie had been the goal, they'd achieved it with ease.

"Who brought wine?" Raven asked, looking expectantly at Mia.

"I stashed a few cases in the back of the beaver," Mia answered. "It was easy enough to bribe the pilot."

"We can't drink tonight," Cobra said.

"There are rules?" Marnie asked. She'd thought this was a casual, lighthearted competition.

"I have rules," he said.

"And we all have to follow them?" she challenged.

"Only if you want to win."

COBRA HELD HIS BREATH, WATCHING THROUGH BIN-oculars while Marnie lined up on the next target. They'd practiced the shooting event a couple of times after returning to Paradise, so she'd known what to expect. The course was a series of targets of various shapes at various distances with short sprints in between.

She had a harder time shooting accurately while she was out of breath, as most people did. But since the points were awarded based on both speed and accuracy, shooters didn't want to waste time recovering at each target.

Two of Cobra's strengths were long legs and a fast breathing recovery time.

She hit in the bull's-eye at fifty and one hundred yards. Now she was lining up at one fifty.

"Relax," he muttered under his breath, seeing her movements go jerky. "Take five seconds."

As if she'd heard him, she seemed to slow herself down.

"That's it," he muttered.

"How's she looking?" Brodie asked from his elbow.

"Just a—"

She pulled the trigger.

Cobra quickly focused on the target. "Nailed it."

"Good?" Brodie asked.

"Good," Cobra said as Marnie slung the rifle over her shoulder and took off along the pathway at a run.

She was in the middle of the pack speed-wise. There were at least a dozen women who were faster runners. But her accuracy was going to be hard to beat.

"Heard you took first in the Chainsaw Chuck," Brodie said.

"I did." Cobra watched Marnie approach the final target. At two hundred yards, and with the competitors tired out, this was the toughest one.

"Nice," Brodie said.

"How'd T-Two do on the hill climb?" The Snowmobile Hill Climb event was held down the valley of Paisley Peak. They ran it in the morning before the avalanche danger could build from the sun.

"Second place."

"Three points to Team Paradise," Cobra said, happy for T-Two, knowing he'd be thrilled with that finish. The snowmobile event was one of the most competitive.

"Plus, your five points in Chainsaw Chucking."

"Fingers crossed for Marnie," Cobra said, holding still again while she aimed.

Her chest rose then fell. She put her eye to the scope, then pulled back from it and swiped at her hair.

"Come on," he said under his breath, acutely aware of the seconds ticking past.

Brodie knew enough to stay quiet while they waited.

Her shoulders relaxed, and Cobra could have cheered. Then she placed her finger and squeezed the trigger.

Cobra moved his view to the target. She was slightly off this time, but still caught the edge of the bull's-eye.

"And?" Brodie asked.

"We'll have to wait and see."

"She missed?"

"She got it into the bull's-eye, but—"

"What do you mean, but?" Brodie clapped him on the shoulder. "Our girl hit the bull's-eye."

"Not dead center." Her first four shots had been flawless.

"Do you think maybe your standards are a little high?" Brodie asked, eyebrows raised.

"I don't want her to be disappointed."

"Her or you?"

Cobra looked at Brodie. "What's that supposed to mean?"

"That you're pretty invested in her results."

"You don't want the points for Paradise?"

"Sure, I want points. But it seems like you care more that she's happy."

"You're starting to sound like Silas."

Marnie was making her way back off the course, chatting with the other women who were gesticulating as they obviously compared notes on how their races had gone.

Cobra was itching to congratulate her, but he had to wait in the spectator area.

"What does Silas sound like?" Brodie asked.

"He thinks I'm him and Marnie is Mia."

"And?"

"And we're not. Totally different situation. You know that." Cobra was keeping things under control with Marnie.

Marnie handed her gun to the inspector and pulled off her safety equipment then spotted him in the crowd. She grinned and came his way.

He met her, lifted her in his arms and hugged her tight. "You were fantastic."

"Did you see?" she asked, sounding enthusiastic. "I nailed it."

"You did," he agreed, happy that she wasn't rattled by the final target.

The loudspeaker crackled and squeaked, and they went silent to hear the results.

She took first place, and they both whooped with delight.

Brodie approached, and Cobra set Marnie down.

"Nicely done," he said. "Paradise thanks you."

"How's our team doing?" she asked.

"In an early second place," Brodie said. "But there are plenty of events to go."

"How soon are you up?" Marnie asked Cobra, nodding to the shooting course. They'd set up for the men's event next.

"I've got a couple of hours."

"Did you see the setup for the Old-Time Pie Baking Contest?"

"Are you interested in that event?" Cobra asked.

Marnie nodded enthusiastically.

Mrs. France was the baker for the Paradise team, while John Reed ran the wood stove for her. Cobra understood that keeping the heat up to temperature and even throughout the oven box was key to a successful pie.

While Brodie headed out on team captain duties, Cobra and Marnie crossed the open field to the gazebo where the pie baking contest was under way.

Smoke chugged from two dozen chimneys on two dozen wood-burning cookstoves set up around the perimeter of the raised gazebo. Each stove had a woodpile behind it, and contestants had a choice of sizes, species and dryness.

The bakers were working at tables in the center of the gazebo.

"Tell me she's using wild cranberries," Marnie said as they found a good spot to stand and watch Mrs. France.

"Likely. They each use their own Alaska wild berry blend. The recipes are closely guarded secrets."

"I love that they use local ingredients."

Mrs. France and the others were putting the finishing touches on the pie crusts.

"I've tasted that pie," Cobra said.

"Braggart."

"It's good."

"You think she has a chance?"

"A good chance—they bring judges in from Anchorage to keep them neutral."

"Seriously?"

"There was an unfortunate scandal one year."

"A pie scandal?" Marnie laughed.

John opened the firebox on their cookstove, peering in at the flame and poking the coals, before making the decision to add another stick of wood.

"The Greyson Township mayor was accused of making a backroom deal with the judge from Pottersville, something about the use of his luxury fishing chalet." Cobra held his palms apart and made a three-foot space. "Huge king salmon."

"Was he guilty?"

Cobra glanced around and leaned down, speaking in a mock cloak-and-dagger tone. "We'll never know for sure. But Greyson won that year, and the mayor mysteriously left office a month later. We all have our suspicions."

Marnie looked skeptical. "Why would anyone take that risk?"

"For the coveted Klondike Challenge championship plaque."

They watched Mrs. France slide her pie into the oven, with John carefully opening and closing the door.

A small cheer went up from the Paradise spectators.

"There's a plaque?" Marnie asked.

"You haven't seen it yet?"

"No, I thought this event was for fun—or just bragging rights."

"It's an original 1896 gold pan, silver plated and decorated with a gold nugget from each of the team's communities."

"It sounds valuable."

"I suppose, depending on the price of gold at the time."

"Might someone be tempted to steal it?"

"They haven't so far." Cobra could only imagine the frenzied recovery effort if someone stole the Klondike Challenge plaque.

BY DAY THREE OF THE KLONDIKE CHALLENGE, PARAdise was running a close second to Balsam Ridge, who had the home field advantage.

Marnie and Cobra both won their pistol competitions,

and Mrs. France was thrilled to win for Pie Baking. Sadly, both Paradise competitors had fallen during yesterday's Snowshoe Race, and Marnie had been edged out of the top three spots in Ax Throwing. Raven came sixth, and the two women had consoled each other.

This morning, Paradise had made a good showing in the Green Energy Challenge. Mia had ridden a bike for the team, and they'd managed to get third—an important two points, since Paradise was nipping at the heels of Balsam Ridge.

Firewood Stacking was under way now, with Raven and Brodie working furiously together. Most of the Paradise team was out to cheer them on in the marquee event. The competitors were scored on both the speed of their stacking and the density of their final stack.

Brodie used a chainsaw to buck the logs into specified lengths, while Raven used a gas-powered log splitter to cut them into halves then quarters. Then she stacked them in the rack. Marnie was in awe of Raven's ability to smoothly set up, split and stack piece after piece. It looked like exhausting work, but Raven just kept going without faltering.

"Does Brodie have the easy job?" Mia asked Silas from where they were standing next to Marnie.

"Easy?" Silas asked back, looking puzzled.

"The saw goes though the logs like nothing," Mia said.

"You ever used a chainsaw before?"

Mia gave Silas an incredulous look, drawing out the word. "Right."

Marnie had used a chainsaw a few times—enough to learn how. The one she'd used was smaller than Brodie's, and it was tough enough.

"It weighs close to thirty pounds with full fuel," Silas said.

"And there's resistance," Marnie said.

Silas gave her an approving nod.

"Brodie's only making it look easy," Marnie added.

"Here I was feeling sorry for Raven," Mia said.

"I'm still feeling sorry for Raven," Marnie said. "That's tough work."

"I feel like such a wimp."

Silas gave Mia a squeeze around the shoulders. "I like you wimpy."

"Thanks tons."

"It makes you lighter to carry in the Wife Packing Contest."

"Partner Packing," she corrected him.

"When are we getting married, anyway?" he asked.

Mia looked incredulous. "You want to talk about that *now*?"

"What's wrong with now? The subject of wives just came up. It's a natural question."

Marnie stifled a laugh.

Mia gave her a sidelong glance. "Not funny."

"Kind of romantic," Marnie said.

"How so?"

Silas jabbed his thumb in Marnie's direction. "What she said."

"Even with all these distractions," Marnie continued. "The minute the word *wife* came up, he thought of you."

"Well, we *are* engaged," Mia pointed out, flashing her ring in front of his face.

He grasped her hand and kissed it.

Cobra arrived. "How are we doing?"

"Silas is doing some wedding planning on the sidelines," Marnie answered.

Cobra looked back to Marnie, eyebrows raised. "How'd that come up?"

She made a rolling motion with her hand. "Wife Packing, wedding, something, something. Raven and Brodie are doing great."

The words were no sooner out of her mouth than Raven faltered after placing a piece of wood on the pile. She stared in horror at the splitter then hit the lever. The splitter shuddered and stilled.

Marnie saw gas leaking out, and her stomach sank.

Brodie was oblivious to the problem—wearing hearing protection against the noise and focused on his saw and the log in front of him.

Cobra swore under his breath, rushing toward their station, approaching an official and meeting Raven there.

Brodie saw what was happening, but Cobra motioned for him to keep going.

After a brief discussion, the official nodded, and Cobra headed for the splitter. He pulled a multi-tool from his belt and cut an end of the hose. In moments, he'd reattached it and restarted the splitter. It roared back to life.

He got out of the way, and Raven went back to work, trying frantically to catch up to the other teams.

Although her effort was valiant, it was clear they weren't going to be the winners. Still breathing hard from their efforts, Brodie hugged her tight and offered what were obviously consoling words as Marnie, Cobra, Mia and Silas went to offer their own reassurance.

"There's still the Partner Packing," Brodie told Raven when it came out they'd only managed third place.

"We'll need the full five points in that," she said, sounding worried. "Plus, we'll need Balsam Ridge to finish third or worse for us to win."

"Doable," Silas said.

Cobra touched Marnie's arm and motioned her away with a tilt of his head.

She followed him a few steps.

"You and I could enter Partner Packing," he said. "Paradise is allowed two teams."

"Oh, no," she said, taking a step away in protest. "I've already told you I'm not doing that." She'd seen pictures of the undignified race. She was, frankly, astonished that Mia had agreed to enter.

"We'd win," he said eagerly. "I promise you we would win."

"Silas and Mia can win."

"They won't." Cobra shook his head. "I've seen their competition out practicing."

And Marnie had seen how the women were slung over the men's shoulders in a completely undignified fireman's carry and cringed. No thanks, not her.

"They might win." She glanced to Silas, trying to decide if he looked confident about his and Mia's chances.

"It's for the championship," Cobra said.

"I'm not a sack of flour."

He chuckled at her protest. "Neither is Mia. Neither are any of the competitors. Nobody will think less of you. You'll be a hero."

She didn't appreciate his humor. "I don't want to be a hero."

"Marnie."

"Cobra."

"It's a guaranteed five points. It's for the town."

"And if Balsam Ridge comes second in the race?"

"Then we don't win the plaque."

"And my sacrifice would be for nothing."

He was silent for a beat before speaking. "So, you're thinking about it?"

No, she wasn't. Was she?

The last thing in the world she wanted to do was enter the stupid race. But Cobra was fast, and he was strong, and she was even lighter than Mia. They were Paradise's best shot at the championship.

She hated that he'd put her in this position. She didn't even care about this competition; she was only participating to help out.

"Well?" he prompted, looking hopeful.

"Let me think about it."

"No. Don't think about it. If you think about it, you'll talk yourself out of it."

"I will not."

"You will." He leaned in. "Just say yes. Right here, right now. Let me go tell them all that we have a fighting chance."

Marnie glanced Silas and Mia's way again. Brodie was talking, and some other team members had gathered around. They all looked worried.

She closed her eyes and gritted her teeth, telling herself it would be over with quickly.

He took her hand in his. "For the town," he repeated.

"Fine," she said, hating her answer but knowing guilt would haunt her for days if she said no. Win or lose, Cobra had better know how much of a sacrifice she was making.

Chapter Seventeen

AT THE STARTING LINE, COBRA SETTLED MARNIE ACROSS his shoulders. He held her effortlessly, barely feeling a strain—this would be easy.

"How long is this thing?" she asked, raising her head and looking out across the field.

"About a half mile."

"A *half*—"

"There are a few obstacles, but don't worry, I won't drop you."

"Wait . . . obstacles?" The apprehension in her voice was becoming more pronounced.

He hadn't described the details of the race, not wanting her to worry, or worse, back out. "A few logs to jump over, things like that."

"Cobra."

The whistle blew three times, signaling for the runners to put their toe on the line.

"It's fine," he assured her. "It's all good. You're easy to carry, and I have great balance."

"You didn't tell me there'd be—"

"Take your marks," the official's voice boomed over the bullhorn.

Cobra tightened his grip and put his toe on the line.

The starting gun sounded, and he took off running.

Marnie made an inarticulate sound of horror and clung on tight.

A half mile was a short jog but a long sprint. Cobra checked the pace of the other runners, putting himself slightly into the lead. He wanted to stay out front, because he couldn't count on having a kick at the end, not while carrying an extra hundred pounds.

The competitors strung themselves out, the front ten staying within a few yards of one another. Cobra glanced to the side and saw Silas was sticking with the front pack.

The competitor from Balsam Ridge upped the pace, and Cobra stayed with him. The ground was uneven, and Cobra had to focus on his footing to make sure he didn't stumble.

They came to the horizontal log obstacles.

"Hang on," he warned Marnie through his heavy breathing. He hurdled over the logs, jumped the creek, then sprinted a few strides to zigzag first through the vertical logs.

Balsam Ridge was hot on his heels.

He hated to up the pace, because his thighs were already starting to burn, and they were only halfway through. But Balsam Ridge pushed, and Cobra had no choice but to run faster.

His lungs labored. His heart pounded. His muscles went from burning to trembling, and he knew he was in trouble. There were fifty yards, then thirty, then twenty. Balsam Ridge was coming up fast. Cobra would have dived across the finish line if not for Marnie on his back.

He pushed through the tape to the cheers of the crowd.

He didn't know for sure they'd won until he saw the expression on Brodie's face.

Cobra dropped to his knees, Marnie still on his shoulders.

"Let her go," Brodie said with laughter.

"Let me go," Marnie echoed, sounding annoyed.

It took Cobra a minute to get his cramped hands to release her, and he hoped he hadn't hung on too tight.

"Are you okay?" he asked as she slithered to the grass beside him.

"Who the hell came up with *that*?" she demanded.

Brodie laughed again. At the same time, Raven dropped to her knees to give Marnie a hug.

"That was some race," Raven said.

"Balsam Ridge came second," Marnie said, looking around at the competitors.

Cobra sobered, knowing they'd won the race but lost the plaque.

"Mia and Silas took third," Raven said with a grin.

Brodie nodded confirmation, and Cobra laughed through his heavy breathing. They'd taken the championship by one point.

"Where's Mia?" Marnie asked, coming to her feet and looking around.

Brodie offered his hand to Cobra.

Cobra took it and pulled himself upright, stretching out his cramping muscles.

"Walk it off," Brodie advised.

"Yeah," Cobra agreed, taking a few steps to get the blood flowing. "I thought it was going to be easier than that."

"You left most of the pack in the dust. It was just you and Greenwell." Brodie paused. "Track star, apparently."

"He's good." Cobra looked around and spotted the competitor.

He made his way over then shook the man's hand. "Nice race."

"You too." Greenwell grinned. "Thought I had you there at the end."

"Another thirty yards and maybe," Cobra agreed.

"Get you next year," he said.

"You're on," Cobra answered, though remembered he wouldn't have Marnie to carry next year.

Chances were very slim, but maybe she'd come back for it. They were already planning more matchmaking events. Maybe one of them could sync up with next year's Klondike Challenge and they could do it all over again. He shook his head, wondering why he was even thinking so far in the future.

He took a step forward, stretching his cramped muscles, deciding he'd have to train if he wanted to do next year's race. He didn't want to go into it cold again.

A firm hand clamped down on his shoulder. "You're the man," Silas said on a laugh.

"You're the one who got us over the top," Cobra said back. He let out a breath. "Wow, that was tough."

"Hell yeah," Silas said. "I can't believe you stayed ahead of that guy."

"I almost didn't."

"Well, we won the plaque."

Cobra grinned at that, even as he looked around for Marnie, wondering where she'd gone. "The women take off?" he asked Silas.

"Probably off to open some wine."

"I could sure use a beer."

"Bar'll be open for the presentation," Silas said.

Cobra would have rather gone in search of Marnie, but he walked with Silas to the main gazebo where the Paradise team would be presented with the championship plaque.

They bought themselves cold beers and accepted congratulations from the other towns, chatting with people they knew, everyone relaxing now that the competition was over. There would be a party tonight, and tomorrow, teams would pack up and move their gear back to the hometowns to hunker down for the first big snow of the winter.

Hating the thought of hunkering down alone, Cobra looked around for Marnie again. He spotted her talking with Mia, and he headed that way.

"Tell them to come up and sign off," Silas called out behind him.

Cobra gave a wave to show that he'd heard.

"You didn't find the wine yet?" he joked as he approached the two women.

Marnie frowned. "I'm not exactly talking to you right now."

He knew she was joking. At least he thought she was joking.

"We should go sign off," he said to Mia.

"That'll be fun," Mia said with a grin.

"What's that?" Marnie asked.

"Accepting our prize. The plaque—which will hang in the Bear and Bar for the year—and a check for the charity of our choice."

"The Paradise Volunteer Firefighters Association," Cobra said in case Mia didn't already know. "It'll put us over the top for a new pumper truck."

"You're a firefighter?" Mia asked.

"We all are." Cobra cast a worried glance Marnie's way, afraid she might have been serious about not talking to him. "Shall we go sign?"

She didn't answer, but she did nod, and he took that as encouraging.

The three of them stepped up in the gazebo. Silas was already there signing. Mia lined up behind him then signed her name and handed the pen to Marnie.

Marnie stared at the sheet for a long minute.

Cobra assumed she was being a lawyer and reading it. It was boilerplate. They used the same one every year, but he didn't interrupt her.

She tapped the pen on the paper as a line grew behind him.

He finally bent close. "What?"

"I can't sign this," she said.

"You have to sign it." What was she even talking about?

"They want my address."

"Put down Mia's, Mile 5, Airport Road."

She pressed her lips together. "I don't live there."

"You do right now. Come on, Mia will back you." He glanced over his shoulder as more team members crowded in behind them.

"It's a lie," she said, making way too much of a technicality.

"At worst, it's an exaggeration," he said. "There's no time limit on how short or long you've lived there. Just sign it."

"If I don't?"

He couldn't believe she was seriously considering that. "Then we don't get the plaque. And we don't get the check."

She took a beat. "Or the new pumper truck."

"Exactly."

"Fine," she said, wrote down the address, signed her name and handed Cobra the pen.

By the time he finished, she'd disappeared into the crowd, leaving him wondering what all that had been about.

THE WINDUP CELEBRATION WAS UNDER WAY WITH MUsic blaring from the central gazebo into the Paradise team camp, coming easily through the canvas tent walls.

Marnie heard footsteps outside, and her stomach clamped with anxiety. She'd known Cobra would come looking for her, but she'd hoped it would take a little longer. She felt sick thinking about what she needed to say and do.

She wished she didn't have to face him and say goodbye, wished right now that she'd stayed away from him altogether. But she'd walked into this thing with her eyes wide open, stayed in it with her eyes wide open too. She had no one to blame but herself.

"There you are," Cobra said, sounding happy to have found her as the tent door yawned open. "They're firing up the grill if you're hungry."

His gaze moved to her open suitcase on the bed and stopped.

"I'm not hungry," she managed. The very last thing she felt was hungry.

"Why are you packing?" He moved closer, his brows knitting together.

"Silas has a WSA flight in the morning," she said breezily, pretending it was only a matter of practicality. "He's heading back to Paradise tonight, and I'm hitching a ride." She turned back to her bed, pretending he'd simply accept her explanation.

He sounded cautious now, confused. "Why would you leave early?"

She refolded a pair of yoga pants and a T-shirt and took her time placing them in the suitcase to keep from meeting his eyes. "I was always planning to leave after the competition."

"The competition isn't over."

"The events are done. You're taking home the plaque. That's what counts." She couldn't keep the bitterness from her voice as she took her toiletries bag from the bedside table and tucked it into the end of the suitcase.

He moved closer still. "What's going on here?"

"Nothing," she said with forced cheer, trying to hold it together.

"Marnie." His voice was strained.

"My trip always had an end to it, and this is it."

He paused for a minute. "Is this about the Partner Packing race?"

"No." It was, but that was only part of it.

"It was all in good fun," he said cajolingly.

"I know." The last thing she wanted to do was start an argument about the race.

"You thought it was tacky." He didn't phrase it as a question, so she didn't answer.

She looked around the room, making sure she hadn't missed anything.

Annoyance crept into his tone. "Is *that* what you think of me?"

She was genuinely confused by that. "That you're right?"

"That I'm tacky?"

"No."

"Classless?"

"No!" The denial leapt from her lips.

"Then *what*? Why are you doing this?"

She saw bewilderment in his eyes and fought a sudden wave of heartache. "It's not you."

"Yeah, right." His tone was bitter.

"I have a life. I need to get back to it." It was true.

"So, go tomorrow, or the next day, or the day after that. Don't leave like this."

"The longer I put it off—"

"What?" He sounded exasperated now. "The more fun we'll have together?"

"No." She held his gaze. "That's not—"

He reached for her hands, but she pulled away.

"What?" he repeated. "Tell me."

"You're a great guy, Cobra."

He gripped the back of his neck. "Well, that tells me nothing."

"You're smart. You're strong. But you're also bold and completely overwhelming."

He shook his head in denial.

"You push me into things," she said.

"This *is* about the race."

"It's not."

"You're lying. Why are you lying to me?"

"Okay." She owned up. "It is about the race. But it's not only about the race. I told you I didn't want to do it."

"And then you changed your mind. Was it that bad? Was it really that bad?"

"You know it wasn't." It was the principle that upset her, not the race itself.

"All I know is that you're packing your bag, and I feel like I'm never going to see you again."

Marnie's stomach wrapped itself in a knot. "I can't live like this," she said, trying to put her anxiety into words.

He looked around the tent. "You mean one more night here?"

"I mean *you*," she blurted out, giving up on trying to tiptoe around.

He went dead still, his eyes hardening.

"You're a great guy."

"So you said."

"Because you are."

"Just not a lawyer or a doctor or an engineer."

"You know it's not that."

"Do I?"

She was angry now, angry that he could think that about her. "Yes. Yes, you do. I've worked for years to chart my own path, to shake it all off and be my own person. But along you come, all bold and swaggering, and I let myself—" She snapped her mouth shut. This was exactly what she'd hoped to avoid.

"Let yourself what?" he asked coolly.

"I can't stand up to you." It was partly him, but it was mostly her.

Trouble was, she didn't want to fight him. She wanted to please him. Even now, she wanted to throw herself into his arms and do as he asked, stay here a few more days.

"You don't have to stand up to me," he said.

"I want to leave," she said bluntly before she could do something stupid.

"And I want you to stay."

"You see?"

He looked baffled.

"Do you *see*?" she repeated. "That's exactly what I'm talking about."

She couldn't let herself be swayed, no matter how desperately she wanted to spend another night or two or ten in his arms. If she didn't stand her ground now, she'd be lost.

"You're not making sense."

"You're *trying* to push me into *staying*," she practically shouted.

"I'm—" He snapped his jaw shut.

"You're a great guy, Cobra."

"*Stop* saying that."

"But you're—"

"I get it," he drawled, his tone dripping with sarcasm. "Just not the guy for you."

She'd wounded him, and guilt cut her like a knife. She wanted so badly to tell him that wasn't true, but it was better this way. If he thought she was a snob, he'd despise her and stay away. She needed him to stay away.

Mia called from outside the tent. "Marnie?"

"I'm on my way." Marnie broke away and turned to zip her suitcase.

"Don't," Cobra said, a crack in his voice.

She swallowed her heartache. "I have to."

"We're battling daylight," Mia called out.

Marnie hoisted her suitcase from the bed.

Cobra grasped her hand. He shifted so he was looking her straight in the eyes. "Not like this."

"I'm sorry."

He closed his eyes and clamped his jaw. Then he whisked the suitcase from her hand and pivoted to walk out the door.

She followed in time to see Mia take in Cobra's expression.

Mia's eyes widened, but she didn't say a word, just led the way to the pickup truck that would ferry them to the airstrip.

Marnie couldn't bring herself to look at Cobra as he dropped her suitcase in the box of the truck. She kept her gaze down and focused on climbing into the back seat of the crew cab. When she finally looked up, he was gone.

Mia opened the other back door and stepped inside, her eyes full of sympathy. "You okay?"

Marnie shook her head, not trusting herself to speak.

"Did you fight?" Mia asked.

Marnie nodded to that.

"The Partner Packing contest?"

Marnie drew a shaky breath. "That and other things."

When Mia spoke a moment later, her voice was gentle. "What other things?"

"Him. Me. Signing that stupid form."

"Form?"

Marnie bent to cover her face with her hands. "The disclaimer. I put your address down as mine."

It took Mia a moment to respond. "So?"

Marnie straightened again, whisking her hair back from her forehead. "So, I'm a lawyer, and that was a false declaration."

Mia looked behind them. "You want me to go . . ."

Marnie shook her head. "It's done."

"And . . . Cobra made you do it?"

"I let him convince me to do it. I let him push me into doing something I shouldn't have done in the first place. And I'm through with . . ."

Mia waited again. "Through with . . . ?"

Marnie tried to frame the right words. "He's so . . . He swallows me up."

"And you don't want that." Mia nodded, reaching for Marnie's hand, squeezing it in sympathy and understanding.

"The problem is . . ." Marnie admitted it out loud. "I *do* want it."

Silas vaulted into the front passenger seat, slamming the door while one of the event volunteers got in and took the wheel.

"All good back there?" Silas asked over his shoulder.

Mia blinked at Marnie in silence.

"We're good," Marnie forced out as bravely as she could, promising herself she'd feel better soon. She'd made the strong choice, and it was the right choice, and she'd made it before it was too late.

COBRA THREW HIMSELF INTO WORK. LUCKILY, THERE was plenty to do to close off the season, and he exhausted himself with long hours in the hangar, falling into unconsciousness as soon as his head hit the pillow. It was the only thing that kept him sane.

He missed Marnie every second. He avoided Mia and Raven because they reminded him of her. Plus, he was afraid he'd crack and ask them about her, how she was doing back in LA. He wanted to stay angry at her, but he couldn't even manage that.

He'd thought a lot about the Partner Packing contest. He wouldn't have chosen to enter the event, but the town had needed the points. They'd needed him to step up. And he'd do it again. At least, he thought he'd do it again. Cold truth was, he might hesitate if he'd known for sure it would lose him Marnie.

But as he rolled it over in his mind, he couldn't help thinking he was missing something. Sure, she hadn't wanted to race. But the Marnie he knew was tough, a team player. He'd watched her do something she hated to support her estranged family who didn't even deserve it.

No, it went beyond the race. It had to. But maybe he didn't want to know what it was. At the end of it all, she'd decided to leave him. It was her right to do that, and he'd just have to live with it.

He'd taken to avoiding Silas on top of everything else, afraid an I-told-you-so from the guy would set him off. Plus, Silas's happy relationship with Mia twisted a knife into Cobra's gut.

Sweaty and exhausted, Cobra paced through the little flakes of snow falling from a bitterly cold sky to the wooden sidewalk. He was too late to get a hot meal at the WSA cafeteria, so he made his way into the Bear and Bar instead and hoisted himself up on a barstool. He nodded a greeting to Badger, avoiding looking at the Klondike Challenge plaque displayed prominently on the wall.

"Beer?" Badger asked him, walking over.

"Whiskey. Double."

"You got it." Badger fished out a clean glass. "Just getting home?"

"Long day," Cobra said, though the last thing he wanted was chitchat.

"Looks like we'll get a few inches tonight."

"That time of year."

Badger set the double shot of whiskey down in front of Cobra.

Cobra downed it in one swallow.

"You want me to ask?" Badger asked.

"Nope." Cobra pushed the glass forward and pointed to it.

Badger poured him another one. "I've got a theory."

Cobra stiffened. "I don't want to hear it."

Badger hesitated, seeming to debate whether to push Cobra.

"I wouldn't," Cobra said darkly.

"Good enough. Super Bear Burger and fries?"

"Yeah."

"Coming up." Badger headed for the kitchen.

A shadow came up beside Cobra as someone took the stool next to him.

He turned his head to tell them to back off.

It was Silas.

"I don't scare as easily as Badger," he said.

"You should." Cobra took a swallow of the second whiskey.

"Mia is worried about you."

"Mia doesn't need to worry about me."

"That's what I told her." Silas set his beer mug on the bar.

"Good."

"Thing is, she doesn't much listen to me."

"I'm fine." The first shot of whiskey was hitting Cobra's system, and he felt better than he had five minutes ago. That wasn't saying much, but it was something.

"I know how you—"

"An I-told-you-so is going to get you thrown into a snowbank," Cobra warned.

"This isn't that." Silas shook his head.

"Pity?" Cobra challenged. "That's even worse."

"Empathy. I've been there."

"It's not the same thing."

Silas waved to Badger and pointed to Cobra's glass. "Whatever he's having."

"Burger too?" Badger asked.

"Sure."

"You're *with* Mia." Cobra hammered home his point.

"I wasn't always with her."

"But you always had a chance with her."

"I—"

Cobra held out his hands as evidence. He'd washed them at the hangar, but grease still lingered under his fingernails. "Look at me. Look at me and picture Marnie."

Silas fell silent.

"Yeah," Cobra said. "Ain't never gonna happen."

"Marnie's not a snob."

"Deep down, every outsider's a snob."

"That's cynical," Silas said.

"She told me I wasn't the guy for her. And she was adamant about that. How else was I supposed to take that?"

"She said that—those exact words?"

Cobra thought back. "Maybe. Or maybe I said them. But she didn't deny it, and she left. She made it clear I was not what she wanted in life."

Silas went silent, drumming his fingertips on the bar. "I don't think the issue's your job."

Cobra twisted his body and drew back, sarcasm dripping from his voice. "You don't? *Really?*" Like Silas knew anything about it.

Badger poured a whiskey for Silas.

Cobra still had a bit left and decided to pace himself. Nothing about his current mood was going to be helped by a hangover.

"Did she say anything to you about the form?" Silas asked, rocking his glass back and forth in contemplation.

Cobra frowned in confusion, his anger still simmering. "What form?"

"The Klondike Challenge disclaimer."

"Are we still talking about Marnie?" Cobra wondered if Silas had decided to change topics.

"Yes, Marnie. Did she say anything to you about signing the disclaimer form?"

Cobra thought back. "She didn't want to use Mia's address."

"And?"

Cobra shrugged. "And she did anyway."

"And?" Silas persisted.

"And that was it. She signed and left." He finished his drink, thinking back to their exchange. The next time he'd seen her, she was packing.

"She told Mia she shouldn't have signed it."

"Why the hell not?"

"Because she doesn't really live in Paradise."

"Who cares? Nobody cares."

"Marnie cared."

Her words echoed in Cobra's brain. *You push me into things.* "I thought she meant the race."

"I don't know what she meant. All I'm sayin' is the form was a thing."

Cobra stretched out his hands, palms up, taking in the calluses, rough skin, sinewy muscle and grease stains. He almost couldn't believe she'd let him touch her with them.

"It's all a thing," he said quietly. "And it's a done thing."

Silas clapped him on the shoulder. "I'm really sorry it went this way."

"Wasn't like you didn't warn me." Cobra was only now realizing why Silas had spoken up. "I shouldn't have been such a jerk about it."

Silas gave a mocking grin. "You can't know until you know."

"And I thought it was bad with Shelby."

"The girl from high school?"

"That was nothing." Cobra would have laughed at himself if he didn't feel so much like shit.

"Don't leave and join the air force," Silas joked.

"I won't." Cobra didn't know what he was going to do. He had absolutely no idea.

Chapter Eighteen

MARNIE WAS DETERMINED TO SHAKE OFF THE INTERlude in Alaska and get back to her regular life. She met with Henry and Hannah and discussed plans for modernizing Lafayette Fashion by switching to new suppliers and expanding into teen apparel. Hannah came up with some terrific ideas for engaging influencers.

Marnie was also still working with Scarlett and Willow as they put together their film project. Hannah had stepped up on that too, reaching out to some Hollywood contacts and pulling together an impressive guest list for a Halloween party. The plan was for Scarlett to mix and mingle with members of the entertainment industry to see if she could find a director.

Henry had started dating Olivia Axler, an odd combination since Henry was uptight and completely by-the-book, while Olivia struck Marnie as somewhat free-thinking and spontaneous. But they seemed to be having fun together, and Olivia was a huge supporter of Scarlett and Willow, so everyone was throwing themselves into party planning.

Marnie's boss, Gretchen Miller, was enthusiastic about the firm moving into entertainment law. She'd given Marnie all the support and flexibility she needed to pursue new clients. The Lafayette party was shaping up to be a great opportunity for Marnie to network as well.

There was plenty going on, and it was all good. But she couldn't get Cobra off her mind. She dwelled on him during the day then dreamed about him at night, waking up sweaty and frustrated. In weak moments, she wondered if she should have stayed a few days and made love with him until she got it out of her system.

The workday was over. It was coming up on seven o'clock, and Gretchen, Emilia Marsh, and Bexley had already left the office. Marnie dreaded going home to her apartment, letting her guard down and having Cobra crowd her mind.

Knowing she couldn't put it off forever, she logged out of her computer, locked her file cabinet and gathered her purse. Then she stepped into a pair of flats for the twenty-minute walk to her apartment. The sunny day had been unseasonably warm, and the concrete and asphalt would hold its heat for hours. So she also shrugged out of her black blazer and folded it into her shoulder bag along with her high-heeled pumps.

Her sleeveless white blouse would be cool in the evening air. She raked her hair into a high ponytail to keep it off her neck. Then she locked the office door behind her and took the elevator to the lobby, pushing her way through the revolving door onto bustling Empire Street.

The signal light at the corner was green, the white walk sign still on. She pivoted quickly, wondering if she'd make it before it changed. A man sitting on the sidewalk bench caught the corner of her eye. He was staring intently her way, and she reflexively braced herself, not breaking her stride.

"Marnie?" the man said.

She did a double-take, sucking in a breath in surprise and stopping in her tracks. "Ethan?"

Her bother rose from the bench. "I'll understand if you don't want to see me."

"What are you doing here?" Her knee-jerk reaction was concern. He shouldn't be out of Kansas. He was breaking parole.

"I got permission to come and see you."

"From the parole board?"

He stepped closer. "Yes."

Her suspicions rose. "What did you tell them?"

"Only that I wanted to visit my sister."

"And they believed you?"

He shrugged. "It was the truth."

They both fell silent, as she eyed him up. He looked good, really healthy, clean shaven with a tidy haircut. He was dressed in a blue striped shirt with the sleeves rolled up and a pair of black jeans with brown hikers. The outfit looked crisp and new. She supposed all his clothes must look like that right now.

"What do you want?" she asked, still wary.

"To talk. Just to talk." He looked up the busy sidewalk, the sounds of engines, tires and car horns wafting around them. "You headed somewhere?"

"Home," she said. Then the late hour hit her. "How long have you been waiting?"

"Awhile." Uncertainty came over his expression. "I didn't want to accost you at the office or show up unannounced at your apartment, so I thought this way—"

"I could walk away," she guessed.

"I hope you won't."

"Why shouldn't I?"

He paused before speaking. "You came to the parole hearing. I took that as a good sign."

"I came to the parole hearing to end this once and for all."

"End what? Being a part of the family?"

"Yes."

He gave a sad smile. "You know it doesn't work that way."

"It can."

He nodded in the direction she'd been headed. "Can I walk with you?"

She wanted to say no, but he'd come a long way. And at least he was alone. If her father had been with him, she would have frozen them out already.

"Fine." She turned for the crosswalk, and he fell into step beside her.

They walked to the corner. The traffic signal changed in front of them, and they crossed with the rest of the crowd. Then they turned north on Empire, walking past ground-floor shops and restaurants with office buildings towering above.

"You like it here?" he asked as they cleared the next cross street.

"I do."

He gazed around. "It's sure big and noisy."

"I don't mind the noise. I like the energy."

"Hmm."

"You don't like it?"

He coughed out a little laugh. "I like being out of prison."

"I guess anywhere is better than a cell." She hadn't thought much about Ethan's life inside. Her focus had been on their father and his betrayal and her anger with him.

"I'm pretty sure I've eaten at least a dozen takeout burgers in the past week."

"You're going to have to expand your palate."

"For some reason, that was the thing I craved inside. I've become a fan of sweet potato fries."

Marnie had an appreciation for sweet potato fries— although she had to eat them in moderation. "You'll need to get plenty of exercise to counteract those fries." She looked him up and down then, noting again that he seemed incredibly fit.

"I'll join a gym as soon as I get settled."

"Are you taller than I remember?"

"Maybe an inch. I'm definitely heavier." His expression sobered. "Not much to do in prison besides work out. I hung with the boxing crowd. Being strong and fit keeps you safe in there."

Marnie didn't want to know about his life in prison. She particularly didn't want to feel sorry for what was his own fault. But she couldn't seem to stop herself from asking. "Was it bad?"

He gave another shrug of his broad shoulders. "It wasn't good. I think it was harder on Dad and Uncle Stuart. It's no place for old men."

Marnie remembered how haggard her father had looked. But he, of all people, had himself to blame. "He's out now," she said because it seemed like Ethan was expecting a response.

"I hated him for a really long time," Ethan said quietly.

Marnie didn't know how to respond to that, so she waited.

"For what he'd done to me, to Mom, to you."

"You knew what was going on." Marnie had been in the dark.

"Eventually, I knew."

"And you hid everything from me." They turned the corner onto Boxler Street.

"That got harder and harder," Ethan said.

Thinking back, she'd admit she'd been naïve. The repair business hadn't made sense—cars trailered in then parked behind the solid fence of the yard. She'd never paid attention to which ones went in and out of the shop. But there'd been a steady stream of out-of-state license plates.

"I should have asked questions," she said.

"By the time you were old enough to ask anything, you had your head down studying."

Again, she wondered about Ethan's experience. Back

then he'd seemed so much older than her, so much more capable and worldly-wise. But he'd been a kid.

"When did you find out?" Marnie pointed to a walkway that led to the twelve-story concrete and glass building where she lived.

"Right after Mom died. You remember the day I got my driver's license?"

Marnie shook her head. There'd been nothing notable about that day for her. She would have been twelve, maybe thirteen at the time, still lost in grief.

"You and I drove all the way to Garden City."

She searched her brain, coming up with a distant memory. "I do remember. There was that little café with the bear statue." She unlocked the lobby door, pushing it open.

Ethan held the door above her and followed her inside.

"That's the one."

Marnie also remembered miles and miles of highway. "Where were we going?"

"Denver."

She pressed the elevator button. "Why were we going to Denver? Wait, Dad was there too."

Her father hadn't eaten lunch with them, but she remembered him being in the parking lot, arguing with Ethan. And then an image all but blew up in her mind. "He *hit* you."

Ethan nodded, and Marnie stood staring at her brother while the elevator doors opened. Then they closed again.

"Why did he hit you?" she asked, her throat dry.

"I was taking you away." Ethan gave a chopped, self-conscious chuckle. "I thought we could make it out of the state before he caught us and—I don't know—that I could get a job or something. It was absurd."

Marnie's chest went hard, like it had filled with concrete. "Why did you do that?"

Ethan's expression hardened. "Because I found out what they were doing. And with Mom gone, Tumbleweed Fuel and Service was no place for you."

* * *

COBRA STARED AT SECTION 2.12.7 OF THE LEGAL CODE of conduct document he'd tracked down online. He rose from the desk chair in his room and swore under his breath, his fingertips turning white where he gripped the tablet. After his conversation with Silas, he'd worried he'd made a mistake. Now, he knew for sure, and it was much worse than he'd feared.

Dropping the tablet on his bed, he headed out the door, not even bothering with a jacket in the falling snow as he paced over to Brodie's unit. He banged on the door before opening it up.

The room was dark and empty.

Amped up on adrenaline, Cobra marched down the sidewalk to the Bear and Bar and found Brodie at a table with T-Two.

"What's up?" Brodie asked, taking in Cobra's expression.

"Got a minute?" Cobra asked, sliding his eyes meaningfully to T-Two.

"Want me to get out of the way?" T-Two asked. His beer was still half full, and he hadn't yet finished a grilled turkey sandwich.

"No," Brodie said. Then he looked at Cobra. "Is this private?"

Cobra preferred to keep it private, but not enough to argue the point. "Okay if I take the Cessna tomorrow?"

"Sure," Brodie answered, popping a fry into his mouth. "Where are you going?"

"Balsam Ridge."

"You forget something down there?"

"No." Cobra shook his head. "Maybe Vantage Crossing too. Depends."

Brodie looked puzzled. He motioned to an empty chair. "Depends on what?"

Cobra plopped down. "On where I have to go to track down all the Klondike Challenge board members."

"Clive is in Vantage Crossing," Brodie said. "Rebecca's over in Greenville but I think Bruce Carter was going to Anchorage for a couple of weeks."

Cobra nodded. It was going to take him a while, but he'd get it done. He'd do whatever it took to get it done.

"You want a drink?" Brodie asked, motioning to Badger.

"Yes." It wasn't like Cobra could fly anywhere tonight. He called out to Badger. "Beer's fine."

Badger nodded.

"What do you need with the board?" Brodie asked.

"I made a mistake." Cobra glanced T-Two's way again, not anxious to have the whole town hear about what he'd done.

T-Two held up a palm. "I'll get out of your way."

Brodie's brow furrowed, his gaze turning accusingly to Cobra. "We were talking shop before you got here."

"It's fine," Cobra said to T-Two. "Stay."

Brodie was right. Cobra was the one barging in, and he was the one asking a favor.

Badger dropped off Cobra's beer.

"Marnie signed the disclaimer for the Klondike Challenge," Cobra said as Badger walked back to the bar.

T-Two looked confused.

"And?" Brodie asked.

"And I was the one who backed her into a corner and forced her to sign. She's a lawyer, and it's against their code of conduct."

"To sign a disclaimer?" Brodie asked.

"To sign a false statement."

"We won fair and square," T-Two pointed out.

"She used Mia's address."

Brodie still looked confused. "That's where she was staying."

"Temporarily. It was a thing. I could tell it was a thing when we were signing, but I pushed her into it anyway."

"Nobody cares," T-Two said.

"I *know*," Cobra responded.

"So, why would you fly all over Hell's half acre looking for board members?"

"I want them to say it was approved . . . in writing . . . in case it ever comes back on Marnie."

Brodie and T-Two shared a look. The look said that Cobra had lost his mind.

After a contemplative french fry, T-Two was the first to speak. "You think somebody, somewhere, sometime in Marnie's future is going to track down the Klondike Challenge prize disclaimer and accuse her of legal misconduct?"

Brodie smirked. "Have you *seen* the board's filing system?"

"That's not the point," Cobra said.

"Point or not, I'm not sure it's worth burning the aviation fuel."

"I'll pay for the fuel."

"Damn straight you will," Brodie said.

"What if they take away the plaque?" T-Two asked.

"They're not going to take away the plaque," Cobra said. "Nobody cares how long she lived here."

"Our point," Brodie said with finality. "I just saved you a buttload of money."

"The point is, she's worried about it," Cobra said, taking a drink of his beer.

"There's no basis for her to worry," T-Two noted.

"She doesn't know that. She's worried because of the nature of her job and just plain principle."

"So, you feel compelled to put her mind at ease?" Brodie asked.

"I got her into it in the first place." Cobra couldn't understand why they were giving him so much grief. He was the guy paying for the fuel. What did they care how he spent his money?

"And after you solve this imaginary problem," Brodie said, "you'll . . . what?"

"Tell her." It was patently obvious what to do next.

"Text her?" Brodie asked leadingly. "Phone her? Send her an email?"

Cobra wanted to deliver the letter to her in person. He wanted to see the look of relief on her face. He wanted to see her face under any circumstances, and this gave him an excuse to do that.

"He wants to be the hero," T-Two said.

"Snow's steady now," Cobra said. He had the airplane maintenance well in hand, so it was the perfect time to take days off.

"What do you expect to happen?" Brodie asked.

"Why is this an interrogation?" Cobra returned.

"Because you want my plane."

"You don't want me to use your plane, fine." Cobra guzzled down the beer.

"Did I say that?" Brodie asked.

"We're messin' with you," T-Two said.

"You should ask yourself why you're letting us get to you," Brodie said easily.

"You know why," Cobra said, glaring Brodie's way.

Brodie's expression went dead serious. "All the more reason to stay in Alaska."

"Are you serious about her?" T-Two asked.

"No," Cobra answered. "I don't know. I like her, sure. She's great . . . make that fantastic. But she's her, and I'm me." He knew reality. He just didn't like it. And this might be the last chance he got to see Marnie, to apologize to her and end their relationship on an even keel before he settled into the rest of his life without her.

"I knew this whole matchmaking thing was a bad idea," Brodie said.

"It was a terrible idea," Cobra agreed.

"Well, I had fun," T-Two said.

Brodie looked as incredulous as Cobra felt, swinging their gazes T-Two's way.

MARNIE COULDN'T HAVE IMAGINED EVEN TOLERATING her brother's company, never mind enjoying it. He'd slept on her pullout sofa, and after a busy day at work, she'd come home to him waiting with a large takeout pizza and a six-pack of beer.

"There's something wrong with you city people," he called out to her as she changed from her work clothes to a pair of yoga pants and an oversize T-shirt.

"What's wrong with us?" she called back through the door.

"They put chicken, eggplant, sun-dried tomatoes, avocado and goat cheese on this pizza."

She emerged from the bedroom with a grin. "I'm so glad you're expanding your palate."

"They looked down their noses when I asked for salami and pepperoni."

"You stopped at the Obverse Gourmet?"

"I didn't know it would be so bougie. There was a picture of a pizza in their window."

"They make terrific pizza."

"I bought some weird beer too," he said, sounding doubtful. "The pizza place recommended it."

"You didn't have to buy me dinner." Marnie knew Ethan couldn't have much money to his name.

"It's the least I can do," he said, opening the pizza box in the middle of her compact dining table.

The living room of her apartment opened onto the balcony with a distant view of the ocean. She was lucky enough to have a corner unit, so there was a window in the kitchen too, and one above the dining table in between. The view wasn't great, just the apartment building across the street, but a row of palm trees dressed it up a little.

Ethan opened two bottles of beer while Marnie set two plates on the table.

She sat down, and they each served themselves a slice of the fragrant pizza.

Ethan took a bite.

"Well?" she asked him after a moment.

He swallowed, dubiously eyeing the rest of the slice. "Better than prison food."

"Maybe don't post a review," she said on a laugh before biting into her own pizza.

"It's good," he admitted. "Better than I expected. The sun-dried tomatoes are chewy."

"But flavorful," she countered.

He nodded. "Do you eat like this all the time?"

"Not pizza very often, but it's easy to pick things up from the deli and the bakery." Marnie didn't do a whole lot of cooking for one.

"Are you happy here?" he asked with a glance around the place as they continued eating.

"In this apartment or in LA?"

"Both, either." He set down his pizza and sobered. "You know, I was *so* glad when you left for college, so relieved that you were finally getting away."

"I worked hard for that scholarship."

A bleakness came into his eyes. "I know you did. I wish I'd left too."

"Why didn't you leave?" She'd never wondered that before, but she did now. It hadn't sounded like he'd been in favor of fencing stolen cars.

He gave a cold chuckle. "After we ran that one time . . . well, let's just say I didn't want to risk it again."

A cold chill came over her, her voice dropping to a whisper. "He beat you."

Ethan nodded. "Said if I ever tried again, it'd get worse."

"Ethan, I'm so—"

"Not your fault. Don't you ever think it was." He took a

drink. "I knew their secret, so I was a threat. As time went on, I got sucked deeper and deeper into the operation." He smiled then, running his fingertip around the beer label. "But you, you were so smart, and you worked hard. You deserved everything you got."

Marnie had always been out of step with her family. But Ethan had seemed to fit in. Even when the truth had come out in court, he hadn't complained, never protested that he'd been unwilling. He might have been able to reduce his sentence if he claimed he'd been coerced by their father.

Ethan squared his shoulders. "I'm inspired by you. And I'm done with him."

"What now?" she asked, impressed.

He shrugged. "I haven't figured that out yet. It's tough to get a job with a criminal record, and I don't have a mechanic's license or anything."

"Could you get one?" she asked.

"First thing I need to do is earn some money."

That made sense. He couldn't go to trade school without a way to support himself. She wondered if she should offer him a place to stay, or maybe some cash to get started.

"Oh, no you don't," he said with conviction, correctly reading her expression. "This is my problem, and I'm going to solve it on my own."

"But—"

"I'm here for a couple of days, and then I'm going back to Kansas."

"Not to Merganser." Staying with their father seemed like a terrible idea.

"Not to Merganser," he agreed. "The parole thing is easier if I stay in the state. Wichita doesn't appeal to me," he joked.

"Maybe Topeka?" she suggested. "Or Salina? There must be jobs you could get there."

"I'll find something." He took another drink.

"Do you need—"

"No," he said flatly. "I didn't come here to sponge off you."

"I can loan you—"

"No. And don't say it again."

She looked at the serious expression in his eyes and realized it was important for him to do it on his own. "Okay."

He helped himself to another slice of pizza. "You can give me some advice, though."

"Sure. Legal stuff?"

He shook his head. "Not that. I've been thinking about this, thinking about it a lot, especially over the past year when I knew I might get out. There was this psychologist I had to meet with in prison—it was a mandatory thing, and I hated it."

"You saw a psychologist?"

"There was some do-gooder organization that pressured the governor, and we ended up with this woman, Dr. Sackett, trying to make guys open up and share their feelings."

Marnie couldn't help smiling at the image. She had sympathy for Dr. Sackett.

"I wasn't going to blubber on about anything. But after a while, some of what she said made sense."

Marnie was fascinated now, wondering if an epiphany had brought Ethan to see her.

"I know I can deal with the physical stuff," he said. "I can find a job, get a place to live, feed myself in a new city." He met Marnie's gaze. "But what about the rest?"

"The rest?" What Ethan had just outlined sounded like a great starting plan to her.

"How do I let go of the way we were raised, our values, our world view, the core of our psyche?"

"Is that Dr. Sackett talking?" Marnie joked.

Ethan stayed serious, and she felt bad for making light of what he was saying.

"I don't want to think like him," he said. "I don't want to react like him. I want to leave everything about Merganser and Tumbleweed in the dust."

"That's a lot to take on."

"You did it."

Marnie had tried. But now she thought back to the barbecue in Paradise, where she'd fit so comfortably into the event, how easily she'd taken to the shooting and the ax throwing, how she'd been attracted to Cobra of all men, so immediately and completely. He'd fit in fine in Kansas—the antithesis of the sensitive and urbane men she'd dated here in LA.

"I don't know that I have," she admitted, not wanting to mislead Ethan.

He looked around the apartment again, then he raised a slice of pizza. "Look at the class of this place, and you like goat cheese and eggplant now."

"I just took first place in a sharpshooting contest."

Ethan grinned. "Good for you."

"I entered ax throwing too. Does that sound like I left my past behind?"

"They have ax throwing in LA?"

She shook her head. "I was in Alaska."

Ethan drew back in obvious shock at that statement. "What were you doing in Alaska?"

"It was for work, and I have a friend up there."

"Ahh," Ethan said, as if something had just dawned on him.

"What, ahh?"

"Mountain man who came over to Wichita with you."

"He's from Alaska," she admitted, wishing Cobra hadn't come up.

"He's sure into you," Ethan said. "I could tell. We all could."

Marnie didn't answer, but her chest tightened, and her heart beat deep and solid. She took a swallow of her beer, hoping to cool her skin. It would be mortifying to blush in front of Ethan.

"Where is he now?" Ethan asked.

"In Alaska," she answered.

"Oh." Ethan looked puzzled. "I thought you two were a serious thing."

She swallowed, giving herself a moment. "Just temporary."

"Really?"

"Yes."

Ethan twisted his bottle back and forth on the table. "I learned a lot about men while I was inside. I learned to pay attention to their expressions and their body language." He paused. "That guy was ready to launch himself across the table and throttle Dad."

"He wouldn't do that."

"I know. But he wanted to. I'm surprised he's not still here."

"He's—" Marnie struggled to put it into words. "He's like Kansas. He's part of what I need to leave behind."

Ethan's gaze narrowed. "Wait. You think that guy's like *us*?"

She nodded.

"Marnie, that guy's nothing like us. Dad wanted to use you. I couldn't save you. Alaska would protect you or die trying."

Chapter Nineteen

COBRA STOOD AT THE DOOR OF MARNIE'S APARTMENT, bracing himself for his next move. He'd walked into her lobby behind a repairman and a couple who were obviously returning from a shopping trip. Nobody asked any questions as he rode the elevator upstairs. Then again, he was a whole lot neater and cleaner than usual, dressed in a crisp white shirt and a steel-gray blazer.

His goal wasn't to impress Marnie, only to put her mind at ease. It also didn't hurt not to stick out like a sore thumb. But if she thought he cleaned up nicely, well, he'd take that too. He had the signed letter from the board tucked into his inside pocket and a peace offering in his hand.

She might not appreciate the peace offering, but she was sure to be happy about the letter.

He took a breath and knocked.

There was the sound of footsteps inside, and he felt a wash of relief. At least she was home.

But a man opened the door.

Jealousy hit Cobra with the force of a twelve-gauge. Had

she forgotten him already and moved on? What the hell was this guy doing in her— And then he recognized Ethan. Marnie's brother was standing in front of him dressed like a pirate.

Cobra would have been flat-out furious at Ethan for tracking Marnie down after everything he and his father had put her through, but he was thrown by the pirate costume. "What are you doing here?"

"Hey, Alaska," Ethan said, clearly surprised to see Cobra, but not the least bit confrontational. "Marnie?" he called over his shoulder as he stepped back to let Cobra inside. "Someone's here for you."

Cobra entered the tasteful apartment, package in his hand, taken aback by the turn of events. The door swung shut behind him.

"Who—" Marnie stopped short in a doorway, her emerald eyes going wide. She was dressed as a ballerina in a pale pink bejeweled tutu and a pair of satin slippers.

Cobra looked from Marnie to Ethan and back again. "I'm going to guess Halloween party?"

"Cobra." Marnie seemed to recover. She looked gorgeous with her hair in a neat dancer's bun, her makeup bold and exaggerated. "What are you doing here?"

"I have—" He stopped himself, looking to Ethan, wondering why he was even there. "You left Kansas?"

"I've got permission." Ethan met his gaze. He showed no animosity but no defensiveness either.

Cobra looked back at Marnie. "And you're good with . . ." He canted his head Ethan's way.

"We've been reconnecting," Marnie said. Then her tone and gaze turned wary. "Why are you in LA?"

"I brought you something."

She glanced to the package in his hands.

He'd planned to lead with the joke, but now he was having second thoughts. She didn't seem to be in the mood for humor. And he sure hadn't expected an audience.

"Brandywine Specialty Cupcakes," Ethan said, reading the name on the box.

Marnie blinked then swallowed. "You brought me a cupcake?" Her tone was incredulous.

"Not only a cupcake." Cobra tried to salvage the situation.

"A very fancy cupcake," Ethan put in.

Cobra slanted him a glare, but Ethan only looked amused. Brave of him, considering how Cobra was starting to feel.

"It's not my birthday," Marnie said, the first hint of softness coming into her tone.

"I didn't want to wait for your birthday."

She moved hesitantly forward. "What kind of a cupcake?"

"Confetti vanilla with pink buttercream, silver sprinkles and a star on top. They custom design."

"You remembered," she said.

"Of course I remembered. Who could forget your crime spree?"

"Crime spree?" Ethan asked.

"I'll tell you about it sometime." Marnie gave her brother a playful grin.

"I take it the reunion is going well?" Cobra asked, thinking maybe he should tamp down his animosity toward Ethan.

"She's taking me to a Lafayette party," Ethan answered.

"That's tonight?" Cobra asked. Mia had mentioned Henry and Hannah were putting on a party, but he hadn't known it was for Halloween. He wouldn't have guessed rich people liked to dress up in silly costumes.

Not that Marnie looked silly. She looked more beautiful by the second, and he was fighting a powerful urge to reach out to her.

He cleared his throat. "My real reason for—"

"Can I see it?" Marnie asked, coming closer still and testing Cobra's resolve to keep his hands to himself.

He held the box out. "It's all yours."

She took the box then set it down on a small island counter. She took a knife from a drawer and sliced through the seal, opening the lid.

Ethan moved in to get a look.

Marnie smiled, and Cobra's heart skipped a beat. Her eyes lit with humor. "They got it pretty close."

"All I had to go on was your description."

"Are you going to share?" Ethan asked her.

Cobra scowled at him again, but it was good-natured this time. "Back off. It's her cupcake."

"I've been eating prison food for years," Ethan defended himself. "And that's a really big cupcake."

Marnie laughed. "I'll think about it."

Cobra removed the envelope from his pocket and handed it to Marnie.

She eyed it suspiciously. "You got me a card?"

"It's not a card."

Ethan took a step back, obviously sensing this was the real purpose for Cobra's visit.

Marnie watched Cobra's expression while she opened the envelope. Then she looked down as she unfolded the letter.

She read the first few lines then grasped the edge of the counter, reading further. She blinked hard and looked up. "This . . . ?"

"I didn't know," he said.

"And they all . . . just . . ."

"I asked them, and they did."

Ethan had to be burning with curiosity, but to his credit, he didn't ask.

"Thank you," Marnie said, holding the letter against her chest, a catch in her voice and relief in her eyes.

"I didn't know it was such a big deal."

"I tried to tell you."

"And I didn't listen. I know. I was too busy trying to push you into something you didn't want to do."

Ethan's posture stiffened and his expression tightened.

"You were right," Cobra said to Marnie. "You were right about everything." Then he turned to Ethan. "I got her to sign a paper, that's all."

Ethan's guard didn't go down right away.

"It's fine," Marnie said to Ethan.

"She stood up to me," Cobra continued, taking in her delicate ballerina costume, thinking how effectively it hid her strength. "She's smart, and she's tough, and she was right."

Silence fell over the room.

He hated to leave her, but there was no reason left to stay. He'd indulged in a version of this reunion that ended with Marnie in his arms forgiving him. But that obviously wasn't going to happen—especially not with Ethan standing there watching.

She was clearly grateful for the letter confirming the Klondike Challenge board unanimously accepted her two-week residency as being valid for the competition. It could never come back on her now, and Cobra was glad for that. But it obviously hadn't changed anything between them. He wasn't the kind of man she wanted—end of story.

Fighting hard against the dejection that was overwhelming him, he took a step backward for the door, striving hard to speak in a measured tone. "I'll let you two get—"

"Want to come to a party?" she asked him.

COBRA HAD BROUGHT BLUE JEANS AND A T-SHIRT IN his overnight bag, and they'd borrowed Marnie's neighbor's tool belt to make an instant construction worker costume. He looked sexier to her than ever across the great room in the Lafayette mansion.

The house was full of costumed partiers, spilling from the great room into the big front foyer and out the opposite corner into the conservatory. The conservatory was extensively and thematically decorated with glowing pumpkins, purple tree lights and waves of white gauze hanging beneath the glass panels of the ceiling.

The music was quieter there so that people could carry on conversations. Earlier, Marnie caught a glimpse of Scarlett in the conservatory. She was dressed as a mermaid, talking head-to-head with a fortysomething cowgirl. Marnie hoped the cowgirl was from the film industry.

"It looks like your Alaska trip was successful," Hannah joked, nodding Cobra's way. She was dressed in a very classy Halloween-themed dress—a black bodice with lace cap sleeves, tight at the waist, with a full, flowing skirt covered in bright orange pumpkins and cat silhouettes. She looked beautiful in subtle glitter makeup with an orange band holding back her thick brunette hair.

"He's just passing through," Marnie said, keeping her tone light.

"Well, he sure looks like he could conquer the wilderness."

"He's definitely got skills." Marnie had yet to find anything Cobra couldn't do.

"Marnie?" Scarlett appeared at her elbow in a shimmer of aqua and purple with a sparkly tiara on her head. The cowgirl was still with her.

"Hi." Marnie put on a friendly smile for them both.

"Natasha Burton, this is Marnie Anton, and Hannah Lafayette is our host."

"Nice to meet you both," Natasha said from under her white Stetson. Then she looked to Hannah. "It was generous of you to invite me."

"I'm happy you could come," Hannah said.

"Natasha directed *Off the River* last year," Scarlett told them.

"I saw the trailer for that," Marnie put in, recalling the title on her streaming service. The film had looked action-packed. "It's just been released, right?"

"To acclaim," Scarlett said. "Critics and viewers are loving it."

"Congratulations," Hannah said.

Marnie caught Cobra's gaze from across the room, and he gave her a smile. She couldn't help smiling back, her chest expanding with a mash-up of emotions. Attraction, sure. And gratitude too. She was grateful to get the letter from the board. But she was also anxious—worried that seeing him again would mess with her resolve.

She should have let him leave right away instead of inviting him to the party. But she'd given into temptation, and she was imagining his arms around her even now.

"Do you think that would work, Marnie?" Scarlett was asking.

Marnie quickly tuned back into the conversation. "What would work?"

Hannah gave her a sly smile, obviously noticing where her attention had wandered.

"Bringing Natasha up to Paradise to scout out the location and meet with Mia," Scarlett repeated.

"Mia's the executive producer?" Natasha seemed to be asking Marnie.

"Yes." Marnie had set the business structure up that way. "We might look for a few other investors, but Westberg Productions will remain the majority shareholder." She caught Cobra's gaze on her again and fought against the distraction.

"So?" Scarlett prompted her.

"You two have an agreement already?" Marnie asked, surprised Scarlett had found a director this fast.

"There's a reason I put her on the guest list," Scarlett said. Then she looked guiltily at Natasha. "I confess, I targeted you."

"Target away," Natasha said, sounding delighted. "The story has a great premise. I love a good high concept." She looked to Marnie. "Scarlett's going to send me the script, but I'm not worried if we have to polish it up. When the bones are good, there's always a way to make it work."

"Wow," Marnie said, surprised and pleased that the event had been so successful so quickly. "Then call Mia and set it up."

Scarlett and Natasha began to excitedly talk logistics, while Hannah was approached by another guest.

Marnie glanced Cobra's way to find his conversation group had broken up. She felt a disconcerting flash of emptiness and told herself to buck up. It was a party, a fleeting evening—nothing had changed.

"Hey there," Cobra's voice startled her from behind her left shoulder.

She turned to meet his dark eyes and smiled.

"Thirsty?" he asked.

"Sure." She fought the urge to take his hand, lean in, stretch up for a kiss. It was far too enthralling to be near him again.

They headed for a bar that was set up in the formal dining room.

"Witches' Brew or Magic Margaritas?" Cobra asked as they came to a display of premade thematic drinks.

"I like the look of the Black Magic Punch," Marnie said.

"Is it possible to get a beer?" Cobra asked the bartender.

"Certainly, sir," the man answered with a smile, extracting a bottle from a well of ice and producing a frosted glass.

Cobra handed Marnie one of the highball glasses filled with what looked like pomegranate juice and a skewer of blackberries.

Drinks in hand, they made their way through the crowded great room into the dimly lit conservatory. It was more peaceful there, with lush plants and furniture groups dotting the glass-enclosed space. A storm had burst in the skies above and fat droplets streaked their way down the panes.

They settled into a corner in two upholstered armchairs with a small wooden table between them. Ferns dangled above their heads while the trees blowing outside added to the spooky atmosphere.

A wave of calm contentment came over her, and she took a sip of the drink. It was tart, with a distinct vodka burn.

Cobra leaned forward. "I missed you." His deep voice sent a shiver of awareness through the deepest reaches of her body, lighting her up, frightening her with the intensity of her emotions.

"Don't—"

"I'm sorry I chased you away."

She struggled for an equilibrium. "You didn't. I was leaving anyway."

"I know . . . but—"

"There can't be any *but*s." She forced a lightness into her tone that she was far from feeling.

"But—"

"Cobra."

He gazed at her in silence for a full minute. "I honestly thought we could pull it off there for a while, the fun, the fling, then go back to our own lives."

"So did I," she admitted. Things had gotten so much messier than she'd expected. "It should have been a fond memory, not a bitter fight."

"I don't want to fight with you."

"Neither do I." She didn't trust herself to say more. Her emotions were too raw, and Cobra was too captivating, and she was afraid of blurting out the truth.

The rain spattered around them, while music wafted from above and voices rose and fell around them.

"What are you thinking?" he asked softly.

She mustered her strength. "That we leave it the way we should have."

"And that is?"

"Friendly. Thanks for a few laughs." She forced a laugh out now. "I had a good time. See you when I see you." She couldn't believe how much it hurt to say the words. Her hand felt shaky as she took another sip of the drink. She set down the glass.

"Is that what you really want?" he asked, his eyes deep and dark with regret.

"It doesn't matter what I want." It took everything she had to keep her voice from cracking.

He took both her hands in his. "*All* that matters is what you want."

She wanted to pull away from him, but she couldn't bring herself to do it. Instead, she looked down at his strong fingers against her pale skin. "What I want isn't good for me."

"Why not?"

"Because it'll hurt me in the end."

"You mean I'll hurt you."

She shook her head. "It's not you, it's me."

He gave a ghost of a smile at her trite words.

"That didn't come out right," she said.

"Don't worry about it."

She tried to explain. "I'm lost with you."

"Yeah?" His hands convulsed around hers. "Thing is, I'm lost without you."

"Cobra."

"You have to let me make it better."

"You can't."

"I have to try."

"It's you. All of you. Every bold, brash inch is overwhelming for me. I can't cope with all that you are."

"That's a lie," he said.

"It's not."

"I pushed. You pushed back. You won."

"You call this *winning*?" She was miserable.

"You got what you wanted. It sure wasn't what I wanted."

"Cobra."

"I'll change."

The very thought was appalling. He was perfect the way he was.

"What are you going to do?" she asked. "Be less of what you are?"

"I love you."

She pulled her hands from his. "No, no, you don't."

"Yes, I do."

"You can't love me." It only made things worse.

"I can't not love you, Marnie." He touched her chin with his fingertip, lifting it.

He leaned forward. She didn't try to stop him as he brushed a ghost of a kiss across her lips. Desire glowed like a flame inside her.

"It doesn't solve anything," she whispered, knowing in that second that she loved him back.

"It solves everything."

Her heart was breaking; loving Cobra made everything a thousand times worse. "I'm not Mia. This doesn't end with me moving to Paradise."

"It doesn't end with me moving to LA either."

Her eyes welled with tears and she blinked them furiously away.

He brushed her cheek. "Don't. Don't. Have some faith in us."

She miserably shook her head.

"What about something in between?" he asked.

"There's nothing in between." There was Seattle. But her life was in LA and his was in Alaska. There was nothing for either of them in Seattle.

"Would you visit Paradise? Maybe in the summer? Do some work up there for Mia and the crew?"

She opened her mouth to say a few weeks a year would only be torture for both of them, but he put a gentle fingertip across her lips.

"I don't have to be in Paradise all winter," he said. "A few weeks here and there, but I can move to LA at the end of the season."

Marnie's eyes widened and she straightened in shock. "You'd move to LA?" she asked around his finger.

"I would."

"And live here all winter?"

"Most of it."

Her mind started moving a million miles an hour. "And I could—"

"You could. As much or as little as you wanted. I'd build us a house. Not as big and fancy as Silas and Mia's, but the same idea."

Marnie pictured it in her mind. Her and Cobra, together, in a house in Paradise for weeks at a time. Cobra in LA for the winter. It felt too good to be true.

"Are you sure?" she asked, not trusting it could happen.

"Are you?" Then he looked around. "This isn't the right place for this conversation. Can we find somewhere private?"

COBRA AWOKE TO A FEELING OF EUPHORIA. MARNIE shifted where she was spooned in his arms, and the night came flooding back. He kissed her hairline.

She muttered something under her breath.

"I love you too," he replied, thinking he'd never get tired of saying it.

She turned her head and her eyes fluttered open. She smiled up at him.

"Morning, my sexy ballerina," he said.

"Morning." Her grin widened and he kissed her lips.

The coffee grinder droned in the kitchen.

"Nice of Ethan to make coffee," Cobra said, inhaling deeply and anticipating the first cup of the morning.

Marnie slithered abruptly out of the bed, stepped into a pair of worn sweatpants and pulled a hoodie over her head.

"In a hurry?" Cobra pulled himself into a sitting position, his hopes of her coming back to bed diminishing when she pulled on a pair of socks.

"My coffee maker only makes two cups," she said.

"What?" Cobra straightened.

She laughed.

"Nicely played," he said with admiration.

"You did want a woman who would take you on."

"Not over coffee," he protested with mock irritation.

She scooted out the door, and he grinned again, feeling on top of the world. He'd walk a mile for coffee this morning if that's what it took.

He changed into his jeans and T-shirt and padded into the kitchen.

"Second pot is on," Ethan told him. He and Marnie were sitting at the dining table for four.

"Thanks," Cobra said.

To his credit, Ethan hadn't asked a single question about Cobra coming home with them last night. And he'd acted as though it was perfectly natural for Cobra to sleep in Marnie's room. Cobra appreciated his discretion.

Instead of waiting for the whole pot to brew, Cobra held his cup under the spigot, then he joined them at the table.

The cupcake was sitting in the middle of the table, neatly cut into three pieces.

"Is this what we're doing?" Cobra pointed to it.

"I hope so," Ethan said.

"I know how to share," Marnie said, looking offended that he might think otherwise. Then she took one of the thirds.

Ethan took another. They both bit down on spongy cake and fluffy icing and smiled their appreciation.

"Mm," Marnie said.

Cobra gave in and took the remaining third. He had to admit, it was delicious—a little early in the morning for something that sweet, but he gave kudos to the bakery.

Marnie looked back to her tablet where she was reading,

and Ethan continued scrolling through his phone. Cobra's first drink of coffee washed the bites of cupcake down and gave him a satisfying hit of caffeine. He hadn't had much sleep last night, and he hoped he wouldn't get much sleep for a few more days to come.

"I think Topeka is my best bet," Ethan said. "I can check out Lawrence from there too."

"You're not going home?" Cobra asked, thinking privately that it was a good idea. Ethan seemed more than a cut above his father and uncle.

He shook his head. "Marnie inspired me." He smiled fondly at his sister. "If she can break away, I can break away."

"For what it's worth," Cobra said, "I think it's a good idea to break away."

"Cobra's family's difficult too," Marnie put in without looking up from her reading.

"Difficult how?" Ethan asked.

"They're snobs," she said.

Ethan's brow furrowed. "Marnie, your family are felons. I don't think snobs are on the same level."

Cobra chuckled. "He's got you there."

"They sound like *the* most judgmental, sanctimonious people," Marnie said, looking up.

"I'm a disappointment to them," Cobra explained to Ethan.

Ethan drew back in obvious shock. "*Why?*"

"I work with my hands," Cobra said.

"Snobs," Marnie repeated.

"Better than felons," Ethan said again.

Marnie scowled at him.

"I'm just sayin'. Who would you rather have in the family? Car thieves or—" He looked to Cobra.

"Doctors, engineers and accountants."

"And a senator's aide," Marnie said.

"State senate," Cobra pointed out.

Marnie rolled her eyes at him.

"You're a lawyer," Ethan said to her.

She frowned in confusion.

"That's gotta help his rep." Ethan pointed to Cobra with his thumb.

"They'd think she was too good for me."

"See? You class him up."

"Ethan!" Marnie sounded horrified.

"He's not wrong," Cobra said.

"He sounds as bad as them."

Cobra reached out to take her hand. "They're not all bad. Miles is good. Mom is fine. Dad is . . . well, Dad. And Barrick is married to Josephine, so he's got his own problems." He finally got a smile out of Marnie.

"You've made me curious about Josephine," she said.

"You'll have to come to Seattle sometime," he said.

"What? Why? No way."

"Just to meet them," he said, knowing he wanted to show her off. He absolutely wanted to show her off to his family.

"No," she said, shaking her head.

"Go for it," Ethan said.

"You," she said back, pointing to his phone, "have your own things to worry about."

"True," Ethan agreed on a sigh.

"What are your plans so far?" Cobra asked, going back to his coffee, knowing any talk of his family could wait.

"A job to start," Ethan said, returning his attention to his phone.

"What kind of a job?"

"Mechanical, maybe." Ethan looked doubtful.

"Are you as good at it as Marnie?"

Ethan coughed out a laugh. "I'm way better than her."

An idea came to Cobra. It seemed so logical, even perfect. "You ever consider aircraft maintenance?"

Ethan looked blank.

"It's apprenticeship training."

"Who'd hire a felon as an apprentice?"

Cobra shrugged. "Me . . . Brodie, technically. My boss."

Marnie gaped at him in astonishment.

When Ethan spoke, his tone was hushed. "You serious?"

"Paradise is way off the beaten track," Cobra warned.

"Cobra," Marnie interrupted, looking worried.

He shook his head at her. "The pay is good, but the hours are long. Winters are cold. But we need young, skilled guys who aren't afraid of hard work. If you're anything like your sister—"

"I know how to work hard," Ethan said.

"Cobra, you can't," Marnie tried again.

"Brodie's increasing the fleet this year, and I have more than I can handle already. We've talked about getting another guy. Plus, I need someone who can take care of things when I want to come down to LA." He smiled at Marnie. "Which will be frequently if things go my way."

Ethan looked at Marnie, and then back to Cobra. "If you're serious, I'm in. I'm *so* in."

Chapter Twenty

—✈—

MARNIE COULDN'T BELIEVE HER BROTHER, ETHAN, WAS in Paradise.

She couldn't believe she was back there herself, and that she was with Cobra now.

Brodie had welcomed Ethan into the company, saying he had complete faith in Cobra's judgment, setting her brother up in WSA housing. Ethan was busy learning the ropes of the WSA, while Cobra and Marnie were busy taking over the caretaker suite above the hangar.

A bunch of the local guys had pitched in to clean out and repaint the suite. They'd pulled down some plywood and discovered some hidden windows that brightened it up considerably. They'd swept and washed out the grit, then painted the walls a fresh butter yellow, transforming the space.

Raven rushed new appliances and furniture in from Fairbanks while Mia stepped in to help with the decorating. The concrete floor was now covered in a variety of gray and burgundy rugs. The bathroom fixtures and kitchen counters had been scrubbed to within an inch of their lives, and a new hot water heater made the open-plan suite a cozy home for Marnie and Cobra while they built something permanent.

"You should build something upriver from me," Raven was saying as she and Mia helped unpack dishes and cutlery into the corner kitchen while Cobra, Ethan and some others positioned furniture in the living area. "That spot at the bend is beautiful. And you'd be super close to the airstrip."

"I want her next to us," Mia said. She looked pointedly at Marnie. "We've got too much property anyway. We can sell part of it to Cobra."

"Don't you want a great view?" Raven said cajolingly.

"Everywhere in Paradise has a good view," Marnie answered. It was true. The mountains were so high around them that it was beautiful whichever way you looked.

"They can build a dock north of my place," Raven said as she stripped the Bubble Wrap from a stack of plates. "The current slows down in the wide spot."

"Do you need a dock?" Mia asked. "They don't even have a boat."

"They can always buy a boat," Raven reasoned.

"We're building a dock in the spring. We'll share."

"I don't see us doing a lot of boating," Marnie said.

"See? She wants to live beside me," Mia said saucily. "We wouldn't even have to put in a trail. The meadow's already open. I'd be able to see you coming."

Cobra came up behind Marnie and wrapped his arms around her waist. "See who coming?"

"Marnie," Mia answered.

"We're fighting over her," Raven added.

"Well, you can't have her," Cobra said on a low chuckle, rocking Marnie back and forth a little. "She's all mine."

She looked up at him and smiled.

"As a neighbor," Mia clarified. "Wouldn't you like to

build across the meadow from us? You and Silas could hang out, have a beer, grill meat, stand around campfires. You know, manly stuff."

Cobra quirked his eyebrows. "Manly stuff?"

"You are a manly guy," Marnie told him.

"You'd get a better view next to me," Raven said. "You know, that point of land across from Red Peak."

"Where do you want to live?" Cobra asked Marnie.

"With you."

He grinned and gave her a kiss on the side of her neck. "Good answer."

"What are you planning to build?" Raven asked. "Big? Small? Elaborate? Plain?"

"You can borrow our plans," Mia offered. "They're tried and true all over central Alaska."

"We've got all winter to decide," Marnie pointed out.

"You'll be in LA all winter." Mia didn't look happy about that.

"We can look at house plans in LA."

"But I won't be there," Mia complained.

"You need to take in the scope of the building site," Raven said. "See how your house will fit, where the windows and deck will pick up the best views, where you want the garage and the driveway."

"She's right," Mia agreed with a nod. "Plus, you also need my advice."

"You could visit us in LA," Marnie suggested.

"Who's going to LA?" Silas joined the conversation.

"You are, buddy." Cobra clapped Silas on the shoulder. "Apparently there are floor plans to design."

"We could stay at the Waldorf," Silas suggested to Mia. "I have very fond memories of the Waldorf."

"Who doesn't love the Waldorf?" Raven asked.

"You want to go to the Waldorf?" It was Brodie's voice this time.

"*I* want Marnie and Cobra to build a house next door to me."

"What does that have to do with the Waldorf?" Brodie asked.

"Nothing," Raven said.

"Everything," Mia said at the same time.

Brodie looked at Silas and then Cobra. "I think I'm tapping out here."

Both of the other men chuckled.

Finished unpacking the box, Mia set it on the discard pile. "I'll come help some more tomorrow," she said.

"Only if you have time," Marnie said. They'd made it through the bulk of the work already, and she really appreciated everyone's stepping in. But she was also looking forward to being alone with Cobra for their first night in the suite.

His arms tightened around her, pushing his warmth against her back. She guessed he might be thinking the same thing.

It seemed like a natural ending spot and, with a chorus of goodbyes, everyone made their way down the stairs and out through the hangar.

As the voices faded, a low background buzz wafted up from the shop. Marnie gazed around at the comfortable living room furniture. There was a partial wall that closed off the bedroom area with a small bathroom beyond. They didn't have a closet, just a freestanding rack in a corner alcove. But the guys had carried in a dresser and a king-size bed, and Marnie knew they'd be perfectly comfortable.

With the sunshine streaming across it, she couldn't help but smile at the result of everyone's work.

"This is way nicer than I expected." She wandered to the coffee-colored sofa strewn with throw pillows from Mia. She sighed and sat down, kicking off her shoes to curl her legs beneath her.

"You won't mind this while we build?" Cobra asked.

"Not at all." She stretched out her shoulders, tired from the long day of moving. "Did I see Mia leave a bottle of wine?"

"You did. She told me it was a housewarming present."

"Well, don't just stand there." Marnie shooed him with her hands.

"There's something you have to see first."

"Really?" She was comfortable now and tired, and she wanted wine.

He reached for her hand. "Up you get."

"Do I have to?"

"It'll be worth it," he said, hoisting her to her feet.

The carpet was cushy beneath her.

"Fine, fine," she said on a pout. "I'll come and see."

He grinned, still holding her hand as they rounded the end of the partial wall into the bedroom area.

She saw it right away, in a corner by a newly discovered window. It was a desk, a beautiful pale maple desk, credenza and a matching shelving unit. There were plenty of drawers and a huge screen set up where she could plug in her laptop. There was also a comfy-looking ergonomic chair and a square white box tied up with a pretty silver bow in the center of the desk.

"Cobra," she said on a note of awe, taking steps toward it.

"I knew you'd want to work," he said. "I wanted you to be comfortable."

"This is amazing," she ran her fingertips along the smooth desktop. "And you got me a present?" She couldn't imagine why.

"It's a housewarming gift," he said.

"I didn't get you anything." She was teasing, not remotely worried about offending him.

"I don't need anything." He came up behind her, touching her again, giving her a kiss at her temple. "Well, nothing but you."

She smiled, her heart filling with more joy than she could have imagined. "Have I told you lately that I love you?"

"Not since this morning." There was a mock censure in his voice. "To be honest, I was getting worried you'd changed your mind."

"Not when you get me presents," she teased back.

"Open it," he said.

"Is it cupcakes?" she asked, realizing she was getting hungry.

"You want cupcakes?"

She reached for the ribbon and tugged at it. "I want something tasty. It's been a hardworking afternoon."

She pulled off the bow and lifted the lid, gazing down to find a set of headphones. She picked them up to see a high-end logo. They looked state of the art and were obviously noise-canceling.

"It's going to be noisy downstairs during the day," Cobra said.

"What a thoughtful gift." She couldn't believe how hard he was working to make her comfortable in Paradise.

The light in his eyes said he was pleased by her reaction.

She laughed in delight and put them on. "What do you think?" She turned her head one way and then the other.

"I think they suit you."

"They fit perfectly."

He moved his lips without sound. It was obvious he was messing with her.

She leaned up to kiss him. "Thank you, Cobra. They're perfect."

His arms went around her, and he pulled aside one of the earpieces. "I love you so much, Marnie. I want you to be happy here, really happy."

"You're here." She realized now that her happiness was

with him. "And Ethan's here." She took off the headset, feeling herself get unexpectedly misty-eyed as she settled into his embrace. "This is more, Cobra, so much more than I ever hoped could be possible."

"That's you, Marnie. You're so much more than I ever hoped could be possible."

ACKNOWLEDGMENTS

An ongoing and heartfelt thank-you to my husband, Gordon Dunlop, for his expertise as a bush pilot, a technician and a northern outdoorsman. There was no way to write this book without you.

Thanks once again to my editor, Angela Kim, and my agent, Laura Bradford, who have supported me unfailingly throughout the series.

A big thank-you to the entire Berkley team, from editing and cover design to marketing and promotion, for turning my story into such a wonderful package.

Also, a special thanks to my Yukon friends and family for decades of love, support and unparalleled life experiences.

Keep reading for a preview of
the next Paradise, Alaska, romance

Strangers in Paradise

Coming soon from Jove!

IT WAS A GLASS HALF-FULL KIND OF DAY FOR HAILEY Barrosse. Sure, it had been a slow summer season in the tiny town of Paradise, Alaska. In fact, it had been an excruciatingly slow year, particularly for the bush pilots who flew for West Slope Aviation. They were paid by the mile. So, no miles, no money.

Not that Hailey had a lot of day-to-day expenses. She lived in WSA staff housing, a small rustic room, just a bedroom, a bathroom and a tiny sitting area. But it stayed warm in the winter and had a great view of the mountains during the long summer days. The company provided three tasty meals plus snacks in the staff cafeteria, so if her bank balance suffered a little in the short term, she could live with that.

Today, however, was a bright spot for the entire town. It was the first day of principal photography for the superhero action movie *Aurora Unleashed*. The production had brought new jobs to town. Local residents had been hired in catering, carpentry, hair and makeup, as well as in logistics. That wasn't even counting the business spin-offs for everyone from Galina Expediting and West Slope Aviation to the Bear and Bar Café and Rapid Release Whitewater Rafting.

Today, practically everyone had assembled at Mia Westberg and Silas Burke's house on the banks of the Paradise River to check out the action. It was a picturesque location with a newly built two-story villa in a wildflower meadow with soaring mountains and snow-capped peaks in the distance. The spectators clustered behind the surveyor's tape boundary that ran to the river's edge. But as official pilot to the location scouting team, Hailey was allowed on set with the rest of the crew.

"Grab a snack," Willow Hale told her, stepping up to the heavily laden craft services table.

"Is eating all anybody does here?" But Hailey joined Willow to check out the assortment of fruit and nuts, cookies and treats. In addition, enticing smells wafted from the catering tent, even though they were halfway between breakfast and lunch.

"We have to keep up our energy level," Willow said, selecting a peanut butter granola bar and peeling away the wrapper.

Hailey was tempted by a bag of white chocolate–covered cashews. The delicacy was new to her, but how could you go wrong with cashews, white chocolate and crunchy toffee?

You couldn't, that was the answer. She picked up a package.

"Besides," Willow continued between bites, "they're tossing me off the sundeck into the river this morning."

Hailey stopped tearing open the crimped foil. "They're *what*?"

"That's the first scene. I mean, not the first scene in the movie, but the first one they're filming. Probably want to get it done before the weather cools. I have to say, I'm all for that." Willow took another bite.

"Do you know what you're doing?" It was a twenty-foot drop from the sundeck into the water. And the water was freezing. Well, nearly freezing, just barely liquid. The river was fed year-round by glaciers high up in the mountain peaks.

Sure, Willow was athletic. But she wasn't a professional stuntwoman. She was a Californian who loved adventure sports and had been drafted by the production based mostly on her enthusiasm for Paradise and the project.

"Not exactly," she said.

"Well, did you rehearse it?"

"Are you kidding?" Willow's voice rose. "Do it *twice*?"

"Good point." Hailey had to agree. "Plus, the first time might kill you."

"Well, hopefully not dead, dead," Willow said matter-of-factly. "There'll be a safety diver in the water."

"It's three minutes to hypothermia in that river." Hailey didn't see how a safety diver would help in such a tight race against time.

Willow pulled the high collar of her shirt down to show a patch of white fabric. "Dry suit. I'm brave, not suicidal."

Hailey felt a little better about that precaution. She tore open the bag of cashews. "What about the current? If the diver misses, you'll be swept all the way to Weaver Lake."

"Riley and Nicholas are downstream in rafts. If it all goes bad, they'll catch me."

"Oh." Hailey popped a nut in her mouth.

"See that?" Willow grinned and squeezed Hailey's arm. "You're not getting rid of me today."

"These are delicious," Hailey noted, taking an appreciative look at the shiny blue bag. "Where have you been all my life?"

"So, that's it?" Willow asked with a pout, gesturing herself up and down. "No more worrying about me?"

"You said it yourself, Riley will save you." Riley'd had a soft spot for Willow since her first trip to Paradise nearly two years ago. Hailey held out the bag. "Have you tried these things?"

Willow took a couple of nuts, biting one in half and checking the inside. "Yum."

"Right?" Hailey ate another.

Willow focused on a spot past Hailey's left shoulder, her gaze holding there. "Oh, hello. Who is *that*?"

Hailey turned to look then compulsively swallowed. Who *was* that? Had they replaced Cash Monahan, the actor playing archvillain Dax Vanquich?

"Is he the new Dax?" She was embarrassed by her fangirl reaction. She wasn't a fan girl of anyone. But this guy was . . . it was hard to find the right words: rugged, sexy, buff. The camera had to love those dark mysterious eyes.

"They didn't replace Dax," Willow said. "They'd have replaced his stunt double too. And look." She pointed to where the crew was getting the shot set up on the sundeck. "Buzz is still here."

Hailey didn't want to look at the stuntman. She wanted to keep watching the man striding their way with such power and composure, like he owned the place.

"He looks like money," Willow said.

Hailey agreed with that. "An executive producer?"

"Mia's the executive producer."

"Maybe she needed another backer. Does he look like he's from LA?"

The film's financial backer Mia Westberg was a former fashion model who had moved up from LA nearly two years ago to marry local pilot Silas Burke. Not that this guy's demeanor said fashion industry, not by a long shot—although he was wearing a custom-fitted suit, dark with a crisp white shirt and a blue silk tie, so he was definitely dressed the part.

"I wouldn't say LA," Willow answered. "No tan, and that body doesn't look like it was sculpted in a gym."

"It looks good," Hailey said, trying to keep her voice even but wanting to sigh like a teenage girl.

The stranger caught her gaze. He stopped walking, and his eyes narrowed, as if he were trying to place her but couldn't.

It was then Hailey noticed the woman beside him. She was dressed as suavely as he was in a black-and-white checkerboard blouse, a short, tailored steel-gray jacket and a matching slim skirt. Her dangling earrings looked terrific below her short, dark hair. But she'd made a bad choice in shoes. The heels were too narrow for walking over the meadow.

"She looks more like New York," Willow said.

"What are they even doing here?" Hailey wondered.

"On set?"

"In Paradise."

The woman said something to the man. He tilted his head to listen but kept his quizzical gaze on Hailey.

"He's staring at you," Willow whispered.

"Do I have something on my face?" Hailey wondered if she'd smeared chocolate in her enthusiasm over the cashews. But even if she had, the chocolate was white. He wouldn't see it from that distance. She glanced down at her mottled blue T-shirt and gray cargo pants. Nothing seemed off with her outfit.

Her leather hikers might be scuffed and worn, but they were eminently practical. And she'd popped a WSA ball cap over her ponytail to keep off the sun. There was nothing remotely noteworthy about her appearance.

Willow studied her for a minute. "You're good."

Then a bad feeling came over Hailey. "Oh, no."

"Oh, no what?" Willow asked sounding worried.

"He might be from Atlanta."

"Atlanta?"

"My family might have sent him." Hailey's stomach turned queasy at the notion.

"Why would they do that?"

"Because they want me to come home." Hailey's sister

had sent three texts yesterday alone, and Hailey had flat-out ignored the recent phone calls from her mother.

"They'd send a guy?" Willow sounded skeptical.

Hailey knew it was unlikely they'd send someone to fetch her. Sure, her family wanted her home for the annual shareholders meeting, just like they always did. But she never attended. She just gave her sister Amber her proxy for the votes.

Then again, unlikely wasn't impossible.

"He's coming this way," Willow said with a thread of excitement in her voice.

The man's attention had definitely zeroed in on Hailey.

She considered making a run for it, but he looked like he'd have some speed. And even if she made it to her pickup truck, what then? Head for the airstrip and commandeer a plane?

She wasn't letting this guy run her out of Paradise.

He was only yards away now, and she braced herself, planting her feet, squaring her shoulders and lifting her chin.

"Hello," he said in a deep honey-smooth voice that sent a ripple up her spine.

She waited, gaze narrowing, prepared to tell him she wasn't leaving Paradise and he could march right back to where he came from.

"I'm looking for Raven Westberg."

Surprise tumbled through Hailey, and it was immediately followed by embarrassment. He was clearly not here for her.

She almost laughed at her own absurdity.

"I'm not sure she's on set right now," Willow said, glancing around.

"Is Raven expecting you?" Hailey asked.

He might not be here for her, but this guy didn't fit in Paradise, not by a mile.

"We don't have a specific appointment." His assessing

gaze told Hailey it was none of her business. Unfortunately, the smoldering look also made her heart beat more deeply in her chest.

Residual adrenaline, she told herself. Not that he could have bodily removed her from Paradise. But she hadn't wanted to argue with some brash stranger about returning to Atlanta.

The professional-looking woman handed Hailey a business card. "If you do see Raven, could you ask her to call?"

The card read *Dalia Volksberg, PQH Holdings* embossed in gold letters.

"What can I tell her?" Hailey asked, growing curious and slightly uneasy. Were these people lawyers? Headhunters? What did they want with Raven?

The man answered, an edge to his deep voice. "That we'd like to speak to her."

"About?" Hailey wasn't going to be intimidated by him.

His lips thinned, as he stood in pointed silence.

Hailey's back stiffened in response. People obviously hopped to it for him in his world. But she wasn't part of his world.

She handed the card back to the woman. "I don't expect to see Raven anytime soon."

She felt Willow's surprise. The man clearly noticed it too, because his suspicious gaze slid to Willow then back to Hailey.

"Alaskan hospitality?" he challenged Hailey on a drawl.

"Urban entitlement?" she returned with the same level of defiance.

For some reason, he smiled at that. "I guess we'll track her down ourselves."

He turned to walk away then, tossing a steely-eyed look over his shoulder.

"Wow," Willow said.

"High on himself or what?" Hailey asked rhetorically.

"I wonder what he wants with Raven."

"I hope he doesn't find her."

"How could he not find her?"

Willow was right. A person couldn't hide in Paradise if they were trying.

PARKER HALL HAD GROWN UP IN ALASKA, BUT PARA-dise seemed quirky even to him. To be fair, he'd spent the last ten years in Anchorage refining his image to better fit in with his expanding business circle.

He'd expected the town's mood to be gloomy, given the tough times they'd faced over the past year. But what he'd found was optimism, almost a festival air.

"You do know it's going to come out," his business manager Dalia Volksberg said as they threaded their way through the trailers, equipment and people crowding the set. Pickups and semitrucks were parked in a neat line beside the long gravel driveway and multiple generators rumbled in the background.

"I know it will," Parker agreed. "But not because I gave it away to a curious woman."

"You cut her off pretty quick," Dalia observed.

"There was something about her," he defended himself.

He couldn't quite put his finger on it. He'd sensed an underlying hostility, then a stubbornness, and he hadn't wanted to give an inch.

"Well, those shoes for one," Dalia responded airily. "I mean, seven pockets in your slacks are bad enough, but there's no excuse for mismatched laces and mud-caked hiking boots."

"You're a pocket snob?" Parker hadn't noticed what the woman was wearing. He'd been too busy taking in those clear blue eyes. He could admire the intelligence he saw behind them, even the curiosity. But her obstinance sure put him off.

Not that they weren't beautiful eyes. And not that she

wasn't a beautiful woman. Even without makeup her eyelashes were thick and dark in contrast to her light wisps of auburn hair beneath the olive-green ball cap. Her cheeks were flushed against her pale skin, and he'd caught the slightest hint of freckles on her cheekbones.

He couldn't help but be fascinated by her deep pink lips that looked highly— He stopped his thoughts in their tracks, giving himself a mental shake.

"The women here . . ." Dalia's tone was searching as she gazed around at the people they passed.

He resolutely redirected his attention but didn't see anything strange. "What about the women?"

"They don't even seem to . . ." She paused, clearly searching for the right word. *"Try."*

Parker gave a wry smile. "It's a working town, Dalia."

At least it had been a working town. It was more of a depressed town now. Well, except for this film. He hadn't known about the film until they'd arrived. It had to be a one-off, a temporary respite from the economic downturn. There was nothing about Paradise that would qualify it as Hollywood far, far north.

Everyone's attention suddenly swung in a single direction, so Parker looked too. There were three cameras in place on the big sundeck, their operators at the ready and the lighting bright on the actors. A man and woman were circling each other like they were about to engage in a fight.

The woman was the quieter of the two he'd just encountered. He glanced over his shoulder, scanning the crowd until he caught a glimpse of the obstinate one.

Ready to find
your next great read?

Let us help.

Visit prh.com/nextread

Penguin
Random
House